A PRECISE DECEPTION

An Enchanted Mountains Tale

Brandon D. Conner

Books By Brandon

A huge thank you to Deb Weatherell, a resident of Cuba Lake, who supplied the gorgeous and stunning pictures for both covers.

First off, I would love to thank the people of Cuba, NY for using my former hometown in my novel. It is a wonderful town and a great spot to visit with loads of charm and history.

There were a few people who meant a lot to me that I would love to dedicate this book to.

Patricia Furman was a special woman to me who loved Cuba Lake and has a special place in my heart. Her zest and love of life captured all of those around her.

Jared M. Kraft, an amazing, brilliant soul who left us all way too early, yet left me a permanent mark in my life and soul.

Austin Starr, my dear friend who also left his world far too soon. I miss you so much, and I love that you now have a place in the literary world forever, one hobby that you always adored.

And lastly to my late mother, I love and miss you so much.

A Precise Deception

I

Radiant hues of red and blue light danced and reflected off the icy, crisp stark white snow that embraced the petite lawn, quaint cottage, and the vast expanse of beautiful Cuba Lake, which was essentially the home's backyard.

Six months prior, give or take a fortnight, those same tones of illumination captivated a multitude of lake goers for the Fourth of July fireworks spectacular show right on the rear deck of the abode being mentioned. Allen Marshall hosted the best parties of the summer right there on the same pristine water. Traditionally his aged and weathered dock had been proclaimed as the perfect spot for such aquatic shenanigans. Much laughter and an abundance of smiles, along with friendly embraces and kisses on the cheek were exchanged that specific evening two seasons before, and happiness was one of the special guests in attendance.

But during this wintry date on the calendar, this house was one of horror rather than one of joy

A few minutes earlier Allen's teenage son Jared had just stumbled into a sight that no son should ever wander upon in a cabin where he spent so many festive years of his upbringing. Being that his father had missed his Christmas band concert, something that was extremely uncharacteristic of Allen since his son was the star trumpet player of the group, and of course the apple of his eye, a blanket of worry had consumed the horn player. Jared had ventured a few miles from his soon to be alma mater and headed to the seasonal escape that transitioned into a year-round home that he and his father had been inhabiting since the separation that severed their once nuclear family the year prior.

As he turned the tarnished and weathered brass doorknob, an original piece to the 1925 craftsman shelter, Jared felt that something was a bit off. Upon pushing the fire engine red door with a leaded glass window open he felt the burst of hot air from the main heating system. This was caused by the ornamental fireplace in the front living room being lively ablaze and radiating a massive amount of heat. This was not something that his frugal and environmentalist father would do under any normal circumstance.

"Dad? Dad! Where are you?"

These ordinary greeting calls were left without a response.

Jared's senses were heightened, he knew that no good was about to unfold.

Each of the two first above ground rooms, these being the foyer and living, passed their impromptu and brief survey that the youngster performed.

Except that once he entered the dated rear kitchen, which included the back door leading to the picturesque water, it was instantly clear that there were several obscurities that presented themselves to him.

Boot prints of fresh snow, slowly melting with each increase of temperature and every added second, led from that entry point and down the basement stairs with remnants of a squabble in between. Jared recognized those prints... But not from any boots he could remember being at that address with just him and his father, the only true occupants. Plus, his dad's particular mannerisms of tidiness prohibited any messes in the beloved cottage, which included not allowing shoes, especially snow-covered boots, to ever patter across the flooring. They were quickly melting alongside a second set that was smeared and unrecognizable.

Another objection that stuck out to the lad was the fact that the small three-piece bar height cherry wood dinette set appeared disheveled. Even though its finish was worn and battered a bit from years of use by many visitors of the dwelling, it was always meticulously placed in the same spot in a caring way. Totally ambiguous, the chairs were pushed across the room, one totally off of its legs, like a tortoise stuck on its back. While its counterpart had skidded a few feet away from its original position. The table itself was moved in a bizarre, ajar fashion eighteen inches from its normal placement. Again, something that was causing an instantaneous internal stirring of the adventurer that night.

A simple pink glass candy dish with curved edges, a beloved family heirloom, had catapulted from its home as the table's centerpiece and was shattered into dozens, possibly even close to one hundred sharpened and jagged pieces across the linoleum floor. A doily crocheted by their late, and amazing, Aunt Charlotte was also disheveled, and was hanging halfway off of the tabletop. Disastrous was the aura of the setting.

Something definitely was awry there.

Each creak of the hundred-year-old battered wooden steps heading to the barren basement added extra distress to the situation. A part of Jared wanted to say that it was a good search, and even though his father's government issued white truck was parked right out front, that his loving patriarch must be somewhere else, anywhere else at that moment, and not in that frigid dirt basement.

The slightly swaying shadow that became the main display of the sunken quarters sent quivers down the high school senior's spine, and goosebumps raced up the snow toned skin of his freckled arms.

But he pushed every part of his being with all his might to keep moving.

Dropping to his knees by instinct, he knew that this was all wrong. The moist earth ground against his joints had him suddenly shivering, and in turn stained the pleated khaki pants that he wore. It all felt so very wrong seeing his father swing softly from a light draft of the cellar.

This must be a joke... It all can't seem real.

Why was his tried-and-true hero, an honestly good man, an agent of the country that he loved, without a pulse, and robbed of so many future moments.

Using what little he could of his logical mind Jared

refrained from hugging his father, and the most challenging part was that he did not try to cut him down. There was no point, every indication pointed to the truth that his father had expired long before his arrival.

Shaking and sick to his stomach, Jared wobbled back up the timeworn stairs, then over to the corded phone hanging on the kitchen wall. Fumbling, he managed to dial 911 on the banana yellow telephone and communicate, with much difficulty due to acute grief and shock, that his father, the USDA federal agent that had friends and foes in Allegany County due to his work, was hanging from a noose.

But most of all, that it was under suspicious circumstances.

*

Nestled in the Enchanted Mountains of Western New York State, Cuba is a cozy countryside community, so small that there are two stop lights in the entire town and village. Being such a petite incorporated establishment, all of the first responding medics are volunteers.

A dominating and howling sound came from the town fire whistle indicating an imperative event as Jared was frantically trying to answer the questions from the emergency response operator. The roaring noise was summoning those who pledged to assist their quaint municipality in such instances, and in turn invigorating the area of a pending tragedy.

Once he heard the sirens from what he could tell were a few close by volunteers in their personal vehicles. In response Jared's hands went limp, permitting the antiquated communication device to drop, allowing the cord to fluctuate and the receiver to sway in the twilight of the moon. Next, he proceeded towards the front door in order to greet the essential visitors.

The door grazed open, and Jared walked back into the blistering cold, the wind chill being a dozen degrees under zero.

"It's my father, but he's gone. He's dead."

Two EMTs glanced at each other, then back to the grieving family member. "Did you try CPR?" Before waiting for a response, they tried to push through him.

"He's dead. He isn't breathing, he looks like he is stiff." Grief riddled him. "Even I can tell he's fuckin' gone."

Luckily a navy blue and gold state trooper cruiser raced to the front of the house and haphazardly parked on the narrow side of South Shore Road. The car was even a bit off skew since it used a well-developed snowbank as a ramp.

After placing his Stetson on his head, per protocol, the lawman slushed through the seasonal precipitation and up the front steps, greeting the medics he has come to know through various disasters in the area, then engaged with Jared.

"What is going on, Son? I am Trooper Wingard."

Holding back tears, the newly orphaned boy barely managed a response, "My father is in the basement hanging."

The lawman was taken back, "So your father committed suicide."

"I don't know," tears were mercilessly falling from the teenager's eyes at this point, "it doesn't make sense."

"What's your father's name?"

"Allen Marshall."

"The agent for the USDA?"

"Yes."

Looking intensely at the EMTs and purely using his trained instincts he wasted no time directing them, "This is now a crime scene, whether or not he ended his own life. Allen Marshall is a federal agent. That changes the game." Next, he engaged his radio from its mounted spot pinned to the shoulder of his distinctive uniform. "Dispatch, this is a bit out of rank for me. I am securing the scene, back up needed. Notify all available units in the area to please come and assist."

With a quick motion he released the button for his radio and reached into the front right pocket of his uniform trousers where he retrieved his state issued smartphone. Rapidly dialing a familiar contact, he informed his superior officer who answered after a few quick trills of the device. "Hey Sarg... So, I am on the scene of this deceased person. It's Agent Marshall over with the USDA. We need the feds in here, this is going to be a shit show." A hesitation due to the fear of what was ahead and a cough from the chill followed. "I haven't even entered the scene yet."

Sighing at a dramatically higher level than was necessary, the boss relayed his instructions, "Go inside immediately, confirm that he has passed and identify him. You have worked with him before, correct."

"Affirmative."

"I will make the appropriate phone calls up the hierarchy and keep you in the loop."

The responding cop next ended the call without any pleasantries, and then he headed into the macabre house to do as instructed.

The enhanced heat from the wood fireplace was also noticed by the policeman upon his entry. Using the skill set that he learned half a decade prior from his academy days, he was careful to preserve the potential crime scene. As he turned the corner in the kitchen he also noticed the challenging boot prints, and that the back door was closed, but not locked.

Carefully he avoided the shattered glass maze around him, and cautiously made his downward trip into the simplistic basement, then to where the homeowner was hanging and lifeless. It was easily noticeable that rigor mortis had started to set into the body.

These two men, one with a pulse, one sans, had worked a few cases together. Allen tended to be more of an examiner who focused mostly on procedure and paperwork, while the copper was more of the brawn and enforcement. Each of their attributes and efforts had complimented the other one nicely through the investigative process.

The man in blue checked for a pulse, confirming that this was no hoax, and retraced his steps through the lakeside cabin and up to the front, just as the blue and red lights from an Allegany County Deputy's car slid to a stop, almost colliding with his own vehicle. Nerves from the condition of the call and the slippery weather caused the near hit from the joining patrolman. All was not okay on Cuba Lake.

*

By dawn on that cold December morning the portion of the South Shore Road bordering the cottage owned by Allen Marshall was completely closed off. With it being a narrow passageway due to the layout of the lake and homes, parking was a complete disaster, especially for the caravan of vehicles that were joining the investigation. Probably the largest crime that this wonderful, All-American town had ever seen.

Just around one am the first FBI agents from the Buffalo office had arrived, tired from being summoned so late at night and unexpectedly from the largest city in the district, and closest field office in the area. With its parade came the forensic team and their vehicles, along with any moderate to high-ranking official starting to migrate down as details of this incident, now close to being qualified as a homicide, were starting to reveal themselves. Upon this hour of the new day they had established some control of the field, yet were still waiting for other key players to make their grandiose entrance.

As the moon was disappearing, and its counterpart rising, rays of fresh sunshine glimmered off of the icy lake, a duo of jet-black SUVs, these also from the same bureau, started to crest over the hill. The fresh light was starting to wake up the area and notify all inhabitants of the fiasco unfolding in their little niche of the world.

FBI Investigator Jake Morris, who was nursing his black coffee, a purchase earlier from the only gas station in town, was slowly taking pictures and processing the scene with his Forensics Specialist Isaac Morray. Both were standing in the basement, a few feet away from where Allen Marshall was hanging still.

The lifeless form before them was simply dressed with a red and blue checkered button down oxford shirt, tight-fitting medium blue jeans, and white socks.

"There is no possible way that he hung himself. There isn't a stool or anything to stand on anywhere in this basement. Plus, his toes are clearly six inches off of the ground. And he is in the middle of the cellar. No way to even stand on the ledge of the wall and pull a Peter Parker over."

This observation came from Morris.

"Or a Peter Pan," added Morray, then he tilted his head and pulled his Maglite from its holstered position on his hip while he engaged it in order to add illumination under Allen Marshall's left eye. "Look at this. He has a small shiner. That does not happen naturally when you hang yourself."

Morris leaned in and shook his head, concurring with this most recent, and accurate, finding. "You don't smack yourself in the eye while in a noose."

"And having a government issued piece, wouldn't you rather shoot yourself and make it quick, rather than hang yourself and torture your soul for a few minutes, then exit stage left, correct.?"

Nodding, Morris agreed, "Quick is best. So, this feels very off to me and my experience with other suicides."

Moving the battery powered torch a few inches down and to the left, he brightened the area on the corpse's neck. "But now here we have the normal ligature bruising."

A familiar shadow led its owner down the steps and into the underground crime scene.

"Gentlemen," said the fresh addition to the incident, and higher-ranking agent, then he cleared his throat as an informal way of announcing his entrance. "What are our preliminary findings?"

The man inquiring such details was Special Agent in Charge Thomas Washington. He was a distinguished looking black man with short, cropped salt and pepper hair, both tones equally dispersed on his head. Being around sixty years old, he held a strong maturity that resonated with him, and also aligned with his professionalism. Reaching around six feet tall, he still had a muscular, sturdy frame that he acquired many years before when he was a rookie agent for the same bureau.

Crows' feet were etched around his concentrated eyes, and there was an aura of leadership that attracted others, including all of the agents who reported to him in that specific third of New York State. With this came a rich sophistication, and the resemblance of Colin Powell or Morgan Freeman was noticeable.

"Sir," stuttered Morris, "it appears that we have an agent down, and a very feeble attempt to make the scenario look as if it is actually a suicide."

"What besides the disheveled kitchen above us, do we have thus far to support this theory?"

Morray took control of the conversation and used his right index finger to highlight what he was explaining. "Looks like our victim, Agent Marshall, took a minor blow to his right eye. It's slightly bruised. Probably from a struggle of some sorts. Maybe a punch."

Nodding, Special Agent Washington scanned the damp dirt cellar. "Have we bagged into evidence whatever he used as a way of standing before he hung himself, if this is indeed a suicide?"

Morray shook his head thrice, "No such object was down here when he was discovered, Sir. I mean, if this is a homicide, they did a very poor job of covering it up."

Washington exhaled aggressively, letting his cheeks and lips vibrate as his breath exited his lungs. "Now that we have this as our running hypothesis, let's work the crime scene backwards, starting here from every detail all the way out of the back door."

The other men nodded, and being the sole forensics specialist on the scene Agent Morray took the lead. Peering upwards, initiating the other men to follow, he pointed at a half inch hole in diameter drilled into the aged and rustic wood beam that housed the rope which Allen Marshall was hanging from. "So, it looks as if this is a freshly cut opening. Look at how lightly colored the wood inside of the joist is. This house is probably a hundred and fifty years old, and as you see the timber down here shows its age. Someone drilled this within the last week, if not a day, ago."

Silent semi-nods were conveyed from the two-man audience showing their combined agreement.

"Now if we find the drill bit, then we can match it like a bullet from a gun. Tool markings are just as distinctive as ballistics these days."

"That should help us figure out this quagmire if we find it somehow." Agent Morris felt obligated to add at least some commentary, even if it sounded derogatory.

Morray started again, this time using his pointer finger to indicate the bright yellow braided rope that had been used, which held a glossy shine to it. A thumb would contain the same thickness as it. "The rope is obviously newer, and a nylon material. The noose is tied in your typical hangman's knot. There are normal skin abrasions from the rough fibers rubbing against his neck. Also note the bruising which is consistent with a suspension hanging. There is probably some slight fracturing of the vertebrae, but not to the degree that we would see of a true hanging, where this is more of a strangulation."

Washington adjusted his standing position, then spoke through his fingers which were slightly covering his mouth. "The local undertaker will go more in depth on that. I have a consulting coroner enroute and traveling here from Monroe County to act as a second opinion, and also because, well down in these parts you don't find many suspicious incidents. Since the deceased happens to be one of us, I want every avenue pursued."

Morris mirrored his superior officer's position and started with his own thoughts. "That is most of what we have down here. It is a pressed dirt basement floor, so no footprints or drag marks would be possible to help us either way."

The basement was a spartan two room space. Since the home was heated by a single fireplace in the living room, there was no need for a furnace. There was an obvious need for a hot water heater, which was in the small side room.

The trio ascended the antiquated stairwell and entered the kitchen, which still had a kaleidoscope of broken glass accentuating its flooring, but all of the snow and slush from the previous evening was dried. Each man carefully maneuvered their steps to find an evidence free zone.

Morray restarted the conversation. "My technicians are on their way from headquarters as we speak. They will be collecting all of the evidence and cataloging it. This is clearly where an obscure interaction occurred. If we have a murder case, why did the killer not clean up the mess?"

"That is what you two are going to figure out together over the next few days, gentlemen. I am also working with officials at the state level for some local assistance in the matter." Clearing his throat he pressed on. "Either I want the case either ruled suicide, or have a perp in handcuffs as soon as possible. I don't like messes, and gentlemen, we are in the middle of one. Literally.

*

The slightly tarnished teacup sized copper bell which hung over the single orange painted door of The Four Corners Cafe sang a short and simplistic tune as Trooper Cecil Wingard entered. Its song being one with a metallic melody. This was the hotspot for residents of the 14727 and surrounding areas to get an enjoyable casual meal. Per habit he removed his sharp, professional headwear, which revealed his freshly cut high and tight light blond hair. Then using his crisp blue eyes he glanced to the right, next to the left, and he used his investigative skills in distinguishing who he was meeting in that cozy diner.

Since only four of the available dozen tables were occupied, not including any seats at the luncheon style counter, that helped him narrow down his search. And due to the fact that he had written various tickets for differing infractions of the law to members of three of those four tables, he easily concluded where his required seat indeed was.

A native to that portion of the state, the policer was built for the job. Being twenty-eight years young, he still possessed the physique of his high school youth where he was a three seasoned athlete. Football, wrestling, and track all worked in various factions to bulk him and thicken his body formation evenly.

After finishing his bachelor's degree at nearby Alfred State, he successfully pursued the journey of becoming a New York State Trooper. Luckily Cecil was placed close to his hometown of Scio, so working the streets and roads of the area was second nature to him, and ensured that he was positively giving back to his own area.

Sliding in, then across the hunter green booth cushion that had a single worn strip of duct tape mending a five-year-old tear, he positioned himself into a comfortable seat. Utilizing proper etiquette, he stretched his right arm across the lacquered oak wood table, which held two glossy single page menus, and shook the hand of someone he had met around ten hours before, but for just a moment as he passed off the crime scene to the bigger guns.

"Agent Morris."

"Trooper Wingard. You can call me Jake."

"Cecil here."

"You came highly recommended by Sergeant Longo. Thank you for pairing with me on this case."

"No problem. A week or two off of the roads here, especially this time of year, is a nice variation to the norm."

A waitress with overly curled and poorly colored blond hair, around forty-five years old wearing a stereotypical restaurant industry uniform including a bland yellow color, some tacky lace edges, and a frilly skirt, approached the table. The attire was quite dated, yet still the memorable kind for this profession. With a nicotine and coffee-stained smile she asked, "Coffee, gentlemen?"

Agent Morris nodded, "Black."

"Same for you Trooper Wingard?"

"Of course, Becky, and my usual."

"Number three, sunny side up, rye toast."

The server grabbed the laminated menu from Cecil's side of the table, "Do you need a minute?" This was directed at the visitor.

Wrinkling his face as he thought, and being extremely hungry so he did not want to delay, he blurted out, "Same as the statie here, guess it will be a surprise."

Revealing another yellowed grin, Becky retrieved his menu also and made her way to the kitchen service window.

"So, rumor has it that you worked with Agent Marshall out on the field in this district?"

"Yeah, the Southern Tier is mostly farmland, so we work with the USDA quite a bit in these parts. Agro-terrorism is not too common down here, but still can be a threat. We worked on a lot of issues dealing with the operation of the farms. Especially fraud when it came to grant money. Also, some animal cruelty and theft."

White coffee cups with a worn pink and green floral pattern around the lip that were housed on matching saucers and filled with hot, aroma filled freshly brewed java were gently placed in an unobtrusive way before them by Becky, who then politely excused herself.

"Now I assume that you haven't spent too much time down this way since federal cases are a rarity."

"Nah, I worked a case down I-86 over in Olean a few years back. Parental kidnapping. Was only a federal case because they brought the kid over the border from some Pennsylvania town called Shinglehouse."

"That's the first borough you hit going into the

commonwealth."

"But when you cross that state line, even as close as that, we get involved."

"So where do we stand with what you found after I left last night?"

"Pretty cut and dry so far," started Jake, "we are ninety-nine percent sure that this is a homicide, which was poorly staged as a suicide to cover it up. When I left an hour or so ago the coroner was cutting the victim down and bringing him over to some town called Belmont for the autopsy. My SAC, Thomas Washington, had one of our own consulting coroners come to assist this morning, starting at the preservation of the body at the scene, and will be with the county mortician through the autopsy and such until everything is definitive and ironclad. Mostly, we want to have all of the facts before us as soon as humanly possible."

"So let me lay out everything, facts and rumors, about Agent Marshall."

"Shoot, Cowboy."

"Currently married, one son. But that cabin is a summer home. He has a nice homestead a short ways up Beebe Hill. Big yellow ranch on an acre. Julie, the wife, works at the cheese factory on that end of town. A mile walk from their home."

Morris looked up briefly from feverishly taking notes, shared a professional smile, then nodded, indicating that he was staying with the pace, and absorbing every morsel of information about the Marshall family.

Satisfied that they were on the same page and understanding, the local fuzz continued. "You may be wondering why he was at the cottage and not home."

The FBI agent glanced up and shrugged, writing utensil still firmly in his hand.

"See, the following is confirmed gossip. Allen left his wife just about six months to a year ago from their main residence and started staying year round on the lake. Julie and some co-worker at the plant were seeing each other on the side. Allen figured it out and left. The son, Jared, has mostly been staying with Allen up on the water since Julie moved her new beau in with her."

"Well right there we have a motive wrapped up in a nice little box for us."

"Yeah, and to be completely honest, Allen loved his son too much to ever kill himself. He was furious that he was missing his son's swim meet two years ago since we had to execute a warrant over in Bolivar. We can fill in the blanks that I don't know when we start interviewing the people closest to him."

"I guess that leads us to his professional life. I am fully aware of how us feds can make some enemies. A year back I had the brother of a guy I put away for racketeering sit outside of my house for three months, just staring every time either my wife or I left our driveway. And nothing I could do about it since he colored within the legal lines."

"I can get in touch with his partner in the USDA, Frank Lyons, quite easily. They worked together for about ten years. Right about now to be completely honest, this is probably the talk of the area, so chances are that almost everyone pertinent to the case has been notified. Small town, big mouths."

Appearing with a lovely sunflower smirk, and their food, Becky swiftly sat the heartily filled dishes down. The plates were oval shaped, eggshell white, and edged with a goldish brown inscription of ribbons all tied together into one solid pattern. Of course, she brought a coffee pot to refill their half empty cups, and used her head to indicate the assortment of condiments at the far end of the table as she exited their space.

The number three special consisted of three eggs of your choice, but sunny side up in this instance, two sausage patties, nice and greasy, a generous mound of hashbrowns, sliced not shredded. Two silver dollar pancakes were squeezed on the side, and the buttered rye toast was laid across the glistening yolks.

Wingard slid a clear glass container of maple syrup, which had a light brown plastic cap and handle between them for convenience. There was a sliding metal spring powered mechanism that when pulled by one's thumb opened to help dispense the natural sweetener. "They use real maple syrup here. None of that sugar water. A couple up the Haskell Road makes it. You won't be getting that up in Buffalo."

After the hometown host applied his portion to the flap jacks, Agent Morris did the same. "Nah, we miss out on that homemade goodness."

Cecil licked a dab of the syrup from his forefinger. "So how do you want to execute our initial approach on this?"

"First let's go back to the scene. I wanna get a feel for everything in the daylight, and with the body gone so that we can see how probable it was for both scenarios to play out."

"That makes sense. I am assuming you have a command station and space somewhere that we can work out of."

"That's affirmative. The Cuba Police Chief is clearing out a few cubicles and their conference room for us to use."

"Well, that works quite well. Are you going to be running back and forth from Buffalo every day?"

"I have a room reserved indefinitely at the local motel over by I-86. Agent Washington doesn't want me to leave the area until we feel that this is a suicide beyond reasonable doubt. Or we have the killer in custody. My wife is running down a few suits and clothes to last me a week or two. My forensics specialist is in the same boat and will be here for the duration. Plus, you and I luck out in terms of back-up if needed. A few rookie agents will be rotating as our assistants and back-up in case of any danger. And one of the local patrolmen is going to watch over the headquarters during the day. Kid named Dylan. So, we have a small team to utilize when needed."

As almost if planned, the lawmen tossed their used and ketchup covered napkins onto the voided plates in perfect unison. Then they pushed their china into the middle, a sign that they had enjoyed their diner style breakfasts.

Looking as if she had just been struck by lightning with her eyes wide open and mouth ajar, Becky neared the table and let the check and its plastic presenter fall onto the table with a soft thump. "Cecil Wingard, how dare you sit here and not tell me that Allen Marshall was shot to death last night." Pointing to her right she revealed the gossipers. "The Burdicks over at table six just told me so."

Avoiding the temptation to engage with village false gossip, Trooper Wingard looked from Becky's direction and straight to Jacob Morris. "Welcome to small town investigating. Where hearsay is our biggest opposition."

*

An Allegany County Sheriff's deputy, fully dressed in heavy apparel for the vividly cold weather, nodded and moved the sawhorse style barricade aside, allowing Agent Morris's government issued black SUV to pass through, followed by Trooper Wingard's state cruiser. Even in a foot of accumulated snow the perimeter of Allen Marshall's cottage with a postage stamp plot surrounding it had a bright yellow with black lettering cordon which said, "Do Not Cross." About half a lot on either side of the street deputies were enforcing the blockage of the winding country road, and in the paved space between half a dozen or so various modes of transportation belonging to differing agencies were haphazardly parked.

One of which was the large box truck that had "FBI" written with giant block letters in a vivid yellow hue against its ink black side. Just as the men who were rejoining the lively scene found their desired parking spots, Forensics Specialist Isaac Morray was descending from the double doors in the back of the portable laboratory. Due to the frigid weather, he was blowing into his ungloved hands as an attempt of gaining warmth; the clouds of fog escaping his mouth and casually passing through the gaps between his pink fingers and through the hairs of his neatly trimmed goatee.

This vehicle was his main workstation, and the man of approximately forty-five years old had maneuvered his way into being the master of his domain. His chestnut hair was slightly receding on his head, which at the top, while he was standing up straight, would hit the five foot and seven inches marker. Naturally he possessed a thin build, with only about ten pounds of extra weight around his midsection. Being that he was more of a support piece of investigations, and not on the front lines as an enforcer of the law, he was wearing his usual snap button navy blue windbreaker that had the name of his bureau in bright white letters on the back. There was a government issued black digital camera that hung from around his neck from a synthetic lanyard, and it swayed as he lowered himself from the lorry.

The three converged in the middle of the impromptu parking lot, almost as if their rendezvous had been planned.

"Agent Morray, you remember Trooper Wingard from last night?"

"Of course, I had him email me the pictures that he took of the boot prints from the kitchen before they melted away. Good thinking with that." This was a firm compliment relaying his gratitude. "Without a doubt it will help the case down the road."

The two men shook hands, and Morris took the lead again. "Luckily, he will be working with us on this investigation, and is a great liaison into the community. So, what has transpired since I left to get a bite to eat."

"Come on, let's do a quick trip around the house, then get back into some heat. What little warmth there is."

With a head bob, which was tilted to the right side of his body, Morray started the progression through the snow, which now had a somewhat established path due to the traffic of those working on the case doing the same traveling many times along the property.

Using his open right hand, he signaled to what he was about to inform them on. "The most notable sign of foul play outside is the boot prints along the edge of the home, which was here when we arrived, then carried around the house. These are not consistent with any boots that we found in the house, and they are kind of blurred in some spots as if they were obscured somehow."

Once in the rear of the cottage they took the walkway down to the edge of the lake near the dock.

Agent Morris took a breath, and also a moment to see the lake in sunlight. "This is a pretty massive lake."

Trooper Wingard explained some history, "Cuba Lake's perimeter is six miles. It was the largest manmade lake of its time when established in 1858, and initially fed the water which eventually led to the Erie Canal."

Morris smirked, "Did you have a project on it in the Boy Scouts."

A little embarrassed, Wingard went on, "Nah, when you are raised here and work these roads for so long, you learn it all fast."

They saw some footprints that led onto the hardened water, and then a small opening in the ice. "What is that hole then, Cecil?" asked Jake.

"That is probably where Allen did some ice fishing." Smiling, he brushed this obscure observation off. "Anyway, keep us moving Agent Morray. Even the hometown boy is feeling a bit frozen."

With a semi-quickened pace, they headed back towards the house and the main focus of the inquest.

"So, the boot prints go along the side and to the back door where inside was the struggle, and then they double back as if someone left using the same route."

"Is it okay for us to enter that way then?" asked Cecil.

"We have made plaster casts from the tracks left on the back deck and have taken a plethora of pictures this morning in this area also, including the lake itself and the dock. You are free to mess the snow up a bit."

As Agent Morris, the last of the pack of men, had his foot on the first step of the weathered hardwood deck, something in the snow to his immediate right caught his eye. Being a bright yellow color, it was somewhat easy to spot with the midmorning sun enriching and dancing off of the brisk snow.

"Gentlemen, backtrack a second. Isaac, do you have an evidence bag?"

Turning around, the summoned man took a step closer and pulled the requested item from his left coat pocket. "What do you see?"

All three of them then squatted down, and the camera man realized that this was significant and started to take numerous pictures of the newly sighted clue. Slowly, after enough photos were captured, Jake withdrew a pen from his front dress shirt pocket and moved the first of two pieces of curled nylon rope, each about four to five inches in length. It was apparent that they had formerly been in loops since there was a knot tied within a centimeter of where the cut opening was. It was as if someone had used them as a restraint, or to tether something, then cut them off, rather than untying it, when they were done."

The NYS cop spoke up immediately. "That looks like the rope that Allen was hanging from downstairs."

Cocking his head to the side, Jake pondered out loud, "So far, we haven't found the rest of the rope. Why would two pieces, which are so small, be outside of the house."

Cecil stood up, crossed his arms, and tapped his right forefinger onto his bent left elbow. "It's right next to the footprints rounding the deck. And it would have been dark. I bet it fell out of the pocket of someone trying to be quick with their escape."

Morray bagged the crucial hint that was just unveiled, and motioned to continue their way into a warmer climate area.

Just before he grabbed the doorknob, Isaac Morray turned to the other men. "Before you ask, yes, we dusted the door for prints. It was completely barren of anything, even smudges. No doubt, someone wiped it clean. Or were wearing gloves."

A silent understanding followed that this was indeed a premeditated act, rather than one of spontaneity.

As the trio entered the rear entry of the cabin, it was

obvious that the three-piece dinette set was still in its obscure positioning as it had been discovered in its initial occurrence the night before. However, they noted that the shattered glass had been cleared, yet each piece had been outlined in black permanent marker. Perplexed, Cecil pointed at one of the oblong style sketches. "What is up with the new polka dot style floor design?

Laughing, Isaac explained, "We have collected all of the actual pieces, but this way we can study any trajectory or angles that the dish was catapulted in and analyze how they landed and such."

"So, a lot of geometry and physics is going on in here." Cecil chuckled again as he delivered this joke.

Morray was quick to recapture the expedition rate of the scene. "So, it is clear that we had a struggle. Perp was probably at the back door waiting for the victim to come into this room and blind side them."

Trooper Wingard put his finger into the air, pausing them, "This just popped up onto my radar. Agent Marshall was a trained federal agent. And he had taken some pretty well-built suspects down in the field. Even in a sneak attack, he would be able to neutralize most guys. I feel like we are looking at a team of probably two suspects that did this."

Agent Morris chimed in. "The victim had a few bruises that were visible even from a quick evaluation. The autopsy should be done by tomorrow morning, so we will know by then if, or what, they found hidden under his clothes."

Quickly Agent Morray removed the previously discovered strands of rope from his pocket, which were still encased in the clear evidence bag. "I would bet my life that these were used as restraints during the attack, then they cut them off of him to help cement the appearance of a suicide."

Pointing down the stairs, Wingard continued, "Also to get a very well abled man down the stairs, without a broken neck from falling due to a push, it would require two people."

"Well," started Jake, "might as well migrate that way

now."

Each investigator, while using the side wall for support by leaning against it with their elbows and taking the steps one at a time and at an awkward angle due to the age and settling of the stairs, finally made it safely into the moist, chilled cellar of the cottage.

Even though the vacated body of Allen Marshall had been removed a few hours prior, after of course, pictures were captured and notes had been taken, the basement still had a morbid aura that sat heavy in the air. Per procedure the rope had been meticulously removed, and a giant gauge, about six inches in length, had been removed from the beam where the federal agent had hung from byways of a small hand saw. This sample was taken, as was the noose, to be analyzed by Agent Morray and his team at their annex lab which was being set up by the higher-ranking officers in the nearby village.

There was a minute or so of silent observation, and a bit of mourning among them, whether or not they had ever met the person who drew his last breath in this same spot. It was a reflection of what had transpired in that space, and how they could hone in on that frequency. Maybe it could even whisper a secret or two that was now hidden in the stone foundation around them.

Finally, Jake Morris broke the tranquility. "As for the layout, this is one of two rooms down here. And well, it's pretty bare. Let's see what the other room has in it."

Leading the way in he turned on the light, which was an antiquated push button switch in a rusted square metal box with some exposed wiring. In response a single hanging bulb illuminated the small room, which was constructed from decades old plywood.

Cecil tried to give an explanation, "These basements are all around a hundred years old, and very wet due to being right on the lake." To coincide with this statement he pointed at some wet areas at the base of the foundation. "Such as you see in here there's noticeable water seepage. Basically down here is just for storage of sturdy belongings. Usually outdoor equipment."

Huddled together in one corner, a few of the odds and ends even leaning against the exterior mortar wall, was a grouping of items, all in a diverse spectrum of ages based on their design, wear, and raw materials.

Pointing to the cluster of belongings Jake spoke again, "Well, I kind of understand the hand cart being here. Plus, that's a nice chainsaw that he had. And that old hand saw seems a bit different than the norm. But what are those other tools around them?"

What the visiting FBI agent was referring to were three metal utensils that were foreign to him. The first was what looked like a giant set of tongs, the next was a massive hand drill, the bit itself around eight inches to a foot long, and last was what resembled a giant arrow. There were different amounts of rust on each piece, and one could tell that they have a score or two of use under their belt. Probably items that had passed along the sale of the cabin in past generations. Moisture radiated from them due to recent use.

"I guess you have never been ice fishing," laughed Cecil, "those are used to cut a hole in the lake, like you saw out back a few minutes ago. Allen probably was ice fishing before dark, and prior to being attacked. Poor guy."

The rural policeman proceeded to explain to the city slickers what the equipment was technically used for.

"Pretty much you use the pick to start a hole, the chainsaw will cut the chunk, use the ice tongs to pull it out of the water, and the hand cart makes it an easy one-man job to move the block."

Jake smirked and grasped onto the pun, "Did you get your Eagle Scout badge for that report."

"You're quite the jokester," snickered Cecil, then his mood changed back to one of stoic professionalism, "nothing compelling in here, let's go back to where he was found."

Calmly the men retraced their steps and migrated back into the scene of the crime, where they all returned to a moment void of sound, yet full of pondering.

Being the newbie to this small crime fighting team Cecil stayed lowkey, but since he was the only one who knew Allen Marshall, he also tried to focus on any bits of information and/or memories that he could muster together to help any facet of the case.

Jake was mystified by the coziness, yet frigid feel of the cabin. They would eventually tour the home that Allen had temporarily surrendered to his philandering wife, but for now he was concentrating his attention on the current surroundings, trying to get a feel for the man who exited via those stairs in a sterile, cold body bag previously.

Isaac was taking his own approach to absorbing the abode before him. Wanting to get back to where the struggle had supposedly occurred, he was the first to wander up the stairs. From there he looked for details on the wall as to exactly where the candy dish had ricocheted from, along with any scuff marks or subtle details that could thread together more of the deadly tale that was written eighteen hours before.

Seeing his comrade ascend the stairs, Jake decided to follow suit. Except he continued this trip further into the home, and actually took a seat on the love seat in the living room, right across from the now smoldering open fireplace.

The small davenport was at least twenty years old, but had aged finely. It had a soft, yet durable texture to its blue toned plaid upholstery, including the fabric buttons and pleated skirt. The arms were a bit overstuffed, and the seats had been moderately worn through the years by those who enjoyed it many summers before.

Members of the squad had brought in a small space heater to help keep the temperature of the room over sixty degrees. They felt as if keeping the fireplace ignited could be a liability, or even result in destruction of the house. Plus, none of the men were keen on chopping any of the firewood that rested against the east side of the structure. Too many of them had been to instances where using an ax did not end up well for anyone.

Suddenly Cecil came bolting up the steps, taking two at a time, and was so excited that he could barely form the words that he was thinking until he was close enough to the FBI agents to relay them. "What are we trained to do when we are in danger? What would any law enforcement agent do?"

His face was an intense beet red hue from exerting such energy during his path upstairs, and also from the thrill of cracking an obvious clue that should have come easy to all of them.

While still sitting Jake rotated his wrists and let his hands drop, palms up, almost in the pose of when someone does not know the answer, but then stopped when indeed the correct response electrified in his head. "You go for your weapon."

"Right. Now I didn't check for a weapon on him. Was anything like that cataloged, Agent Morray?"

Shaking his head he supplied the answer, "No, we would have removed it immediately for multiple reasons."

"Okay, but do you remember seeing a holster on his hip earlier? I was too far in shock to think about that right then."

"No, but I have the pictures of him still elevated before he was taken down and to the morgue."

There was a cranberry red wingback chair with oak curved legs angled towards the brick fireplace and to the right of the love seat which Isaac sat in and configured the digital camera in such a way that he could turn it on and review the photos from earlier.

Still working off the enthusiastic energy he was generating, Cecil paced along the battered hardwood floors with his index finger curved over his lower lip. A perfect gesture for such an instance, even if it was completely stereotypical.

"Damn Wingard, we would've caught it at the autopsy later today, but this helps us now. Sure enough, he has an empty holster on his belt." This discovery was important, and the elation in Isaac's voice with this statement was proof of it.

Jake rose, and Cecil neared Isaac, then together they then bent over opposite shoulders of Isaac's in order to view for themselves the revelation. Attached to his right hip was a tan colored leather holster for a small handgun. And it was obviously vacant of any firearm.

Shrugging his shoulders Isaac asked, "I don't obviously carry a weapon in my position, but would you keep the holster on you even if you aren't carrying the gun?"

In response, both of the men who carried light armory daily shook their heads in a negative connotation.

"Well, where would the gun be then?" This came from Isaac again. "You guys are the experts when it comes to packing heat."

Cecil motioned his head upstairs, "I have a lock box under my bed if I am going somewhere where it's not kosher to have my Glock on me. And when I sleep, I have it in my nightstand drawer."

Nodding Jake agreed, "I have it locked in my gun cabinet, or it's under my pillow."

Abruptly Isaac stood up, allowing the camera to fall, in turn the strap around his neck kept it suspended while they went upstairs. "I haven't really looked up there either. Let's see what the second floor has to bring us."

The steps ascending were quieter than their subterrain counterpart. This pathway had a mahogany stained banister, which had a semi-bright shine, while each step was painted a dark blue, and had a small carpet pad on each elevated spot. There was a small, ordinary landing, and three simple hardwood doors, painted in a glossy eggshell white, all of which were open and untouched by the investigation thus far.

On the left side, and immediately off the landing, was the only bathroom of the structure, which was in a square shape. The original octagon white and black tiles, in a respective three to one ratio, covered the floor. Subway tiles in a lustrous finish, all in the same white hue except for one vertical strip which were narrower that was in noir black, encompassed the walls. One small rectangular window was built into the bathtub space, around the height of anyone's head, and in fogged glass for the appropriate privacy level.

A pedestal sink and matching stark white toilet, all older than the men who were surveying it, completed the lavatory.

The middle room had a simple twin bed with a copper toned piped headboard and footboard, with larger sized tubed focal points on each corner. Burgundy was the choice color for the decade old comforter, and teenage style clothes were randomly placed, probably by a soft throw, throughout the space.

Sitting on the soft pink carpeted floor were two suitcases that were open and had clothes draped along the sides, looking as if they were lava expelling from a rectangular black canvas volcano.

Without having to apply much logic, they came to a quiet assumption that the final room had to be that of the deceased. Before entering, Isaac gave the other men bright blue latex gloves to wear, which he also dressed his hands in since this was previously unexplored space, and they needed to take such sterile precautions.

Breaking up their quaint cluster they searched the small room that had a double sized bed, with a less ornate frame, a navy blue comforter, and this room actually had a small walk-in closet.

Morray went through the beaten maple wood nightstand which had a drawer on the top and a single door underneath, both with a worn nickel knob. No guns were currently being housed there.

Cautiously Wingard removed the blankets and adjusted the pillows on his limited search, yet no luck.

Finally in the walk-in closet was where Morris found the waist high gun safe, which had the secure door slightly ajar about six inches, and nothing inside besides some unused ammunition.

Isaac looked in and commented a rapid theory, "Maybe the killers stole it?"

Cecil looked up at the ceiling, then back to the other men.

"That is feasible, but he could be like a squirrel and hide it somewhere bizarre, and difficult to find."

For the next fifteen minutes or so, give or take a few clicks of the clock, the truth seekers were more thoroughly exploring rooms and closets, dressers and drawers, and anywhere else that the late agent would have used to hide his gun, or anything else that was pertinent to the inquest before them.

A few legal documents were bagged pertaining to Allen Marshall's life insurance policy and other such paperwork that were indicative of any financial motives. Which also would help the team of forensic accountants who work for the FBI and pursue such matters for justice in the very near future.

Again, they converged in the kitchen after all were content with their impromptu search. Located there all of the investigators were gazing in different directions, all seeking for some type of hidden message within those walls of where the supposed initial contact occurred that caused the downfall now before them.

Looking at Cecil, Jake conveyed an idea. "On several cases Agent Morray and I have re-enacted the struggle or attack. There's three of us, and evidence is showing that there were probably three of them total, so let's roleplay and see how everything ended up."

In perfect unison they all nodded a wordless agreement.

"Cecil," initiated Isaac, "I only saw the victim hanging. Out of our trio, who best fits the body build of Agent Marshall."

"That's easy, that would be Agent Morris."

Which was the truth, and very accurate. Both men had quite a few similarities in their body builds, and other physical aspects. Jake was forty-five, while Allen was a few weeks shy of fifty. They both had a solid core from both previous and current work necessities. Starting as a young man in the academy twenty-two years before, Jake had a notable physique that was slowly softening from age yet still impressive and up to par with the others in the bureau. While Allen had grown up on a farm where throwing hay bales was his first, and a very intense, workout as a teen. They both were around six feet tall, give or take an inch, so their frames were quite comparable.

Redish hair that brushed his ears and nape of his neck adorned Allen's head, and a decent amount of it even to the day he died was firmly there, while Jake had a rich and dark black toned high and tight cut style. A striking stud soap opera star style enriched Jake, while Allen had the true looks of a handsome hometown grown guy.

Facially Jake had the more defined jaw line and higher cheekbones, while Allen had a bit more of a rounder face, yet still slim. But for the essential purpose of the day, Jake was the best fit for the experimental performance.

The kitchen light was turned off, then Isaac and Cecil exited the back door. Retreating back into the living room, Jake next turned and entered the kitchen, then turned on the light as anyone would do during a normal winter evening. Once near the refrigerator he was acting as if he was looking for something to eat and/or cook. Or more likely contemplating a beverage.

That was when the other two, who were acting as intruders, entered abruptly and blitzed a fake attack on Jake. Using purely his instincts the seasoned pro turned and pulled his imaginary handgun for his defense. This was when Cecil, who was trained in such matters, used his right hand to push Jake's right forearm, which would in turn push the victim off balance and disarm him, allowing the metaphorical gun to hit the ground.

The assailants then wrestled the victim to the ground. In this instance they did so slowly and methodically so no one was hurt, yet they felt as if it would be accurate to the actual rush attack on Allen Marshall. In the midst of the fall, they did come in contact with where the small dinette table and chairs would have been placed, therefore launching the glass candy dish and initiating the breaking of it afterwards.

Jake was lying on the floor, getting a feel for how Allen would have landed, when he looked at the hidden space between the linoleum tile and a small wood curio, its color choice matching exactly the dinette set, and let out a single laugh. "I found the missing piece guys; his Glock is beneath that china cabinet."

*

"**G**od these hills are gorgeous down here, Cecil." The navigator looked side to side, then confirmed their route. "Do I keep going straight into town?"

"Those are the Enchanted Mountains of New York. And yes, keep going past The Expressway entrance and below its underpass, then at the three-way intersection take a right at the light."

The two men were now driving in Jake's black SUV together to try and stay somewhat lowkey in the highly gossiping small town. A marked cruiser would not allow them a stealth-like appearance. This was also the best vehicle for the heavy, wet lake effect snow that covered Route 305 and the adjoining fields and hills.

Coming to a slow, sliding stop Jake pointed at the burgundy brick building which had a large painted piece of cheese, and a fat mouse enjoying a chunk of it. "They have a cheese store and a cheese factory?" laughed Jake as he slowly and cautiously took a right turn after making sure the intersection was clear of other motorists.

"It's the largest employer around." Using his index finger the navigator did his job by indicating which direction to go. "The police department is just up this hill, so take a left. I'd name off local hot spots as markers, but you would have no clue what I was referencing."

"Affirmative on that."

Changing back to business Jake followed directions and relayed his thoughts on their next investigative steps. "We have to get this gun into evidence and examined by the two associate forensic technicians that are down here. It's doubtful, but I would like to see if it was discharged recently." Pausing at an intersection he confirmed a safe passage, then continued with his thoughts aloud. "I would like to go over to wherever Belmont is and check in on the autopsy. See what's going on there. Then we could question the son and ex-wife. Get a few names from them about who else to talk to. Also get in touch with his USDA partner. So, a lot of running around to do yet and we are pushing one in the afternoon already."

Thankful for the four-wheel drive, Jake pummeled through the snow of the gravel parking lot and to one of the many open spots in front of the large metal building that housed not only the police department, but also the department of public works for the village. Some parts of the steel structure were still painted in an orange and yellowish hue, while others were aged and rust was crawling along it such as ivy would to a scalise. The building was weathered but had given the town many loyal years of service, and many more to follow.

In this instance the dual-purpose structure was coming in quite handy. A few hours earlier Allen Marshall's USDA issued truck had been towed and brought into the garage portion via a locally owned tow truck which was contracted to perform such duties. It was placed into a private enclosed bay where welding usually occurred in the space. Forensic technicians were intensively working at combing through that vehicle for any other crucial clues.

With a small cardboard box in hand, Cecil made the short trip to the law enforcement entrance of the bi-plex facility. Being a manner minded professional, Jake hustled a little faster in order to open the glass door which had a curved aluminum handle. Once inside both men dragged their glistening ebony-colored boots on a commercial style small rectangular rug in a rugged, yet professional style in order to rid their soles of snow, followed by three stomps each to complete the cleansing job of the frigid precipitation.

There was a single CPD officer sitting on watch at the front of the semi-open bullpen style space. Included in the space behind him were a dozen or so cubicles, far too many for the six employed members of the department. Off to the far right were a few doors including an interrogation room, the chief's office, and a conference room.

Sitting to the right of the guard was a skinny redheaded young man who had strikingly similar features to the man that they were finding answers about.

"Trooper Wingard."

"Hi, you're Jared, right?"

"That's right."

"He's been waiting for you guys for the better part of an hour." This came from the weary watchman. "I told him I would take his number and give it to you, but he insisted on waiting here."

Wingard smiled, "We really cannot talk to you unless your mother is here, Son."

"I am eighteen, and we need to talk."

"Use the last room on the right, that's the interrogation room. First room is the conference room, and the forensic agents are in there working."

"Come on then, and this is Agent Morris. He is also working on your father's case."

Briefly, the new acquaintances shook hands.

"Trooper Wingard, get him comfortable in the room, I will drop this off to Morray's team in order to start their analysis, and then I will meet you gentlemen in there."

As proposed the three men dispersed, then congregated in the assigned room at a round yellow linoleum table with flecks of various colors. They sat in hard plastic chairs with bright aluminum frames. There was a small six cup coffee maker in the corner which Cecil turned on and started to brew some java since he was familiar with the room having questioned a handful of suspects within these walls for previous cases.

While the beverages were being prepared Jake started the conversation. "We did not plan on having you find us so promptly. Please excuse us if we haven't really created too many questions as of yet."

"Well, I think my mom's boyfriend did it."

Both investigators looked at each other, then Cecil took the lead. "I understand that it's very shocking to find your father like that. I highly recommend some therapy for you. Knowing your dad from the field myself, even I was put back by seeing him like that."

Using some skills by buffering the initial complaint, he was hoping to figure out why the deceased's son also thinks that this is a homicide, regardless of the name of a potential suspect. It had not yet been mentioned to anyone outside of the immediate law enforcement circle, even to Agent Lyons, Allen's partner, that murder was indeed the buzzword.

"But let's not say things that could really hurt or affect people negatively." The FBI interrogator was going to cover his bases with this comment.

"I know my dad would never kill himself."

"Depression hides in everyone, look at Robin Williams." This came from Jake who was also sending out feelers as to why the offspring of the deceased would venture down this highway.

"Well, he missed my band performance. Even if he was going to kill himself, he wouldn't have ruined my senior concert like that."

Pouring three cups of the rich, dark coffee Cecil dispersed them around the table, tilted his head to motion that there were condiments for their brews on the same small table as the pot, then continued with this type of inquiry. "Something will just click in their head, and nothing will stop them."

Getting irritated from the lack of sleep the night before, and of feeling that he was not being heard, Jared flared his nostrils and started to show aggression through his tone of voice, and deliverance of his words. "How would my father hang himself with nothing to stand on? Why were Clayton's boot prints on my father's kitchen floor? And around the outside of the house?" With each fine point of the scene that he was conveying his voice rose such as a crescendo in a piece of music. "Why was my Aunt Charlotte's candy dish smashed to smithereens? Something that my father would never do since it was cherished." With zest the teen went from being on the defense, fighting a strong offensive line. "Why did Clayton throw a fit when I wanted to go see why my dad wasn't at my concert. Maybe I should be the detective here."

Feeling the tension rising, the intended inspectors read the other's mind. It was apparent that the details which were leading them to know that it was a slaughtering were obvious to their witness also.

After tapping his fingers three times on the tabletop Cecil sighed and caved in on bluffing the lad. "So, what we say to you now does not leave here. Especially if you have someone in mind who could have hurt your father."

"Deal. You got it. My lips are sealed. I want to know what happened to my dad."

"Well, we have the FBI investigating, that is who Agent Morris works for. And we feel as if it might be a homicide. We are not releasing that to anyone."

"Good. I want Clayton and my egg donor to burn."

The cops looked at each other, then paused, both knowing that it was two men who took down the late father. But keeping the information flowing, maybe they could figure out more from the mourning child.

"Hold up. We have to investigate every avenue first. Your father might have made enemies working for the USDA. And we must follow that road thoroughly also."

Jake took over with a few ideas that could help reign the questioning in. "Was your father a handyman? I didn't see a tool shed, or any tools downstairs."

"No. My dad just had a few old tools for when we ice fished when I was a kid. Which we haven't done in years. Too much hassle." The storyteller shook his head. "He never tinkered around the cabin, or house for that matter. He would hire someone to do it." A memory caused the lad to make a stoic smirk. "Kinda funny, my dad hired Clayton to do some chores on Beebe Hill before he found out that he and mom were fooling around."

Leaning in, Jake tilted his head forward and rested his arms on the table. "So, your dad wouldn't have a drill somewhere."

"No. My father was a talented man in many ways, but he could barely paint a room, let alone use a power screwdriver."

"But this Clayton would? I heard from a very credible source that he and your mother were messing around on the downlow."

"They were. I found out about it first. And Clayton does odd jobs around town. His truck is full of tools and stuff like that."

Absorbing this knowledge Cecil leaned back in his chair, his coffee cup empty and on the table. "So does anything else seem a bit bizarre about last night, or even leading up to it between Clayton and your dad. Has to be some animosity going on through the breakup."

"Well usually I stay with dad. But yesterday was my mom's birthday. And for the past week she and Clayton have been begging me to stay the night up on Beebe Hill. To celebrate, and as a gift to Mom to see more of me. But after Dad didn't come to my concert, I wanted to go see if he was okay. Which obviously he wasn't." Softly he shrugged. "Mom and Clayton had a fit about me going to the cabin to see what was going on. They wanted to do cake and presents before they went to bed and kept saying not to worry. They were furious at the end that I left. Clayton almost wrestled the keys from my hands at the school before I got away and into my truck."

Midway through this tale Jake began to take notes about the whole scenario and the motive that was unfolding right there before them.

"Wow," started Cecil, "that is quite a lot going on."

"Is it enough to arrest him?"

"Not yet, I need substantial evidence. Physical evidence. But here's my card."

Both of the interrogators handed the solemn boy their business cards. At the same time Jake transcribed Jared's cellphone number into his notes so that there could be easy communication among them through the unfolding case.

As they were leaving the room Cecil asked a question that popped into his head, and was very relevant. "Do you feel safe staying at your mom's with Clayton there? Especially since we haven't released the cabin yet."

"I am at my grandmother's over on Wolf Creek. She's quite upset, so it's good for both of us."

Jared was exiting the facility and walking to the entrance, ready to shake some of the grief off. While the lawmen were about to discuss their next steps in the investigation an assistant forensics technician named Jay opened up the conference room holding a single piece of freshly printed paper with a look of surprise and urgency on his face. "The IT department just sent me this. They unlocked Allen Marshall's work email account. For nearly six months he has been getting death threats and not reporting them. One that he got last week said quote-unquote, 'I am going to filet you like a fish and mount you on the wall.'"

This breaking news was a game changer to say the very least.

*

"**A**llen was the type of agent who wouldn't want to add more trouble for a criminal, even if they did the damage themselves." The storyteller cleared his throat and held back some tears. "He was always trying to find the best in them, since he knew how hard it is to run a farm in this overtaxed state. So, he let them blow off some steam that was directed at us when we had to investigate them for fraud. Or when maybe they just simply misfiled a tax return, or made a subconscious error on some miscellaneous form with a clerk." The small, whimsical smile on his face dropped off when the type of suspects they were privy to changed. "But a lot of the time they knew what they were doing, and tried to play the dumb card. That's when I played the bad cop, or agent, and called their bluff on their bullshit."

Cecil tapped the printed out picture and information from the New York State DMV about a specific member of the Cuba township. "I agree, Frank. He was a bit lenient at times. Now I remember going to this Brian Swartson's property about a domestic dispute with his old lady a few years back. Threatened his live-in girlfriend at the time, but she refused to press charges. Come to think of it, the neighbor called it in because he could hear them fighting from an acre away and was afraid for the girl's safety."

"Yeah," started USDA Agent Frank Lyons, Allen's now former partner, "he is a real piece of work. We knew he was guilty of ripping off two grants specifically, and we were getting all of the paperwork ready to file an indictment with the federal prosecutor in the next few weeks. He has been on our radar for close to a year and has known we were investigating him the past six months."

Jake looked up from his notes with much interest, "How much was he stiffing the government for?"

"Around twenty thousand, give or take. Fabricating who he was employing and how long they worked there. Especially minorities and past felons since some grants will pass along a nice check for hiring them."

Shaking his head, Cecil laughed, "Gotta love how he used his own internet connection, but a fake email address to send all of those threats."

Frank shrugged, "Might be the prime reason to hurt Allen then. Greed and arrogance." There was a bitter moment of pause. "Can't believe he's gone." Mourn captivated the aura of the saddened man and paused their momentum again, but in a respectful manner.

"Oh, that reminds me," Jake shifted a few pages in his notepad to a fresh leaf, "when did you see him last?"

"So, we finished up at the office at, oh hmmm, three

thirty. We start our mornings early since the local farmers do the same. He said that Jared had a concert at seven, but texted me at five twenty about another case. Nothing at all seemed off with him."

Cecil and Jake looked at each other, and the former announced his tentative findings. "As usual protocol we won't get an official time of death until the autopsy. But I responded at nine fifteen to the call. His last message was to you Frank at five twenty. We dumped his phone and that was the final correspondence he had. Therefore the time of death for now is between five twenty one and let's say nine."

Nodding Jake agreed, "I can feel comfortable about that finding. So where does this Swartson live?"

"Well," started Cecil, "up Rawson Road, about seven miles from Allen's cabin."

"Which down here," said Jake, "is not that far of a length. Let's get out there and have a chat with him. See if he was all talk, or if he had some bite in him. You riding up with us, Frank?"

"I got my work truck with me. I will be right behind you. This guy can be a bit squirrely, to say the least."

In the interrogation room where they were having their impromptu briefing all three lawmen proceeded to buckle their holsters onto their bodies, then secure their department issued weapons. Afterwards they applied their desired types of Kevlar and body armor, then their official jackets. In such frigid weather they did not mind the multiple layers, in fact they appreciated them for a variety of safety and warmth reasons.

Thinking ahead, the men also borrowed three walkies from the CPD for smooth communication, especially heading to a rural area where cell phone reception is far from superior. Nodding to one another they knew their mission, then proceeded to head into the parking lot, ready to lay down some justice.

Frank Lyons rolled out first in his hunter green extended cab truck which showcased the USDA seal on both sides of the vehicle, plus it had multiple emergency lights hidden in the grill and hood of the four-wheel drive. Jake followed suit in his black SUV that also had the camouflaged illumination. Both modes of transportation had enhanced engines to keep them up to pace with any dire situation.

As they negotiated the turns around the lake a steady stream of chunky, heavy snowflakes, some the size of a half dollar coin, fell at a hurried speed from the puffy gray and white clouds down to the earth where they quickly and enthusiastically accumulated on the grass, and on the road before them.

Rawson Road is a narrow two-lane country passageway between Cuba and its neighbor Rushford, who share the same school district. The houses are normally acres, if not miles apart from their neighbors, and often set a substantial distance back from the road.

The multi-mile route was a peaceful time for all the responders to ease their minds for a few minutes.

With a sharp turn onto a large driveway Frank led the way to the Swartson homestead, with Jake and Cecil two hundred feet or so behind. Snow was thickening and multiplying on all that it landed on. With heavy clouds and hefty precipitation falling, the midafternoon sky was darkening and adding some difficulty to their overall vision.

A modest Dutch style two story home with a detached garage, both two toned painted in mustard yellow and aged white colors, sat on a small knob of the land around three hundred meters from the road. A small circular trail of the driveway ran in front of the structures. This all sat on an open expanse of approximately fifteen acres of fields, with a weathered and beaten bare wood barn about a half mile to the east on the acreage.

In the middle of the loop was a ten-year-old truck idling, smoke billowing and the country air molested by the roughness of the motor. The driver's side fender and the hood were of different colors and the back panel of the bed was mostly rusted out. Its emaciated metal hung loose and was shaking with the vibrations of the struggling, yet powerful, engine.

A surprised bottle blond female passenger was inhaling hard on a long cigarette, its ash close to a quarter inch and glowing red. When she saw the growing images of the two new vehicles in the area her eyes electrified and smoke pummeled from her lungs and through her open window as she let out a boisterous cougher's voice yell, "Brian. Get your ass in gear. The fuckin' pigs are already here."

Immediately the front door flew open, and out came a distraught man of approximately forty years old and of a lacking physical build. There was some muscle to his body, but also the wear and tear of many years with more emphasis on the playing hard compared to working hard mantra had shown its invasion of his being. Beneath an aged trucker's hat, which bore the name of a minor league baseball team from nearby Bradford, Pennsylvania, he had a curled mullet in a dark brown, almost invading of black, with a few strands of rogue silver. His hands were gritty and dirty, as they always were no matter how many times he applied soap and water. In those labored mitts he was grasping onto a basic mauve colored canvas well-worn suitcase. It was fully packed to the max, and ready to hit the road with the fugitives.

To match his baby momma, he also had a well enjoyed lit cigarette drooping from his left lower lip.

When it registered that this was not a meeting about the simplicity of polishing some information on employees on forms, and instead in reference to the raging morbid gossip of the county, Brian Swartson tossed the aged luggage into the bed of the vehicle and ran, to his best out of shape abilities, around the hood of the struggling pick up and into the driver's side.

As this movement was transpiring Jake was already on the radio with Frank. "We got us a runner. That never looks innocent."

Violently throwing the steering wheel shaft mounted gear shift into drive, and simultaneously tossing the lever running on the floor bed from two-wheel drive to four, the now leader of the chase slammed on the gas pedal, throwing a wave of snow behind him before grasping proper traction to get the pursuit started.

In a first, and futile attempt, Jake steered his vehicle to the right section of the base of the exit for Brian. But this did not phase the escapee in any capacity. Instead, he revved his motor in order to gain some much-needed motion and made slippery, yet effective movement through a patch of his front yard and around the first line of defense. Agent Lyons was trying to keep the action at the property rather than complicating this interaction by adding it to the local roadway, which was far from ideal for any type of chase.

Swerving back onto his driveway Brian applied more speed and then took a right onto Rawson Road, heading away from Cuba and towards Rushford. Even possibly into the Buffalo metro if the caravan ran in his favor and his back hills driving skills were proven successful. Although this was unlikely since it was close to eighty miles to the north.

Luckily equipped with a scanner/radio in his truck, Frank was spinning his own U-turn while communicating to the dispatcher that there was a suspect on the run.

Being on his home turf Brian knew the rises and lulls of the road, along with each angle of the pavement close to his abode. With that he could predict, even in the ever-worsening torrent weather, how his old truck would react with each foot of the blizzard covered decades old asphalt and how he could somehow escape from the trouble that he had just had caused.

Sitting shotgun to him his girlfriend was furious. "Brian, I told you not to do this shit."

"Shut up, Kelly Ann. No one forced you to run with me."

"Well, you had no reason to run."

Since he was somewhat familiar with these back roads Frank was able to stay within a quarter of a mile behind Brian, which the runaway was not pleased with this fact. Also since his truck was half a decade newer than the clunker ahead of him, this also helped Frank close in the decently sized gap between them.

A large bend, which inclined exactly at its major curve, was ahead. There was a blindness caused by a large patch of evergreen saplings that were generously enveloped in rich needles. Brian knew this path his entire life, and knew that so many predicaments ahead could be an obstacle, but being a gambling man with extremely poor judgment he swiftly forged ahead with his only focus being on victory.

Feeling the truck sway and slide he kept pressing the gas and steering as taught as a teen into the turn, and then forced more acceleration than he should have through the twist of the road. With much confidence he let out a mischievous grin as he cleared the pines.

Unfortunately, this was extremely premature since at the break of visibility was an Amish horse and buggy, going at a much slower speed and without any means to pull over abruptly in such instances as a truck barreling in the snow towards it.

Instantly seeing the many errors in his risk taking, Brian bolted the truck to the left in hopes that he would not tap the edge of the cart, which was probably full of a family, and possibly adding manslaughter charges onto the many problems that he had to face ahead of him in the very near future.

An erupting whinnying of the horse cracked through the air as it revolted back and onto its hind legs in fear and horror of the near collision of the invading enemy.

In response to this fresh obstacle his truck began to shift and slide so that it was going sideways alongside the now panic-stricken operator of the mare. His rear tire struck the sand and grit of the shoulder of the road causing the truck to abruptly reposition itself to the proper driving format. This caused the driver and passenger to turbulently whip from side to side in their seats, both striking their head on their respective side window, Kelly Ann's movement causing a small spiderweb crack in her side.

Her answer to this unnecessary addition to their already

plight ridden journey was to jab her lit cigarette, one she ignited during the chase knowing that it might be a while until she got one again, right into Brian's fleshy elbow.

In turn he muttered a few names for a woman's genitalia and female dogs beneath his breath as nicknames for her current, yet justified, behavior. But the evader knew that he was so far into the wrong that he should keep his explicit comments to a low mumble.

Thankfully the Amish family had pulled over and into the field, afraid and filled with the shock of what was conspiring around them by the time that Jake and Frank had rounded the devil's curve. This allowed both of them to gain some space on Brian. Which enraged the head truck's fears and caused him to gun his engine again. His antiquated muffler rumbled like thunder, and blasted tar colored smoke in the air behind him. Causing a small hole in the overhead ozone. The unsteady footing under him down to the currently dropping flurries caused his truck to again fishtail.

Due to the season and weather, a dusk like feel was coming around them. Their headlights were on while guiding their way and keeping them on the road. Fifteen minutes and eight miles had transpired so far, and no one was willing to call it a defeat yet. And the reinforcements that Frank had called out for on the scanner were at least six minutes away, depending on what turns Brian led them down next.

A long, even trail of the aged asphalt was coming up before them. Trees were on either side of it for a mile, but Brain knew that there were no turns ahead, or even any motorways that fed onto it. So this was his chance to achieve max speed and really put some space between him and the fuzz.

About half a mile into this speedway Brian's headlights reflected off of three deer, which all began an aggressive sideways advance. Being spooked, one doe and a buck had enough notice to jump up the embankment and into safety. Sadly, the third ten point trophy buck clipped Brain's front bumper while the truck was barreling in at approximately fifty seven miles an hour.

This caused a massive spinning motion using the momentum of the truck and the effect of the deer setting if off balance. On the right of the road the truck dipped into a two foot deep ditch causing it to ramp up and then to start rolling into a small open field. The rotating truck missed the larger trees, and the four maple saplings it encountered helped slow the truck before it could do massive damage.

Frank gunned his truck up and over the ditch safely while Jake and Cecil came to a sliding stop. They in turn dispersed from the SUV, guns drawn, running in the field maintaining their focus on the pursuit's vehicle roll. This was while many pieces of the body ripped and flew off, littering the space around it. Glass was rapidly shattering, and mirrors were bending with each rotation then ripping and detaching from the frame, then ricocheting off and settling in the snowy ground.

With a final revolution around, the vehicle bounced off of its tires again, then slowly flipped one final time, quivering as it steadied itself. Massive damage was apparent, and it was no longer drivable.

Once his truck was stopped, Frank leapt from his door and began sprinting, his Glock also drawn and ready for battle since they all knew that a country boy like Brian would not enter any appointment including the law without some type of impressive weaponry.

The tattered assorted color jalopy finally came to a rest on its hood and roof. The chasers were unsure of the state of those who just landed. It was a quandary if they could be hurt, dead, trusted, or in fact aiming at them, ready to disperse slugs.

Cecil got his sights on Brian first. His hand unwavering as he pointed his handgun between Brian's eyes, a patch of skin which was bloodied due to the accident that just unfolded before them.

"Police! Don't fuckin' move, Swartson. I should reshape your forehead for almost killing that family back there."

Jake trudged at a sprinting pace to the other side of the

crushed truck. "Passenger, hands where I can see them. You don't want to meet Jesus today, do ya?"

Shaking from shock, the cold, and pure fear, both occupants of the total vehicle stuck their trembling hands out of the broken windows that they were seated on.

While Jake was steadfast on his gun pointed at Kelly Ann, Frank went to the driver's side, grabbed Brian by his forearms, his nails gripping and cutting into the fugitive's skin, then yanked him full force and over a blanket of shattered glass out of the crunched four by four and onto the blistering cold ground. Flipping him with no mercy he then shoved his knee into the middle of the detainee's back and wrestled his arms to the same spot, then tethered his wrists with the cold handcuffs.

Cecil holstered his piece, then took over while Frank went to assist Jake, replacing Frank's knee with his boot, but adding more pressure to the piece of scum.

Frank manhandled Kelly Ann in the same fashion, no leniency was given to the female as she was an accomplice, and just as guilty as the driver in everyone's eyes. Per procedure she was also cuffed without haste.

A parade of four Allegany County Sheriff's cars, every single one that were running the roads that day, parked along the tree lined road as the arrested duo were thrown into separate back seats of two official vehicles. Reports were being filled out in the heated front seats of several cruisers, and a tow truck was coming along in order to haul the ruptured pickup to the Cuba DPW/PD building so that it could be analyzed and inspected properly by Isaac Morray and his waiting team.

Fuming mad, and ready to tear apart the subject at hand, Frank Lyons opened the door of the patrol car where Brian Swartson was being detained in. "So, you really put your money where your mouth is and offed my partner."

"I ain't did shit. I have a fucking alibi. I didn't snuff out that fucker."

"What do you mean?"

"I was in Buffalo at the hockey game last night."

"Then why'd you run?"

"Cause you're gonna pin it on me anyway."

Suddenly Agent Lyons realized that the stupidity of the suspect was limitless if indeed the story was true.

*

A few gray, textured cubicle walls had been moved and repositioned in the CPD bullpen style office space, then two vacant unpainted silver metal desks had been pushed together as a mirror image of each other. The shades of each were drastic, and did not match. But this setup was more for function than a design competition. Staging the business furniture pieces almost as if they were one single partners desk was vital for their purpose. Cecil and Jake had configured the furniture this way with the optimal arrangement for the duration of their investigation. Three mismatched tables in a variety of wood stains, all with differing styles of scratches, and a bent and worn brown metal file cabinet outlined their impromptu workstation.

Glossy white cardboard takeout containers with thin aluminum handles containing different forms of rice were alongside black plastic rectangular containers with matching clear lids which contained sauce-covered meats and various vegetables were strewn over the desk blotters. The men were using simple snow colored paper plates to fix their own combinations from the buffet, which had five different entrees to choose from. Cecil had driven a few blocks away to the only Chinese restaurant in town to pick up their much-earned dinner while they worked on the mountain of paperwork that their road adventure had caused.

The two appointed investigators were in their respective office chairs munching on their cuisine while Frank had pulled up a single hard plastic chair, yellow in color, to the end of Jake's workstation as a casual way to sit as a team. The policeman had grabbed three liters of soda; one regular cola, one diet, one lemon-lime, from the take-out joint. Using styrofoam cups that were found in a supply closet off of the conference room they were washing down their smorgasbord as they were discussing what they knew so far about Brian Swartson and Kelly Ann Clark, and what charges they would be filing against which one while they waited for Brian's lawyer to finally arrive.

"So, for Kelly Ann," started Cecil as he was mixing some white rice into a healthy portion of shrimp and lobster sauce on his plate, "let's charge her with resisting arrest, then drop it after she talks to us about what she knows when it comes to the question of the night if Brian did it or not."

Deep in thought about this idea Jake rotated his cup of diet soda in small circles, causing the liquid to swirl and for the carbonation to increase resulting in a multitude of bubbles to release. "I wouldn't be opposed to that. But the kicker is that Brian swears up and down how solid his alibi is."

In response Frank laughed while scraping a few pieces of rice with a plastic fork from his plate. Due to the grief of losing his partner of several years and the stress of the earlier chase, he was lightly eating, mostly just for show. "Well, he said he was at the hockey game in Buffalo last night. They did play, but does he expect us to accept a ticket stub that he could have ripped apart himself?"

Swallowing, Jake shrugged, "I have a call out to someone who owes me a favor. Bagged his ex-wife who was sending threats through the mail, trying to intimidate him. Luckily, he works as an event coordinator. In turn he has access to the footage from the game. I sent him pictures of Brian and Kelly Ann, along with their seat numbers. That was forty-five minutes ago. So, we will see."

Rolling his eyes Cecil then lamented, "His alibi was definitely not going to a Mensa meeting." A smirk helped glue the joke together, then he pressed on. "But why would you fuckin' run from us, with a packed bag, if you're innocent."

Quickly Frank fielded this question. "Down in these parts, they are big on conspiracies. But in turn they want you to believe their tall tales. From what Brian said before he requested his lawyer, he was afraid that I would pin it on him, just like how we were, quote-unquote, 'pinning the fraud charges on him since we want to take his land.' When in truth he used family members' social security numbers, without their consent, on forms claiming grant money based on attributes that these people didn't qualify for. Period. He has told himself these lies so many times that he believes them and that we just want to throw him in federal prison so that the county can take his land and sell it."

"Afraid that the government is going to steal from him, but he is stealing from the government?" Jake scooped some pork fried rice while stating this obvious point, then put it on his stained plate. Opening a packet of soy sauce with his tooth while grasping it with his forefinger and thumb, he then squirted the sodium filled flavor enhancer on his newly added ration.

"That's one way of simplifying it," added Frank.

Dylan, the CPD officer who was on desk duty at the station to keep watch on the entrance and next door DPW garage, and to aid the investigators, walked back to the gentlemen and knocked on the cubicle wall out of respect. "The infamous leech on Allegany County society Joseph Stevvins is here, and is claiming to be Brain Swartson's attorney."

"About time. Send him to the interrogation room. I will run back and grab Swartson from his holding cell." This direction came from Agent Morris.

The reserve cop returned to his post in order to instruct the solicitor as to where to go, while Agent Lyons and Trooper Wingard took a few final bites of their chow and then headed to the intended meeting space.

As expected Brian Swartson, covered in bruises and cracked, dried blood from the senseless crash was sitting in one of the two plexiglass-encased cells that the department had. Being such a small holding facility they did not have any prepared food for inmates, so the two suspects were given a variety of dollar menu items from the in-town arched quick burger joint. Brian had picked at some of the food but did not consume much. Although it was steadily becoming a common fact that he probably would not see fast-food for the next few years he should have indulged in it. Although he may not be the right fit for the homicide, the wild expedition that he took the lawmen on will be resulting in numerous charges, and serving a significant time in the New York State penitentiary system was a given.

"Come on Swartson, hands through the opening. You know the drill, I've heard that you've spent some time in here on and off throughout your life."

The prisoner stood, shook a few crumbs from his clothes, still the same attire that he wore earlier, turned around, and backed himself up to the door of the unit which had a waist-high rectangular opening that he put his hands and wrists through. This spot was where Jake handcuffed the reckless citizen, then he unlocked and opened the door.

Guiding the detainee through the small station by the shoulder, they entered the interrogation room where the lawyer and other men were waiting.

Joseph Stevvins was a slim man, clean shaven, with a full head of vibrant black hair, dyed bi-weekly by the best salon in Olean. Appearance was part of his clout. Being a man of forty-five, give or take a birthday, he had aged quite well. With a large nose as the main focus of his face he wore it well, especially since it was large and hooked downward at the end. It possessed an authoritative essence, and gave him a hawklike aura, which he not only enjoyed, but owned with pride.

Even late on a Friday he wore a well-tailored black pinstriped suit with a canary yellow dress shirt and a sky-blue tie, which had a flat fabric with no shine. There was a simplistic, yet refined presentation that it exuded.

His ink black shoes registered far on the other side of the spectrum and were shining as if they had a coat of ice over them. To add pizazz, his argyle socks helped by having added some sort of fun to his style, which in turn acted as an endearing trait that warmed people up to the controversial lawyer.

Being six feet tall, his hands were plentiful and dense, yet soft due to the type of work he was sworn to do. The lengthy fingers with substantial girth that he held were tapping the tabletop waiting for his client, who had already paid a large retainer, cash of course, a few months before pertaining to the fraud case, was being sought and escorted over.

Although he was silent during the short walk from his cell, once he saw his lawyer in the room he became arrogant and boisterous. "It's my buddy Joey! You piggies are so screwed now. We are going to sue you for so much money that your grandkids will be paying mine in restitution."

With a single lifted hand with an open palm his advisor silenced the rowdy offender. "I need some time alone with my client to discuss everything. As of right now what is he charged with?"

Ready to unleash on both men for every sin that Brian Swartson had committed lately, Jake Morris started rambling them off. "For starters 18 U.S.C. section 241."

"Threatening a federal agent? And who are you?"

"FBI Agent Jacob Morris."

"And he threatened you? Well, when you trespass on my client's property and refuse to leave, therefore causing him to retreat for his own safety, that is not a threat."

"I am not the one he threatened. We have several emails sent from your client's IP address at his residence that contain death threats against USDA Agent Allen Marshall."

"I will be happy to clarify those when I question him on the stand."

Cecil smirked and shook his blond head. "Can't badger a dead man, Joseph."

"Trooper Wingard, I haven't even had time to greet you yet. Plant any evidence lately?"

"Nah, have you finally looked up the word 'ethics' in the dictionary yet?"

"So what other falsities are you constructing against my

client? I did hear about the plight of Agent Marshall. However, the rumor mill strongly states suicide. But please, amuse me with what charges I will be having dismissed very soon."

"Fleeing and eluding federal agents. Reckless driving." Jake took back over the laundry list of offenses. "Endangering the welfare of a child. Speeding. Hell, I am going to count every single blasted time that he turned the corner without using his blinker."

"I need time with Mister Swartson, if you don't mind."

The truth-seeking trio left their counterpart duo alone for their legally sacred time. Being that an escape, even with Swartson handcuffed, was a possibility, they stayed close by to tackle the man if necessary. Which they would enjoy too much, especially taking him down on the rigid concrete flooring in the building would add much pleasure on such a somber day. But at the same time, they had to keep a big enough bubble from the interrogation room that they could not be accused of eavesdropping and jeopardizing many parts of their case.

Straightening his tie as he opened the wooden door of the interrogation room, he engaged again with the investigators. "Please join us so that we can settle the matter, and all of us, including my client, can leave."

The three beckoned men headed back to the space, all rolling their eyes, and Cecil made the comment that they were all thinking, "Or you and your client can share a cell tonight if this gets out of hand."

Regrouping and finding seats in the small room, the attorney cleared his throat. "We can lightly discuss the tragic death of the USDA agent, but don't be surprised when I shut down the majority of such inquiries."

"That's usually how it rolls with you and me, Joe." This jab came from Cecil again. It was apparent that the men had a sordid history with differing sides of the law.

"Anyway. So first and foremost, I want to emphasize the fact that my client has an alibi two hours away for when Agent Marshall committed suicide."

Shaking his head, Jake commented on this statement. "I have sources within the hockey arena who are reviewing video content from the game, specifically focusing on the area where your client claimed to have seats with his accomplice. And at this point it is a murder investigation. It is clear that foul play, and a cover up, are all involved."

"And what evidence do you have that Mr. Swartson was involved in this incident?"

"Well," Jake cleared his throat, "my forensics team gained access to the late agent's federal email, and several were sent from an email address, the first part being 'fuckusda,' and all coming from Mr. Swartson's address on Rawson Road."

"Anyone could have hacked into that Wi-Fi network and framed my client."

"That ain't possible." This was the first time that the defendant spoke, and the look on his attorney's face relayed the fact that he should stay quiet. "I got me a VPN and all the software to keep me protected. I don't want the government reading my messages."

Joe Stevvins whispered, using only the lower left part of his mouth, in his client's direction. "Shut up Brian. Let me throw some reasonable doubt around."

"Well, I don't want them thinking that they can just infiltrate me like that."

"Let's move on," the discouraged defensive mediator cleared his throat and shook his head, "what other evidence did you have before raiding my client's home without a warrant or any type of clause?"

Shifting in his seat, Frank Lyons fielded this question, "There was no 'raiding' done today. We pulled up to ask him a few questions. Our sights were focused on someone else until we found the death threats."

"But you barged down the door just to ask questions to Mr. Swartson?"

A grand feeling of puzzlement arose among the coppers who were at the scene and had experienced the interaction.

Cecil spoke up in response to the falsities, especially since he did not want to have them avalanche into larger problems down the line for everyone involved. "I am unsure of what information that your client gave you during your phone call earlier, but we never left our vehicles."

Solicitor Stevvins looked at his client, and again spoke softly, "I thought that you said they were drawing guns forcing themselves inside of the dwelling?"

Brian crossed his arms and shook his head one time. "It felt as if they were."

Grasping onto any straw available at this point, his counselor moved on. "But fleeing, how can you say that? He felt threatened and left the property in duress for self-defense due to being intimidated by law enforcement."

A smirk came across Cecil's face, "Did he mention that he was coming out of the front door with a suitcase packed, then tossed it into the bed of the pickup and jumped into the cab as we were coming up the driveway? We didn't even have our lights on."

Redness crept up Joseph Stevvin's neck through his jawline and up to his cheeks. Irritation was accompanying the change in coloration. Again, he tried to subtly speak to his, now possibly terminated, client. "Why did you not mention this to me before Brian?"

"See, I can't even trust you. I need someone on my side."

"I am on your side, but I need the facts, not a fairy tale." With anger and frustration, the law interpreter karate chopped the top of the table.

The semi-cracked screen of the ink black smartphone belonging to Agent Morris illuminated, and the body vibrated leading the device in a crooked escape, lastly sending a pulsating tone in the air. Quickly he picked it up from the tabletop, slightly juggling it, then swiped across the face of it and answered, making sure to click the speaker mode option. "Hey Tony. How did your research go, finding my suspect in a haystack."

The unknown voice answered, "Do you want me to email

you the pictures? I matched several shots throughout the night with the two you sent pictures of."

"You are completely sure?" Jake was not expecting it to be so easy to rule out Brain Swartson.

"Sure, as you and I are talking, friend. We can zoom in on any seat and replay any shot from any point of the game."

"Thanks again."

"No problem."

The agent ended the call and looked at the suspect. "Well, I am not going to charge Kelly Ann with any crimes since she seemed to be an unwilling participant. I should charge you with kidnapping her, but I won't. But talk to your lawyer Brain. Because I am still nailing you to the cross for fleeing and almost killing that Amish family."

Abruptly Joseph steadied himself in his seat. "What about an Amish family?"

Looking up towards the ceiling the detainee sighed, "They pulled out in front of me, and I almost couldn't stop in time."

"Well, we can negotiate those down to probation at the most."

Frank Lyons grinned ear to ear, "Don't forget threatening a federal agent, and I have all of those fraud charges that will be expedited through the courts now buddy. You won't be watching those hockey pucks in person anytime soon.

*

Checking to ensure that the aged, stained cream metal door numbered room seven of the Cuba Lake Motel was securely locked with one hand, and juggling a paper coffee cup with the other, Agent Jacob Morris firmly slammed it shut. Ensuring that the lock had engaged he then attempted to push it back into the daily rental's space. After this test he was quite confident that it was indeed secure. With so much to do, he was ready to take on the day, even if it was just after six in the morning on the first Saturday of the investigation. This fell two days after the death of Allen Marshall. Quickly he made the four snow riddled steps to the passenger side of Trooper Cecil Wingard's police cruiser, who was waiting quite patiently with the heat at the right blaring temperature.

Opening the awaiting door, he hopped inside. "So, you're driving today?"

Whipping the steering wheel to the left, then popping the car in reverse, the cop then answered as they were exiting the ten space parking lot. "Snow should be melting, and I know these county roads and how to get to Belmont fastest."

Cecil accelerated onto the adjoining I-86, which the locals call "The Expressway" since it was the only one of its kind in the region. All other roadways were less urban-like and more like the inspiration of a country song.

"So, the FBI sent down our coroner from Rochester, Dr. Christopher Hemple. Awesome examiner, very detailed and thorough. Nothing passes by him." For a moment he glanced out onto the wonder of the land, then was pulled back into the conversation. "I was told by my SAC last night that they should be done with everything and waiting for us at seven am so that we don't miss a beat investigating. And our guy wants to get back to civilization as soon as possible."

"Oh yeah, those city slickers." The Patrolman snickered. "Roger is a good undertaker. You'll see his funeral home. It's absolutely gorgeous. Second generation in the field, he took over for his dad before I was born, and he is the only show in town."

"Oh," said Jake, taken back, "we aren't going to a morgue?"

Shaking his head Cecil laughed, "Oh you urban boys."

On the rest of the forty-five-minute trip the duo discussed how Kelly Ann had been released within an hour of their interrogation of Brian Swartson, and how naive her thinking was that Brian would be released, or at least given bail that night. When in turn he wouldn't see a judge for a few days, and bond was unlikely, with solid reasoning behind that.

They also outlined their plans for the rest of the day

after the morbid trip that they were taking on was scheduled so early. This included talking to Allen's mother, along with the estranged wife and new boyfriend. Feeling unsure of how solid this investigative path would lead them they were also discussing potential other routes to explore in respect to the late agent's demise. These being as far-fetched as a disgruntled neighbor at the lake, to maybe a sin the man had committed in his past. Going so far back that the revenge would be served ice cold.

The Expressway led them the majority of the way to their destination, and then they took a few winding country roads until they entered the village of Belmont, which was similar to the ones of Cuba. Historic Victorian and Colonial style houses added character to the community and the streets were beautifully lined with endearing maple trees of every stage of life, from the young saplings to the girthy beasts who had a century or two under their belt.

Carefully Cecil braked the cruiser as he came to a halt in the stone parking lot, which during brighter seasons grass was mingled among the gravel and rocks. On their right was a simple white compact sedan with federal plates. Obviously, this was Dr. Hemple's official loaner for the business trip down. There was also a cranberry red minivan that they assumed must be the proprietor's own personal vehicle, along with a midnight black luxury brand hearse which was backed flush to the rear of the establishment, and obviously the professional mode of transportation. Behind it was a single garage door built into the structure which allowed privacy for transporting any passed clients.

Many in the county were dying to give Roger Winters their business, and in turn he made a killing at what he did.

The sun was shining, which allowed the temperature to peak at a nice thirty-nine degrees Fahrenheit and enabled a small layer of snow to start melting. This change in weather would usually be short-lived, as later in the night the temperature would drop again below freezing and cause any of the liquid released from the form of snow to become ice again, only adding more complexity and hazard to the land of Allegany County.

The red brick home, which doubled as the business, stood proudly on a large corner lot with various trees adding character to its presence. A stately building that was quite unforgettable in the area from both its appearance, and its saddened purpose. Along the porch, which faced the two sides that were adjacent to the street, there was a bright, glossy white wood railing, and curved, accent trim along the top of the porch also, matching perfectly. In compliance with town ordinances there was a wheelchair ramp that led onto this entrance, along with a few short steps next to it. This provided a choice in styles of ascending to the single front entry, which had an aged screen door and then a sturdy hunter green wooden one. Securely fashioned on the wall next to them as they approached with a brushed nickel sign that said, "Winters Funeral Home Est. 1967."

With two raps of his closed fists on the outer door, Cecil's knuckles announced their arrival, and in turn a graying Caucasian man with a rotund belly, short T-rex like arms, and a push broom style mustache happily greeted them. "Trooper Wingard. Always a pleasure, even though the reasoning behind our encounters is not that pleasurable." The pun teller gave a hearty, full stomach laugh, then opened the door fully to allow his guests to enter further.

"Roger Winters, the comedian, and mortician. This is FBI Agent Jacob Morris. You had the pleasure of working with his colleague Dr. Christopher Hemple last night and into today."

"Of course. My overnight guest is just finishing breakfast. Let's head into my workstation. The breakfast nook is on the way."

As they progressed, Jake hung onto a detail and needed an explanation. "Is this a bed and breakfast also, Mister Winters?"

"Call me Roger. And no, except for this case." With his exclamation his hands moved in a calming way. The professional tendencies that were warm, yet precise and educated. A richness and genuine quality was in his aura. "Since you were delayed yesterday with that unexpected chase you had with a suspect, we decided to let you rest and come this morning. The FBI did not plan accordingly, they should have booked him a room at the hotel in Wellsville. And it is plainly impractical to drive all the way to Rochester and back. Therefore, with so many open rooms, most without caskets, I was fortunate enough to be able to host."

A muscular black man with a similar age to Cecil, wearing a paisley button-down shirt, mostly in purple hues, and sharp tan khakis stood up, brushed crumbs from his English Muffins off of his slacks, then smiled. "Roger does make the best eggs benedict in the 585. And saved me finding a hotel or driving back with a less than desirable vehicle for the season."

"I bet you would like to investigate more murders in these parts then," laughed Jake to everyone, then he turned to the five-foot ten-inch clean shaven co-worker who had a short, trimmed hairstyle and a smile with a small gap between his front two teeth. "This is Trooper Cecil Wingard, my co-investigator on this case."

The men shook hands as the host led them into the official side of the dwelling. First, they passed through the receiving portion of the funeral home, which had another entrance where a casket would usually be laid out, and mourners would congregate to pay their last respects. This room's walls had a waist height chair rail where the upper portion was designed with decades old, yet still firmly affixed, pink and white floral wallpaper with a deep blue background. Its lower counterpart had wainscoting in a rich mahogany color which the ornate molding perfectly matched. Burgundy commercial type carpeting, knitted with a tight weave to it, was the flooring choice. Due to thousands of services occurring on them over the years it had not aged as well as other parts of the abode.

Inside the more technical part of the facility was a complete contrast to the rest of the structure. It was a barren space with cold stainless-steel counters along with a bank of metal refrigerators with square compartments with matching rolling trays specifically for housing the unalive. Cold, gray painted cement encased the ground, keeping with the sterile feel of the environment. Two rolling stainless steel exam tables were in the middle of the laboratory style zone, one of which had the corpse which was the primary subject of this inquest.

It was as if Dr. Jekyll and Mr. Hyde were leasing the entire property together. Drastic differences through a single doorway.

Laying there nude, except for a simple folded ivory flat sheet across his hip and genitalia section, was the expired Allen Marshall. With an already pale complexion, he had even a more blank and frigid skin tone than when he was alive. There was a Y shaped incision starting between his collarbone and pecs, then meeting at the middle of his chest, and going down to his groin region. There was significant bruising on his neck where the noose had been, and right cheekbone was showing more of a purplish coloration, which was suspicious from the beginning of the case.

"Gentleman," started Roger, as he rubbed his plumb hands together in a friendly way, "I am going to let the expert here lead with the autopsy summary, since he is better suited than myself, but it was a pleasure to work alongside him."

By instinct Jake removed his notepad from his coat pocket, but Dr. Hemple waved it down, and walked to the workstation in the corner. There was a basic standard computer, printer, and other miscellaneous office fixtures and accessories all on a massive corner desk. Included in this inventory was a three-tiered organizer, and from the top shelf of that he grabbed four documents, each with around twenty stapled pages.

"No need to make your hand cramp Agent Morris. Everything is printed out for your convenience, and to lessen my OCD."

Upon dispersing the booklets, he led the presentation. "Our subject was forty-nine years old, and of relatively good health. No visible signs of heart disease, or any other natural causes of his demise. The time of death is somewhere between five and nine thirty pm Thursday night. We determined this by taking his body temperature at the scene, and then again last night. Both of the readings point to this time frame."

Jake butted in, "His last contact with his partner, and as of right now anyone not involved with the crime, was around five fifteen that night, and he was found by his son around nine-fifteen.pm."

"Poor kid," the medical examiner shook his head with a sympathetic reaction. "Okay, so that narrows it down a bit more, thankfully. Excellent." Smacking his lips he moved on. "We found what resembles some pasta and marinara sauce in his stomach, and gaging the digestion process I assume that this was consumed an hour or so before his untimely death.

"There were also no traces of illegal drugs or alcohol in his system, so that clarifies quite a bit there. Some opiod pain relievers, but nothing substantial. Barely a trace." The specialist exhaled. "It's pretty cut and dry, and of course finding him suspended by his neck with a rope, we all can assume how he died."

The audience nodded.

"If it was not included in the preliminary paperwork that I received that there was no way for him to stand on something to jump off, and also if it failed to mention the struggle in the kitchen, I would have ruled out anything but suicide. However, everything else points towards foul play, and I found a few hidden details that may help corroborate your case.

"We have the normal bruising from the fibers of a ligature consistent with what he was found hanging from." While he spoke, he pointed at these areas on the deceased and the others observed. "The actual death itself is caused by the constricting force caused by the gravitational drag in response to the victim's body weight pulling them down. As for the shiner, well, that was probably given to him by someone else, or some type of unknown accident. No way of explaining that from a suicide."

Briefly the orator looked up from his own collection of

notes to ensure that he had the others captivated, which he did, then continued. "We did take Agent Marshall on a small detour to the Cuba hospital where we commissioned their CT scanner and X-ray machine to help us with what only a superhero could see."

Pausing, he waited for a laugh from his dry pun, but there was none. So again, he pressed on.

"There was substantial fracturing of the hyoid bone and the thyroid cartilage. Which is consistent with the drop from about six inches and not being cushioned by his feet hitting the ground."

Indicating that he had a question, Cecil motioned his single index finger of his right hand up. "I have been on the scene of a few suicides by hanging. Rarely do they end up like this, most of the time they lean away from the noose and use their weight that way."

Confirming that he understood the question, Christopher helped differentiate the variety of such types of ending one's own life. "That is more of a hanging than being hung. Hanging is using your weight and most of the time their feet are still on the ground. They lean in such a way until they are unconscious, then pass out, then away from lack of oxygen to the brain.

"While being hung is similar to how executions were a hundred years ago. With a drop then suspension bones will fracture, as in this case. He still asphyxiated, but there was damage to the spine."

Cecil and Jake looked directly at each other, but Jake spoke. "As if someone's head and neck was fed through the noose then dropped down."

"That is a great theory there." His head bobbed in agreement. "Now moving on. We found some slight ligature marks, and reddening of the skin around his wrists. There were also some fresh quarter inch scratches running vertically through these horizontal rubbings."

The same duo made the same look at each other. "Like if he had his wrists tied together then cut off?"

The morticians were both taken back and quite surprised by this idea. "That would run perfectly in line with these subtle injuries," stated Roger Winters.

Jake chuckled, "We found such pieces of cut rope, two sets, probably the other for the ankles, behind the house. We are considering that they were dropped by one of the suspects during their exit."

The doctor in the room cleared his throat, "All of the other minor details are in the reports you received. The federal prosecuting attorney was emailed the same information. I am ruling it as a homicide caused by compression of the trachea leading to asphyxia with noticeable trauma."

"It's official Cecil, we are investigating a premeditated murder of a federal agent."

*

"I am not familiar with these roads, but even I can tell that this is not the same path that we came."

"Nothing gets past you Jake," snickered Cecil, "this is the back hills way to see Allen's mother. While we are there we can also see if Jared is around so that we can talk to him a second time. The boy did say he was staying with her on Wolf Creek."

"Might as well interview them now since after they release Allen's body, they are going to be busy with the funeral arrangements and such." The FBI agent adjusted his positioning in the passenger seat of the cruiser, then continued sharing his thoughts. "So, according to the rumor mill, how messy has Allen and his wife's separation been?"

"Not enough for any police intervention, Allen held himself to a higher standard than that."

"Opposite of our buddy Brian Swartson."

"Exactly," laughed the local, "even though Allen was the breadwinner, he probably still would have walked away better off than Julie when the divorce was finalized. She makes okay money at the plant, and she was in the wrong. So, if he lived, he probably would have kept the house, and the camp has been in his family for generations. But with him dead, unless he changed his will recently, then Julie would be the beneficiary."

"That screams motive. I have seen people get killed for less, and sadly get away with it on a technicality. Plus, with how Jared was saying that the new boyfriend and mother were acting sketchy when he wanted to go check on his father, there is probably some reasoning behind it."

"I bet that they wanted to go back and clean up a bit. Maybe ran out of time, or got spooked and left, but intended on returning later on and the boy stopped them."

"I think that reasoning is dead on."

A charming driveway between two towering hunter green pine trees accented with an abundance of snow on its branches appeared which had a mailbox that read "V. Marshall" where it met the country road. Taking a hard right onto the camouflaged entryway Cecil continued down the path and through a small wooded front yard to where, on about an acre of cleared land, was a quaint wood cabin. Leading away from the right of the homestead was a slight opening with a two-rut path to where an old barn stood and many outbuildings. A few weathered pieces of farming equipment with a yellow paint and rust accent tone stood in a barren spot now, but with long, untamed grass area during the warmer months. Currently it was just deeper snow than other used zones. Many blue moons ago this would have been a top tier agriculture facility beauty. However, age and loss of the patriarch showed its cause for desertion. It was obvious that it was long past its days of producing goods for the world. A bittersweet vision of a farmer's dream.

The abode of the property was quaint and rural. Its roof was built with red and black asphalt shingles and had shutters around the various windows in a matching burgundy hue. The exterior logs were stained in a flat, grayish tone where snow had accumulated and was resting peacefully in the nooks and crevices of the rough, weathered logs. Around the entire cabin was a redwood deck with a waist high railing. Every side of the wraparound porch had its own small set of stairs.

As they were pulling up closer to their destination two medium sized brown and white huskies began to bark and circle the intruding vehicle, protecting their fortress.

The burnt sienna wooden front door opened a foot, and a blue haired head popped out in order to inspect the situation, and to tame her beasts. "Zeus, Alpha, get back here and quiet down. Jared finally fell asleep, and don't you boys be waking him up now."

Cowering, the dogs did so as instructed. The commander of the pups stepped onto the deck and pulled a fuzzy navy blue robe tightly around her. Her protectors sat to her left, both cautious of the visitors, but heeding to their master.

With his Stetson on his head Cecil walked up to the homestead first, with Jake close behind.

"Morning, Mrs. Marshall."

"Trooper Wingard, I was expecting a visit from some type of law enforcement. And I am glad that it is you. Come on in and out of the cold." After one step inside she looked back at the arrivals. "Of course, bring your compadre."

Both lawmen entered the home, stomping their boots free of snow on the deck. The impromptu hostess then motioned for them to take a seat at a four-piece dining set, one side of it pushed flush against an exterior wall which held a single pane window above it. Condensation was accumulating on the edges of the glass and moisture was softening the surface of the bare wood forming the sill.

"Virginia, this is Agent Jacob Morris with the FBI. We are working your son's case together."

Due to the emotional exhaustion that she had been a victim of, a simple nod was her only form of exchanging pleasantries with Jake. Respecting the situation he exchanged his own bland smile.

Using her right-hand Virginia pulled at the string

hanging from the teabag of a cold cup of Earl Gray sitting in front of her. Not being a stickler for proper etiquette, she was using a brown coffee mug made from a thick, durable ceramic. Being a country woman she was more focused on practicality than formality. Just like her home and its furnishings, she embraced a less frivolous life.

Before her unpredicted company came by, she had been watching the steam come off of the liquid while staring out of the window. Unable to eat or sleep in the past thirty-six hours, she had been sitting there with a continual supply of these heated beverages, only a few ever receiving a sip. They were more of a companion than a source of nourishment

Thoughts of how just a few short hours before "the incident" happened that her son, her only child, had been there talking with her, and trying to drum up some quick conversation. Busy wanting to watch her stories, and not desiring to drive in the snow to see her grandson's concert, she had brushed the visit off and cut it short for her own gratification. Never did she think that that moment would be her last with her kin. There were thoughts of guilt that she had not turned back when he said goodbye. Emotions of grief that he was gone, and feelings of rage that she was supposed to be the one who departed first, not him. And not in this way. Not in the form of brutality and malice.

A mother's love was tearing at her that her baby boy was apparently ambushed and viciously hurt before being forced into an early grave. Jared had walked through the small amount of evidence that he had seen with her as they discussed the horror of it all, and those signs pointed to a played out scenario that was of a foul theme. And there was nothing that she could have done to save her own flesh and blood.

And she knew in her heart who could be behind this massacre.

"Mrs. Marshall?" Cecil touched her left hand, which was nearest to him and motionless on the tablecloth.

"I am sorry. It's been a turbulent day and a half."

"We have been riding a similar rollercoaster, Ma'am." This empathetic comment was made by Jake. "I came down immediately from our Buffalo office."

"I appreciate that. And I also safely assume that if this being categorized as a suicide, that you boys have left by now."

Nodding with politeness and authority, Jake confirmed her accurate statement. "That is also correct, Ma'am."

Gritting her teeth she drew a long nasal inhale, closed her eyes, then released the depleted oxygen again. "I know that you will think that I am batshit crazy, but I am certain that she and that McBride boy have something to do with this. Ever since Allen found out that she was screwing around on him, she has been just, well excuse my French gentlemen, a twat."

Both men were taken back by such language from a grandmother, and in turn had to stifle laughter.

Keeping his composure, Cecil pressed on. "I am only a bit familiar with the professional gossip. You know how the Southern Tier is. Lots of chit chat, but who knows what the actual truth is."

"Since my Allen is gone now, I can give you some of the details."

Smoothly Jake withdrew his pen and notebook from his sportscoat interior pocket, slightly pausing as the writing items were partially exposed. Virginia nodded an approval of his record keeping of what she was about to inform them of.

"My boy and that Julie Adams have been married just around nineteen years. If you do the math and account for the fact that Jared is eighteen, you can safely assume what kind of marriage that was. A very hastily thrown together one, and a theoretical firearm pointed at my boy.

"Now back then I really didn't have too much bad to say of her. I mean, I always did assume that she roped my Allen into marrying her all that time ago, and until a year or so ago they seemed happy. But as we have seen the past few days, life can change at the drop of a hat."

With that feeling of misjustice the narrator fought back

a few tears and stifled a solitary whimper of the heartbreak that she was currently enduring.

"What gets me so mad is that she ran around on him for a few years before he caught wind of it. Of course, he and I never talked of his intimate bedroom life, and it's best that way. But the day he came up here back in May to tell me that he was gonna live at the cabin until things were settled was when he said that he should have seen the signs over the years. That he would have just let her go and do her thing.

"Why would she tangle him up with a baby and want a ring on her finger, then go about cheating on him?" Elevating her hand and lowering just its index finger she jabbed the tabletop a few times. "Allen let her go to the bars, and he stayed home with Jared. He never cared what time or what condition that she came home from St. Joes." Looking at the foreigner, she informed Jake of what she was explaining, "That is the bar in town."

Trying to get her to hone in on information that was helpful to them Cecil softly guided her back. "How did the affair get discovered?"

"Poor Jared. Now that he has that little truck of his, he was more independent. And one day during school he ran home to get his trumpet that he forgot. Well, there his mother and Clayton McBride were, stark naked in the living room. The audacity of that woman to be so bold."

The storyteller huffed and shook her head in disgust, which rightfully so was a correct response. Joining her with the same feelings were the members of her two-man audience.

Jake stuck his thoughts into the conversation. "So that is why Jared sided more with Allen?"

The matriarch agreed with both her body language and her verbiage. "That, and Allen and Jared were always together. Allen was a dad, and Julie... Well, she was a guardian. A parental unit, perse. More in favor of the title rather than enjoying the actual progression from baby to adulthood. Which was fine by Allen. He loved rearing a boy. And would have had more if

Julie was more inclined to. But she shut him down at just the one child. Although I am glad that he's a boy to keep the name going, and also keep the house on the lake roaring for another generation. Even with this tragedy."

"And of course I will pass it down to my kids, Gramma." This came from a voice originating from the small hallway off of the living room about fifteen feet away.

"Oh sweetheart, I thought that you were sleeping."

"Sorry if we woke you, Son." Cecil was offering half an apology since he actually wanted for the young man to be awake in order to ask some questions.

The lanky young man, adorning classic casual wear came closer. That wardrobe being a faded gray tee shirt and plaid pajama bottoms, such attire for a dreary day.

"Nah, it's fine. I dozed off for a second, but I'm just too lost at this time to fall asleep." Casually he proceeded to the kitchen sink where he poured water from the faucet into a mug, which exactly matched his grandmother's. Then he casually tossed a tea bag from one of the knotty pine upper cabinets and put the concoction into the microwave, firmly pressing the number two button, which in turn heated the beverage for precisely two minutes.

As it was starting its journey to a boiling state Jared grabbed another one of the chairs and sat a few loving inches away from his grandmother. By crossing his ankle over his knee, and placing his tender hand on Virginia's shoulder, he finally got settled in and comfortable.

Clearing his throat as he stretched backwards and cracked his knuckles, Jake made an announcement, one that was not a surprise. "The coroner is classifying Allen's death as a homicide. I will stay down here on the case until it is solved, and Trooper Wingard will be my partner."

"Fucking Clayton."

Virginia slapped the leg of her grandson who just cussed. "Young man, even if you are an adult don't use that language."

"Gram," he sighed, "we both know it was him up to no

good."

"We both know that, but foul language is not necessary to emphasize it."

"Yes, Gram."

"So," started Jake, "I am the stranger in a strange land down here, and I have no knowledge of anyone in, or around, your family. I am a blank slate." Adjusting his hands to more of a conversation state, open and at his chest level, he pressed on. "Why do you feel that it is your stepfather?"

With a sharpness to his tongue, Jared spoke, "First, he is not my stepfather. My real father and my mother are still married."

"Sorry, again, not from this area." In a way to defend himself he did throw his hands up, palms facing out as a plea for leniency. Although this question had been done on purpose by Jake in order to fuel some aggression from the boy, and to see if there really was bad blood flowing up on Beebe Hill.

Without prompting Jared softened his tone, and did as Agent Morris wanted, which was to fill in details about the sordid family affair. "My mom acted as if I should just let Clayton merge into the house and take over as my stepdad. Just because she had been cheating on my father with him for so long, she thought that I would just create an instant bond with him, and even wanted me to get to know Michael as a sibling."

Positioning himself forward, and in a more professional seating, Cecil released his thoughts on the matter. "That is just impractical for her to force you into loving the man that she was cheating on your dad with."

"But my mom never really grasped how important my father is, well was," the orator corrected his proper verbiage use, "to me. This is because of how she never bonded with me. She never understood the word sacrifice when it came to her child. Kids in my grade, well their parents will do anything to see their play or concert. This week was the first time in two years that she came to my concert. Or so she said. They were there when I was done, but I couldn't see them when I was on stage."

The brothers in arms investigating the bizarre case looked at each other while Jake took intensive notes on this detail. This is when Cecil poked around for more information. "You mentioned something yesterday about Clayton almost getting physical with you at the school after our performance?"

"He what?" blurted out Virginia, shocked and appalled at this new information laid before her.

Not wanting to draw away from the essential plot of the story Cecil redirected the mourners, "Let's focus on what went down specifically bit by bit. Start at the beginning of the concert. You said you didn't see them there, but they appeared at the end?"

"Yes."

"How did you get there though?"

"I drive myself everywhere now that I have a license."

"Did they say that they were going to be there, or just show up at the end?"

"So, it was Mom's birthday. And of course, she was mad that the concert was also that night." Kicking his head back and expressing a sarcastic smile he continued. "They both even acted as if it was my fault." Then he returned to a stoic state. "To celebrate we had an early dinner at Four Corners Cafe. They said that they would see my concert, then we would all go back to the Beebe Hill house and have cake and ice cream afterwards.

"Well, I looked and looked while we were playing, trying to find dad. I understood Gramma didn't wanna come because of the weather. But dad never misses a concert. That was odd because he usually sat in the first few rows.

"Now Mom, the few times in my entire life that she has ever come, she would sit in the back of the auditorium, even if she came with Dad. He still would sit up front, that's something that he never did back down to my mother about."

"But when did you see Clayton and your mom?" This came from Jake since he wanted accurate notes about this period of the evening since it would be the time frame that Allen would have been killed.

70

"At the end in the front foyer of the school when parents would greet us after we put our instruments away. I connected with them immediately, and even when I said that I didn't see them in the crowd they swore that they had been there the entire time. I also asked if they had seen Dad, and of course they said no."

"Can you give me an exact time?"

"Eight-thirty... Eight forty-five."

Fiddling with his pen for a moment Jake asked, "Did they seem agitated immediately? Did they explain their absence? Or anything about your father not being there?"

"No. They just said that maybe I didn't see him. Or he had to be out in the field working a case longer than he expected and couldn't make it. And as for them they said they were in the back." Pausing he rolled his eyes. "And to hurry up even."

"When did things seem to boil over?" Cecil really wanted to know if they were covering up their tracks, or if this was a case of an oversensitive teenager.

"I was getting embarrassed, so I went outside, and they followed me to the patch of grass by the senior parking lot. Clayton tried to have me brush it off and told me to hurry up and get to Beebe Hill so we could cut the cake before bed, since they had to be up early in the morning. I told them that I was going to check on Dad at the lake first, then head to that part of town. Next thing I know, he has his finger stabbing my sternum and telling me that my pansy ass of a father is fine, and I need to shut up and get home since it's my mother's special day and enough of it had been wasted on me."

It was as if a silent nuclear bomb went off in the room. Everyone was blown away by the guilt that this man was inflicting on Jared, along with how this was only cementing the case against him even more.

"Sweetheart," started the doting grandmother, "keep going. You are only helping your father by telling them more."

"Well, I stormed off because I was, and rightfully so, worried about my dad. He tried to follow me out, but people were starting to look at us weird. Thankfully he was fed up with the dirty looks and comments from people."

"I am assuming that we can talk with some of your teachers or classmates, and they will confirm this with us?" Cecil stated this since he knew exactly who to ask, and also that the lobby of the Cuba-Rushford School had multiple cameras, along with various ones in the parking lot and in the semi-forested multiple acre lot.

"Of course."

"What else can you add that you think is pertinent that you haven't mentioned yet?" Cecil was trying to dig hard.

"Well, also because Clayton is such an asshole, sorry Gramma," he glanced over for a moment as an apology, "all the time, life was unbearable the little bit of time that I did spend with him. If my mother and I argued over the smallest thing, he would flip out and defend her as if she was his queen. Mom has him wrapped around her finger, and he thinks that she is God's gift to the world."

Sharply the justice partners glanced at each other, both sending telepathic messages of the same genre; that Julie was the second person involved in the ambush, and most likely the organizer of this slaughter.

"So, before you said that your father never had any tools, but Clayton does. Are they kept up at your mom's house?" Honing in on his FBI mindset, Jake wanted to get to the forensics, the bones per se, that will help certify that these two were the culprits.

"Oh yeah. The weekend after dad moved to the lake, I was grabbing some of my stuff and sure enough, Clayton's tools were moved down into the basement. Hung up everything on the walls like it was his own little workshop."

"Well, I don't want to rain on your parade boys," started Virginia, "but I heard on the scanner that you chased that Swartson kid down with his girlfriend and arrested him."

Looking confused, Jake looked at Cecil, who in turn explained the local social media replacement. "Down here many civilians have their own personal police scanners to hear all the gossip. True or not." Then he directed his information back at the homeowner. "And yes, we arrested him, but he never laid a hand on your son. And he has an alibi for Thursday."

"Then why in the dickens did he run from you if he didn't do it?"

Agent Morris laughed while he answered that question, "Well you just can't fix stupid, as hard as you may try. It just won't happen."

Everyone engaged in a much-needed round of chortle, and Cecil felt that it was time to wrap things up with his interviewees and head back to their command center to get the ball rolling on the somewhat new information they had just received. "Well, we will leave you two alone so that you can have some peace and privacy. Is there anything else that you want to share with us before we leave?"

Quickly, or as quickly as her aged body could, Virginia stood up, using the shoulder of a still seated Jared for stability, and headed to the fridge. From the face of the freezer door of the appliance she moved a magnet aside and removed a curved white business card with baby blue writing on it that was previously affixed there. "This is Allen's lawyer. Well, was." She flipped it over and on the back in red ink was a 716 area code phone digits. "I called him yesterday and he gave me his cell phone number. With everything going on he said to call anytime, even during the weekend."

Using her frail, liver spot colored hand she gave Cecil the card and touched him on the shoulder. "Anything that I can do to get justice for my baby boy, I will do."

*

"So that's Beebe Hill? That's pretty close to where Virginia lives." While they were heading back into town Jake said this while pointing to the road to his right. Then rapidly he pointed to the left side of the road. "And that's the cheese plant? Allen did live in the center of everything he and Julie needed."

"Yup, all three in a two-mile triangle... perfect little paradise that all came crumbling down."

"Let's see what the attorney has to say. That will show us the tone of how the divorce was going, and either make or break the motive so far."

"Yeah, I picked up what you were thinking about with the toxic relationship that Julie and Clayton must have. She's the perfect planner and manipulator while he is the main assailant and lovesick puppy."

Nodding they went another a mile when Jake pointed the right side of the road and laughed. "That is quite the barn. Has to be the size of a football field."

"That is called the Blockbarn. One of a kind architecture and brings in visitors."

"Might as well have their own derby down here with how many horses that they can house in there at once."

This was said as Cecil was slowing down the cruiser and heading up East Main Street and maneuvering a well-known knoll in the village, then turning right and then into the parking lot of the Cuba Police Department.

Agent Morris rolled his eyes and signaled his index finger towards a black SUV with government plates. "That's my Special Agent in Charge. I didn't expect him to be back until Monday, and he never works weekends. Especially weekends when he must travel two hours each way."

As they entered the main door of the station, a not-so-enthusiastic Dylan faked a smile. "Some really important guy from the bureau came about an hour ago. I was going to call you guys, but he insisted that I don't. Said he didn't want to interrupt you and the field." With some reddening coming to his face, he shrugged. "I've given him some of our coffee, and he seems okay."

"That's my boss," replied Jake, "his lack of charisma is part of his charm."

The duo progressed through the vacated bullpen of cubicles and found SAC Thomas Washington seated, with said coffee, comfortably in the cubicle next to where Jake and Cecil had created a double desk.

"Gentlemen."

"Special Agent Washington, it is nice to meet you finally, Sir." Trooper Wingard extended his hand, which was received with a firm, professional shake.

"Sir, I did not expect you down here until Monday at the earliest."

"Agent Morris," stated the man as he was playing with a stapler in his right hand. "I thought that you enjoyed my company?"

Realizing his error and possible social faux pas, Jake tried to digress back a bit. "No, Sir. I just mean that I was not privy to the information that you were coming down to join us again." Grinning, he tried to make up for his mistake to his superior officer.

Smirking, and enjoying how he was getting a rise out of the agent, the higher ranker looked at Cecil, "He really can never take a joke from me." Addressing both men he pressed on. "My higher ups wanted me down here to see how the direction of the case was going. Some local news stations have heard the words USDA Federal Agent and homicide floating around, and we need to get our ducks in a row before we can release any information to any media source. This will make national news." Washington rose from his seat then softly, and silently, clapped his hands together. "So, what do we have thus far in the investigation?"

"Bring your chair over to our workstation," instructed Agent Morris, "first things first we need to give a call to Allen's lawyer who was dealing with his divorce. Virginia Marshall gave me his cell number and relayed a message that he was expecting our call."

Thomas nodded, and leaned back in his chair, letting his protege take the reins and reach out to the solicitor.

There was a basic black corded phone on Cecil's desk, which Jake slid closer to himself in order to dial. Placing it on speaker mode he dialed the number and sat waiting with the others as the trills rang out a few times.

"JT Dove here."

"JT, this is Agent Morris, I am with my superior officer Special Agent in Charge Thomas Washington, and Trooper Cecil Wingard with the New York State Troopers."

"Ah yes, I received a call from Virginia yesterday, and then saw in today's Times Herald about it, which is being described as a suspicious death."

"Between the four of us, it's a homicide."

"I see. Shame. I am guessing that Julie is your main suspect. She and that Clayton McBride."

"Things are leaning that way. We just need a feel from you, uncensored, for how the divorce was progressing."

"Not good for Julie. She would've been out of everything but her car. Title of the Beebe Hill house and the camp were in Allen's name. The lake house defaults to Jared since he is eighteen now. As was his will. Had it been six months ago Virginia would have gotten it. He did it that way to stay in the family blood line.

"The main house would go to Julie; he did not change the will. But if she is involved in his death then it would default to Jared now."

"I have seen that before," started SAC Washington, "in a few cases. Even if she is found innocent, if there's enough proof then Jared still keeps it."

"Exactly," replied the attorney, "same with the quarter of a million-dollar term life insurance policy that Allen has through the USDA. If she is arrested, then it goes into limbo. And if convicted then Jared gets it. Since the term was about to expire next month when he turned fifty, he had no way to change it to Jared until the new term was beginning."

Cecil smirked, "That is one giant motive. House and a quarter of a million. That's retirement kinda money in these parts."

"Julie was trying to take half of his retirement plus the house. She was fighting like hell. But since she was the cause of the divorce, it would've been a battle for her and her lawyer. And Jared would have had to testify since he was the one who discovered the affair."

"Half of a federal pension?" clarified SAC Washington.

"Yup. But wasn't getting it. I can ask for a unicorn, but doesn't mean I will receive one in the mail. Now if she is innocent, then she would get the whole thing."

"Thanks JT for the help. I don't have any further questions," Jake looked at his counterparts to see if they had any. Neither responded. "And no one else does. We will be in touch if we need anything else."

"No problem, guys. I have known the Marshalls for twenty-five plus years. I did the closing on the Beebe Hill house when Allen bought it just before meeting Julie. And if she did it, like I think she did, then crucify her. He was a damn good man."

"We will do our best."

With that the line went dead, and Jake returned the receiver to the base of the phone. "Let's go over what we have found out so far. Then I want to talk with Agent Morray, he's in the conference room with the evidence. Lastly, we need to pay a visit to the estranged wife and new lover."

Perfectly on cue Dylan came in a rushed motion pulling a giant whiteboard which was on wheels over the space and dropped a handful of dry erase markers onto the desk blotter. "I wanted to wait until you were off the phone first. I thought you guys might need something to plot out evidence and any other case findings. We only use this about once a year when we have a major crime. If you need anything else like this let me know, gentlemen."

The useful gumshoe left, and Jake grabbed a marker and glanced at Cecil, who nodded. It was an understanding that the agent should present the information to his boss and let the Trooper sit shotgun at that time.

Using a green hued option for writing Jake penned their victim's name in large capital letters, then enclosed it with a sloppy circle. Taking three large strides he then placed the words "death/autopsy" in the far right corner and underlined that twice.

"Let us start with a recap of what we know in death." In sloppier writing he then wrote "homicide" and put a star next to it on the right. Then "suicide" underneath it and grabbed a red marker from the desktop. With apple hued ink he drew a straight, yet declining line through that word. "Obviously this was poorly staged as a self-hanging, but we all know that it in fact was not."

Quickly he scrolled in hunter hue "injuries" with an arrow then "face/wrists/neck bruising" and then "struggle?!"

As another thought dove rapidly into the presenter's mind he side-stepped two trots to the far left of the board and wrote "suspects."

Facing his two-man audience he then jotted down "Brain Swartson" in green, and then crossed him out in crimson. "Our paranoid possible perp fell apart." Grabbing a navy-blue marker he then pivoted back and wrote "Julie/Clayton" and drew an outline of what looked like the outer edges of a cloud. Bolting again he snatched up an orange pen and hastily, and in very sloppy shorthand wrote "motive $$$ house pension."

Leaning back in his chair Thomas Washington tented his fingers over his nose and mouth. "How about we pause this outline for right now. I want to go with both of you in the next hour and talk to the estranged wife and this new lover. How were their names brought up as suspects, and not as mourners."

Using his index and middle finger to flag his desire to field that question, Cecil then informed the high ranker of what their morning had consisted of. "I had a decent professional connection with Allen Marshall. With being a Southern Tier boy myself, and working these parts, I can tell you that the separation was getting ugly, as JT Dove described. Plus, we spoke with the victim's mother and son. These two are looking pretty guilty, so my gut feeling, in and out of the uniform, is that we need to get to them, and drill them."

A blushing Dylan interrupted the meeting. "Sorry guys, but there is someone on line one saying he has some information."

Nodding, Cecil picked up the receiver and pressed the correct buttons to access the extension. "Trooper Wingard."

Click.

"Hmmm...." Pushing down the receiver he then pressed the right code to call back whatever number previously had called and selected the speaker option.

"Friendship Hardware Shoppe."

"Hello, this is Trooper Wingard with the state police. Did you call Cuba's police department?"

"No, no. That's a misdial." The voice was of a young male and was riddled with signs of anxiety.

"But the caller said they had information on..."

"No, it's a misdial." Click again.

Shrugging, Cecil hung up the phone. "Strange."

"Even stranger is that someone would name their store 'Friendship Hardware Shoppe," announced Washington.

Cecil chuckled. "Friendship is the name of the town over."

Standing up the SAC began the small procession out of the cubicle space and towards the conference room of the department. "We learned what we needed to, and what to keep our eyes open for during our visit. Catch them off guard and downplay our suspicions."

After three quick knocks Isaac Morray was fast with answering the simple wooden door and allowed his well-known guests to enter. "Come on in, gents. Special Agent Washington! Thanks for joining us down in the sticks."

Laughing, the head investigator crossed his arms. "We are going to head over and speak to the wife and her lover. What should be on our stealth radar as we speak with them. Any smoking guns that could help us?"

"Well at the scene we had boot prints. They are work

boots, and here is the dried cast." In response to this Isaac pointed at an ivory white copy of the prints found at the scene. There was some coloring to show the slanted, willow leaf like grooves in the soles of the footwear. "Size nine boots. From the autopsy notes emailed to me from Dr. Hemple, Allen Marshall was a size thirteen. Also, any offensive wounds on either one of them. We never found the rest of the rope, same with the drill bit and power driver."

"Aren't all drill bits alike?" asked Washington.

Pointing to the chunk of wood with a single hole in it that was cut out of the beam from the basement belonging to the lake home Agent Morray expanded on the differences. "They used what is called a spade bit. This made an inch wide hole, allowing the half inch rope to nestle nicely in."

Since he was not a handy person either Cecil used his smartphone to research on the internet browser a picture of what was being described. Tipping his head quickly he then rotated his hand and showed the image.

On the screen was what looked like a rectangular popsicle with a stick in the bottom, which was inserted into the head of the power drill, then a small tip on the top, which was sharp and intended to first penetrate the wood, then allow the opening to gain more girth after multiple revolutions of the bit.

After a solid fifteen seconds of exposure, the sleuths were confident in their new wisdom of home improvement aides.

"And of course anything else that is suspicious can be brought back if it is exposed. Or any inkling, write up a search warrant and I will have a look when we seize it." This advice came from Isaac.

Confident of what to seek for, they then exited the small police station as a unified group and jumped into Agent Morris's black SUV, excited to be venturing up to see what answers were laying before them on quiet Beebe Hill Road.

*

Rogue slush and salt soared over the front tires of Agent Morris' ride as he turned into the (now broken) Marshall residence. Decades old pine trees accompanied each side of the property line for the first half of the property, perfectly defining the residence's perimeter in an arbor style. The home itself was a ranch, but larger than most built in its era. In contrast to a rectangular home, it was a U shape with creamy yellow color vinyl siding and hunter green shutters. In the front was a deck that connected two solid glass French doors, and bay windows balanced the glass front door at the inlet of the abode with a solitaire Japanese Maple in its center, one with a few decades of growth in its bark.

Weeping willows hung lower with heavy snow in the back portion replacing the evergreens in its duties as land markers. There were of course many acres of wooded land that belonged to others behind the dwelling providing a quiet boundary to the world, and across the road was a dramatic embankment followed by a trickling creek.

The car doors closed in a triplicate cadence. Slam. Slam. Slam.

Due to the blizzard-like accumulation of precipitation, entry through the front door was hazardous and not possible during this wintry season. Rather a basic side door opened which had two stairs flush with the worn black top driveway and appeared a woman who was slumped over trying to balance a greeting along with keeping a young black labrador at bay.

"Afternoon gentlemen. Come in and let me put Piper in Jared's room."

The visiting trio did as instructed, all standing on a small patch of hunter green tile next to the entryway until the hostess returned. She had corralled the pup, which was a year old so into the room adjacent to the family room which they were in. The basic bedroom door closed rapidly ensuring the containment of the canine.

"Please," started Julie Marshall, "take off your boots and come in. Have a seat."

They brushed their boots off, but did not remove them per protocol. But they did have a seat at the curved sectional sofa in the room which had an off-white basic fabric along with splashes of vibrant colors of greens, reds, and some pink.

The recent widow was a woman of approximately forty-five, and her years showed, even daring to appear that she had five more than she actually had acquired. Her hair was dark brown, almost black, with a generous proportion, almost three to seven, of gray, almost white hairs. They were held together in an intertwined style which was straight and to the nape of her neck. Overly curled bangs squared off her puffy, and unevenly shaped face, which had some freckles and wrinkles typed into her fair skin.

Light blue eyes did accent and reflect the light, adding some character to her mundane appearance. A maroon, chunky sweater looked disproportionate to her lanky, yet unfit body. Tight black spandex style yoga pants did not help the fashion statement that she was pursuing, and all together she did not appear to be the degree of a woman who two men were supposedly fighting over.

As she sat in the mauve recliner opposite of the men her dry hands, whose nails were painted, yet chipped and unfeminine, slid on her outer thighs, resting on their inner counterparts. "I assume you are about to show me your badges."

"That is correct, I am Agent Jacob Morris, and I am an investigative agent with the Buffalo branch of the FBI. This is my superior officer, Special Agent in Charge Thomas Washington, and you may be familiar with New York State Trooper Cecil Wingard."

As if they had rehearsed perfectly for a performance all three flipped their identifications holders open revealing their respective shields.

"Well jeez, they really bring out the big guns for an asshole hanging himself."

This uncouth statement took the surprise of all three seasoned lawmen in the room. No one was sure what direction to go into next, or even what to say following this for a solid forty seconds until the direct shooter spoke again.

"It is no secret that Allen and I split, and everyone in the county knows that I moved Clayton in right away. Our marriage was dead, so I guess he offed himself because of it. I am not going to make the arrangements. Jared and Virginia can have that fun. I may show up to the funeral. But for legal issues I am assuming that you need me to sign off on a death certificate or something since we were technically still married."

Clearing his throat in order to receive everyone's attention and to set some dominance in the upcoming conversation, Cecil decided that since he was the local authority that he should deliver the next blow to her. "Allen's death is officially a homicide."

"A what?"

"Homicide, Julie."

"Since when is a man depressed over his wife leaving him, who out of spite kills himself on her birthday, a case of homicide."

"Ma'am," started Jake, "we cannot go into details yet. But we do have some questions, if you would not mind."

Immediately the avalanche of surprise became apparent on her face since she was not expecting the line of questioning to venture down this avenue. "Well, I guess so." Her hand rose with a bent wrist, and she motioned her fingers up and down twice. "Ask away."

Opening his notes, Jake began trying to ask any relevant inquiries. "Has Allen been acting differently lately?"

Julie glared at the interviewer. "Have you spoken with Jared? I haven't seen Allen in two months. So, I cannot gauge anything like that."

Thinking of an alternative line of questioning, Jake

paused for a moment, which only irritated the woman more. "Here's the deal gentlemen. I am the guest of honor in just over an hour at my mother's in Portville for my birthday party. I have to finish laundry and still get ready. So, you have twenty minutes to ask me whatever you please, then I must break up this little interrogation since I refuse to have Allen ruin any more of my celebration weekend. Now you may join me as I rotate the laundry in the basement."

The annoyed speaker rose, and so did the three lawmen at this invitation. Wanting not to reveal any further excitement of being allowed a tour of the space Jake asked his next question. "So please help us understand why you were contesting the divorce so much if you were already over Allan."

A few steps out of the family room and directly in front of Jared's bedroom, where the pet was being held in time out, was a metal door which Julie opened as she answered. This passageway was into the two-car garage. "Well, being that I helped Allen build half of this house, the two portions sticking out looking like tits are an addition, shouldn't I get something in return? At least pay me back the forty grand I helped invest into it?"

With a disgruntled look on her face, she led them into the garage, which was where the basement steps were, which was the route in order to get to the washer and dryer. As the three men trailed Jake motioned his head to the right where a pair of work boots for a man were sitting. They all glanced at the footwear and saw a white tag which had the number nine in black ink printed on its tongue.

Heading up the rear Cecil nonchalantly lifted the boot while Julie's back was to them as she walked, and all of the eyes of the cops lit up as they noted the unique slanted leaf like design of the soles of the boots.

During this Jake tried to feed some more bait for Julie to nibble on and divert attention from their clandestine actions. "Well, we spoke to JT Dove, and you will end up with the house now."

Nodding quietly, they were excited at this small piece of evidence handed to them on a silver platter.

"I am shocked at that. I pictured that snake having Allen change his will immediately after he walked out on me. But at least I get some part of a victory."

Each person used their elbow to stabilize their downward journey of the red stairs as they entered the cement basement. In comparison this cellar was much more useful and beneficial than the one at the lake home. It was not livable, but there was a giant built-in shelving unit to the right which housed various tools and lawn equipment.

Really pitching to Julie's blatant denial that her crime would go unnoticed, Jake kept pressing on. "Yeah, and since it's a homicide his life insurance will pay out. If it was a suicide, you would've missed out."

After breaking the halfway point of the expanse of the underground zone there was a washer and dryer. And then to the far-right corner was a small, freshly assembled workshop with several pieces of painted plywood attached to the wall, and a variety of tools hanging alongside their accessories.

Again, the detectives honed in on this.

The one controlling the conversation, Jake, continued with his distraction techniques while Thomas and Cecil went to the handyman nook, snooping around a bit. "Yea, we chased down that Brian Swartson yesterday. Ran like a guilty man and lawyered up after we caught him."

With wet clothes in one hand Julie turned to answer. "Really. Wow. I've heard the name. Heard he's a real menace to Rawson Road."

In a small stretch of various drill bits in a multitude of sizes, one that seemed to be a one-inch spade bit hanging a little ajar, with a few small slivers over freshly drilled wood scraps on it, caught the truth seekers' attention.

Cecil cleared his throat, and Jake quickly spun his head and saw what they were discovering. A second valid suspicious clue.

Watching as Julie stared straight ahead and yapped on about some story based solely on the Cuba rumor mill about the first suspect of the homicide case from ten years prior Cecil slowly crept behind the floor to ceiling shelves and saw a bit of yellow nylon sitting on the third shelf from the cement floor. Perfectly half an inch in diameter and roughly cut at an angle.

"Found the last of the trifecta, Agent Morris. The rope and drill bit are back here." Next the trooper faced the high-ranking bureau man. "Agent Washington, your call?"

"Arrest her. Let's get the cordon up, find the accomplice, and get Agent Morray here with a forensics team."

Before Julie Marshall could fully turn around Jake was slamming her against the front of the washing machine, the full bottle of detergent violently hitting the floor and spraying its contents among the rough concrete. Coldness from the metallic handcuffs made her entire body shiver as they clicked into place, securing her arrest for the premeditated murder of USDA Federal Agent Allen. J. Marshall.

*

Two Allegany County Sheriff Deputy cruisers swiftly, and in a stealth like fashion without red and blue lights, slid to spots on the country road in front of the home where Julie Marshall had just been arrested. This detainee was handcuffed with Agent Morris softly using his right hand in the nook of her left elbow to guide her down the driveway. "Can one of you guys take her to the holding cell at CPD. The other please start a cordon. Agent Morray and his team will be here in the next ten minutes to wait for the search warrant to be signed and emailed from the federal judge. Special Agent in Charge Washington is on the phone now with him."

The pass off of the arrested woman occurred as directed, the deputy putting her into the back of his car while another kept a chilled post at the end of the driveway. Morris and Wingard stood at the end of the driveway waiting for the senior officer to join them.

Thomas Washington was ending the call from his smartphone with his judiciary counterpart and started to jog down the slippery passageway. "Judge Forrester is issuing a search warrant for this address, and also an arrest warrant for Clayton McBride. By the time we get to the cheese factory it will be on my phone."

"Sir," started Cecil, "that's less than a mile away."

All of the men piled into Jake's black SUV while engaging in this conversation.

"His Honor is aware of that. But he is privy to the information that this is such a small town that news flies fast, so consider it done. We do not want one of his nosy neighbors letting Clayton know while he is at work that we are taping off his house and that they saw his lover getting thrown into a paddy wagon."

Going down the bumpy country road the SUV had its hidden warning lights flashing, although they only encountered one other vehicle in their travels. After a safe traverse across Route 305 and into the parking lot of the cheese plant they came to an abrupt halt at the front entrance of the dairy production facility.

Filing out without haste they entered the aluminum and glass double doors to where a very startled secretary greeted them with a yelp and a bunny hop in her seat. This was due to their brazen entry with each man using one hand to display a badge, and one hand embracing their unholstered handgun.

"Cheryl," demanded Cecil. Being a tightly knit area the local gumshoe had been to the processing center a few times for various issues. "Where is Clayton McBride?"

"Sector C2." By pure instinct she grabbed the radio used for inner factory communications.

The men were gliding across the foyer, allowing Cecil to guide them. Lifting his hand slightly he directed the greeter. "Do not warn him we are coming."

With fear in her eyes, and the assumption that it was best to not ask any further questions she put down the walkie talkie and sat in a timid fashion. Being a lawful citizen of the area, this was not a scenario she had ever endured. There was a grandmotherly essence of her with a floral-patterned blouse on a royal blue hue, and a baby blue shawl over her shoulders. A simple faux pearl button clasped two crocheted pieces together at her neckline in order to keep it fastened and proper.

Although she was not instructed to, and did not need to, she did raise her open hands as if she was being hunted.

With speed and an instinctive awareness and defensive mantra they rounded past a few of the portions that consisted of the layout for the plant and finally found the zone labeled "C2."

There was a waist high large glass window, around six feet wide and three in height, that looked into a production section of the establishment. Inside included four men were wearing what appeared to be hazmat suits, but instead of giant masks their heads were exposed except for "Cuba Cheese Factory" baseball caps. These outfits were actually utilized to keep the space sterile as they were working machines that shredded large amounts of golden yellow cheddar cheese which eventually fed onto a giant conveyor belt.

Three raps on the glass by Cecil's closed fist achieved the working men's attention followed by all of the officer's shields being pressed against the lightly teal tinted glass.

Each man froze, unsure of who rolled the unlucky dice in this match. Using his stern index finger, he pointed at Clayton McBride.

"McBride, out here now. Hands up, do not pull any shit."

All three warrant enforcers then tapped their respective handguns on the window to verify that this was not a visit trying to sell the wanted man tickets to this year's police ball.

As if springs were in his shoulders Clayton McBride's

hands flew into the air, and one of his cautious co-workers opened the door connecting the two areas. In response Jake pushed the suspect intensely against the cold cement block wall and tethered his hands with the government-issued steel manacles.

While doing so the bureau man grunted out "Clayton McBride, you are under arrest for the premeditated murder of Federal Agent Allen Marshall. Whatever you have to say can, and will be held against you in a court of law."

"What the fuck man. Dude hangs himself and you arrest me? When I get my phone call, I'll get Julie to hire me an attorney."

Jake ripped him off of the wall and they started their exit out of the establishment. "Maybe you will luck out and find an attorney who does a two-for-one deal."

Heading down the hallway a young man of twenty years ran around the corner. "Dad. What is going on?"

"I don't know, son. Call your grandmother, then an attorney."

"What about Julie?"

Gladly Cecil answered this inquiry. "They're both heading to federal prison for their twenty-five to life honeymoon."

Shocked, the only child of the suspect, and maintenance man for the factory, stood in disbelief as to his life also crumbling before him.

Clayton then hung his head down low and pushed his chin into his collar, embarrassed of his final departure from his long and steadfast employment being one of a suspected slaughterer.

*

"**I**t really sucks when they both lawyer up so fast, doesn't it?" This casual, uncharacteristic comment came from Special Agent in Charge Washington, and brought a small smile to Agent Morris' face.

Cecil intercepted this statement with his version of its interpretation. "In the Southern Tier there is very little support, and of course trust, of the police. So, they are afraid that any law enforcement will try and quote-unquote 'screw them over.' Tons of locals traveled hundreds of miles and stormed the Capitol a while back. They even claim to be sovereign nations and exempt citizens sometimes. Truly, it was no shock to me that they both lawyered up."

His pink lips grinned and illuminated their contrast against his ebony face, then the SAG snickered, "But they both want the same lawyer."

"Which they can do. Had this happen in a case a decade or so back." Jake was trying to include himself in the conversation, and did so conveniently with this tidbit. "They have to all sign off on it, and have a hearing concerning it, but it is kosher at the end of the day."

Laughing, the Trooper let them in on some small-town knowledge. "Joseph Stevvins has never met a dollar that he didn't like. So, of course, he will squeeze that turnip until he gets blood."

"Is he that bad?" asked the highest-ranking gentleman as he perched his head up and leaned back a bit, returning to a more professional, stoic essence.

"That lawyer probably bills by the nano-second," laughed the statie.

"I go by the quarter hour Wingard, but I like how you think. Maybe you should jump to the more profitable side of the law."

The three men turned in shock to see their unannounced guest, and the subject of their gossip, behind them.

"Your little doorman, the kid I almost made cry on the

witness stand last year during a DWI trial that I won, must be in the crapper, and not at his post."

Perfectly on cue, Dylan exited the bathroom while drying his hands on a brown paper towel, causing everyone to shrug and laugh.

"Well Joe, which client do you want to meet with first? We are entertaining a courtesy by not transporting them immediately to Batavia to the federal holding center."

"Well, both at once works fine since they are going to be co-defendants."

Blushing a bit since he realized his faux pas, Dylan disappeared to the back to retrieve the suspects one at a time, both handcuffed to their fronts, while Cecil guided the attorney to the well-known interrogation room.

Once the advocator and his clients were settled in the neutral space, the protectors of the law took their customary seats in a nearby cubicle in order to be vigilant of any attempted escapes, yet far away not to be accused of spying on the detainees and jeopardizing the case at hand.

For the most part of the conference only normal mumbles were heard from those walls while the solicitor was receiving information on the long, lengthy path before them. At one point Clayton did yell that they were innocent when it was apparent that the litigator was ensuring that even if they were guilty that his goal was to have the charges amongst them dismissed, or an acquittal when before a judge and jury.

This muffled outburst was an isolated incident that did not require any of the security members to make a grand entrance and break up a scuffle between a lawyer and his retainers. At least not in this situation, although other moments such as those described have occurred in that exact meeting space, with that exact lawyer.

After an hour and a round of coffee and pastries retrieved from The Four Corners Cafe by Dylan, Joseph Stevvins emerged looking exhausted and dripping with sweat, his suit jacket draped in the crook of his thin elbow. "So, are they over to

Belmont now to be held?"

"Straight to Batavia, Joe," laughed Cecil to his old nemesis.

"Give me time to file an injunction on that, come on."

"Sorry Mister Stevvins," started SAG Washington, "orders from Judge Forrester, he wants them up on his playing field under the United States Marshals' lock and key."

Rolling his eyes, the attorney turned to leave as Cecil spoke up, "That's right Joey, looks like you are going to put some miles on your car for this case."

*

Three slaps on the back of the paddy wagon completed by Agent Morris alerted the driver of the armored vehicle that the rear doors were locked securely, and all was good to go. With that confirmation they pulled out of the CPD parking lot and headed on their two-hour journey with the suspects contained in the back, each in a separate compartment.

The three investigators on the case looked at each other in the frigid parking lot, and Cecil nodded his head. "Well, you know how to reach me if and when you need me to testify. But it was fun playing a Federal Agent for the past few days."

A wily grin crept up on Special Agent in Charge Washington's face, "Not so fast, Trooper. I have been granted permission to have you stay on the case up to, and through the trial."

A noticeable surprise overcame Cecil as he leaned back, and his eyes grew wide. "That is quite unusual."

"I had the pleasure of speaking to the prosecutor on the case, Jackson Steele. They are seeking the death penalty. Even if the state does not allow it, Steele will request so in federal cases. And being that this was a brutal murder, they will be striving for the ultimate punishment."

"Oh wow," Cecil was again blown away by this revelation. "They are going for blood with those two."

"During our conversation he was more than confident in

our evidence. Beyond what you two have discovered, he did pull cell phone data on both. Their phones never reached the middle-high school until after eight thirty that night. They were inactive during that time. Meaning they may have turned them off during that time period, which makes them appear even more guilty. Especially since they were not sighted in person either."

Raising his finger, Cecil interjected. "There are some dead zones in these parts. But traveling from Beebe Hill to the school there would be at least one spot that would pick up a signal."

"Exactly," said SAC Washington as he pointed at the commentator. "Now go and let the son and mother know about the arrest. I am confident they will be excited. Arraignment will be Monday at nine in the morning at the Federal Courthouse on Niagara Square in Buffalo. Trooper Wingard, you will have accommodations at a hotel nearby to work on the case, especially during the discovery process, and help investigate any other tips that may come in. Once this hits the news, who knows what tidbits may find their way to us."

All three men nodded in a solemn acknowledgment of the nearby future process.

"Agent Morris, enjoy the motel down here tonight. Both of you can rest tomorrow and migrate up before the arraignment in the evening. My office will let you know where your hotel is Trooper Wingard. Chances are it's the usual accommodations on Delaware Ave, very close to Niagara Square, where all of our action is at."

As the superior ranking officer was heading to his vehicle he turned back to face the two truth seekers. "Fantastic job gentlemen. Your files will have notes exemplifying your work. Now we will keep it up until they both have needles in their arms for what they did to our fallen brother."

*

A familiar ring of a familiar bell rang through the most popular eatery in the village, introducing Cecil and Jake to the crowd of about two dozen diners. Utilizing his flirtatious grin, Cecil greeted a friendly face. "Becky, aren't you usually on breakfast detail?"

Grabbing menus, she returned a feminine, small-town smile. "We are a few short this week, so I picked up some night shifts. Now let me get you into a booth so you can tell me all about Brian Swartson's trial."

Both of the investigators looked at each other and rolled their eyes, then followed the hostess to their table.

Sliding in, both men ordered regular colas, and Becky headed back to retrieve them. After SAC Washington had made his exit, they had finalized some paperwork, and were anxious to refuel, dreading that they were again heading up to Wolf Creek Road and disturbing the Marshalls again.

"Wow Cecil, this really is homestyle comfort food. What do you suggest."

Not even considering any other options, the local expressed himself, "I always go for the hot roast beef sandwich."

"Sold," Jake let the laminated menu hit the tabletop.

Perfectly timed Becky returned with their soft drinks. "Before I allow you to order Cecil, I need all of the details."

"Becky, then I guess we will be mummies before we get our hot roast beef sandwiches." Sternly he shook his head while Becky faked an over exaggerated pouty lip. "I will tell you that Brian Swartson, and his old lady, are innocent of this. Not of their fraud cases. But they had nothing to do with Agent Marshall's death."

"What about the commotion up on Beebe Hill a few hours back. Ya reckin' that we won't notice that Mister Statie. Five or six houses with that yellow tape up. None of the county cops will tell us squat." This announcement came from a customer at the luncheon counter.

"Mister Carpenter, that I cannot comment on."

"Well," rearing for an argument, the resident continued, "should I be locking my doors and sleeping with my shotgun under my pillow?"

Inhaling deeply, Cecil rebutted this. "You are fine. There is no threat to the community." Looking back at the waitress he smiled, "Is that good enough for my official statement? My comrade and I would love to have two hot roast beef sandwiches with those world-famous mashed potatoes."

Deeply rolling her eyes the server realized that she could not blackmail any further details of the Enchanted Mountain's hottest topic. So instead, she turned the order into the cook and relayed to them the few tidbits of gossip to the rest of the wandering staff.

Clearing his throat, Jake pulled Cecil back in for some business talk, while the nosy ears were away. "Currently we are pushing seven o'clock now. Let's go and notify the Marshalls and call it a day."

"I second that motion."

"I will be selfish and want to sleep in until nine tomorrow morning. I have to check out at eleven. So, let's meet down at the DPW garage at noon to discuss with Isaac what they are analyzing."

"Sounds good," Cecil peeked up from his mobile device. "Just got an email. My hotel in downtown Buffalo is booked. Right on Delaware avenue near the Federal Courthouse."

Being an easy cuisine choice to prepare, Becky was fast with delivering the platters to the hungry coppers. Knowing not to push her luck, she eased off on interrogating the duo any further.

There was a comforting silence among them as they ate. The need to fill the void of conversation had subsided. Bonding had occurred during their tumultuous few days together, so at times when any intense action subsided, they could truly relax. Any buffering in getting to know the other was gone, so now they could assimilate as a newly formed partnership.

With their discarded napkins being the only substance left on their plates, besides a hint of deep brown toned beef gravy, the men were off to their next task. Obviously after paying the tab and leaving Becky a semi-generous tip.

Twilight enriched the eight-minute drive as they made their way to the Virginia Marshall's homestead. The snow had ceased falling, yet still decorated the lawns and fields as they passed. The quarter moon allowing its glisten to dance among the crispness of the fallen precipitation.

The protecting pooches of the estate greeted the men, yet this time Jared was quick to corral them, putting them at ease that these were not intruders, yet welcomed guests. There was even a small grin on the greeter's face. Which only consumed a quarter of his mouth. Yet was the first sign of anything positive to escape his lips since he stumbled upon his new traumatic moment.

Exiting Jake's black SUV, the men nodded in the direction and headed to the doorway. Once there they entered freely behind Jared and the dogs, knowing that an invitation to join was readily available.

Instead of the dining area as their last conference was, Jared led them into the front living room. There was a large, eight foot by four foot, picture window where the lovely front lawn and driveway was a quaint view. Virginia was settled in an aged hunter green recliner. Her feet were only semi-elevated. Some knitting laid on her lap, and a popular trivia game show was playing on the television.

Opposing his grandmother's seating arrangement was a cranberry red recliner of approximately the same era of assembly, which Jared immediately reclaimed as his spot. This in turn left the new additions to the pow wow to sit on either side of a floral print sofa. Which was fine by them. Any padded seat after the past few days was heavenly.

Quick to the point Jared was the first to strike up the conversation. "Earlier my neighbors called here and said something about a hostage situation at the Beebe Hill house? Did Clayton have my mom at gunpoint? I wouldn't mind that much after all of this."

The couch sitters glanced at each other while sending telepathic messages about how the gossip runs this town a bit sideways.

Being the local voice Cecil clarified. "No. Your mother was arrested there. And Clayton at the cheese plant."

Adjusting in his seat, Jared leaned in, the rocker pulling him closer to the men. "You were able to do so just that fast?"

"Well son," Jake wanted to interject politely, "we stumbled upon some evidence at the Beebe Hill house. We will have men in there for a day or two more. You can't go back there for a bit since it's a secondary crime scene. Long story short," he nodded, "there is enough forensics that we discovered in plain sight for the arrest to be justifiable."

Grasping her knitting needles Virginia whimpered and allowed a few tears to disperse over her rosy cheeks. In an attempt to soothe his beloved Jared stood up, but the mourner motioned for him to sit back down, which he obeyed immediately.

"Now, what do we do from here?" Jared was showing his anxiety, his voice a bit strained and his fingers white from grasping the arms of his seat.

Since this was Jake's field of expertise, he fielded the question. "You will definitely be a witness during the trial process."

Rolling his eyes, the inquirer sighed, then relayed his thoughts. "I see those true crime shows. They will probably plead to manslaughter and get ten years."

Shaking his head, the FBI agent expressed the truth. "This is a federal death penalty case." Then he switched to nodding. "The prosecutor has already put this into action. There is no bond. There is no plea deal. You will testify." His noggin swayed in rhythm with this, then stayed stationary. "No doubt about that Jared. And death, or at the very least, life in federal prison, will be the outcome for both."

Mustering up some strength Virginia responded with her own doubts. "And in those gosh darn shows, a lot of the time there isn't enough evidence to prove that the person did it. And then they are back out there."

"Virginia," Cecil intertwined himself in the discussion, "from what we have already, there is no reasonable doubt that they did not commit this crime. Either way, they are only going to leave jail in a body bag. Depends on if it's when God decides, or Uncle Sam."

Suddenly a burst or light ran across the yard and shot a flash through the front window. Startled, all four occupants began to rise to see who had just molested their peaceful rendezvous.

"Oh shit," stated Jared.

"What?" inquired Cecil.

"Fuckin' Michael McBride is pulling up."

"Language, Jared." With a mild enforcement her hand slightly raised, fist clenched around a wrinkled and used tissue.

"Sorry, Gramma."

With ill intentions, the son of one of the accused leapt from his simple red pickup truck and swamped through the snow. A dog was howling in the cab of the vehicle. "How dare you pin your father's fucking suicide on my father." Looking back, he scolded the puppy. "Shut up, Piper." Then he kept walking and screamed even louder. "And your own God damn mother. Come out here and fight me like a man. Something your old man never was."

Tears streamed down the faces of both residents of the spot, while the lawmen began to grasp for their pieces.

"Boys," started Jared as he opened the side door where the intruder could be easily seen. "Fass, sacken."

"Don't do that Jared," yelled Cecil. For he knew that those two words were attack commands for the German protectors. Phrases that they did not take lightly. The only thing that they would take would be chunks of the invader.

Both powerful mutts were showing teeth and jumping up into the window for Michael to see. In turn he covered his wrist with the ending of his coat, and smashed the back taillight of Jared's little truck.

This is when Cecil and Jake went past Jared and the dogs. Jake exclaimed, "Do not release them. It's the end of my day, and I don't feel like doing any more paperwork."

Rolling his eyes with much disappointment, Jared set out the next commands. "Bleiben Ruhig. Steht Noch."

Per their meanings, the dogs wandered to free spaces in the kitchen, still with their masters in sight, and laid down.

Whipping out their badges, the enforcers were quick to calm the situation. In response to the surprise of the extra occupants of the home Michael threw his hands up in the air, regretting his timing for the invitation to brawl.

Cecil walked over. "Listen kid. This is not how this is all going to go. Okay."

Embarrassed at the results of what happened, the McBride son let his head hang.

"You are going to pay for this. I am not going to arrest you. But."

"Yes, Trooper Wingard."

"If you come around, or talk shit again like that, I will be sure to lock you up. Don't complicate this situation any further." With authority his finger jabbed the air, and his voice owned the tone of authority.

Looking back at the deck, which Jared was on, Cecil proposed, "How about you get the car fixed down at Bump's autobody. And then Michael here pays for it. I will let Bumpy know."

"That's fine," assured the victim.

"Fine." Replied the disgruntled vandalizer as he opened the door to his truck and swung himself inside, the engine revving up and snow splattering behind him as he descended the small knoll of a driveway.

*

B right, blinding sunlight invaded Agent Morris' eyes as he left his hotel room, causing him to scrunch his face and squint a bit. Being that this was his third trip out to his black SUV, he should have been accustomed to the environment, and its intense manner on that unusually warm December morning.

The prior two trips to his vehicle consisted of his arms being loaded with luggage and his pull along briefcase of all the information and notes he had typed in that motel room and deep into the night. Many keys had been slammed on his laptop before dropping into a dead sleep in the mediocre mattress of the room. Necessary reports and filings are quite vital to his job. Paperwork was the less than exciting part of the gig, but one essential in keeping said charges to stick in a soon to be courtroom setting.

Without haste since it was close to eleven and he needed to meet up with the others, Jake proceeded to the inn's office and swiftly followed through with the check-out procedure. The clerk was a local, and did make a comment about how glad he was to get those killers off of the streets. Then he tried to strongly explain his belief that Brian Swartson had paid them off to commit the deed.

Small town conspiracy theory.

It was only a three-minute trip into town, which did take a total of ten since the investigator swung through the drive through of the local arches for some breakfast. There was no time to spend savoring a meal at The Four Corners Cafe. Plus, he believed that Becky was starting to imagine a love triangle happening.

When in fact it was only a dot.

Chowing down as he pulled up and parked next to Wingard's cruiser, he was ready to get moving and back to his own playing field. The case was far from over, and both of the truth seekers had a stressful road ahead of them.

Entering the now familiar station he tossed his wrappers from his meal into a small refuse can. Dylan was seated at the main desk appointed as the standing guard. As an excited puppy would to see their master the patrolman smiled up at the seasoned investigator. "Hey Agent Morris. Trooper Wingard is waiting for you, Sir."

"Thank you, Officer!" The lad did remind the Bureau expert of himself as a rookie beat cop. There was an innocence about the rookie, yet a distinguishable drive that was likable about the newbie. Relating to this, Jake did smile as he wandered back to their communal workstation.

Wingard was sprawled out with his legs up on the desk, and the local Olean newspaper stretched out before him. Dropping it down slightly he welcomed his partner. "Let's wrap up here so that we can mosey up north."

"You got that right. When we get up to those parts I am going to treat you to some of my hometown cuisine."

"If it's within a cab ride to my hotel, and has a beer or three involved, I am in."

The bonded pair ventured to the front of the building with Jake's arm patting Cecil's shoulder as they left the CPD and entered the DPW front entrance. Which was the impromptu forensics lab for Isaac Morray.

A majority of the forensics team was busy boxing and cataloging the evidence before their own trip up to their main laboratory in Buffalo. That would be where intensive study of their samples would be analyzed and evaluated. Meanwhile in a corner to their right Isaac was busy with one of his technicians inspecting the last few pieces collected the day before. More from the Beebe Hill crime scene would be taken directly to the main center as the progress continues before the trial, but the annex locale would be given back to the snowplow drivers and road workers in the very near future.

"So, Isaac," belted out Jake to his long time comrade, "did we strike paydirt with the few tidbits that we retrieved. Afterall, that is our smoking gun, per se, for probable cause. And I want to nail these two to the wall when in front of that jury."

Smiling, the professional winked as they approached. "You might as well have them killing Allen Marshall on live television. This is bulletproof."

Intrigued, the newcomers came closer, Cecil was even rubbing his hands together as if he was eyeing a delicious turkey dinner, and ready to devour it.

"First off, we have retrieved the laptop of Julie McBride. We were able to access it easily. Did not even have a password." Disbelief at such ease, the leader shook his head and smirked. "And in the past month there were searches about neck trauma from hanging, along with some legal inquiries on her internet browser having to do with estates. Like really in-depth digging about taking down an armed person. Plus, how to disarm someone with a weapon.." His eyes broadened. "They did some demonic homework."

"They really were blind when it came to hiding evidence," stated Wingard. Tittering came from all of the men in response to this ironic truth. Continuing, the trooper asked, "What else do you have to help us? Some internet surfing is not solid for a conviction."

"We have closely monitored the precise cuts of the ropes we acquired on the primary crime scene. Those being on the back porch of the lake home. Then the larger samples in the basement on Beebe Hill. Well, just like a fingerprint, or even the edges of duct tape, they are distinct, and a match." With ease and precision, the orator picked up a manila folder and opened it revealing a few various photos of the ends of the rope. "See how clean and exact that they are, and yet match perfectly like a small puzzle."

All three nodded in amazement at how nicely these lined up for them, and of course they shook their heads in disbelief that the perpetrators would not have thrown such incriminating evidence away after their murderous adventure.

"This will make for a nice forensics show on television."

This cockiness came from Cecil as he clapped his hands aggressively while insinuating the validity of the key pieces of evidence from the secondary location of the crime.

"How about the boots?" inquired Jacob."

"There is no way to perfectly match the boots. The snow is wet and of course with sliding while walking, no two impressions are perfectly aligned." Slightly lifting his shoulders, he tried to lighten the strike of that, and then went on. "But they are both the same size and design. Very small window for argument there. With a melting environment we could not get exact imprints, but the size nine matches, and so does the leaf design on the soles. The other set was too messy to get any reading from."

"And do we have a strike out with the drill bit."

"Swing a miss for the slaughtering duo. That bit matches just right. Again, fingerprint or duct tape precision. The wood sample will need to be tested. Just like DNA for humans. But it's probably going to match."

"With confidence, we would say that they struck out pretty miserably, and we have our probable cause firmly intact so that we don't sink on a technicality," mentioned Cecil.

"Nailed it gentlemen," confirmed Isaac, "now we are going to pack it up so we can get into a real lab setting for the rest of our analysis."

"I am joining you guys for a few more weeks during the discovery and trial, so you will get to see this mug for a while." Ensuring their bond, Cecil vigorously shook Isaac's hand.

With that the trio dispersed, Isaac began to pack more of his professional essentials with his team, as the investigators went back to the police side of the establishment. This was where Dylan met them with several large sturdy boxes for them to move their files and other necessities.

Since they had less of the bulk to move, their packing procedure took just about half an hour. There was a tinge of sadness when they separated the two desks apart and watched their workspace disintegrate into an empty cubicle. But with all semi-closed cases, the show must move to where it is necessary to progress further.

Outside in the crisp, fresh air the men loaded their government issued vehicles and hit the road.

"Are you taking Route 16 Cecil, that's what my GPS is telling me."

"Oh, city boy, I am taking the back woods way via 219. I'll be settled into my room by the time you get to West Seneca."

"Slow and steady is fine for me, Pal. I don't know these hollers and hills like you do, Wingard."

With that they set forth on their journey to the semi-bustling metropolis of Buffalo. Both with a plethora of thoughts on their minds.

Agent Morris was focused on the fact that even out of his normal setting the case went smoothly. This was the point when prosecutors would get deeply involved, and there would be motions and subpoenas. Without a doubt Jake and Cecil will be testifying to various details and dealing with Joseph Stevvins trying to bully them around.

The FBI sleuth has dealt with worse in the past.

There was also a bit of satisfaction that swift justice was served for a fellow federal investigator. Whether or not they had met before. It was a sense of pride, and hope that others would take care of him, like he had taken care of this poor soul. This stunned victim.

As he passed through the small town of Freedom he thought of the poor boy Jared, and his life shattered on that lake.

Quickly as Cecil sailed over Chapel Hill and through Humphrey his own thoughts were percolating, however they were of doubt.

Even though he was a seasoned trooper, he still had never seen a murder case close so easily and with so many mistakes by the slayers. From the failure to provide anything as a way for Marshall to get his head through the noose, to a shaky alibi and pretty much retaining more evidence as keepsakes. Was this even possible for any foolish criminal to do? Why was it so sloppy? Or was he overthinking it.

Trying to divert these thoughts as he traversed through the ski village of Ellicottville, he browsed up at the slopes, which were lively with partakers in their snow-enhanced rides up and down the small hills. Smiles and joy radiating so much that he could feel it from the lanes of Route 219.

As the twilight fell early, just around five in the evening, both men returned to thoughts of the road and avoiding any deer that may sprint before them. Their focus back into real life, and away from the monstrosity of a case that they were in the midst of.

*

The crisp, clear taste of an ice-cold Canadian beer in a frosted pilsner glass made everything seem okay at that moment for Cecil Wingard. The last portion of his trip was peaceful, and the check-in process into the glamorous downtown hotel near the federal courthouse was a breeze. Now he was at the hotel bar waiting for a call from Jake so they could meet up for some food, and a bit of relaxation before the hectic nature of the next day.

This was truly his first time to semi-travel for work. Mostly he stayed in the Southern Tier region for any investigative matters since all local municipality judicial systems were within a somewhat reasonable drive to his own homestead. Since this was his first federal case, and the workload would be leading up as they pummeled more evidence into the discovery, the show was on the road and must go on folks.

Flutters of snowflakes with girth and substance, yet fluffy in nature, were dropping rapidly along the busy avenue that split the city of Buffalo. The block that he was on was one of the few starter segments of the urban motorway. Passersby were going to swanky dinners, and over to concerts in the area. This was a hustle and bustle that was not quite foreign to the small towner, yet something he embraced and partook in on a very erratic schedule.

Never would he give up sitting in hunting stands on a cold November morning for a twelve-point buck in lieu of this on a nightly basis. His education enabled the ordinance protector to appreciate both of these contrasting worlds.

Breathing in and enjoying the chic aura of the space he also enjoyed being dressed in an eggplant colored buttoned oxford shirt, and dark gray khaki style slacks. Maybe he could find a spot on the bureau. Maybe he could use a change.

But you really could not take the Allegany County out of the boy, and vice versa.

Amidst his thoughts circling the glass encased and gold trim lined revolving door spun with life and in entered his loyal partner for this macabre case. Being that he knew this establishment from many instances of other guests of the bureau staying here, Jake moved to the tavern area without much haste, smiling at his new comrade. "Cold beer on a chilly night seems to work nicely, now doesn't it."

Swiveling with a jovial purpose, Cecil spun to great Jake. "A brewski after some handcuffs is a nice feeling. Are you going to kick one back now or take me to our surprise destination."

"Come on, our DrivR car is outside, and we have four minutes to get into it. I am not having a drink and drive in this disaster outside. I like my shield way too much."

Cecil spun back and threw a few crumpled ones on the bar top as a tip for the barkeep. Being a down to earth kinda guy, he was always good to those employed in the hospitality field. Standing up he then placed his long cut midnight black peacoat on and followed the local man outside and into their awaiting ride. The frigid temperature and true lakeside weather did not go unnoticed by both of the men being couriered to their next destination.

Streetlights illuminated the sedan's path as they headed up Delaware Avenue in the Allentown area of the Buffalo proper. Beautiful historic brownstones were mixed with more modern buildings, the architecture of this city was a smorgasbord of concepts, yet they all nestled together and brought unity to the Queen City.

Pointing to his left Jacob played tour guide. "On that corner, the building is long gone now, was a house that Mark Twain lived in back in the day." A smile rose as his finger fell. "There is also a story about him living in the Southern Tier, about an hour's drive east of Cuba, living on a farm and having close friends there. Nice place called Elmira."

Nodding, Cecil appreciated this gesture of friendship. Happy that the host was proud to help the visitor.

With a rapid right the driver went down a side street, then took a sudden left onto Main Street, and halted before a skinny brick building, which was painted in a dark red, almost purple hue. There was a leaning belonging to the structure to the right side of it. Quite noticeable the shifting was, yet obviously safe even though some of the second floor hovered over the sidewalk and part of the side street.

Exiting safely they wandered up the nicely shoveled walkway and into the historic establishment. A giant sign with an anchor read, "Sailor Bar."

"I've heard of this legend, Morris," Cecil chuckled, "but I never had enough time up in these parts to swing through and try some true Buffalo Wings."

A bland, petite brunette hostess was busy on her phone, but held her head up high enough to give a semi-smile, then raised two fingers to indicate the correct amount of guests. The coppers nodded in response, and in an unprofessional silence they passed an inlet to their right with the distinguished bar area.

But this was no ordinary ale spot. It was a giant horseshoe shaped bar in a fifteen by twenty-five-foot space. The bar was lacquered with a prominent gleam, and the wood was done in a dull oak finish. Matching in the same color, the barstools were basic with an aged, wild west style with ornate pillars in the back.

At elbow level for the drinking enthusiasts there was an array of taps with lively pull levers, each its own work of art. They were changed regularly and sporadically to different tastes and types of brewskis.

Up above everyone's heads was a generous shelf that ran the full U of the tavern top, full of various liquors and spirits. This was open to all the participants to see. Along any other free wall space were various license plates from various states dating to any time period from when the first vehicle identifier was created, up until current day. Some had basic jumbles for their combinations, while others had hidden names such as "wingz4life" from Maryland, or "sp1cych1x" from Texas.

It was a nice spectacle to add to a unique grill.

Past the booze center and through an archway was a small dining room with about a baker's dozen full of tables. All in the same basic wood tone, but with simple red and checkered plastic tablecloths dressing them up. There were also a few license plates adorning the walls, but also celebrity pictures with their signatures decorating the larger expanse. Giving it a "the place to be" kind of aura.

Far in the left corner the maître d' placed two basic paper menus, folded in the middle, onto the three-seater table. With an ordinary smile she exited and headed back to her mediocre post. Being in the law enforcement game, the gents sat with their backs against the wood paneled walls and facing the expanse of the eating hall. This was both by instinct, and made them both the most comfortable in any situation.

An insert of the menu included the current draft beer selection, which was numbered at between three and four dozen, coming from the taps at the bar. These were selected by the management and barkeeps of the inn.

A well-kept and semi-flamboyant waiter walked up to the table. "Hey guys, what beers have you chosen to kick off the night with?"

The server's name tag exclaimed that his name was Charley.

Jake introduced his order. "Southern Tier Ale."

"Ditto," rang in Cecil.

"Do we need time with the menus still fellas."

In the mood for whatever, Cecil shrugged in Jake's direction. "Want to just share wings and such? This is your area of expertise."

"You read my mind, Trooper." Flicking the menu before him the order giver then spoke. "Let's do two dozen hot wings. Two dozen garlic parm. And a large basket of your fries. Does that sound good, Charles?"

"It's Charley, and I guess you guys are the boss. Right." With some attitude the order taker descended from the table.

Attempting to turn the vibe back around, Cecil cracked his knuckles and looked up at the various influencers on the walls who had dined in the same spot. "So, your wife didn't want to join us."

"Nah, she isn't one of the details of the job, or even interacting with the others from the field. Reminds her of the danger that I am in the front seat for every day."

With less sass and a semi-smile, Charley brought over the frothy pint glasses loaded with suds and hops.

With indulgent gulps the men began to relax again together. But the case was close in their mind, and on their tongues. And the statie had some thoughts that had been congesting his noggin. "Do you have any slight doubts at all about Julie and Clayton being involved?"

Perplexed, Jake lowered his glass and set it on his cardboard coaster. Then leaned a bit back in his seat. "I really can't think of anyone else who would have done this?

"Do you think Allen staged it?"

"Pffft," in a jovial mood Jake sat back up and reached for his brewski. "Could he hover? Because that's the only way he could do that."

Defeated, Cecil decided to move on, and actually admitted to himself that it was an off kelter idea. "How is the federal prosecutor?"

"Well..."

"Just be blunt. Good, bad, ugly, and all the gossip."

A skewed eyebrow showed his disbelief to his friend/ professional ally. "You have never heard of Jackson Steele?"

Nearly snorting a decent amount of hoppy pale ale from his nose, Cecil then tried to recover by coughing and grasping onto the edge of the table top. "I totally forgot that he is the federal prosecutor for this region."

Using a folded napkin, he tried to do some damage recovery and maintain some decent state after this unintended obstructive response. The mentioned lawyer was well known in the area for his stern stance on crime, and also his potential political career. Word on the street, and in the political circles, was that he was chomping at the bit for a spot on the ballot in the next two to six years for any position possible for him to win.

Some even insinuating Deputy Governor.

"Wingard, have you seen the news about him in the past few years?"

"Yeah, I just had a lapse of memory right there. He is a pit bull."

"That is an understatement. He is already calling for no plea deals. Death penalty. It is clear that he wants to make a mark in the area, and this is his jackpot."

Raising his brew for a more cautious sip, Cecil proceeded, but first made a counterpoint. "What if this becomes a mess. What if people decide the 'fuck the machine' route is better, and this all blows up in his face." A hearty swallow followed.

"Touché," Jake took his own indulgence in a mirror fashion, "but when you select the right jury who sees an ambushed, then hung, not suffocated, but hung, federal agent who sees that the animals and land of a sacred country area are protected, then no one will claim any machine."

"Damn Morris, sure you aren't interning for him during this trail."

Both men exploded with chortle as the wings and taters, both fried perfectly, landed on the table via Charley's arms and hands. From under his bicep he released a small wooden bowl and a plethora of napkins cradled within and sat them in the center of the eating display. Without words all parties were aware that this was intended for the plentiful sauce, and the aftermath of many bones from the fowl themed cuisine.

From this came a silent agreement, a treaty almost, that the rest of the meal, and the two beers afterward, would be kept sterile from any talk of the case. There was a necessity for the men to have boundaries and space so that they could rest and replenish their souls from the case, which was just getting started.

Stirring up some conversation, Cecil questioned Jake about his life and wife a bit. Finding out details that he was comfortable sharing about his spouse. There was also the subject of how Cecil was still single, and in response there was a chat about how the trooper wanted to keep climbing up the law enforcement rankings, and then settle down a bit. There was no race in his mind to mix the two life objectives.

With a solid fight, and a victory on his side, Cecil declined to be dropped off by Jake's DrivR ride while he ascended to Tonawanda. Instead, he opted for the ten minute jot down some frigid side streets, then back to Delaware Avenue to his glimmering glass encased hotel on the main drag.

Again, he had a desire to have some life and depth blown into him from the crisp breeze coming from the Niagara River and Lake Erie. Life to begin jolting his soul, and more passion was fueling his mind in order to fight for justice for the life that Allen Marshall lost.

*

Murmurs upon whispers were drilling noise into the marble floors and highly domed ceilings of the main courtroom of the federal judicial space in Niagara Square during that intimidating Monday morning. The judge and staff had been more than accommodating for the petite blizzard that snuck across the Great Lakes the night before and dumped twenty monstrous inches over that third of the state. Whether the attendee was driving from the Southern Tier, or from the east leaving the federal prison, or a few miles away from within the city itself, all needed much extra time, and there was no way to postpone this arraignment.

This was due to the fact that a small press release late into the evening beforehand had snowballed, pun intended, into a headline that was now worldwide. This media blurb was unveiled by Jackson Steele as a plea for attention, and the plea grew into a demand from all sources of news casting for more details on this unique court battle to begin.

Since it was a rarity that a federal agent was killed, and in this case intentional with premeditation, news outlets were eating it up. Throwing in the fact that the prosecutor had mentioned the words "death penalty" in a state that normally does not in itself allow such a consequence enlarged the flames and drew in more moths to its enticement.

Since it was a federal crime, and federal jurisdiction, the needle into the arm was the ultimate goal for the brazen solicitor. And a few tidbits from the case showing the viciousness and depravity of said offense really allowed for a full explosion of interest of all types.

In response, a slew of national journalists were rolling into the downtown zone of the state's second largest city. A new spark to thaw out the cold northeastern winter. A long trial that will keep an audience glued to their seats.

A segment of the population dying to see the downfall of murderers.

Wrapped tightly in their winter's best head to toe, her arm slinging to the crook in Jared's elbow, the devastated duo ventured into the large art deco styled stately building where the proceedings were to take place whenever the defendants finally made it through the snow plastered Interstate 90 from Batavia. The initial ten am hearing was delayed until all was settled, and that was fine by the two travelers since their trip from Cuba had taken nearly three hours, double the normal amount, due to the inclement weather.

Confused and overwhelmed, they finally found the third-floor hallway where room 312 was boldly plagued with "Jackson Steele, ADA." Nodding to each other in assurance, Jared then boldly knocked thrice.

With thrust and emotion, the door flew open, and a dashingly handsome man in his mid-thirties, with a solid build, soap opera star like jawline, and a perfect hairline with ink black hair combed to enhance his perfect bangs, was eager to meet the first rounds of guests for the pre-arraignment gathering.

With vigorous, yet respectful tempered handshakes, the law debater welcomed Jared and Virginia, and had already known their names, and a bit about them.

Jackson Steele was a man of the people. This was a middle-tiered rung position on the ladder of his ever-earning success. And with each rung he knew that as a committed public servant he had to make stellar impressions on all that he interacted with . And if he wasn't precise in his movements at this level, how could he ever rise to become a politician who actually had integrity. There was a standard disgust in his soul and body that despised the past politicians of the Empire State. An angst and dread when another one was taken down for a sex scandal, or debauchery, or just plain old embezzlement would fester with Jackson. They would ascend as he was starting, and then fall onto their double headed sword and leave the voter, and New Yorker, in disbelief that they had yet again been tricked.

Fool me once...

And for the past ten years since he left law school he had been thriving in the western portion of the state, first as a clerk, then higher up in the judicial system, and traversing from state agendas to the full-on federal system. And this was his second-year prosecuting, and in his eyes protecting his fellow brothers since he himself was from the Rochester region, and wanted to play close to home and do some good in the extremely hazardous field of public duties.

"Marshalls, please sit down." His slender, generous hand with slim, perfectly kept manicured nails and fingers motioned for the distressed kin to have a seat on a tufted leather sofa in a rich cinnamon hue. Almost that of ground light blend coffee pre-brewing.

Pairing them in the same abbreviated davenport was a well devised plan in order to have them feel safe close to each other, comforted in the furniture, and appreciated for their time.

This dude was not a bad person.

"As you have likely heard," started the host, "the paddy wagon heading west with the suspects," precisely he avoided the words "mother" or "they." This way any attachment Jared had with his maternal parent would not be aroused. "Has been slowed down tremendously due to the snow. As I know you have been heading this way you must have encountered the storm also. And we want this done today." With the smile of a politician, he pressed on. "We have a small caravan of officers, two vehicles, in front and back. And they are far below the speed limit. But I am insisting that they can get here. Because I want nothing to go wrong with this case, especially this early on."

"We understand," was a muffled response from Virginia. Her aged and wrinkled hand, one embroidered with liver spots and moles, grasping onto Jared's, clinging to the last part of her family tree that was above the ground. "Especially since the funeral services are on Wednesday. We appreciate that."

Embarrassed, he had not thought of this factor, Jackson slightly blushed, but pushed onto his own reasoning behind a swift appearance before their Honor. "We need to make sure that on my end there are no holes, or mistakes. If we delay, they could say we are slowing down their speedy trial, and in turn make a mess for us. I play by the book. And only win fair."

"And by winning," Jared's voice failed and wavered a bit in strength and volume, "you mean that you truly are going for the death penalty."

With a robust nature the prosecutor boldly looked at

the attendees, "Absolutely. There is strong, and deliberate premeditation." Before pressing on he cleared his throat. "And sorry to say this, but it was a malicious and vicious crime. There needs to be vindication in this."

Trying to obtain some power in the conversation, Virginia pitched in, "But as Jared has said before, those crime shows on the tv show plea deals for manslaughter, and they get out in ten or fifteen years." Her hands moved as if she was having a small fit over this potential injustice.

Fielding this question Jackson carried on. "That is in a scripted film or show. This is real life. If we back down, it will set a precedent to the state, and nation, that they can kill our federal agents. And your father was a loyal veteran to the USDA. What they did was greedy, and selfish." True emotion showed from the orator at this point as his clenched fist pounded twice on his desk blotter. "I entered this field and profession to make sure that the law is obeyed, and the easy path isn't enjoyed when it comes to due process. I am going to forge this case, and Agent Marshall's death will not be in vain."

Goosebumps were a common answer to this vivacious impromptu speech. A quivering silence, much needed and enjoyed by all followed. And those words were sinking in just as another knock on the door peacefully brought them back to the moment.

*

With some preplanning Wingard and Morris had coordinated their entrance together. There was a need for a sense of solidarity and camaraderie to continue with their partnership in a steadfast fashion through the entire lurid litigation process. Cecil had strolled around the first floor waiting for Jake's text announcing his arrival. By doing so he had missed the Marshalls' entry. Which was best so that they could pow wow with the head attorney first and alone.

And once the agent had arrived, they met in the foyer.

A PRECISE DECEPTION

Casual handshakes and greetings were exchanged while they progressed to the lifts. Hopping into the elevator together they were ready for the day.

The previously joined guests both allowed their faces to light up with contentment that they knew the two new joiners. That led to a bit of comfort and trust resonating in the room. Being from such a small-town area, these two did not like to trust those who worked in big buildings and wore shiny suits. They were afraid that they were only in business for themselves. But there was a trust level with Jackson that they were starting to admire.

Being the local up in these parts, Jake furiously shook Jackson's hand and rubbed his shoulder during the grasp. "Hey, Chap. I am glad you were assigned this case." Peering over to the fallen hero's family, the agent conveyed his confidence in the avenger. "Mister Steele is the best man on duty. Not just for his convictions either, which he is at like, what ninety-six percent rate of convocation."

"Ninety-eight."

"Ninety-eight. My bad. But the man has some morals. And true ethics."

"Thank you," started the younger Marshall, "I didn't think we would see you anytime soon since your job is done. Especially you, Trooper Wingard."

"Oh," started the cop, "I am the case on and off until the trial is over. Which could take years."

"Not here," smiled the knowledgeable host, "in these cases they want a speedy trial. Now we have an abundance of evidence before us." A grin of a man with a winning hand was painted over his face with these details. "The shaky alibi, the financial gains, the physical evidence and forensics. We don't need to keep fishing the creek for the smoking gun. We have it all. Therefore, if they want a speedy trial, they will get it. I want this wrapped up by Easter, if not sooner."

"That's fast for even you, Jackson," replied Jake.

"This is my first time trying a capital murder of an agent.

116

And I want to make a true statement for anyone who is thinking of the same. Or if they are pulling a gun on an agent in two years. You pull that trigger; you will be going down. And fast at that."

Some type of bittersweet pride rose in Jared. "So, my dad is a martyr?"

Inhaling deep, Jackson was unsure how to word the next statement, but did so with respect to the family, but yet maintaining stamina in his field. "This is a tragedy, and we all wish we were not in this room together for this occurrence. However, the only silver lining in this thunderstorm is that maybe he could prevent the slaughtering of an agent in the future."

There was an awe, and a pleasant remembrance in the room at this small, yet poignant, focus of view.

With a robust ring, the static style break in chatting was disrupted again with the ink black phone laying on the mahogany desktop of ADA Steele.

"Yes," he answered in a mild, simplistic manner. The line coming through was his secretary, so he was courteous, yet was not forced to go through his whole well-mannered spiel as if it was anyone else trying to connect with him.

Without a farewell he slightly dropped the receiver onto its matching base. "The defendants have arrived and are being offloaded now. Judge Forrester will proceed with the arraignment in twenty minutes since we are quite a bit off schedule as is. And we want to get the media out of the lobby as soon as humanly possible."

Shocked, Virginia blinked her eyes rapidly and shook her head in an attempt to wrap it around how major this case is. "All of those news trucks outside are here for this?" Curiosity ravaged her voice and mind. "I thought that they were here for the blizzard outside. Not for my Allen."

A menacing sob ensued.

"Let's head down," the attorney was ready for a small spectacle starring himself versus Joseph Stevvins. In response all the occupants of the room rose and flocked to the solid wood door which held a steamed glass window from the waist height up. "National news outlets willl be all over. This is a very rare case of when a federal agent is killed outside of his duties, and the death penalty being blatantly displayed from day one. Come on," he closed the door behind them as they headed to the elevator, "you will see the circus, and remember, when any reporters ask, 'no comment' is your instructions by me."

*

U nforgivable flashing of cameras flickered and roared off of the ceilings and shining beige marble walls of the lobby for the federal building as soon as the party of five left the elevator and proceeded to the side entrance of the courtroom. Murmurs amongst the photo takers and their journalist counterparts ensued. Whispers of "that must be the family," and "that Jackson Steele goes for blood," shimmied their way to the ears of all of those in the progressing mob.

A tear ran down the somber face of Virginia in the realization that her son's massacre was now a public headline. A single rivulet that was again captured by picture seekers and notes on that detail written in small notebooks by the newspaper creators.

This was juicy content that the world was about to eat up.

As a proper leader should, Jackson opened the right door of a set of two. They were solid, and rich in their wood grain and color. There was a girth and substance behind them, those being similar in how justice should be handled in this supreme space. It was on the right side of the assembly zone, that way they did not have to fight the masses of yet more of the tabloid mongers and local looky-loos who wanted to see some of the hottest gossip in the region. It was a feeble attempt at keeping the Marshalls a bit pure before more madness would ensue during the rest of the damned process.

Inside the actual courtroom was scantily assembled with just a few people at that time. The official front doors had yet to be opened, so this allowed the Marshalls a chance to take in the atmosphere sans the circus raging at the door. And the tranquility let them absorb the start of their rollercoaster, and feel at peace for a singular moment.

On the far back wall was a memorable built in shrine to the judge. With a massive structure and detailed trim work, it spoke of his stature and authority in this domain. Giant flags representing both the nation and of the Empire State were prominently displayed hanging vertically behind him. There was no doubt that he was a patriot at heart. Of course, in dynamic print along the front of his expansive office space there was a sign that read, "Honorable James Forrester."

Intimidation was not a necessity when constructing said sanctuary, but rather it was an unknown product of such architecture in such a power-ridden experience expanse.

On either side sat his clerks and stenographer. They were situated a level lower, yet again intensifying his prominence.

Basic church style pews lined the arena for the audience. A small patch on the front of the staged area behind what appeared to be the table for Jackson Steele had four spots taped off for the quad coming with the prosecutor. There was a knowledge in the back of Virgina and Jared's minds that they would be forced to literally be front and center of the show, but this was another reminder of the suffering that they must endure with now many facets of the country, and possibly planet, spying in on their pain.

Softly they sat, the bench cold on everyone's derriere. Of course, the lawmen sat in the spots next to the mourning family. This was a process that they were used to, yet considerate that those joining them were not.

There were a few court workers meandering about doing their preparatory work. Perfectly on cue, Joseph Stevvins appeared at the opposing table from Jackson. They had never interacted in any facet, nor were really aware of one another even, so the host felt an obligation to greet his sparring mate.

"Mister Stevvins, welcome to my kingdom. I play fair, and

I encourage you to do so also."

Excitedly the defense protector stood from his seated spot, pushing his floral tie close to his body and using the free hand to shake that of his opponent. "Of course. I do have a few motions."

"That is fine."

"Being that both the defendants and I travel quite a ways, we want to get a few housekeeping issues tidied up so that we are not back and forth weekly on this."

"I like to cut the fat and get to the point. So therefore, I have no problems with that logic."

Nodding they both parted ways without a proper farewell. They were heading into a territory between the two scholars that held respect, yet no need for simplistic etiquette. Lives were literally on the line here. Even being a small-town esquire, Joseph Stevvins was eager to step up to the plate, yet cautious and ready to research everything so that his first time at the big league would not be his last.

And especially no terms for being disbarred.

In a pew behind the defensive line was Michael McBride. A deep stare was radiating from his eyes over to Jared and Virginia. One of hatred and despise. One of a man with no one else to blame for his father's new hurdle. One he most definitely will lose.

As if perfectly choreographed, a law clerk used her forefinger to signal to one leading deputy who then spoke to a few bailiffs and nodded to each other. Lastly, they proceeded to the rear and released the prominent duo of impressive doors, allowing a sensational burst of television cameras and their teams enter, along with a vast array of people looking to come in. Even some law students and their professors pushed through in order to get a glimpse of this rare showing that was about to be unveiled.

A soft tap accompanied another one, both Virginia and Jared's shoulders, the ones that were side by side of each other. Virginia's left, and Jared's right. Both turned to see who this was. They were well aware, and cautious of the fact that many onlookers, and even some press members, will be interrupting their quiet moments from time to time. But much to their relief it was a friendly face. It was JT Dove.

"Mister Dove," proclaimed a frail, yet interested Missus Marshall, "what are you doing in these parts?"

"Well I need to stay up to date on all of these proceedings in reference to how I handle Allen's estate." With this intention clear, JT sat on the edge of the pew behind them. "I am working on the term life insurance policy issued through the government. With the arrest and now arraignment it will be moved from your mother's name to solely yours. So in six to eight weeks, you will pick that check up from my office."

"What if she gets acquitted?" This worry came from Virginia.

"With this much evidence against her the policyholder will default the payment to Jared. They need less of a burden of proof to make their decisions than this trial."

Being overwhelmed with all before them, neither thought of asking about the amount that was waiting. It didn't seem to matter, they would barter anything for their patriarch to be here with a heartbeat, rather on a cold slab in Belmont.

"What about the house, we need to go there to find Dad's good suit and a few things for the service this week," inquired Jared.

"Coordinate with the investigators, they may have it sealed off for now. Since you are not a suspect, and still a legal resident, you will have full access."

"That works for us," exclaimed Jared.

"Tomorrow I am petitioning the court on behalf of your father's estate to have the house formally deeded to you Jared. That will take a few weeks, especially depending on how the judge feels about this case being prosecuted. But the law states that if anyone who can benefit from a victim's death is being suspected of said offense, which your mother clearly is, then the estate is to move along the line of successors."

The listeners looked at each other, nodded, then smiled back at the advice sharer.

In a solemn response the visiting solicitor leaned back into his spot behind them, and the mass of visitors had also settled. When there was a small occurrence of peace in the judiciary space two guards nodded and motioned to the far back door on the side wall. Slowly that entrance opened, and a gasp rang through the courtroom as the defendants were led into the courtroom, both with their heads hung in disbelief and embarrassment.

Their wrists and ankles were tethered with stainless steel handcuffs. These cold, silver shackles were wound around their body in order to ensure no escape attempts, or attacks on anyone else would be on the schedule. They were dressed in matching intense orange uniforms, ones that were in the style of a nurse. Therefore, there were two pieces to the ensemble, and the material was a textured cotton, with a single pocket over their hearts.

In pitch black lettering it stated, "US INMATE MAXIMUM."

Without questioning, Jared knew that they were being held in the tightest security, and the depravity of the situation sank into him. For a moment he almost shed a tear to see the woman who gave him life be in such a distressful state.

But for just a moment. Then reality sank in again that she stole his favorite parent away, and this was just part of the karma that would be sailing her way until she was fitted for her pine box.

The suspects were directed to a small seating area to the side of the arrangement of invitees. Both looked frazzled and confused. There were tears rising and then dropping from their own eyes, and frantically they were looking around. For a moment Jared swore that Clayton had waved at him. But then he looked to his right and saw Michael McBride sitting behind Joseph Stevvins.

Rolling his eyes, Jared then squeezed Virginia's bicep as a

way to comfort them both. Although he needed it the most.

Five awkward minutes passed. There was a mixture of voices performing a banquet of duties. Some were recording small introductions for their future audience of their news blurbs. Some were discussing the beginning stages of the trial. Others were even simply discussing the weather.

Except for Jared and Virginia. Silence was just fine for them.

*

A n energetic whisk of air erupted in the abbreviated arena and announced that the main leader had entered the playing field.

"All rise for the Honorable Judge Forrester," rang the voice of a bailiff who was situated next to the front of the stage on its left side.

This was followed by the promised entrance of said civil servant, and all the occupants, chained or not, rose to the occasion. His gown in a satin fabric yet in a jet-black tone waved slightly with the air as he marched in and to his post.

Exuding an aura of prestige, balanced power, and dignity, the professional designated to preside over the upcoming matter entered and smiled. Along with this overwhelming presence he was detailed with semi-curled salt and pepper hair which showed his knowledge and experience. While his face, aged fifty-three and a quarter, held stamina especially, with his hooked nose and clean-shaven features. There truly were many strong judicial traits radiating both physically and internally with the jurist.

Using an opened hand at waist level he softly beckoned the crowd to regain their seating in a modest fashion. With this simplest form of acknowledgement exercised it eased the audience and potential convicts slightly. It was also a style in his repertoire that was successful, and somewhat welcoming.

With a strike of his occupational gavel onto the finessed

lumber surface, the court was now in session for a pinnacle fiasco.

"We are here for the arraignment in this matter. Before me I have the charges laid out that the federal district attorney and his fellow council have filed officially this morning." Looking over a few scattered documents before him, the orator continued. "I see that they have two defendants, yet one defense attorney."

Rising Joseph Stevvins decreed to the court. "Yes, Your Honor. I would like to first approach the court and have the two accused tried as co-defendants. If approved I would be acting as their council for said indictments."

During this proposal the decision maker placed a pair of wire rimmed glasses properly and had engaged a stylish ink pen into his right finger and thumb in order to take any necessary notes. With this inquiry he did look up and over the spectacles so that he could view the solicitor asking.

Glancing at the team pursuing the vicious charges asked a singular question, "Mister Steele, any objections."

"None, Your Honor. I am perfectly fine with that."

Clearing his throat, and obviously tussling a few of his own tidbits of the debate in his mind, the magistrate threw his hazel eyes back and forth between the opposing members of the same bar then made his own determination. "I will allow it. With one stipulation."

A small instance of suspense arose among the onlookers.

"I will be appointing a member from the public defender's office as a consultant. If you wish them to be more than such during the process, that is also fine. But I do not want to have this end up unraveling at a potential appeal."

Deep in his mind Jackson Steele of course would have preferred that Joseph Stevvins ran his show as a single man episode. However, there was some gratitude that this small detail in the premiere of the proceedings could cause a snag upon review. Then a higher-ranking judicial enforcer would end up tossing out any guilty verdicts and cause the carousel to spin back around to the entrance and void all of the work that he had managed to place into this cause. There was no time for that on his agenda.

"Any objections to this, Mister Steele?"

"None, Your Honor."

"Moving on. May I have the defendants rise."

The disgraced McBride and Marshall gathering stood to their feet, the metal interwoven links clinked and clanked as they did what was instructed of them.

"In this case, in relation to the following charges, premeditated murder in the first degree of an active federal agent, tampering with evidence in the first degree of said crime, and burglary in the first degree. How do you, Clayton J McBride, plead?"

With angst in his voice, he answered. "Not guilty."

"And to you Julie A. Marshall, same charges."

"Not guilty."

"You may be seated."

Standing and initiating the next part of the hearing Joseph Stevvins nodded at the evaluator, who replied, "I am assuming you want us to discuss bond. Correct?"

"Yes, Sir."

"Unfortunately, there will be no bond in this case. This was a callous act. And being so close to Canada, we are not risking anything."

With too much enthusiasm Jared said, "Yes."

The press had a field day with this reaction in a multitude of publications.

Searching notes Jackson did stand and raised his open palm.

"Yes, Mister Steele."

"There is communal property, well, property that was being disputed in the pending divorce. We want to move for a stay on any attempt to receive a loan from said property on Beebe Hill Road for any reason. In different motions we will be asking for the property to be distributed to their son, Jared

Marshall."

Rocking back in his chestnut hued chair behind the bench, with his fingers tented over his nose, the enforcer exhaled and shared his decision. "I agree with this. Has the home been released back to anyone yet."

"It is a secondary crime scene, but we found profound evidence there. So not yet."

"No loans or sale will be allowed. And please keep me up to date on this issue."

"Absolutely, Sir."

"Anything else, gentlemen."

"Sir," started Stevvins. "I want a speedy trial."

"As we all do. Let's set eight weeks for a preliminary hearing. Is that sufficient for discovery on both sides?" A quiet zephyr allured through the jurisdiction without a mumble or sound. "So be it. If we must extend, we will. However, let's see what the next two months bring us. We are adjourned."

*

Nervously pacing around the main receiving hall of Winters' Funeral Home, Jared Marshall was straightening his navy-blue tie with yellow rose decorations, and awkwardly pecking at the cuffs of his rich royal blue suit jacket sleeves. The outfit was new since it had been years since he needed any type of formal apparel. Due to its freshness there was a stiffness to it, which was how he felt emotionally the past few days. Many instances he wanted to break down and cry, which he did, but only in private. Since any public showing of said dramatic feelings would immediately bring his grandmother to tears also. Trying to be strong for Virginia was taking a toll on his own emotional health.

Flowers in a tasteful assortment of colors and styles were lining the walls and on various tables. The senders were listed on small cards with caring messages plugged neatly into the vase or soil. A small podium was at the mouth of the doors with a small open book, encased in tan toned leather. Its pages were bare, ready for those to leave documentation of their visit to be inscribed with an ornate attached pen, its ink jet black.

There was still another half an hour until the doors officially opened for the visitation, which would end with a modest service immediately afterwards. The grieving center was designed to hold seventy-five seats for the gathering that day. And being a man with expertise in such situations Roger Winters added an extra thirty placement or so just in case. Even with the incident of more than anticipated attending, this seating arrangement would be sufficient. Especially since the burial would have to be delayed a few weeks due to the intensity of the frozen ground being unable to be penetrated by any digging device.

Regrettably this delay would only prolong the mourning process for the grieving family members.

Included in this mass was a distraught Virginia, who entered the room after giving Jared his much-needed space. Head to toe she was adorned in a midnight black dress in a drastic conservative style. Long sleeves and a knee-length skirt to its structure were keeping with her current style of funeral attire. Gold buttons danced along the center of the piece giving it a small, yet sophisticated pizzazz that was appropriate for such a setting. The day prior her winter toned locks, which were fashioned in short curls, were given attention at the local salon. The stylist was courteous enough to avoid any talk or gab about the macabre week that the customer was enduring, which was a small gift to the heartbroken mother.

Every so often one segment of the duo would approach the intimating mahogany coffin that embraced their beloved Allen. Satin, in the shade of canary yellow contoured his body, which was in a solemn black suit, a sharp white dress shirt, a hunter green slim tie with a few keepsakes settled amongst his resting home.

Those endearing possessions that he cherished in this life were continuing their journey to the next alongside him.

With a crisp entrance into the side of the establishment, this being permitted by their lawful status, Trooper Wingard and Agent Morris bowed their heads and politely wiped their shoes on the thick carpet intended for such inclement weather. The Marshalls were only aware of who the newly introduced guests were due to the familiarity of their voices. Upon settling in the newcomers spoke to the proprietor, only making small talk about their trip down from the bustling metropolis on that Wednesday morning.

Two days had passed since the arraignment triumphantly made a vibrant splash throughout the world about such a preposterous case of mariticide, and the loverboy accomplice. A love triangle in a one-horse town. Plus, their failed coverup for a shady replica of a suicide was being analyzed by legal leaders on major networks. Facts were being strewn, and the sleepy town of Cuba was making headline news in this matter.

With an aching obligation to be a proper host of the depressing encounter, Jared wandered from the side of the casket and into the small enclave area where the detectives were removing their outercoats and ending their chit chat with the mortician.

"Thank you for coming." This was a shy welcome from the orphan. "I know things are busy, and thank you so much for letting us grab a few items from the Beebe Hill house."

"No problem, we had some tasks down here to do also. Background work into your mom and Clayton. Things that we can take care of after the service."

"Driving all of that way down here does mean quite a bit to us." This was coming from Virginia as she was entering the group. Her steps were wobbling and dangerous, yet her heart was steady and pure.

At precisely ten in the morning Roger Winters opened the main double glass with aluminum edging doors and allowed the droves of people to ascend into the sacred, somber dwelling. There was a scheduled two hours for visitation and viewing.

With his pristine cosmetic skills on the recently departed, Roger was able to cover up the minute amount of bruising that Allen had acquired. There was still a slight amount of life and realistic measure of blood flowing through the permanent sleeper's veins thanks to shadowing and using proper tones that you almost expected him to rise and join the gathering.

Grief stricken family members from across the state and northeast joined Virginia and Jared as they mourned as a united front the abbreviated life of the hero. Tears and frustration were shared and molded together as one unit. Many times, the mother of the slain was forced to sit and sob in peace. Even Jared's comfort was not enough to ease her ailing.

About ten minutes into the congregation Frank Lyons emerged from the doorway, dressed in his formal USDA uniform, and readily greeted those that he knew, especially the four stable members of the gathering. These were times when a partner dreaded a day like this. Disbelief of a comrade being caught in a type of plight. Even if it was one not on the direct field. It was still a hit to the team, and a blow to his soul as a man. Instead of letting this disaster take him down, he was staying strong for all around him.

Massive vans with long telescopic antennas reaching from their bodies were parked in the nearby streets. Distinctive media logos were painted on their doors and side panels, expressing who they represented. Deputies employed by Allegany County were patrolling the area and ensuring that the lot reserved for the mortician's business was solely for visitors, and not the press. This was easing the traffic flow created by the ebbing and flowing of those who were passing their condolences.

Every so often Jared would have to excuse himself so that he could get some water, or intake some headache reliever tablets. Although he was steadfast with his work which was the dire task of receiving empathy and sympathy from the visitors. Eventually there was the sighting of Jackson Steele which led to some surprise and a sudden growth of respect for the man.

The bar member spoke first, "Jared, I am again sorry for your loss. As another civil servant, we all feel the pain when one of our own is taken short of their full potential."

Wrapping his slim hand around the masculine counterpart's open mitt, Jared smiled, "I am impressed that you traveled down here for this."

"I am not like the rest of the bunch up in Niagara Square. I honor my victims, and fight for their justice." Seeing that a small line was forming he moved on and engaged with Virginia in a similar fashion talk. Yet again that Marshall was entranced with his presence and care for their fallen loved one.

Continual action such as this progressed until approximately ten minutes prior to noon. A large proportion of the partakers were simply there to give and share their sorrows, view the honoree one final time, and merge back into their own lives that were quite cumbersome themselves. There was no need on their behalf to stay and wallow further.

While others did stay, even the Buffalo wanderers. When the time came to convert from informal to a formal procedure, Roger Winters softly alerted those in attendance that it was time to take a seat, and for any idle chatter to cease.

Which the sheep did follow their herder in perfect migration.

Tenderly they sat as Roger Winters rose to the podium at the front of the settled batch of attendees and spoke. "Thank you for joining us today for this memorial service. As you all have been informed previously, the formal burial will take place in a month, give or take a fortnight, pending the ground thawing, as we all know is unpredictable in these parts."

Nods and "mmhhmms" from the throng of people confirming this fact with the orating leader.

"First, we have USDA Frank Lyons speaking. There was a strong, loyal bond between these partners, and in remembrance, he wanted to take some time to voice his admiration for our recently departed."

Rising from the front row, two seats to the right of Jared,

the announced speaker ascended to the focal point of the room. With his palm on his belly button area, he smoothed the jacket of his prestigious outfit and cleared his throat, although as he spoke his voice faltered and vibrated with emotions. "When one works for the federal government as investigators, no matter what facet, there are always a majority of good eggs, and a minute population of rotten ones. Their yolks spoiled from their own demons and faults.

"They only scrounge around for what benefits them, and not society as a whole. And those are the ones we filter out first, although they always leave a tarnish in the world, and on the name of us solid agents. The ones with morals."

Gripping the podium, he pushed through reactions from the shock that he was actually laying his fellow agent to rest.

"However, in the large ratio of the commendable enforcers is the elite crew, the ones who balance right and wrong. Moderators who properly evaluate both sides, and come to a fair, equitable verdict in the end. And in that hair thin proportion was Agent Allen Marshall."

Utilizing every duct in his lungs, Frank indulged in a massive breath, one that took several seconds to partake in, yet so crucial in order for him to keep his composure as memories flooded the enormous silver screen in his mind.

"Allen listened to those that we investigated and took into consideration their struggles and comprehension of the laws that we dictate. Many times, he would lessen the blow, or eliminate charges, because of simple errors that they had understood. Never was he disciplined for such actions, because they were fair. And he had a voice for the people we serve. Well, he served."

A crisp exhale helped his status stay stable.

"And that is not to be translated as letting down the government and allowing wrongs to pass under his nose without justice. When he found fraud, he stood his ground and made sure both sides of the law were fairly represented."

Biting his lip, he pressed on. In his mind he wanted to

speak more, but his raw inhibitions to break down and sob were fighting a mighty battle.

"Not only was he a hero of our nation, and part of the world, but he was a model parent. Jared was his pride and joy. And alongside that notion he was a son to beat all sons. I always wanted to hear what he was getting for Virginia each Mother's Day, so that I could find something of the same caliber."

This story relieved some chortles from the audience, and helped smooth the overall vibe in the space.

"I would love to go on with more anecdotes, but I think someone is cutting onions in the kitchen." To coordinate his pun he wiped his eye, but the tear was serious. "But thank you Allen." With that he faced the open casket. "You helped craft me into being a better member of the USDA, better person, and overall helped this area in being a heartland."

Soft applause radiated from the seats, and Virginia smiled in his direction, confirming her approval of the eulogy.

Hesitation struck Jared at this moment in a paralyzing fashion. One that meshed his body into his chair and was excruciating to expel himself from. Suddenly someone had poured metaphorical concrete in the pockets of his slacks. If he stood up at that moment and gave this speech, it would be confirmation that his father was gone. Sure, the body was right there. But the actual farewell oration was the final nail in the coffin.

Literally...

Noticing the haste in his momentum to take the stage, Virginia provided a slight motivational elbow onto Jared's forearm, letting him know that this was his duty to send his father off in a goodbye sermon. Which by hearing this dictation leave her grandson's lips would also be cementing the fact that her baby boy was gone from them forever.

Knowing his duty he rose, and headed to the designated spot.

This epilogue to his father's life was one that he spent the past few days writing. There were crumpled pieces of yellow paper with faint red lines that had first and second drafts, though all of them were abandoned. Plus, several on his computer that were rapidly backspaced as he buried his head in the open hand and cried over his frustration, and of his loss.

Finally the night before, as he had been previewing tombstones, did he get the ideal idea. One small symbol made the speech possible and motivated him.

Lowering the microphone, Jared swallowed hard and mustered up a small smile. "Thank you all for joining my grandmother and I in bidding farewell to my father, USDA Agent Allen J. Marshall.

"My father was a man who loved the land of the Southern Tier. The soil, the mud, the crops, and the people who worked it. He was never a good farmer himself, he even joked that he had a black thumb." This tale caused the air to lighten a tiny bit. "However, he highly respected those that could work a farm successfully. Especially growing up on one and watching how much his father loved the fields and dirt. And how my dad wanted to assist them, which he did successfully. But in his own niche. Exactly how Agent Lyons just attested. And the majority of the census belonging to Allegany County would agree with that."

Deeply he inhaled, but with vigor and stamina.

"When his tombstone is placed over his grave, there will be his name, the day he was born, the day he was murdered. And between those dates there will be a basic dash. But this dash for my father was anything but simplistic."

To emphasize this, he raised his hand and showed his fore and middle finger an inch apart in the air, signifying the size of said mark on the stone. Moistening his lips, he pressed on, and his voice grew in confidence and volume.

"That dash represents him as a young man, who was an exemplar son, and an outstanding scholar and athlete. A renaissance man who soared through college and broke into his optimal profession, protecting the land in the Enchanted Mountains as he had always dreamed of. Even as a teenager in the Future Farmers of America club.

"But most of all, he made that dash really mean the most when it came to being a parent. There was no doing the minimum or having a latch key kid. He made sure I was taken care of, even when the other unit was failing at their side of the bargain."

A few small gasps were heard at this triumphant statement about his own mother. But he pressed on since she, nor anyone from her side of the family had attended due to the pending charges.

"That dash should be admired, and I am glad that I am praising it today." With prestige and strength, he scanned the audience as he spoke. His hands on either side of the podium, and his elbows bent with some slight shaking from his emotional outburst. "In all that he did, that dash was vibrant, and the purest irony, and tragedy, is that it was slashed and compressed for greed and pride. The world itself has taken a small blow to it, because of my father losing a potential thirty years of his life."

This was when a multitude of eyes widened and began to drip mercilessly from his monumental words.

"But in the end, we all should be grateful for having him. I would not have given up my father for anyone else in the world. And I am going to be blessed if I am half the man that he was in this world." This part of the speech proceeded with a crescendo entailing passion. Then softened for the farewell. "Again, thank you all for joining us."

The single page of paper felt like a load of bricks when he picked it up and proceeded to his seat. Seeing how the phrases and verses of his eulogy had gone, the lad scanned the room and saw sniffling and sobbing, so he knew he said the right words. With this Roger Winters quickly cued the organist who began to play an older hymn.

Those who knew the melody joined in with singing the saddened song. "Come home. Come home it's supper time."

*

"Thanks for joining us back up in these parts," started Jacob Morris, "we would have driven down, but there is so much evidence that we have collected that we need to go over with both of you."

"That is fine by me." Virginia sat with a modest smile, then squeezed the hand of her beloved grandson. "It is nice to get out of town. Between the gossip and the news vans that pull up every so often. And Jared finishing up school under all of this." Sighing, she moved on. "We really need a change of scenery right about now."

"And with it being Easter break, this is a good time to break free." Piped in Jared. "Plus, with the fact that the burial is finally Thursday, we need some reprieve."

"Excellent, and in about half an hour Jackson Steele will be joining us. So, let's get started." Quickly the agent picked up a normal basic asphalt colored corded phone that was sitting on a side table and dialed a familiar extension. After trilling thrice, the intended party picked up. "Isaac, the Marshalls are here. Come on over to conference room one twelve, and let's get going. Steele will be here around one."

This space was about twenty by eighteen feet with a long conference style table in a gray and cream synthetic topcoat. The aesthetic was one of the early 2000's, and the baker dozen count of matching design chairs with basic gray toned tweed style material cushioned pad on the seat pulled the deal together. The space was too much for the intended five, and the room overall felt uncomfortable, but that was within the budget for that region of the FBI.

They clustered close to the far end of the room where a large screen, which took up between one third and a half of said wall, was lit and ready for the show before them. This presentation entailed the vast expanse of information that they had to convey and confirm prior to the overwhelming trial.

Perfectly on cue Isaac Morray entered, sans knocking, and smiled to greet their guests. "I hope that the drive up this way was not too bad."

"Nah," started Jared, making simplistic small talk, "early spring, sun was shining. It was a good day trip for the two of us."

Figuring out which cords went to which plugs, or whether the sockets were in the adaptor for the screen or the laptop, the forensics guru looked back at the Marshalls during this tiring chore. "I heard through the professional grapevine that the bureau was springing for the hotel up here during the trial." This was an attempt at keeping the chatter alive while he explored the electronic source for the gadgets. And to keep down the awkward silence while doing so.

A gush of air entered with the aura of Cecil, "I will make sure that they are on my floor for the duration of the proceedings." Upon everyone looking back at the trooper, he grinned, flaunting his handsome looks, then sat next to Virginia. Softly, yet in a friendly manner, he grasped her forearm, just an inch above the wrist, in a loving, reassuring way that a true friend would do. An act that was held in a very sentimental value by not only herself, but also her kinfolk in attendance.

Once Agent Morray had coordinated the wires and inlets the screen of his laptop was mirrored onto the giant monitor before them. Settling back in the only comfortable office chair available, he hunkered over his computing machine and pulled up some pictures with his mouse.

"Jared, you will be on the witness stand without a doubt." To confirm this the speaker's head bobbed slightly. "Virginia, I am not sure about you. We will see what Jackson says when he joins us. But we want to cover some information now so that you can absorb it before the trial. And see what we have on our side." Clearing his throat, he pulled up a video of a recognizable place.

"That's the entrance to my school," alerted Jared.

"Correct," this came from Cecil, who fielded the question. "Two weeks ago, we swung down to do some more investigating, and I spoke with Principal McClarin. Without a doubt Don did not remember any of your parents there during the event itself. And he gave us permission to pull up security coverage. And well, Clayton and your mother never showed up until the concert was pretty much over. Close to nine pm. We have the full fight of you and Clayton on here also, and how he tried to stop you from going to your dad's cabin."

With grief and anger Virginia shook her weary head. "So, no alibi for them."

"Not at all. We must release this to the defense as part of their discovery. And well, they were claiming to be there this whole time."

Leaning back Jared permitted his eyes to focus on the ceiling. A small tear collected in the border of his eye. This was just another let down of his mother. To not only kill his father, but to do it on such a night when he was counting on her. At this point there were no redeemable qualities in the one who birthed him.

"Unfortunately for us," Isaac pressed on, "there are one or two cell phone towers that a phone pings off of down there. Being in such a rural area that's normal, yet ineffective. And there is no way to pinpoint exactly where they were in that precious time period. But in my professional opinion, there is nowhere else that they can explain that they were at this point. Because anywhere else on the school campus they would have been seen."

"True, because even if they were at the cabin, not too many people are around that time of year. Most are just seasonal cabins. And actually, the two surrounding ours are snowbirds who go to Florida from fall to spring." This source of information was also from Jared after he dropped his head and refocused his energy.

"Now onto the forensics." In sync with this announcement the screen changed to an album of photos. "We don't have a ton to reveal, but the basics before trial." The first picture rose before them which was of the disheveled kitchen. There were pics taken before and after the marker outlines and numbered placards were placed. "We all have seen this throughout the investigation. Jared, you stumbled upon it, which in of itself is a tragedy."

Another emotional scar that his madre inflicted upon the poor teen… the fate of discovering the remains of the blindsided attack.

"There was no doubt a struggle," the images passed as the presenter continued, "and his government issued Glock was found after it was forcefully removed from his person, and slid under the small china cabinet."

Nods from the small mass confirmed their agreement, just as the door opened, and a sharply dressed Jackson Steele entered the gathering as predicted and expected.

To balance out the seating pattern Jackson took the position next to Jared, but not before they engaged in a hearty, masculine handshake. There was a bonding, and also professional respect that they both had for one another. In one corner Jared appreciated how stellar Jackson was at his job. There was no lying or denying, Jared had used many internet search engines in order to dig deep into the attorney's business portfolio. Yet at the opposite end Jackson appreciated Jared's strength and maturity in the conundrum.

Before pressing on Isaac looked at Jacob. Both were on the same wavelength as to the next predicament. They had been wrestling over the quandary if they should be displaying autopsy photographs to the duo with them. During the trial they will be out there, and Jacob had fought that showing them now would lessen the blow. But Jackson and Isaac had proclaimed that during the formal proceedings that Virginia and Jared could leave the courtroom when they are shown as evidence. But if they stayed, the impact of exposing them to the family members would be a drastic, and vital move to help the jury convict, and convict with a vengeance. Raw emotions would be the best style for a gut-wrenching courtroom spectacle.

So instead, they moved on to pictures of Allen's truck and other clues. This included the rope fragment, pictures of Allen's department issued vehicle, various rooms of the cottage, and a few of the basement.

Then came the stretch of shots taken from the Beebe Hill residence showing where the condemning evidence was discovered in very plain sight. When this aspect was relayed by Wingard and Morris to the rest, they just shook their heads. The lack of care in hiding said items held an arrogant aura and statement of the heinous crime that they felt as if the law would never consider them to be the evil doers.

This again resonated with Jared. The intensity of the rotten interior that his mother was showing over lust, and greed, to not only take his father, but to act in such a way that his emotions and best interests were insignificant and minor annoyances in her bigger, malicious dreams.

There was a small rundown of the information searched on Julie's laptop a week or so before the attack. By itself it was not remarkable, yet with everything else exposed it was quite incriminating and damning.

For the final portion of the two-hour rendezvous Jackson Steele went into more detail about the trial. There was no doubt in his mind that it would indeed start promptly as all parties had preferred. A date in one month's time, give or take a pull from the daily calendar.

"So," Jackson started, "they have not marked you down yet, Jared, as a witness. However, I am. Unfortunately, I will be asking you about how you found your father. If you had touched or moved anything on your way in. And so on."

A nervous twitch in Jared's right arm indicated the obvious anxiety already starting in his blood and soul.

"I know that it is tough, but they will try and pin it on you. They will probably be ruthless, and your mother seems to be the type that would push you under the water in order to save her own skin." Pausing he let that sink into the boy's mind. "Do not waver. Do not stutter, do not let Stevvins tear apart your words when you are on the stand, and he is cross examining you. One falter and he will be all over it. You know the truth, and what you saw. Just relay it in an even tone and don't change a single letter."

A surge of the pure necessity, and strength of his role in this overwhelmed Jared. With a smile, he said, "No problem at all. I will avenge their wrongdoing."

*

A soft mist was glistening and attaching itself to the windshield of Virginia Marshall's simplistic older station wagon. There was a stable substance to it, and the rust was minimal on the light green exterior with its wood paneling accents. As per most occasions in the past two years since claiming his driver's license Jared was the operator, and Virginia was nestled in the shotgun position.

Riding in the front segment of the abbreviated caravan was a pure black hearse, its paint crisp and the chrome sparkling in the late March sun. The main gathering was to be at the cemetery on the vintage Elm Street in the village of Cuba. That was where the majority would be meeting the parade of two vehicles, but the saddened ones who shared blood with the deceased wished to escort him on his final voyage across his beloved county.

As they took the side roads and passed many hollers and hills, they sat in silence, yet with remembrance of many times now passed. Ones that can never be duplicated due to the lack of characters in the scene. There was now a wedge. An open spot, per se, in their generation of the Marshall clan. A giant void where a brave one had lived. One link prematurely taken in a chain of their own lineage.

The gentle precipitation was falling and settling in such a way that a faint rainbow would be exposed every quarter mile or so. In like a lion, out like a lamb, as they compare the month to. And it was surely so that spring.

Their windows were cracked open a small bit in order to let in the fresh aroma of the scenery. The snow was melting from the hills into the valleys, which had a revival essence to the region. The world around them was waking up, yet they were laying a piece of themselves to rest.

To make their lives easier, and the walk for the maternal Marshall less strenuous, Jared followed the morgue-mobile as it ascended the small incline into the morbid field. This pathway was paved with asphalt that was probably laid when Virginia had been a girl. Cracked and weathered, yet still was steadfast for accommodating the needs of the cemetery.

Both modes of transportation stopped, and Jared exited his own side first with a steady pace around the front end of the family roadster where he then helped his grandmother descend from her seat. Next, they moved over to where a large tent was expanded over a specific section of the graveyard. One that had been reserved for a few decades with the Marshalls in mind. They had purchased the plots a score or two before. Making sure all lurid instances were covered, they had obtained close to ten of them for such tragedies, that way this part of the plight was taken care of. A somber premonition that Jared's great grandparents had acquired, one that was useful today.

In the far back of the solemn field sat the trio from the investigation. To be swift and efficient they had carpooled together in the noir shaded SUV that was issued to Jake. This opportunity they pledged to be more of a background compilation than in the forefront. Sometimes less was more in these instances. If the Marshalls approached them in chatter would be one thing. But sometimes they felt that the families of the victims needed normalcy in their mourning. Not a reminder of the traumatic onslaught and horror induced into it.

With professional synchronism a host of gentlemen, all suited in black, merged at the rear of Roger Winter's ride. This included Frank Lyons, Jared Marshall, and a few others that were considered kin or residents of their inner circle status. All grieving while receiving the casket from the trunk, and each obtaining, then carrying, equal weight of their loved one. The heaviest portion of this project was the strain on their hearts, not on their muscles.

In a rhythmic progression they faithfully marched to where a plot was dug, and a few chairs assembled by it. With love and care they settled the sarcophagus onto a small scaffolding infrastructure over the open space and stepped back to the seating area. They joined their loved ones, each with a tear or two in their eyes.

A professional man of God was there, one who prescribed the Protestant style of religion. A local preacher who had encountered the agent and his folks a few times in these parts. Virginia and Jared wanted to keep this segment of the transition simple, so the speaker only read the prayer of the Lord. With its ending, the workers who were conveyed with the task of lowering Federal Agent Allen J. Marshall into the soil did so.

Piercing silence was felt in the air, except for the cawing of a single crow a hundred feet or so away. This added to the irony of the peace being interrupted, such as the corpse's life had been. But as the forever box hit the bottom, and the mechanics lifted, Jared walked over to the intrusive gap before them. This was when he grabbed a clump of wet dirt, probably the size of a softball. There he grasped his hand inward, and caused the solid mass to crumble into small bits. From there he rose his hand a bit higher, then rotated his palms, allowing the morsel of the earth to slowly drift onto the casket, finalizing in his mind the permanence of the sullen situation.

*

"The people have no objections to juror seventeen."

"Mister Stevvins, how about the defense."

"No, Your Honor, we are fine with this selection also."

"Excellent. That divides the day in half." Judge Forrester

next glanced at the designer watch on his wrist, then back at his crowd. "Let's take a two-hour recess for lunch and meet back here at one in the afternoon."

With the violent burst from a slam of his gavel, the presiding legal magistrate commenced the pause in the second day of the trial process.

As they had done the day prior, Jared, Virginia, Jackson, Jacob, and Cecil made a small progression out of the courthouse through the side entrance. Such had been the procedure during the arraignment, and currently, reporters and cameramen had been stalking and pouncing on any opportunity that the group had been in public. The need to know more about this mysterious family and the web that were being put on display was mounting and the talk of the networks.

As advised by Jackson, all had turned down a series of attempts for interviews, even paid ones. There was a talk of cashing in on one or two down the road and after a solid conviction. But it would be a while before they would return to ponder these possibilities. However, for the time being a solid front of silence was the best way not to have any hiccups during the proceedings.

A whisk of the elevator brought them to the fourth floor, and out into a glimmering passageway from the art deco era. The building was a stunning, historic staple of the downtown segment of the city of good neighbors. Designs that were handcrafted and could no longer be duplicated due to the deterioration of mankind when it comes to cost versus true quality.

In the conference room numbered 455 there was a large table perfect for such gatherings. At the closest end was a wonderful luncheon set up of the true Buffalo kind. Today's cuisine was a Beek on Weck buffet.

Selected sides were the normal potato and macaroni salads, along with some 'slaw and of course pickles. Presented next was the deconstructed sandwich, which one could build to their liking using the perfect ingredients. The bun was of the kummelweck variety, with salt and seeds baked on the top and was irresistible. A platter of sliced roast beef was next on the hunger tour. Cut thin, and ranging from rare to well done, this was to be placed as the protein of the bunch. A quart sized container of au jus was close by so that one could pour some onto the roll and meat, adding some wonderful moisture and flavoring.

But to pull it all together there was plenty of horseradish. This was to be applied per taste of the diner, but was in fact the zing that adhered everything else on the order into a perfectly blended symphony of flavor.

Once the construction of everyone's platter was finished, and all were seated, Jackson decided to chew into some of the business at hand in addition to their nutrition. "I am really excited about the jury selection so far. There are enough moderate thinking people in the pool that will not only actually look at the facts, but also have enough strength to be in favor of the death penalty."

Nodding while swallowing, Jake presented his own observations. "I have been down this road a few times with juries. They teeter with their own ethics and beliefs. Some are afraid to side with the defendant, but yet have sympathy for them since they have an undertone of anti-law enforcement." Quickly, and in a polite fashion, he wiped his mouth. "But the eight so far have a feel for a story having both sides, and our side telling the truth in this aspect."

"Absolutely," the law scholar grabbed the ropes of the conversation back, "there were actually a few that Stevvins let slide by, that I would have not wanted if I was in his defensive shoes."

Rolling his eyes at the fact of the incompetence of their counterpart in the courtroom, and his past experience with said solicitor, Cecil chimed in. "I hate to say it, but he is way over his head up here. Down there you could swoon a jury, which he has a few times that I have been privy to witness. However, there are giant holes in his strategy so far."

"Even with that co-counsel from the defender's office." Pointing a plastic fork with some potato salad on it, Jake re-entered the discussion, "there is quite a bit that he hasn't jumped on yet like not really questioning the jurors about their beliefs on this being a federal case versus state."

Wiping his fingers on his napkin in a professional manner with precise etiquette, true to his form, Jackson pulled the discussion back to him. "Unfortunately for them, lucky for us, if/when they try to appeal for poor representation, the higher courts will not side with them. Forrester did me a solid by planting a second diploma on their side."

All in the eatery zone were agreeing to this point. Jared and Virginia remained solemn, yet listening, while enjoying the spread of deliciousness. To them, they all were speaking Greek. It was not due to their intelligence level; Jared was enthusiastic about going to St. Bonaventure that fall for his freshman year. This centuries old learning establishment was just twenty minutes down I-86. Before he had planned on staying in the dorms, but now there was no question that he would commute in order to help his ailing grandmother.

Easily he was at the level to comprehend most of the talking points, and Virginia had her associates degree from the local Jamestown Community College branch in Olean from when Allen was a baby. But in these times their hearts were breaking, and they only allowed their minds to waver from grieving to revenge, like an internal, emotional metronome.

*

Per their morning routine, this being the third in a row, Jared knocked on the wall between their hotel rooms to alert Virginia that they needed to head down to the lobby and over to the courthouse, which was a short stroll away. Once in the hallway Virginia walked out of her door and immediately took the bicep of Jared's awaiting bent arm and wrapped her forearm and hand into it. This was their preferred walking stance, supplying them both with strength and comfort. Both physical and emotional, which was needed in both factions.

Once out of the hotel's majestic glass revolving doors and onto the spring filled sunny street, Virginia tapped Jared's shoulder and pointed a bit off. "Over there is where the minor league baseball team plays. Every spring, your grandfather would bring your father here for one or two games, depending on the price. Those were wonderful times for both of them."

Holding back his own parade of tears, Jared bantered back, "He did the same with me. Those were good times."

"Your father learned from the best." A grin followed this statement.

The rest of the three-block wandering was left silent so they could fondly think of these two men, the Marshall guys, in such positive, and still tangible forms. Without words they also were glad to confirm that the men would finally be together.

Again, in sync with their routine, they had members of the Sheriff's Department of Erie County joining them a block or so from the side entrance of the federal courthouse in order to safely convey them to the courtroom. Since it was the premiere day with testimony, precisely the opening statements, of the epic trial, press members were swarming like mad bees in their hive, and trying to grasp onto any unique part of the story that would in turn prevail their headline over their competitor's.

Finally safe from the news mob, they settled into their spots, with Trooper Wingard and Agent Morris on either side of them. Almost like a cop sandwich.

Seated at the defense table with only ankle shackles were the defendants. They were facing straight ahead being that they had no need to look the other way, except for when they looked at each other and tried to keep some upbeat talk going. The family was broken, and there was no going back from here.

The rumbling voices of the crowd behind them lowered to a murmur, and finally halted once the bailiff stood up to announce the judge's entrance. Once he was settled and motioned for the audience to be seated, he started the day.

"Good morning, ladies and gentlemen. We are here for the commencement of the trial, the People versus McBride and Marshall. I have no pending motions or documents, and I want us to be done in the next week or so. So, unless I hear anything," there was still a void of objections, "then let us proceed." Clearing his throat, he pressed on. "Mister Steele, your opening statement, please."

Smiling, the cued one rose as he adjusted his sports coat and straightened his tie. Previously a clerk had clipped a small, wireless microphone to his shirt's lapel in order to maximize his volume. Something they had also done to Joseph Stevvins while preparing for the day.

"Good morning, everyone, we do have a packed house. But with that note, we have a packed case. A complicated case, indeed. There will be talk of blindsided attacks, pre-meditation, and a cruel two on one lynching. But a heinous attack on not anyone, but a federal agent for the USDA. A man in his prime, which was forced to die prematurely. An early demise actually at the hands of the defendants. Yet, for a simple, hardworking man, this was never his intended exit of the world.

"Allen J. Marshall prided himself in family, and his hometown area." With a small remote in his hand the speaker clicked it, and behind him on a large screen appeared a picture of Allen. And of course, Virginia and Jared were in the shot. "Many details will be relayed to you as the jury, and you will hear about the small town, yet giant persona of a man who lived there." For a moment he paused, allowing his thoughts to form for the next portion.

"Also, may I say thank you for your service for the next two weeks." Shifting his body he glanced at the jury box. "It is imperative for our quest for justice to have a pool of willing, and loyal participants." Trying to grin and be smooth with the audience for his moment of gratitude worked, as many were returning the glowing expressions.

Speeding up his tempo, he moved on. "Cuba is a small township, about two hours south of here. And Allen was known all around. It is largely an agricultural area. And this was part of his pride and work. He was a federal agent for the USDA. This man was a hero." Click of a button turned the snapshot to a formal picture of Allen in his full formal uniform.

"Objection your honor." Joseph Stevvins rose to his feet. "That is speculation, he never was given any honorary badges in his line of work."

Such an interruption was already setting a foul vibe in the air for all, although a part of the attorney's plan was to make Allen a less likable victim.

"Overruled, this is an opening statement, and the victim was an agent of the nation. Hero in any other circumstance would have been pushing it, but not in this case." Stevvins sat as Forrester sent a scolding face in his direction. "Moving on, let's continue."

"Thank you, Your Honor." This jolt did push the orator a bit off of track, as were the malice intentions of his counterpart, but he redirected nicely. "Agent Marshall was a family man. In the courtroom today mourning his loss we have his mother and son." With his strong, wide and girthy hands the federal prosecutor signaled in their direction. "Pain etched into their souls for their loss. And also, as they are forced to watch one of their own," he turned and indicated the suspects in this part of his lecture. "Jared's own mother, and the man that she broke their family apart with during a torrid affair, on trial for his slaughter.

"Allen provided a beautiful home, was a caring father, and even left the family establishment when it was discovered, by his own son, that his wife was having a rampant scandal with a coworker. Who is now her co-conspirator and co-defendant."

Pointing with his extended arm, Jackson fired away. "Their jealous lust split a family apart. Never once had Allen been accused of anything but a good person in the world. And even took the higher road and left the toxic situation."

With each word he was pacing, keeping a steady tempo. Never did he allow his steps, or speed of his sermon to get too fast as to confuse the jury, or too slow to bore them. Which he did with much grace and precision.

"Instead of staying put, he moved to the family cottage on a beautiful lake. A cabin passed along for a few generations now. One that sadly is in his son's hands prematurely due to a heinous, cold blooded act that took place in such a wonderful heirloom.

"One of concise planning, and of terrible details." With a smoothness and suave move, he picked up a yellow number two pencil from the tabletop at his assigned area, and lifted it up to his chin. "One that involves a swift and powerful attack on an armed man." For dire dramatic purposes he spun his body and moved his arm as if he was being attacked. His coattails from his suit jacket spun with the breeze, and the jury felt startled. "A man trained to take down any risks. But using the two of them and sneaking in the rear door they blindsided him. Even when he grabbed his weapon, they hit it down. Now disarmed, and apparently battered, the vengeful philanderers dragged him to the basement where they did their deadly deed. And hung a noose from the floor joists where they then fed his head and neck through in order to make it look like he took his own life. With anger they dropped his weight from their arms and let him drop. That fall cracked his neck and killed the man." With the word cracked he used both hands to snap the leaded utensil in half, then tossed it on the floor between himself and the jury, leaving them with their mouths hanging. "They played pretend and wanted it to look like he took the coward's way out of the world, when he was fighting like hell to keep his life together and be there for the two people in the world who needed him."

At this point he glided softly and used a gentle open hand to identify Virginia and Jared. Then with might and gusto he twirled and threw his hand, this time with a sharp, incriminating finger at the defensive duo. "These two selfish, arrogant thugs robbed the world of a truly good man. A man of the people. Over lust and greed. But they were messy." Steele shook his finger again, yet in a mocking, open way to all see.

"There were numerous mistakes that their cocky selves decided to not be careful of. And we have caught those errors. And we will point them out to you. And without a doubt, you will be not only handing over a guilty sentence, but you will be asking for the death penalty as a final way of showing them that what they did was a crime against all of humanity."

Panting slightly, and with a few rivulets of sweat beating down his temples, Jackson Steele bowed slightly and took a courageous seat at the prosecution's table signaling he was finished with his poignant speech.

From the expressions of all in the courtroom, except for the defense table, they were stunned with such an oration.

"Mister Stevvins, you have the floor."

Rising, the defense attorney made cautious strides to the main arena area and quietly cleared his throat.

"First off, I do have one commonality with the prosecutor, Mister Steele. That is mutual gratitude for the jury members who are helping us decide. So, thank you. And it is an honor to represent Clayton and Julie, because it is not often that I can plead a case for truly innocent clients. Hardworking people who deserve justice when a plethora of misconstrued items are thrown together to make a sloppy case."

Using that small town charm and guise, he smiled at the twelve decision makers. Then he pressed on. "You will be given random artifacts that were collected. Then thrown into a totally far-fetched theory." With those words his arms flew out before him with open hands. "And this 'theory,'" Joseph used finger quotes of the word in question. "Is strained and can be broken down easily."

"We will not be denying that the defendants had performed clandestine, unloyal acts." Shaking his index finger in the air, he then allowed his head to make such a motion to emphasize this truth. "We are all human, and humans can make small mistakes, or even medium ones. But that is as far as these two made. When in actuality they were falling for each other and completely love drunk. But not impaired, or awe struck enough to harm anyone physically.

"There is something called 'reasonable doubt.'" Again, he made a finger parenthesis emphasis. "In simple terms, this means that you have to believe one hundred and ten percent that anyone in a defendant's seat is guilty. No ifs, no maybes. You must believe that there is no doubt in your mind that these two committed a crime. A crime against Julie's family. Her own son."

Swallowing hard he in turn used his open palm to highlight Julie. "Even with a pending divorce, and a splitting family, there was no solid reason to harm her husband. The government is trying to shove a round peg into a square hole with the pursuit of my clients." Due to necessity, he cleared his throat and attempted to keep a smooth, steady presentation.

"There will be evidence showing an attack, supposedly by my clients. And a few pieces of very circumstantial evidence found at their residence on Beebe Hill. And once those were found by very biased investigators, they were on a vicious witch hunt."

With aggression and passion in his voice, the solicitor continued onward using an attention grabbing, jagged tone. "The FBI wanted this case closed fast. They rushed their investigation and presumed two random people involved in the case guilty, rather than their constitutional right as being assumed innocent.

"And furthermore, the day after the crime was committed, they had performed an arrest on another quickly assumed suspect that resulted in a high-speed chase, an accident, and a path of chaos left behind."

Jumping into the air as if his seat was consumed with flames Jackson Steele profoundly announced, "Objection your honor. The prior arrest was warranted at the time due to incriminating evidence found immediately after the murder. But then an alibi cleared him. And that should have nothing to do with this case. The jury is now severely tainted, and I want a mistrial."

Gasps erupted around, and even Virginia and Jared

sighed, upset that progress was being halted when momentum should be in its place.

"Mister Stevvins." The judge was exuding irritation at the attorney. "I should grant the prosecutor his request. However, since your verbal dump of the story is vague as to the events, thankfully Mister Steele interrupted you in time. We will press on, and as a middle ground, I want that comment stricken from the record." Guiding his line of focus to the jury box, he elaborated on the call he just made. "Members of the jury. Please disregard the previous statement by the defense. It has nothing to do with this proceeding."

Aligning forward he sternly looked at Joseph Stevvins. "Do not push another button like that again." Losing the roughness in his words, the magistrate spoke again. "Please move ahead with your opening statement."

"Now we will have more evidence thrown against us. And they are hoping that the fluff and glitter that they sprinkle on the small amount of items pushed together will shine in a verdict for them. But it's all smoke and mirrors. A hoax, perse.

"What I need, what the people of America need, is for the selected members of the jury to use a critical eye and mind, to decipher the truth, from an imaginative theory thrown together by Uncle Sam.

"And when you see those scrambled facts, I want you to remember one thing." With a monotone tone and tempo, the lawyer spoke a mantra while steadily pointing at the defendants. "Without reasonable doubt, there is no burden of proof, so therefore they are not guilty. They are not guilty. And don't let a flurry of tall tales make you think anything else."

*

((...the whole truth and nothing but."

"Yes, I do."

Cocking his head to the side in a perfect fashion to allow his midnight black bangs to slightly rustle, Jackson Steele then released his first question to the premiere witness. "Please state your name "

"Jared Allen Marshall."

"And we can assume that you are the namesake of the victim for this trial."

"That is correct."

"Now, we are about to delve into some not so pleasant waters."

"I understand, I want justice for my father."

"Objection," rang from the opposing table, "he has no authority to derive what justice should be in this case."

Another scour was released from the moderator on the bench. "Overruled. Please continue, Mister Steele."

"Would you be so kind as to walk through your day on December 15th of last year for us. I know it's a painful day, one that you will always remember. But for clarification we need to hear what happened that day."

"Want me to start from when I woke up?"

"Sure."

"So, I woke up at the house on the lake around six am. Dad and I ate a quick breakfast before he had to go to work, and I had to go to school. And I left around seven thirty."

"Was your father upset or anything?"

"Not at all. He planned on coming to my concert that night."

"At that point you parted ways, correct. Did you see him again that day"

"Sadly, no."

With a halfway risen hand and his mouth about to open Stevvins was given another look from the judge and sat down silently. The presiding judiciary figure would not allow games when an emotional teen was before them.

"Now after school, how did you spend your time?"

"I went to see my mom right after school."

"And where was she at?"

"Our house, well now mine, on Beebe Hill Road."

"And for what reason did you go?"

"It was my mom's birthday, and even with everything going on, my dad still insisted I go spend it with her."

"Things are kind of rocky with her, even before this ordeal, right?"

"Well yeah."

"Why is that?"

"Well, back in May I found my mom and Clayton McBride naked in our living room."

"Objection, relevance, Your Honor."

"Your Honor, this whole affair is a giant part of the motive. You can't deny that this is a huge factor in the narrative."

"Overruled, go ahead, Prosecutor."

"Thank you. Now how did you celebrate the day, and what else was going on."

"We went to The Four Corners Cafe at around four thirty, five o'clock for dinner. At seven I had my band concert. So, I had to get to the school at six thirty."

"Did everything pan out like this?"

"Yes, and I went to my concert. But I was over the birthday crap already I actually got to campus at six sharp."

"Did you see anyone from your family there?"

"No. I expected my father to be there. And he always sits in the first few rows and is easy to see. But he wasn't."

"Anyone else?"

"My mom and Clayton were supposed to come. But I never connected with them until after we were done playing."

"And did you have plans after the concert?"

"Yes. To have ice cream and cake back on Beebe Hill."

"Did that happen?"

"No. I was extremely worried about my dad, so I wanted to go back to the lake to see if he was okay."

"Did your mother and her lover take this news gracefully?"

"No, Clayton got in my face and was screaming that I

needed to let my mother have a good birthday, and that my dad was probably putting on an act to be dramatic."

"Is that something that your father would do?"

"Absolutely not. He was dealing with the whole mess with dignity."

"I want to present to the court evidence 'A.'" With this command a large projector rose awake, its fan buzzing and light illuminating the main screen. A black and white video of the entrance of Cuba-Rushford school was brought into focus, and then once the viewers had their attention drawn to the attraction, Jackson pressed play. The incident described where Clayton was very brash, and somewhat violent with Jared came to life. There was a muffled sound, but an altercation with Jared being the victim arose. After a minute of the back and forth, when the aggressor was grabbing the victim by the wrist, Jared did break away and leave. A few onlookers gawked, yet it was quite clear of what had gone down.

"That seems as if it was quite traumatic." There was a subtle plea for sympathy from the jury for Jared. And a blunt call for dislike for Clayton. Both were awarded accordingly.

"Were you able to get away from Clayton while he was making a scene?"

"Finally, yes."

"And what did you do then?"

"Went to the lake house."

"What time was this?"

"Nine, or around then."

"Is it a long trip to the camp from your campus?"

"Nah, six or seven minutes."

"And what did you see outside of the house?"

"My dad's USDA truck."

"Did you knock in order to go in?"

"No. It's my house too. So, I went inside."

"By any chance did you go around to the rear of the building?"

"No, I went right through the front door."

"Was it locked, or unlocked?"

"Unlocked."

"What did you encounter inside?"

"The fireplace was roaring. Which is not like him. My dad hated waste."

"Okay, and after that room?

"Then I went through the archway and saw that the kitchen was a disaster. My late Aunt Charlotte's candy dish was smashed, and it looked like something crazy happened in there. I was afraid I might be next."

"But you did not see anyone else in the dwelling, correct?"

"No, just the warzone in the kitchen."

"Which brings me to People's Exhibit B." A giant screen in the background came to life and a picture of the living room, even with a small fire still ablaze, was offered as an optical part of the testimony. Then he hit a small button on a same ratio sized remote that put a picture of the disheveled kitchen into a split screen of the first pic. "As we can all see, these are the mentioned rooms, and the suspicious condition they were found in." When done addressing the jury, he looked back at Jared. "After that room, what did you do?"

"I went downstairs."

"Now what was down there?"

"It is a basic dirt cellar. Nothing fancy."

"But what was off that day?"

"My dad was hanging from the ceiling." With a firm inhale the storyteller was using every ounce of strength in him to keep the tears at bay. And it succeeded.

"I know this is horrible. But did you see anyway that he could have raised himself that high in order to do this."

"No."

"Ladies and gentlemen, this next exhibit, labeled 'C,' is difficult, but so is most of this tragedy." With a snap of his fingers on the clicker a picture of Allen's feet, encased in socks, entered the screen, removing the last two. It was showing that indeed nothing was around for him to stand on, and his sock encased toes were three to four inches off of the ground. This was an abbreviated picture, so it failed to show anything above his shins. It was extremely poignant, yet did not give away all of the shock value of the trial quite yet.

"Even with Allen Marshall being an extraordinary man, he still could not hover in a way that he could intertwine his neck into a noose and be elevated off of the floor where this could be possible coming from one single person."

Different reactions flowed through the gathering. Virginia obviously was distraught and cried but stayed steadfast in her desire to be present at every single crucial moment of the proceedings. Within the jury a few members quivered, some that were accustomed to this morbid section of humanity still had goosebumps. And one felt a bit ill, and needed a small trash can to be put beside her, but it was fortunately not needed.

However, right in the middle of the action was Jared at the stand with a single tear that broke the barrier and drifted down. Being so overwhelmed he did not even brush it away, which only highlighted the immense pain he was feeling at that moment.

"For the moment I do not have anything else. I do reserve the right to bring this witness back to the stand if needed for any other testimonial needs."

"That is fine. Mister Stevvins, you may cross examine."

"Thank you, Your Honor," and said counsel rose with this welcoming. "Now Jared, this is a very intense question. And I need you to answer honestly. But do you favor, or have you ever favored, one parent over the other?"

"Well yeah. My dad my entire life. Mom was never hands on."

From the defense table Julie rolled her eyes and crossed her arms.

"Okay. So, you would do anything for your father."

"Well, yes."

"Now, when you found him, maybe did you move anything? Or change anything in the house when you went inside?"

"Ummm.. No."

"To maybe to protect his honor, because suicide is very taboo." In a weird way he bent down and was trying to seem sympathetic. Like it was okay to confess this little secret that he had been holding. "Did you move the step ladder, or the stool?"

"No. Absolutely not."

"How about any other pieces of rope, maybe you tossed them away?" Shrugging he mustered up a condescending smile. "If you did, you would not be in trouble."

Showing a disgruntled side of him, Jackson fired his hand and propelled himself upwards to a standing position. "Objection, this is badgering the witness. Mister Marshall is clearly distraught and has stated under oath that he did not impact the scene at all."

"Mister Stevvins, move on."

"Okay," his palms went up in the air. "Nothing further at this time from the witness."

"This witness is dismissed, please take a seat.

Feeling proud, the orphan did so.

*

"Lemon-lime soda for the kid, and a double bourbon heavy on the rocks." After instructing the tavern keeper on their beverages, the two men, Cecil and Jared, opened up the menus side by side at the expansive hotel bar. Jacob had ventured home after that day of opening statements and Jared's testimony. Virginia opted to splurge on herself with room service and keep a low profile for that evening. There was also an intentional ploy from the maternal one for the two diners in the restaurant to be together. It was a grandmotherly instinct that Jared needed a masculine role model at this current time to go through this painful process. Especially since the selected mentor had been down this road a few times.

As they were considering their menu choice, the tab being taken care of by the US of A, Cecil cut to the point, especially since the elder was in her room. "Steele made the right move by putting you first."

"Oh?" The learner of the pair was blind to how these proceedings were to be assembled, and the strategic planning behind them.

"Most would have led with myself, or Morris. More seasoned men on the stand. But he wanted to establish the timeline. Which worked out quite nicely."

"Stevvins was really trying to break me at the end."

"Yeah, he wants any tiny crack in the case, because it is a solid one.

The fairly younger ale man laid eggshell white cocktail napkins in front of them and dispersed the drinks accordingly. "Have you gentlemen made up your mind yet?"

With a casual toss he let his menu drop onto the glossy bar top. "Ribeye mid-rare with steak fries."

Due to the intensity of the conversation Jared had pretended to view the options, when in fact his eyes were dead to the world due to stress and pride at the same time. "Exactly the same sounds good."

"Perfect, I will come back to freshen up your drinks."

After a long draw of his potent potable the statie mustered up his own courage in order to have a more personal talk with the lad. "I still have my old man, so I don't know what you are going through." Another glug of the cinnamon toned liquor for less anxiety followed. "So, I can't pinpoint what you are feeling, but it must be a lot."

With nothing to numb his pain Jared was hesitant but proceeded with an answer to that inquiry. Especially since any chances like this to have a discussion with someone he held with such high regard for alone would not appear all of the time. "I have to be strong for Gramma." His head lowered, and he was steadfast with staring directly at his feet for his own sake. "Because she is so frail about all of it. When I really lost both parents."

"I guess that is true."

"I feel deceived. I feel as if my mother pulled a precise deception over me. Mothers are supposed to sacrifice for their kids. Not steal the other parent from them." Rotating his head upwards, then staring at the ceiling in order to hide the malicious tears that were falling, he did press on. "Why would she literally orphan me when I needed my father the most. I am set to go to St. Bonaventure in the fall. I was going to move into the dorms and start my life." Two swipes, one from a duo of his fingers per hand diminished the sorrow releasing from his eyes, and heart. "Now don't get me wrong, I will do anything for my grandmother. I just expected to assist my dad, and not take over for his duties."

"Are you still going to go to college?"

"Absolutely. Just now I am going to commute."

"Okay."

"I won't have to work because of the life insurance policy. Thank God because the policy was due to expire two weeks after my dad died, which would have been his birthday."

"Small sliver of a silver lining, I guess." The cop was unsure of how to deliver, or praise, that small feat.

"Plus, as soon as the trial is over, and JT Dove, or Jackson say so, then I am selling the Beebe Hill house."

"Really? That's so close to your grandmother though."

"Too many mixed memories. I'll keep the lake house forever, but probably will never sleep there again."

Swooping in came two platters with their desired cuts of grilled beef and fried and sliced potatoes. Both men applied ketchup and steak sauce to the appropriate staples, then kept up their engaging conversation while they chewed.

Wingard did order another round of drinks for them.

This time Jared initiated the next topic of conversation. One of just chatting about life in general rather than the depth of his ailing. Dwelling on the pain was not useful, but he knew that Cecil was a call away at all times.

*

In unison the courtroom attendees rose, then settled back down as it had the previous few days when Judge Forrester entered. Soft discussions emerged again as the magistrate shuffled random paperwork that was related to the case around on his desk, this was what his modest eyeglasses were on the bridge of his semi-crumpled nose. Looking to and from at the documents he wanted to make sure his judicial ducks were in a nice, orderly row.

With the first syllable of his statement the crowd hushed immediately. "I see that we have no pending motions to deal with. I do like how neatly kept the paperwork has been." This was mostly a comment to himself since he knew that the advising attorney for the defense, the one he assigned, a Chester Reynolds, had been steadfast with his aiding of Joseph Stevvins. This was to ensure everything in this case was airtight, since appeals on his convictions was something that Forrester was prone to keeping a low ratio of.

"Mister Steele, your first witness of the day."

"The people," speaking as he rose and adjusted his suit, Jackson pressed on, "are calling Trooper Cecil Wingard to the stand."

Standing proudly tall while placing his Stetson on his head, Cecil proceeded to the witness box. The previous, and soon to be future, days that he was at the proceedings he wore his basic uniform. But for being on the stand he opted for the most professional apparel necessary.

This was his formal dress attire, which held a few metals attached to his chest he had accumulated from his half decade of experience. There was a serious undertone to the deep navy-blue fabric of said required outfit. These were meant for ceremonies and galas, even perhaps a policeman's ball here and there. Never worn on duty and was meant to impress. Which it did quite nicely.

Once perched in his civic duty spot at the center of attention, at least for that short fragment of the legal affair, he relayed a professional smile to the truth seeker, who then started the interrogation. "Can you state your name for the record please?"

Leaning into the slim microphone he did so. "Cecil Wingard."

"And what is your profession?"

"I am a New York State Trooper."

"And even though this case is under the FBI's jurisdiction, you were requested to help in this investigation, correct?"

"Yes."

"Were you told the reasoning behind this?"

"That is an affirmative. Since I knew the area extremely well, the bureau felt as if I could be an asset."

"And you happened to be the first officer on the scene?"

"Correct."

"Who else was there upon your arrival?"

"There were a few volunteer paramedics and Jared Marshall."

"Besides the victim's son."

"Objection," rang from the defense table, "at this point in the recalling of events, and until my clients are found guilty, Allen Marshall is technically not a victim."

A glare that could stop rush hour traffic emanated from Jackson Steele's gray eyes.

"Overruled, Mister Stevvins. Technically he was a victim to an incident. I see what you're doing, and you're not doing it well."

Getting back into the questionnaire, the prosecutor moved on. "Could you walk me through the next few steps that you took?"

"Absolutely." And it was easy, since that scenario had played out in his head constantly since it happened. Finding a comrade hanging in a cold cellar will burn a picture into your brain. A nasty image at that. "I made sure that no one was to enter the home, even the EMTs. I wanted everything kept sterile."

"What did you think you were walking into at that time?"

"I knew that it would be a deceased person. Initially suicide. However, after talking with Jared Marshall I felt as if this could not be determined immediately."

"Objection, a high school boy is no expert."

"Your honor," with a sturdy turn backwards to face his opposing counsel, Jackson continued, "anyone is privy to the knowledge of a scene such as this being suspicious and does not need expert status in doing so."

"Overruled."

A slight sense of stability formed in the courtroom again.

"As you proceeded, what other telltale signs made this a questionable scene?"

"There were blatant signals of a struggle occurring, or blind attack, in the kitchen."

"So, this was not just an unkept kitchen."

"Far from it."

"What indicated this?"

"Broken dishes, furniture thrown about and on its side. Telltale signs of something malice occurring."

"And from there what did you do?"

"I proceeded to the basement."

Looking back at the audience he noticed the Marshalls, and was surprised both were still there. Earlier he had asked if they wanted to leave for any of the intense pictures, and left before they could answer. Allowing them some solace was a consideration. But their lack of action speaks words that they needed to see these lurid snapshots for the closure that they must obtain.

"Once in the basement, what did you uncover?"

"A male, mid-forties or early fifties, hanging from a support beam with a noosed rope around his neck."

"Let me show everyone People's Exhibit 'R'."

With a small grimace, and apologies being sent in a telepathic fashion to Allen's family, the crime scene photo of Agent Marshall dangling from the noose, a full photo from ceiling to the dirt floor, illuminated against the screen. This was where Jackson wanted raw emotions from the Marshalls. Keeping them together in the audience assured that the entire jury, if not entire congregation, would focus their sights on their agony of said image.

Gasping from the jury and the onlookers swooped in a single, unison syllable.

As her response, Virginia's body shuttered, her eyes looked like they were welded shut due to the pressure she was using to squeeze them while her clenched fists, one holding a semi-used pink lace handkerchief, vibrated in the air. Her pure emotions were radiating, the onslaught of pain was being felt an aisle away.

As for Jared, a cool sense overwhelmed him. Frozen like he was in the cellar a few months prior. Trying to piece it together. The feeling of being an orphan resonating strongly, and the look of loss in his eyes penetrated whoever was around.

Attempting to regain his pace, Jackson turned back to Cecil.

"Did you check for a pulse?"

"Yes."

"Was that successful?

"No, he did not have a pulse, and he was cool to the touch."

"What followed?"

"I went back to the front porch, called my sergeant, and informed them of the situation."

"That being?"

"With a federal agent down, we needed the FBI to come in."

"And how long did that take"

"I kept a vigilant watch in the front until the bureau came down, which was about three hours later."

"Was that the end of the case for you?"

"No, bright and early the next day I was teamed up with Agents Morris and Morray."

"They have not been to the stand yet, so please enlighten

the jury as to what roles these FBI members perform."

"Agent Jacob Morris is an investigator, and Agent Morray is in charge of the forensics team for the region."

"Excellent. And once united, did you execute a walk-through of the primary scene of the crime?"

"We did."

"Let's summarize a few findings, since I will be going over them in detail with Isaac Morray."

"Outside, and on the rear deck, we recovered two small pieces of rope, similar to that used in the noose."

"What other evidence did you, and Agent Morray, discover in the snow out there?"

"Leading."

"Sustained counselor."

"Sorry, redirect." Jackson coughed under his breath. "Did you find anything in the snow?"

"Yes, at least one set of boot prints, and a secondary track, although those were blurry."

"And inside of the home, what else did you observe?"

"First we examined the deceased."

"Anything stand out?"

"Bruising by his eye, and near the rope's location on his neck."

"Anything seem off to you during this examination in the basement?"

"Yes, his federally issued Glock."

"What was unusual?"

"Well, it was not in his holster."

"Was it ever retrieved?"

"Yes."

"What steps did you go through to find it?"

"At first we went upstairs to the bedrooms and had no luck."

"What brought you up there?"

"We thought maybe he had it in his gun safe."

"Okay. Solid logic. Where did you find it finally?"

"In the kitchen under a small curio cabinet."

With a click of his remote, a new image was revealed. This was of the gun in question laying under a china credenza. It was far enough back that the naked eye could not see it. But once on the ground as the photographer showed, it was clearly exposed.

"In your professional opinion Trooper Wingard, what occurred for this to land there. Strictly theoretical."

"There must have been a struggle. Whenever someone in law enforcement is in danger, they grab for their piece. Clearly the victim did so, and one of the attackers hit his forearm precisely and in turn disarmed him."

"You said two, please elaborate."

"Objection."

"If the witness brings up a possible second, I feel as if we should keep going," argued Prosecutor Steele.

"Overruled, but this is on a tight leash."

"Two sets of tracks outside." The witness had two fingers up, and then embraced them with his other hand and squeezed. "To take down a trained specialist, you had to be tricky and overpower him, like what was evident downstairs at the scene."

"So, two people, but one who has privy knowledge of the structure would be ideal, correct Trooper Wingard?"

"Objection."

"It's fine," Jackson held up his hand, "I am releasing the witness for the defense to question. However, I am reserving the right to bring him back onto the stand if needed." Next, he grinned at Virginia and Jared, proud of the trick of words he was able to slide into the jury members' mitigating minds penalty free.

*

"It was nice that the judge let us out at three today."

"Yeah, Jared," started Cecil, "after the specialist on the rope was released, Jackson would have just started questioning Agent Morris, then call it quits midway through his testimony."

"Yeah, he ran out of questions with the rope fiber guy quickly," summarized the younger of the two.

"Wasn't too much to say about the fibers and the cutting patterns being the same. Plus, Jackson thought that Stevvins would have dug deeper into that evidence to disprove it, but here we are. Didn't even ask a single question." The speaker's shoulders heightened, and his open palms rose. "And I would consider that another win for us."

The duo was seated on two overstuffed caramel-colored loveseats in the hotel's lobby area. A giant television tuned into a national news station was playing before them. As usual it had information about the trial that they were mixed up in. Analysts from various law firms and consultants for the government were discussing the case. There was a staunch argument running through the country about whether Steele should pursue the death penalty or not. The staunch majority of those polled in random surveys were vigorously rooting for the needle as the finality to this conundrum.

Many were saying that it was the trial of the decade in regards to federal and states' rights to prosecute such cases. And it happened to be an enormous election year, so this was a hot topic, and the trial was a Godsend for those attached to a donkey or elephant.

Both of the men were steadily tuned in until Virginia came out of the elevator banks. "Hello, boys." Before she could catch herself, a single tear shed itself. From the back of their heads watching the news station they looked to be Jared and his father, not the policeman. Regaining composure, she closed her purse and moved it over her shoulder. "You called us down here Cecil, what did you have in store?"

"Well Miss Virginia, I feel as if you should have a cocktail, and then we will go on my small adventure."

"I haven't had any such thing in five years." With a small smirk, mostly consuming the left side of her face, she answered.

"I will take a fuzzy belly button."

Returning a gaze of confusion, Cecil inquired, "A what?"

Interrupting, Jared explained, "A fuzzy navel."

"Oh..."

"My grandmother can be quite adorable at times."

This made the matriarch laugh, but then she sat next to her kin on the tanned cowhide sofa. There she enjoyed the moment and appreciated him there.

Carefully carrying the three drinks between his two hands, Cecil successfully delivered them. A lemon-lime soda to Jared. A fuzzy belly button to Virginia, and a regular cola for himself. Jared took note of this unordinary choice. "No bourbon."

"Nah, I am driving us around for our getaway, and a trooper driving a squad car after a drink while in the midst of an epic trial getting stopped. Oh, the press would eat that up, and so would Joseph Stevvins."

All three enjoyed a round of chortle at this analysis.

Finally, after some light non-trial chatter and Virginia fully enjoying the libation, the trio left the building and moseyed over to the parking garage assigned to the extravagant inn. Cecil's state issued cruiser, boasting bold navy blue and gold colors, with of course "New York State Trooper" as a glowing inscription, was parked close to the entrance. After some light bantering and teasing, Jared ultimately ended up sitting in the semi-comfortable backseat, allowing his grandmother the privilege of shotgun.

"People will be thinking that we are partners, and just detained Jared," joked Cecil to Virginia. Then he accelerated onto the onramp of 1-90 and headed in the northbound direction. To their left was the roaring waters of the mighty Niagara River. The current cut and rose, ebbed and flowed from the power it held. The other shore was that of Canada. A funny view for those who commute it daily. Seeing another country so close, yet so far off was a spectacular attraction in and of itself.

The air conditioning was turned off, and the windows

were rolled down. Fresh air and the smell of spring hit all of their senses. Keeping pace at just about eighty miles per hour Cecil ensured their safety, yet was very efficient with their trip.

Finally, Jared made the realization in the rear seating compartment. "You are taking us to The Falls, aren't you?"

"Well of course. It's so close that we might as well ride on up."

This wonder of the world was so conveniently located to where they were congregated for proceedings that Cecil thought it might be a nice way to clear their heads, and finally cut loose a bit. With a status of being wedged in the middle of the investigation was causing him to become heavily hounded by the media, but not to the extent that these two passengers were. It was quite exhausting for all. Especially when Jared's cell phone number was leaked to a pushy, and relentless reporter. This was all thanks to a classmate who sold it for a hundred bucks to a national news outlet. After that it was a nightmare getting calls and messages from various numbers. Being proactive he blocked them at first. But then more and more kept coming until eventually he had to change his number completely.

With Virginia's primary phone being a landline and listed in the ever dwindling phonebook, she just kept the receiver off of its hook, even during their trip. A never-ending busy signal was her way of flipping the bird to all those media hounds harassing her.

There was a strong necessity for closure in this case for a multitude of reasons. One being that Jared and Virgina had to now adapt to a new life that they never would have thought of before. Another being a complete finality to all of the pain and being overly exposed to the entire world.

With a smooth exit from the freeway Cecil maneuvered the city streets on the American part of the liquid landscape. It was a bit nicer overall on the Canadian end of the water spectacle, but for time and energy's sake he wanted to stay on this side of the horseshoe shaped allurement.

Finding a convenient spot, one not legal for a normal citizen, Cecil parked in the semi-forbidden area, and all exited with some relief and pending delight percolating in them. The erupting movement of the liquid diving deep off of the cliff and creating the waterfall could be heard from a mile away. This added to the excitement and thrill of absorbing the monstrosity that was before them.

Walking towards it in a lightly graded path of grassy area made it easier for the eldest, although it still was a slow, yet steady progression. With nothing planned until dinner whenever they wanted, they could enjoy the scenery and all its glory at a leisurely pace. Mobs of visitors from all over the world consumed the national park, and they luckily blended into the massive crowd, which even with such chaos around them, they felt peaceful being just another tourist, and not "them from the trial."

"You know Jared," Virginia reminisced, "your grandfather and I came up this way up on small trips up until your father was two or three. With him walking and being a little trailblazer like he was, we did not want him somewhere that could hurt him." There was a tender smile encroaching on her face as she softly looked to the blue sky. One with a small peppering of white clouds, not large ones. Ones that were non-threatening and quite peaceful. Almost as if they were destined to be painted for a whimsical portrait. "We always intended to bring him as he was older, but other places sounded more exciting, and we just never got around to it."

"Yea, I only went on trips here during school," explained Jared, "Dad and I did trips as a kid, but never here." Moving close to his grandmother as they made strides closer, he wrapped his left arm completely around her in a sideways hug, then kissed her on the cheek, precisely as they needed in such a tumultuous time of their lives. "But here right now is quite special, Gram." With those words he squeezed a bit harder for a second or so.

This of course completed the mission in Cecil's heart, and they moved to the sidewalk area that was adjacent to the main attraction. From there they took casual pictures of the liquified entertainment, and also of each other. There was a smooth, therapeutic sensation that brought it all together. After an hour or so of playing tourist, they walked over to a small casual restaurant where they dined. All chose items that would not be on the hotel's menu, since their taste buds were already depleted with the selection at such an eatery.

As dusk was on their tails the trio dispersed from their wonderful fare and headed back to the police vehicle, still safely parked thanks to its prestigious ranking. They fought some traffic that was heading towards the marvel in search of its gorgeous light display when the night had fallen.

Rather for these three rushing back to downtown Buffalo they enjoyed the twilight trip, which entailed them watching the sunset in the west. Almost as if they were chasing it during some of their journey back to their sleeping arrangements. This twenty-minute commute was without discussions or small talk. The passengers were tired and worn from the entire day, and since the week was not quite over for the proceedings, they had a long day before them.

As they split off of the elevator they nodded goodbyes, Jared snuck another soft peck on Virginia's cheek, and they retreated to their own private oasis from the madness ensuing, ready for a final verdict.

*

The day after the small voyage to the falls, the trial made steady forward progress. Jacob Morris was the first one to hit the witness stand, and his testimony was quite similar to Cecil's. Discussions on evidence found at the lakeside scene, and then over to the Beebe Hill site, were all explored. Legitimacy of the evidence being found by the arresting trio of course was called before everyone by Joseph Stevvins, but all of his pleas for such quintessential clues to be excluded were denied by Judge Forrester. During the interaction with Julie no rights had been violated, nor had any tampering taken place. Simply put by the prosecutor, the suspects poorly covered up their tracks, and it was without a doubt that they had left some crumbs behind. Like an untidy Hansel and Gretel.

Isaac Morray took the stand on the Friday of that wretched week. This was planned out and executed by Solicitor Steele in order to keep a unified front on all of the testimony at hand. This felt monotonous, but did drive the point through that there was no way for the defending duo to talk themselves out of any of the facts.

There was of course the discussion of if Virginia was to take the stand, yet it was agreed that there was no point to it. The jury knew who she was, and of the pain she was suffering. During certain parts of the testimony more jurors were paying attention to the reactions of Virginia and of Jared, than of the words of the witness before them. Emotions were high, and that was another point against Julie and Clayton.

All three of the Southern Tier attendees, Virginia, Jared and Cecil, had checked out of their hotel early that Friday morning. There was no desire to stay the weekend for any of them since now Niagara Square was being marred with pain and stress. The final witness for the day was a medical expert that Jackson had found in respect to the neck wounds and the implements of being hung, versus a hanging. They left this as more of a technical testimony than emotional so that the jury would not feel that they were being manipulated to vote guilty due to the raw feelings of the case, rather than the blunt facts.

This presenter was due to start his testimony at precisely noon, yet the Marshalls had decided to drive back home without hearing his statements on the case since it was not a true decision maker on the matter, and the aspect that they were reluctant to listen to more details of how their beloved had been terminated.

During their hike back down to Cuba Jared was doing his due diligence in keeping Virginia fully entertained in conversation with him. Pure chat in a light manner was the goal while trying to keep their moods enriched. They were discussing going to a fish fry at The Four Corners Cafe after they had gotten home and settled. Neighbors had been taking care of the canines for them, plus housing them, so they would take them back for the two days, as a chance for normalcy.

A sense of relaxation welcomed them as they pulled into Virginia's driveway. A spring thaw had allowed the grass to be fully exposed, with a slight inclination for mud. They both descended from Jared's truck, and they ventured inside. The same pup sitting neighbors had watched over the quaint home on Wolf Creek. As expected, everything was in proper order for both inhabitants.

Jared had moved his belongings into this home, even though he legally owned two others. The estate had been pushed through the courts by JT Dove, and all of Allen's possessions were now in Jared's name. But he had winterized the cabin and locked it up for the chilled season. After a verdict he will open it up again so they can enjoy the lake that year. But at that time there was no desire to be there more than a minute or two a week while he checked in on everything. The sting of finding his patriarch suspended and chilled ached deep, and his soul was not ready to build any fond memories there.

"We need to get some laundry started, so that we can get our good clothes ironed and ready for next week." There was a solid, commanding feature to her voice while relaying her expectations. Except when she said "we," she meant Jared would do the brunt of the work while she did the lighter of the labor. An unspoken mode of the workforce distribution, but it was one that made the matter progress smoothly.

"One second, Gram." This was Jared's request filtering from the room he used as his bedroom while he stayed there. Not really annoyed, she just smiled and waited for him to come out when he was ready. There was no need to rush him, and she was simply pleased with his company.

With a mischievous look on his face, he came to the small dinette set where Virginia was sitting with his electronic tablet in hand. "Not to sound morbid, but you do plan on passing the house down to me someday, correct."

This did throw her off balance for a moment, but she recovered. "That is now the plan, you are the only grandchild."

"Well, I have an idea." There was still some devilment in his voice. "Come outside with me."

Both ventured back outside and to the larger side yard of the plot, which was stage right of the home. It was a nice flat area, which was always an empty zone to mow. Years before there was a small metal playset for Jared, but that had long been retired to the dump. Every decade or so for a summer event it was ideal for parking cars, or a random picnic table. But other than that, it was just there. Part of the multitude of acreage for the long-retired farm.

With a swipe of his hand, Jared allowed the tablet to illuminate the illustration of a two-story home plan. "What if I built myself a house over here? We would be close, but still have privacy." Swinging closer to her he showed the design and smiled. "Two stories, three bedrooms for when I have a family."

"That's nice sweetheart," interrupted Virginia, "but what about the Beebe Hill house? Your father loved that place."

"Gram, I don't want some house where my mom and Clayton McBride have been inside butt ass naked together."

They erupted in a unison bout of laughter at this comment.

"You know I love you Jared, and if this is what you want, then we can do that dear."

"Good, because the excavator is coming Monday when we are in Buffalo."

More chortles erupted, and more change, this time planned, ventured into the Marshalls' lives.

*

"The people call Doctor Christpher Hemple to the stand." With a familiar grin and an excited wink Jackson Steele turned to view his colleague. They had worked together on many cases, and this was part of their routine.

Nodding as he sat, along with his own friendly smile, the first witness of that Monday morning was settled into his spot as the leader of the questioning started. "Would you state your name for the record, along with your occupation?"

"Yes, I am Doctor Christopher Hemple, and I am a medical examiner employed by the FBI."

"And you are the leading expert who conducted the autopsy of Agent Allen Marshall, correct?"

"That is correct, Sir."

"Let's start from the cause of death and work backwards. What was your official stance on it?"

"Homicide caused by compression of the trachea leading to asphyxia."

"Does that coordinate with his death certificate?"

"Indeed, it does."

While he was interrogating the mortician Jackson was walking casually around the space between the lawyers' s and the enormous built-in benches for the judge, clerks, and witness. There was a professional stride that added a casual essence in order to make him more likable, especially in his sleek black suit.

"Now, I am quite familiar with the law side of death, but not with the terms and cause. What exactly killed Agent Marshall?"

Leaning into the small microphone Dr. Hemple explained. "It was from a lack of oxygen to his brain."

"Now is this typical suicide style for said result? Passing away due to a noose around one's neck is a common way to unalive yourself."

"No." Extending his arms he let his hands proceed to move in tempo with his words in explaining this matter. "There is a difference between a hanging, and being hung."

"Oh really," stated Jackson, although he already knew this. "Would you inform us on this matter for clarification?"

"Yes. A hanging is asphyxiation when one uses their body weight as leverage and lean backwards. And is the more common method."

"Is there a way to better explain this?"

"Lucky you should ask, I have two slides prepared for this."

"I would like to introduce evidence exhibits 'L' and 'M.'"

The screen at the side of the courtroom that had been used throughout the process was again brought to life, and an image of a stick figure with a noose around his neck appeared. A clear line indicated where the floor was, and his body was at an angle, his body bent at the waist. One could see he was in a position to lose the privilege of breathing.

"Doctor Hemple, please enlighten us by explaining what is on display."

"This is a scenario of a hanging, where the person uses their body mass as the power to pull down and restrict their airflow."

"Was this the method that Agent Marshall died?"

"No."

With a snap of his finger on a small remote the interrogator brought up the second slide. This image showed a stick figure with a noose around their neck. Instead of their feet planted flat on the ground, there was an indication of space between them. And rather than their body being curved, it was a straight drop from the tied rope.

"And Doctor Hemple, can you explain this to us?"

"Why, yes. This is the definition of being hung versus a hanging. There is a drop of the victim which then causes damage to the bones of the neck and spine."

"When was this used in history?"

"For many years as a way for executions."

"So not easy for one to do."

"If they had something to stand on."

"In the evidence shown so far, this was not possible."

"Then one would not be so inclined to do so on their own?"

"Objection, leading."

"Sustained."

"Pardon me." Jackson knew what he was doing. "This would be very difficult to do under the circumstances shown here."

"Correct."

"Now, was there any evidence of damage to the victim's bones?"

"Indeed."

"Let us proceed with evidence 'N' for the record"

In perfect timing the screen moved from the illustrated image to an X-Ray of Allen's neck. There were noticeable cracks and abnormalities.

Cringes came from the Marshall duo in the audience.

"What are we looking at here?"

"This was taken at Cuba Memorial Hospital briefly after Roger Winters picked up Agent Marshall."

"And what can you tell us about it?"

"Classic signs of being hung from a drop. There are fractures to the bones from the suspension. This led to a slight paralysis and asphyxiation before death."

"So, his death was not instant."

"Objection, unless he was using a Ouija board, the undertaker has no true knowledge of that fact."

"Sustained. Come on Mister Steele, you know better."

He did, but that was beside the point.

"Let me rephrase the question, Doctor Hemple." There was an emphasis on the title to show his ranking since Stevvins tried to downplay the witness' expertise. "From what is shown in evidence, do you believe it was a sudden death."

"No. If the spine had fully snapped, then it would have been instant. With some fractures, he did have some time coming in and out of consciousness before he passed."

"Were there any other injuries on Agent Marshall visible?"

"Yes. There was bruising under his right eye."

"Objection, there is no way to pinpoint when Allen Marshall received said injury."

"Sustained, let the jury note it was there, yet no proof of when it occurred. Move on, Counselor."

"And there was one other bizarre mark, correct."

"Yes."

"And what was that?"

"Abrasions around his wrists."

With stealth and a bit of mischievous energy Jackson approached the evidence table and grabbed the two strands of rope found at the rear of the lakeside cabin. "Could they have been inflicted from friction due to these ropes marked evidence 'K.'"

"Objection."

"Sustained."

"That is all, thank you Doctor Hemple." Nodding at his opponent, he said, "Your witness."

Standing up, and knowing some defeat, Joseph Stevvins simply stated, "No questions for this witness."

*

"The prosecution now rests." This proclamation came from Jackson Steele on the Thursday afternoon of the second week. A few more experts had taken the oath and explained other technical issues pertaining to the case such as the time of death including the mystery of the heatwave in the cabin when Allen was discovered.

Of course, JT Dove had testified to the fact that Julie was going to walk away from the marriage with her clothes and car. That there was no way possible with the specific circumstances to the divorce, especially the betrayal and adultery, that she would have received the house or any significant win. This led to the implication that money was the true motive of the crime, and had they gone undetected for their crime, Julie would have gotten everything that Jared had inherited.

Another profound nail driven into the coffin of the defense.

Now it was time for Joseph Stevvins to walk up to the plate and bat the best few innings that he could in order to keep his clients out of a federal prison, or out of the execution chamber.

Proudly taking center stage, as if he was the main attraction of the show, Joe Stevvins smiled as he pulled at the tufts in his suit jacket. The attire was a shining silver color which flickered in the light and garnered much attraction. A blue dress shirt underneath, and a brilliant maroon tie pulled the outfit together. The blood toned knotted neckpiece was intentional. This was due to his stern belief that red posed a status of power. And he was trying to regain some power in this ongoing legal argument.

"The defense calls to the stand Gary Ferguson."

A middle-aged gentleman wearing a simple polo shirt and tan khakis rose from the pews and headed towards the front. With a medium build, he seemed like an everyday person. His chrome was bald, almost glistening. Yet he had a monk's crown of hair in a light brown with some gray. His push broom mustache flickered in the same colors.

As he passed Julie he waved and smiled. This was not due to his belief in her innocence, he was just a man of the small town who believed in greeting all that he knew. It was actually a fact that he did not want to testify, but his honest mouth got him smack dab in the middle of the drama.

"Please state your name for the record."

"Gary Ferguson."

"And do you know why you are here today?"

"Well yeah," the truth flowed from the witness' mouth. "I was chatting with the investigator that you hired for Julie

Marshall, and I told him that I saw Allen up there a week before he died puttering around."

Embarrassment radiated from Stevvins, while Steele was enjoying how the show was going so far. There could have been an objection on the prosecution's part, but honestly, Jackson wanted to see how the cards fell on this.

"Well first, Mister Ferguson, what is your relationship to the Marshalls?"

"I am their neighbor."

"There were two residences, please be more specific."

"We both live on Beebe Hill."

"And to clear up confusion, you saw Allen Marshall there randomly just before his death."

"Yes, I am unsure of what day, but it was the week before. I had a hernia fixed and was off of work that week because of it. Normally my wife and I wouldn't be home during the day. I would've talked with him, but it hurt to get up. But I was able to see him going in and out."

"So, no one else appeared to be home."

"Nah, Julie and Clayton must have been working at the plant."

"Leading up to this time Allen had not been there much, correct?"

"Nope. When he found out those two were fooling around on him, he left her ass and went to the camp. And now that she's gone and killed him."

"Stop, Mister Ferguson." Stevvins declared this with his open hand up in the air, praying for the witness to stop talking. "Your honor, can we have that stricken from the record."

"Not too often does the defense need their own witness' statement erased, but we will do so." The judge faced the jury. "Please disregard that comment, it is an opinion not a fact."

"I guess to complete things here Mister Ferguson, it was out of place for Mister Marshall to have been snooping around the property,"

"Correct."

"Nothing more for the witness."

The reasoning behind this line of questioning was to add some suspicion to the victim. Throwing in that everything was not right in the entire case. Jackson Steele could have objected to the witness, but instead decided to use it for his leverage.

Rising he walked to the orator and smiled. "Mister Ferguson, thanks for taking the drive up."

"No problem, Allen was a friend of mine."

"Now were you told to watch over the home by anyone?"

"No."

"Did you have to contact the police over the victim entering a home deeded to himself?"

"Not at all."

"So, no crime was committed."

"No."

"Did you fear for anyone's safety or feel that any property was in harm's way."

"No."

"So, you were just nosy, and that got you brought into court."

"Correct."

"That is all for this witness."

*

After another witness with lackluster testimony in regards to the telltale signs of suicide was completed with their spiel, the court was adjourned for the weekend. This was the part of the trial when everyone was feeling true fatigue, yet a glimmer of hope at the end of the tunnel. There was some fading energy from the Marshalls with emotions draining and a desire for it all to just be over... Finally.

Obviously, Cecil and Jackson had been through a plethora of such proceedings and were conscientious of the impact that it had on the family of victims. This is why on Fridays they just let the mourning couple disperse and rejuvenate. Which was what said duo did.

Again, they retrieved the pups and evaluated the digging work that had happened so far in the side yard. There was still a newness, and not quite acceptance that an abode was soon to be constructed. Yet an excitement of change, and of closure, just around the bend. An anticipated curve in their lives, one that was feared, however, at the same time welcomed with open arms.

Once returned to Niagara Square that Monday the defense put on a few days of spectacles for the jury. Again they were not triumphant, nor were they mind changing. And some were just frustrating to all parties and onlookers involved.

Clayton had taken the advice of the silent second chair counselor and was not taking the stand. There was too much on the line in the midst of the confusion, and they wanted to keep it simple. Their true plan of action was to try and throw a tiny bit of doubt in the jury's eyes about the evidence brought before them. All of the witnesses were intended to not be profound, rather to take a small dig at any of the other testimony that the opposition had drawn before them and question the likelihood of the conspiracy at hand happening.

The motto was simple, yet could be effective. "One juror voting innocent means success."

If graded, their strategy would be marked as a D+, at best. There really had not been any huge wins, and only pinholes had been popped in the prosecution's case, especially in reference to the validity of their evidence.

Contrary to what her legal team was emphasizing, Julie Clayton was dead set on testifying. Which she had every right to do, even with it being a detrimental factor to her case in everyone else's eyes. And not only that, but she wanted to be dead last. One last plea of her innocence.

*

"Lastly we call Julie A. Marshall to the stand."

For her testimony the judge had allowed her to wear something other than an inmate uniform. Michael McBride, who had been there for the duration of the trial and was loyally on their side, had purchased a basic lady's pant suit in a dark purple for Julie. There was an abiding and strong passion for their innocence which he held.

As for handcuffs, she was allowed to be restraint-free from her wrists, yet her ankles clanged and clattered with a set by her feet, ensuring her containment in the courtroom, yet letting the jury have an unbiased opinion of her during her questioning.

After her oath for honesty was finished, one that was debatable as to the sanctity of her promise, she nestled in with a small smile on her face, and a desire for a chance to cleanse her name.

Standing proud, Joseph Stevvins had weighed over each and every question that he was anxious to ask of her. "Would you state your name for the record?"

"Yes, Julie Marshall."

"You are obviously the widow of the deceased."

"Correct also."

"First off, sorry for your loss."

"Thank you."

An abundance of eyes viewing the questioning rolled at this feeble attempt at sympathy for her.

"Moving forward, let us state one thing, your marriage to Mister Marshall was ending, correct."

"That is correct."

"And you were coming to terms with the fact that you would not end up with much in the divorce, is that also a truth here?

"Yes."

"In actuality, you were placing an offer on a house in Hinsdale with your co-defendant."

"Yes, we were."

"I would like to add exhibit 'V' into the record." On the projection screen a contract to purchase a property in the neighboring town appeared. "This was created two days before the incident, if I am not mistaken."

"Yes, we were planning our exit from the Beebe Hill house."

"Now, for the record, where were you between six and eight forty-five that evening."

"First at the Beebe Hill house, then at Jared's concert at seven."

"So that means there is no possible way that you and Clayton could have attacked Mister Marshall."

"Not at all."

"So, you are completely innocent."

Leaning into the microphone she looked directly at Jared and Virginia. "I had absolutely nothing to do with his death."

"What do you believe happened?"

"I think that he pissed off the wrong farmer."

"That is all for this witness." Joseph Stevvins smiled for the court and took his seat.

With gusto and excitement Jackson Steele rose from his seat and headed towards the witness box, ready for a mighty showdown.

"Ms. Marshall, before this incident, when you and the victim lived together, did you ever feel frightened of someone attacking him, or your family, due to his line of work."

Frozen, she was unsure of an answer, and meekly said, "Well, there is always that threat."

"But was there a direct one, or anytime that something suspicious happened."

"Not in my memory."

"So, no... Now you are attesting to the fact that you arrived at the school at around seven pm."

"Well, yes."

"You are aware of the significance if you are in fact lying

here, correct."

"Yes," was her answer, that ascended lightly in volume as her face began to flush with embarrassment.

"I am re-entering exhibit 'A'."

"Objection, that was introduced solely in relation to the dispute between Jared Marshall and Clayton McBride," exclaimed Stevvins. "That holds no merit here."

"Your honor," countered Steele, "there was no specific time frame mentioned when entering the evidence, only the date."

Nodding, and impressed with the prosecution's foresight, Judge Forrester ruled. "I am going to allow it. He got you there, Mister Stevvins."

The tape rewound to six forty-five pm.

"We are going to speed this up a bit, however you will see that the only time that the defendants appeared at the school was just before the scuffle."

As promised, he played the segment of recording, but at a speed five times the normal pace, sometimes faster when no one was coming in.

Throughout the period of the concert there was no sign of the presumed killers coming near the main entrance. Until finally at eight forty-five when they viewed Clayton's truck pull into a spot and they both got out and stood in the yard as other parents were exiting the facility. They were acting as if they had also experienced the musical demonstration and greeted Jared when he was done.

When the final clip of the video finished the interrogator faced Julie. "So, are you standing by your alibi?"

Destroyed and distraught, Julie was unsure of what she should do, until she looked over at Stevvins who was quietly showing her five fingers. Similar to a third base coach to a first base runner.

"I guess I plead the fifth."

Luckily neither Steele, nor Forrester, saw this little hand signal.

"I will let the jury decide on that, nothing further for the witness."

This time Steele made a motion of his hands as if he was shooting a basket in the direction of Jared and Virginia, with a quirky grin expressing his pride in a slam dunk

*

"**A** tragedy," proclaimed Jackson Steele in the first sentence of his closing argument. "Pure and simple." There was a solemn and distraught aura to his words. "A travesty to those he loved, and to the Southern Tier of this great state." As he exclaimed these words he wandered about in the open area of the courtroom. The carpet was aged and embraced many lectures such as this on its worn, yet durable forest green threads.

"A man of honor," his hands and fingers worked in unison to emphasize the dramatic nature of his lecture, "who vowed to be a protector of the land, and of the men who farmed it. A man with grace, who even though his marriage had collapsed, and his world was changing, he kept his dignity and was being civil through such matters."

Pausing, he stopped at the mahogany stained railing which was located between him and the jury's quarters and pressed his fingertips on its top. Pressing so that his hand was like a spider this stance showed precision and dramatic appreciation to his speech.

"But our defendants could not respect our victim. They had pushed and pushed with their affair, and once it was known between their attorneys that Julie would not be receiving much from the divorce, they made a plan." With this he stood and crossed his arms. "They pinpointed an exact time that they could sneak attack Allen when he was alone." Holding up his hand, his index finger popped up, emphasizing the first point of his theory. "Julie knew the property, knew how to sneak attack, and where. She was also privy to the schedule for the evening when Jared would be at the school getting ready for his concert.

"So, they stood in wait, rope in hand, toolbox closeby, ready to take down the only obstacle for a very hefty estate. Plus, a federal pension. Dollar signs radiating in their eyes.

"And once Allen entered that kitchen, for whatever greed enhanced reason, they leapt into the door and blindsided him." To add some pizazz Jackson spun in place, his suit coat tails waving in the wind. "Being a law enforcer Allen grabbed for his government issued gun, but a quick elbow down would disarm him and cause the piece to slide and land under the china cabinet. A table and chair are tossed around, and an antique glass dish is shattered, all in the struggle for life."

Rubbing his own wrists, he went on. "Then they tied his hands, and led him into the cold, cold cellar, where again they took the time to drill a hole in the beam and place a noose around the terrified man's neck. And in those few minutes it took, Allen was fearful. Death was on the horizon."

With a petrified stare he looked at the audience for a solid fifteen seconds, trying to emphasize the fear that the victim would have at that instance.

"Imagine being held up by two people, then having a noose around your neck, and then just being dropped. You feel your spine crunch as you fade away. Fade away a bit too soon from the world with so much on the horizon."

Dropping his head, Jackson displayed another silent and stoic moment.

Popping it back to its correct position his voice came to life again. "You will hear 'reasonable doubt' thrown about. And yes, you need to know that term. However, we have fulfilled it. And enough for capital punishment. We have lies, we have motive, we have premeditation, and we have forensics.

"The drill bit and the wood shaving found with Clayton's tools, along with the rope, and his boots that match the prints in the rear and around the crime scene. We have opportunity, we have it all here." With vigor and strength his hands lifted up, highlighting the enormous weight this evidence held. "And now what I need you to do is to make the toughest decision of your lives. But in turn, the most important." Softly his hands dropped, and a more subtle and caring tone reverberated from his being.

"Our federal agents risk their lives, and we need to show anyone wishing to harm them that we will not stand for them to be taken down. That it will not be just some bit of jail time, and then return to their lives. If you take an American hero's life, we take yours. Fair is fair. Let us provide justice to Allen Marshall, Jared Marshall, and Virginia Marshall. You have the power, please use it to its extent."

Upon taking his seat and exhaling Jackson proclaimed, "The prosecution now rests their case."

*

With poise and elegance Joseph Stevvins rose from his reserved spot next to the co-defendants. With a nod, and a sleek smile, he tried to reassure them of the possibility that the trial just might go their way. Somehow.

With a long inhale while facing the jury box, he then proceeded with his final testament. "The past two weeks have been grueling for all of us. The twelve of you have been sworn to uphold the law and decide if justice is due here. My clients have been imprisoned, and their lives have been shattered, and now at the mercy of my debating skills of protecting their honor. And of course, there are those mourning the loss of a notable man.

"However, that death was not one at the hands of my clients. There was no stable motive at hand here. Julie McBride had moved on to a man who fit her better, like a ying and yang situation." With this demonstration Joseph lifted his hands, with his fingers spread, then put them together, his fingers weaving together as harmony. An obvious metaphor for the words he just spoke. "Money was not an issue, nor were any custody battles or land disputes. Things were civil and going to continue that way.

"The few pieces of evidence found at the Beebe Hill home were at best circumstantial. Who has purchased the same boots as an acquaintance, and everyone has rope and drill bits lying about. These are not earth-shattering revelations that should give two clearly innocent people the death penalty.

"And yes, they fibbed about their alibi. Who hasn't told a tiny, white lie to get out of a minute social gathering. Again, this is not a smoking gun.

"I also want to recognize the stress that the dozen of you are experiencing with this being a nationally covered trial. A mysterious suicide has snowballed into a national affair.

"Or was this the result from a suspect in a USDA case? Again. There is more than enough reasonable doubt to liberate my clients and let everyone explore the true story behind this tragic event, that has become jumbled into a larger occurrence. All of these notations of the case are not enough to reach a consensus of reasonable doubt.

"Thank you. The defense rests."

*

"And a fuzzy belly button."

The barkeep turned and gawked at Cecil.

"I mean a fuzzy navel. Sorry."

"Sure, take a seat and I will bring them right over."

With that promise of a round of drinks delivered Cecil joined Jared and Virginia, plus Jackson, who were sitting around a small table by the fireplace. There was a small sofa, and a few accent chairs pulled into a circle. The past two weeks this had been a usual meeting arena for the guests of Jared and Virginia.

"Thank you again Mister Steele," expressed Virginia. With a grandmother's touch she squeezed his hand.

"Not a problem."

"So," started Jared, "how soon until we will hear from the jury?"

"Well," the solicitor cleared his throat, "could be

tomorrow, or Saturday. Judge Forrester hates breaking for weekends with a jury. But they set their own pace."

The tavernist returned with the drinks and then returned to his post. With some light banter Cecil was enjoying his chilled bourbon, Jared a soda, Virginia her fuzzy belly button, and Jackson was actually relaxing with a frothy IPA from the hotel's draft selection.

Each person took a healthy gulp of their refreshment. They had left the courtroom a full two hours before and had agreed to meet there before heading home. The jury would break for the night at seven pm, and Jackson had learned years before to never leave the city proper until they had receded for the night.

Such as that lesson previously learned, this night was the same when the jury finished their debating and pondering at six pm.

A generic ringtone erupted from Jackson's interior suit coat jacket, which was draped over the arm of his chair. With surprise he answered, and his eyes illuminated with electricity and almost disbelief.

"That was the clerk," he took a healthy swig from the beer. "The jury is finished already, We have half an hour to get back to the courthouse."

A few other parties in town for the trial were in the lounge area, such as reporters and consultants. They were all receiving texts and calls, so they were also closing up camp to get back to the judicial meeting spot.

Cecil enjoyed his drink, killing it in a single stride. While Virginia smiled at Jared and let him complete the two thirds of her peachy liquor concoction that she wasn't able to indulge in. This was stressful, and Jared was allowed this one vice, this one time.

There was a healthy stream of media coming in, along with Joseph Stevvins and other essential players to this top story. Anchormen and their associates were trying to get a comment from the Marshalls, yet they stayed true to their solemn commute. There was fear that the jury would acquit Julie and Clayton. A true fear that shook them to the bones.

Murmuring was occupying the pews as court clerks and bailiffs were descending to their spots. The defendants were seated already, and then the jury marched in. Their faces were like settled concrete. Absolutely stellar poker faces that did not hint at which direction they had cast their ballots.

"All rise..."

With gusto and a showman's spirit, Judge Forrester entered from a solid mahogany door behind his bench. This was intended for the cameras to give him an authoritative aura since the next few minutes will be engraved in newsreels around the country.

Bowing, he allowed the others to sit. Then he looked to his right. "Jury Foreman, have you reached a verdict?"

"Yes, Your Honor."

"Please hand the document to the bailiff."

The lead juror did so, and the deputy passed the sacred note to the judge. Upon examination of this historic document, he relayed its transference back through the assembly line and to the jury.

"In count one, premeditated murder of a federal agent, are you in unison in reference to the verdict for both defendants. Do you believe both acted with malice, and together in said offense?"

"Yes, we do."

"How do you find the defendants in said crime?"

"Guilty."

Gasps flooded the room, Virginia and Jared clasped hands and shed tears. Horror encompassed the faces of Julie and Clayton. Jackson grasped his fist tightly and shook it in a winning style. Cameras rolled taking this all in, and complete astonishment reigned king.

There was a steady look on Joseph Stevvins' face, conveying that he was not shocked at said exclamation, yet he went white and felt sick to his stomach. This was expected, but its intensity just sunk into his soul. There was also a sense of failure since he truly believed in their innocence and was hoping that this would be the underdog victory that they deserved.

Slamming the gavel down twice, the magistrate brought control to his domain again. "Quiet, quiet."

Everyone paid heed.

"Did the jury find a unanimous sentence?"

The foreman rose again. "Yes, we did."

"And what did you decide upon as an assembly?"

"Death by lethal injection."

II

"Wow, Dad. The night is so clear, not a single cloud in sight."

"I know, Jared. This fireworks display is going to be amazing."

With that enthusiasm flowing the teen walked across the deck in the early twilight of the Fourth of July evening looking to forage some more of the picnic style food that they had dined on earlier. With a variety of summer themed selections, the spread was quite impressive. The proud father kept his eyes on his only child just as his own mother came up behind her son and tapped him on the elbow. "Allen, this night is so nice."

"Thanks, Mom."

"I can't believe that Jared is a senior this year."

"Yeah, time has flown by."

"Are you two doing okay living up here? It's been a month or two since you left Julie." A worrisome expression invaded her face. "You can tell your old mother, do you need me to come up and cook for you boys?"

Embracing her with a side hug and a kiss on her cheek he went on, "Nah. Julie was never that much of a cook anyway. I did most of the meal prepping. Her best work in the kitchen was calling for delivery."

This dry pun did not create any laughter.

"I know, Dear. But it still is a shock for us all."

"Well, I am fine with it. She never was much of a mother to Jared either. And it was an unspoken understanding that we would get Jared through college and then split ways." Slightly he huffed. "But apparently that Clayton McBride wooed her while they were working together so much."

With a cross look on her face due to her emotions of the failing nuptials Virginia decided upon a seat on a built-in bench that was part of the structure for the rear deck for the camp. Being an adoring son, Allen followed suit.

"Let's enjoy the night some." The property owner wanted to soften the aura of the evening some.

"You are right, Sweetheart."

A slight shadow rounded the house as a man in a tee shirt and khaki shorts rounded the side yard and headed into their direction with a twenty-four pack of bottled beer resting on his shoulder during the small trip.

"Hey," announced Allen, "Frank finally joined us, and he's pulling his own weight for once." This was a lighthearted joke since they both respected and cared for each other.

The new guest joined the party, which had about a dozen or so others. These included some cousins and friends. A simple gathering that Allen casually called his own independence party due to his pending divorce. At that time the fireworks erupted in the sky over beautiful Cuba Lake, initiating the hour-long spectacular show, and a bit of peace and harmony was present.

*

Paperwork overwhelmed the desk of Federal Agent Allen Marshall in his Department of Agriculture office located in Olean. There were many active cases that he and his partner were firmly examining at that point. In the same office was said co-investigator, and together they oversaw Allegany and Cattaraugus counties. Their desks were spaced apart in order to keep their sanity at times, yet in the same room so that they could be effective as a team.

Leaning back in his chair, his left calf and ankle resting on his blotter, Allen shook his head. "Jesus, Frank, this Swartson character is really pushing my nerves. There is no way that he can expect us to believe that it was a mistake when he was filling out all of these grant applications."

"Oh, you know how they are. They think that they can pull one over on us, when he can barely pull a sweatshirt over his head."

Both chuckled.

Looking at his screen he saw some threatening emails from Brian Swartson but decided to delete them. This was the response to Allen when he had asked for verification of some information on workers at the farm.

Sometimes people have a mouth which writes a check to someone that their ass is unable to cash when it comes down to it.

A friendly familiar head popped into the open doorway. It was their shared secretary, Lisa. "Hey you guys. Interoffice mail. But just for Allen."

Being their professional aide, she walked the large manilla envelope over to him. Being so thin it would be correctly assumed to be a single sheet document. The cover of the shuttling folder was used over and over since it had names written on the back of previous receivers of the delivered paper good.

Shrugging Allen unwrapped the single strand that was holding the clasps together and pulled out the mysterious letter. His eyebrows moved up and down while his mouth pulsated reading a few words of the memo.

Curious of its nature, Frank asked, "What is up?"

"Oh," Allen shook his head. "I turn fifty in January and my term life insurance runs out then. In the next six months I need to get a physical with a good bill of health so that they can renew it until my retirement."

"Yea, that's pretty standard.:"

"Yea. I have my yearly physical coming up soon with my GP. I'll have him fill out whatever forms and get it back."

"You got it." Feeling as if that topic was over the other lawman slapped his desk top. "Well, let's head over to Angelica to check out that one farmer. I swear something is up with him. I'd love to surprise him and see how many day laborers he has working right now, and how many are actually on his payroll."

"Sounds good to me," Allen stood up and grinned, "a little impromptu drop by visit reveals a lot."

*

"**A**llen, I told you man. We should've started radiation back in February when it was stage two." The medical specialist was at his desk, glasses in hand, and frustration plus grief on his heart. "We can go for it now, but we have to be aggressive to get this. Or go in and take out your prostate and the growth around it. Since we are now looking at stage three, almost four right now we must act. No dilly dallying. We must do one, the other, or in my opinion both." Shaking his head at his long-time patient he asked, "Aren't you in a whole lot of discomfort?"

"Well, yeah. Hurts like hell if I can piss. Other times it's like trying to shoot a monsoon out of a capped off straw. My lower back is always hurting."

"Then why are we staying at the status quo?"

"If my family found out, everyone would go overboard. Plus, I'm heading into a divorce."

"They can have you for six months as is, or a lifetime after you fight like hell."

"Let me ask you something, Doc."

"Yeah."

"Theoretically speaking, if I needed an okay from you for my term life insurance to be renewed, could you sign off on it with me like this."

"I would lose my license."

"Doctor Lyman, then what if I, hypothetically, went to another doctor who I had never seen before and had my exam."

"One prostate exam and he would know how the cancer is growing and would never sign off on it. He would try and get you into surgery the next day probably. Or getting you zapped with chemo." An annoyed sigh morphed into a grunt. "Any other patients, and I would have scheduled it and been pushier. But Allen, this is no laughing matter, especially when it comes to insurance and such."

A nervous shuffle of his hands and feet on Allen's behalf reiterated that it was actually a true problem he had been wrestling with.

"Listen Allen," the disease curer leaned further onto the table. "I will respect your decision. Some want to fight and get microwaved for years. And they do it." A macabre professional smile rose on his face, "Then I have those like you who want nothing more than to pass away without warning to you or anyone else. This way they remember you, and not the person who will be laying in a hospital bed shriveled up, ready for it to be over."

"I want my dignity, and to leave my boy some money, and to have fifteen more years with him."

"You can't have it all." The physician rose, indicating to an ailing Allen Marshall that their time was up. "Let me know your plan."

Deep in thought Allen exited, unsure of what route he would wander onto.

*

"JT, thanks for seeing me with such short notice."

"Well luckily you caught me when I was not in court. Come into my office."

A simple waiting room with commercial carpet and a bland matching secretary led into a little bit more upscale office for the solicitor. One with a large, impressive desk, and a wall of cabinets with legal files belonging to a large portion of the area's residents since he was one of the few attorneys in town.

"I just finished a call with that Joseph Stevvins. God, I always feel like I need a shower after talking to him. My client is being sued by one of his over an accident on The Expressway two years ago. What a mess!" The story teller's hands flew up. "His client is reaching for dollars when my guy is worth pennies." Both men sat laughing at the legal anecdote. "What brings you in, Allen."

"I wanted to follow up with my divorce, and I want you to pull up my will, it's been a hot minute since I read it."

"Sure, sure." Logging onto the computer the legal expert pulled up notes from his client's case. "So, I was looking into it all, and she can barely afford a lawyer. Which helps us. On top of that she is at fault. The house was in your name before you married. The camp also. She could try for alimony, but she won't get it. She caused the rift in the marriage." Looking up, he inquired, "Jared is eighteen, correct."

"Just turned it."

"Perfect. Let's pull up your will here." Punching more keys he made more progress. "We wrote this about five years ago. Julie receives all property in your untimely death. If she is deceased then it goes to your mother, same with guardianship of Jared if Julie died with you, or before you. Do you want to write a new one?"

"Let's keep this as is until the divorce is finalized. Just to keep it easy." A part of him wanted to change it, but another subconscious voice was pushing him towards keeping his options open. "I do have a dumb question; may I ask it."

"With what I am billing you right now, you get as many as you want."

Light laughter fluttered.

"What is term life insurance?"

"That is easy. Term is set for a specific time."

"Mine is up in January when I turn fifty. And they want a new medical exam."

"Is everything okay Allen?

"Yes."

Blatant lie.

"So that is when they want to make sure you are healthy to re-insure. Pivotal point in your life with health issues. They just want to make sure they are investing in those they can make longer profit from before their pay out."

"Right."

"So just do the exam, and they will issue a new term, probably until you hit sixty or so. With the government I do believe they will let you keep it after retirement even. But don't quote me on that. Talk to your human resources person. That is something that you should switch to Jared when the term is up, and when you renew. Even if the divorce is still in the midst of the proceedings."

"Now, my pension. What is the deal with that?"

"If you drop dead today then Julie gets it for her life. If you divorce her, it is solely yours, unless you remarry."

"Can I pass it down to Jared?"

"I am unsure about that. Someone in Human Resources will help guide you with that part."

"Thanks, JT. I think I know what I need to do now." Yet their lists of what he should do were complete contrasts of the other.

Rising Allen left the attorney's office, really pondering what he should do and how the cards would play out for him.

*

With a closed-door Allen snuck a quick phone call in at the office. After a few trills an unknown voice answered. "This is Jackie in Human Resources, how may I assist?"

"Hi Jackie. I am an agent with the USDA south of Buffalo. I have a question."

"Excellent, we cover all of the federal agencies. Go on."

"I am about to turn fifty and was wondering about my

retirement. But I am going through a divorce. Can I retire and have my son receive my pension after my death instead of my wife, or soon to be ex-wife."

"Is your child under eighteen years of age?"

"No, he just turned eighteen."

"Then unfortunately not. Only spouses who are wed for more than nine months are eligible."

"Okay. Thank you for your time."

Just then Frank opened the door to their office. "Ready to run up and talk to this Swartson character?"

"Sure."

The two proceeded outside and to Frank's truck. The sun was shining, and the ride from Olean over to Cuba and up the Rawson Road was expected to be a nice one. The first two thirds of the tripduring the highway portion was superior since it was just as the end of summer was starting to show itself. But once he saw the exit for Cuba Allen felt somewhat philosophical and wanted to have an open talk with his trusted pal.

"Do you ever worry about if something happened to you."

"Well, of course man." Going along Route 305 just past the school Frank gunned the engine a bit. Their windows were a bit down for some fresh air, and he was fine with this type of chat. They were not only just partners, but true friends after all.

"Well, like do you ever think about if you deteriorated in front of your family. Like either mind or body. Just shrivel up. Especially as the man. The leader."

"I'd hope my family would love me no matter what. Sickness, and in health. And your mom and Jared would do the same. They would take damn good care of you."

"But what if I am the caretaker?"

"That hat in a family has to be shuffled sometimes. You can't always be the healer, fixer, money maker, and best friend. Sometimes you must pass that along to someone else. You have taught Jared well, he would do all of those for you."

"But he's just a kid."

Looking over, Frank glared at him. "When you need him,

he will have progressed into a man by then Allen. Okay. Are you not telling me something? Or is this just divorce talk in your head?"

"You're right, it's just divorce talk."

"I think we are at Chez-Swartson." With a hefty turn of the steering wheel the truck ascended the lot and towards the small home. Once in the rounded part of the driveway they parked and jumped out.

A skinny face looked out the window, cigarette rising and descending in his slim fingers. "Do you have a warrant?" This command was yelled through the window.

"Brian," started Allen, "we are just here to chat. No warrants. I am Agent Allen Marshall with the USDA, this is my partner Frank Lyons. I have sent a few emails and letters via the post office."

"I don't need no feds up on my property."

Brushing it off, the seasoned officer explained, "There are some discrepancies on some documents in relation to grant money that the federal government gave you two years ago. That is all we are looking to chat about."

"Talk to my lawyer Joseph Stevvins, and if you don't have a warrant, get your asses off of my property. I am a sovereign citizen of this here parts."

Turning to walk away they both immediately broke out into laughter and headed back to the truck.

*

"**M**ove that dish back to the countertop and close to the wall, it was my Aunt Charlotte's, and I don't want it broken. Plus, I have breakfast ready."

Coming through the doorway from the living room and into the kitchen Jared grabbed the sacred heirloom and placed it on the small china cabinet across the kitchen space. "It's safer over here anyway, Dad." With a slight twirl in the tight space the younger Marshall headed to the coffee maker and poured himself a healthy amount, then added its condiments.

Laughing, Allen then moved the two plates of eggs, bacon, toast and home fries onto the small dinette set. "Better than The Four Corners Cafe any day. Right, Son?"

"Of course, Dad," replied Jared as he sat and smiled. "I can't believe I am a senior this year!"

"Yeah, when I was a senior, we were still the greyhounds. Anyway," just before sitting Allen pulled out his wallet and handed some currency over to his lad, "here is twenty bucks in case you need anything else. And for lunch of course."

"Thanks Pops."

"And please don't ever call me that."

Smiling, the jokester took a bite.

"Be sure to at least text your mother and tell her how your first day went."

Dropping his fork for dramatic purposes Jared answered. "Fine, fine," he retrieved it and continued eating. "You are so much better about her, than she is to you."

Finishing his own gulp of coffee, the elder continued. "Sometimes in life you must be the bigger person, Son. Even if it takes all that you've got."

"I guess you're right."

"And always make sure that you get married to someone you love."

"Did you love Mom?"

"You are old enough, and have done the math."

"Since I was six, I knew I was a mistake."

"You were a bonus. I would never trade you for anything." Reaching across the table Allen rubbed his kin's shoulder.

"Right, Dad."

"Seriously. Now your mother and I... We were infatuated with each other. It was a great courtship." Swallowing, he pressed on. "But it was not of substance. Then I was surprised to hear she was pregnant with you, and I did what I felt was right at the time."

"Would you still have done the same today?"

"Nah, I would've stayed single and received full custody of you."

"So, we would have ended up this way?"

"Yup, but such is life. Now hurry up before the traffic gets bad and you're late on your first day. Between the buses and the Amish horse and buggies, you don't want to get stuck behind either one."

*

"**O**kay, one more picture with Gramma and Jared in front of the fireplace." A teenage boy and girl walked away from the fiery centerpiece of the room while Virginia blushed and headed to the spot next to Jared. Dressed exceptionally well for the Homecoming formal dance he had a wonderful deep brown suit with an bright nectarine hued dress shirt underneath, and a festive orange and brown tie as a stunning accent. His shining cinnamon shoes matched, and he was excited to go to the school get-together with his two best friends.

After Allen had snapped the picture Jared kissed his grandmother on the cheek and erupted out laughing. "Okay Dad, let us go now!"

"Sure, sure, drive safe, no drinking afterwards. Be responsible."

The teenage trio were exiting the home and waving as the son answered, "Of course, Dad."

"Well Mom, Allen lifted the strap holding his digital camera over his head and placed it on the coffee table. "Want to play some rummy or dice?"

"Not tonight, Son. It is late, and I want to get over the hill."

This was a bit heartbreaking for Allen, since he was yearning for more time with her. Loneliness was creeping upon him during the times he was feeling the depth of his pending illness, and this led to thoughts of what to do about some dire issues in his life. Ones that he could no longer keep pushing to the back of the agenda. Ones that needed some proper attention, and decisions to be made.

Putting on her jacket, Virginia turned to her son and kissed him on his cheek. "Email me those pictures, and have Jared call me tomorrow to tell me all about it, Dear."

With a quick whip of brisk air entering the quaint abode and gushing out, Allen was left alone on a Friday night. These were the nights he had been struggling with. The ones which tore himself into shreds trying to deal with the nearing fate of his life, or the downfall of disclosing his declining health with an intimate audience. In order to taper off these fiery feelings Allen decided to mix himself a cocktail, a habit that he rarely indulged upon. But such serious, and thoughtful matters needed a bit of a potent lubrication to help the process along.

Opening up the china cabinet he withdrew some aged scotch and a tumbler glass. Pouring two fingers in depth he placed the bottle back onto the shelf and closed its protective door. This was an attempt to limit himself to just one, but he knew that those hinges would be swinging again relatively soon in order to add to his intoxication.

Throwing some ice cubes in the direction of the glass he chilled his concoction and headed to the living room. First, he was going to upload the pictures onto his laptop from his digital camera, but he slid into a rabbit hole by opening up a search engine.

Throughout the past few weeks, he had allowed his mind to run rampant and create these ludicrous ideas of how to trick his way into a clean bill of health. One was to hire someone to take the medical exam for himself.

And what was profound to him to cease this line of thought was first that it would not help his own demise. Throwing in a decoy was a very temporary fix. The cancer would still be growing, and it would be discovered that he was a fraud.

And this only led to an outcome of the plot being exposed,

and the whole house of cards to fall around him. There would be shame and embarrassment encircling the hypocrisy of disobeying the law. Plus, he could lose not only the insurance, but also his profession.

And pride. That pride must stay intact.

The unfortunate thought of suicide had passed his mind. This would be the easiest, yet would cause more pain than good for his family. Having a friend who ended their own existence when they were schoolmates left a scar that was still fresh for over thirty years later. The agony of feeling useless when they needed him. Lingering around for ages would be guilt and so many other emotions that had tagged along for so long. Those he would not want to give to anyone, especially his own child.

This method was a permanent solution to a temporary problem when it came to those with depression and such true feelings. And being a mature man, he knew it was best for those with such intentions to reach out, there is always someone willing to listen.

And Allen did love his life, but the fear of not taking care of his family properly when his days were finished was an agonizing part of the enigmatic equation.

Then came thoughts of an accident. Maybe falling down the stairs. Firing up the internet he tried to see how a tumble down the stairs a few feet away from him could be staged into a perfect way of his passing, and all to be right. Property to go to Jared, and his name remains pure. A name his son would be proud to carry on.

But she would get the pension. She would be stingy with the insurance money and not let Jared prosper from the funds.

Also, the chances of hitting the right spots on the right steps was so precise, and if bones did not crack properly then he would be in a wheelchair, still with terminal cancer, and a burden with less money and means than when he started.

Draining this potent potable he rose to the kitchen. Walking in his wet feet he stepped on an ice cube, which had semi-melted. Sliding a few inches, he grasped the counter and steadied himself.

"Wish that little fucker took me out there."

Kicking the half-depleted coolant he went to grab more from the freezer while shaking his head. Grasping a handful he replenished his glass and closed the door. Just as he was twisting away from that wall and to go to the opposite one for more booze the moon hit the light of the lake behind him just right to start stirring in his mind.

Retrieving more of the liquid gold from the bottle Allen lamented about his failing marriage and his soon to be ex. "God, I wish it was her going through this hell. Or at least some way to blame her."

That was when a spark ignited in his brain, and he retreated back to his laptop, this time with a plan, and vengeance in mind.

*

V ivid orange and apple red hued leaves were gaining the majority of the foliage in and around Cuba Lake as autumn was hitting its fever pitch. October had been a busy month for the Marshalls. Allen had been using up some paid time off hours to spend with Jared and Virginia. This was not a surprise to those he worked with, especially Frank, since they all had been insisting that he do so since his two most important people needed him.

And with his plan he wanted to leave them with as many enriching memories as possible, since he knew that the new year could not strike with him still breathing.

The stress of not being in the best health obviously affected the cancer and increased its snowballing. Roaring pain and difficulty using the men's room ravaged every waking moment that Allen had. With his final appointment with Dr. Lyman Allen was able to twist the healer's arm and wrist a prescription for some strong painkillers. These he kept hidden yet used strongly.

But this was not how he would end his reservation on earth.

Building in a steady uproar was a resentment against Julie. A pure hatred brewed in him over the fact that he was the "good" parent. He was the caring father. It was his life he sacrificed to raise their child while she floated along. Yet he was unable to enjoy the fruits of his labor over all of the upcoming future years. Jared would be fatherless, and Julie would be enjoying her life with a new lover. Free from worry.

Not unless he had something to do with it.

So, in his downtime, and when the pain had lessened a bit to concentrate, Allen had hatched a plan. One designed so far from his character that it would never be believed. One that would never be tested. One that was the perfect crime... reversed.

There was much research into hanging to end one's life, versus if there was assistance in doing so. Measuring had taken place and placed in his mental files for when it was time to perform the scenario.

Through October and into November purchases would need to be made. The correct drill bit. What type of rope would be best. But the most beautiful part was that the final factor, the piece that would assist, then confuse them all, was one that even Allen had to wait for the perfect moment to harvest.

*

"**M**om, thanks for having us over for Thanksgiving."

"No problem, Allen. You know that I prefer to host the holidays. And your butts have better be here for Christmas."

"Of course, Mom."

"Now Jared, go put those dogs away so that we can eat."

"I'll put them in my room."

"Sure, Sweetheart, just hurry up." Looking at Allen, she laughed. "That boy has always called it his room. Like he's moving in."

"Let me help you, Mom." Upon standing a terrorizing pain ripped across his lower abdomen, causing Allen to sit.

"Allen, you had better go see that doctor soon. I don't like those pains."

"It's just old man pains, Mom."

"Jared, come help me so your father can sit."

Excited, Jared came into the space to help set up their turkey day feast, all while Allen simply sat. When both of his loved ones were looking away, he slipped another opioid tablet. Begging for the pain to subside. At least for a bit.

With some energy and enacting bravery against the torture of his aches Allen wandered into the kitchen and grabbed the large carving knife and its oversized fork counterpart. This was his part of the tradition, and he made sure that he was fully present to complete such duties. With each slice he held back tears, yet showed pride and joy in this triumphant show. And gratitude to those around him.

Once the smorgasbord was laid before them, including too much food for just the trio, they all started to enjoy the meal. Allen ate in small bits, moving his food around alot and only taking small nibbles. Using all of his might he tried to prove to everyone, mostly himself, that he was keeping up with their dining pace and quantity. Yet in reality, he barely consumed an eighth of what the other two did.

Thankfully neither noticed this fact.

"So, Allen," began his mother, "has the lake iced over yet?"

This was actually something that he had been keeping a very close eye on.

"Not yet, barely a few inches have hardened. But the weather for the next few weeks looks like it is promising to get colder and thicken up. I love seeing everyone ice fish out there."

"Yea, Dad, maybe we could this year. It's been a hot minute."

"We will see, Son."

Yet this was an empty promise. Allen was focusing on

his comfort, his family, and his revenge plot for the next three weeks. Details slowly were threading together and building a perfect tapestry for his final exit.

Allen Marshall had never been a resentful, or even a mean person. During the separation he played everything fair and was proud of himself for that fact. Yet as he felt the tumor grow in him, and as the pain increased, so did this urge to get equal with the world. The desire to right the wrong he was going through. Fix the injustice that he was now nearing. And who would be the best two for a target? The woman who added more pain, and the man who decided to devastate their marriage.

However, for the time being he nibbled on his stuffing, and played the good father and son for this final holiday.

*

With a few stomps of his feet within the first yard of entering the establishment Allen had cleared his feet of any slush or snow. Glancing around he tried to get a bearing on the layout of the store for his clandestine needs.

It is quite strange to have a shopping list for a crime of this nature. Don't forget to burn it, along with any receipts or other telltale signs of his trip, he thought.

These were places he never would normally spend money at. God knows he was no handyman. Born with that skill set it was difficult for him to choose the right rope. A young salesperson with a name tag that distinguished him as "Skip" did help with finding a good deal on the drill and the right bit to use for creating holes for electrical wire through joists.

Decent details of the cover up story, but the clerk never asked at that point.

Brushing off the stock boy, Allen pressed on to find the material for the noose. At first he was being nosy with some twine. But that seemed way too weak. As he moved up to larger ones, he had to keep in mind one that would fit through the freshly drilled hole. So, with various ropes in his hands and around him the lad came again.

"What are you looking to hang?"

This startled Allen of course. But quick with his fable he answered. "Deer. In my garage. I want to drill a hole with the bit you just sold me and get some rope that will hold up a deer."

Allen and a grown deer were comparable in weight.

"Ah," the specialist then grabbed the rope in Allen's left hand. "This will do you for the size needed to hold up that monster buck this year."

"Sure, sure."

"How many feet do you need?"

This was not a question that Agent Marshall was prepared for.

"Eight feet?"

"Most men go with seven but can't go wrong with eight."

"Excellent."

Whew, lucky guess.

"How about some hunting equipment?" The youngster was eager to impress his own father, the proprietor, by adding on some extra dollars to the receipt.

"No, no. Let's just ring this up."

And with a quick cash transaction some of the wares for the dirty deed had been procured.

*

P remeditation is a peculiar word. One that has a drastic meaning in the courtroom, and one that shows evil in so many instances. But this time it was premeditated revenge on the federal agent's mind.

One final email to his doctor requested that his files be deleted and that he was not seeking his livelihood services any longer. There was an intention on Allen Marshall's request to keep his medical history hidden, only known by him at this time.

Going out to the frozen lake behind the cabin he sawed a chunk of ice from it and used the appropriate tools from the basement in order to extract it. This round was acting as a purely experimental purpose. It was nine inches by four inches. Once inside he went to the basement and stood on it. The height was perfect, and it melted in just about three hours, even in the damp basement.

The perfect disappearing stool for the upcoming event.

With care he used the previously purchased tools to drill the hole up high, so high he needed to use his step stool. Then packed it up to take it on the road. Along with the majority of the rope.

Using skills, some would say even close to espionage style, Allen was able to obtain the work schedule for Julie and her plaything. Adulterers never assume responsibility for their treason, but now she would pay no matter what.

The world will think that those hands tied the noose.

Casually pulling into the driveway of the Beebe Hill house he was delighted to see his access code for the garage door still worked. Oh, naive Julie. She thought she could always walk right over Allen sans penalty.

Not today. Slut.

Of course, that damn nosy neighbor, Gary, saw Allen. Who waved and smiled through his window like the creep that he was. Just wave and smile and you will appear innocent.

Once inside Allen opened the small bag he had brought with him, when suddenly he saw a pair of winter boots sitting in the garage. Another detail of the operation appeared in his head. Looking at the bottom of the rubber sole Allen remembered that Clayton wore a size nine. Those can and will be purchased at the hardware store in the town over.

Allen wore a size much larger. Minute details make the difference. Of course, there should be at least one set of tracks that could be traced to them. Another quick trip to see that hardware store wouldn't take too much time.

Downstairs in the ranch's basement he of course found all

of Clayton's tools and materials. What a buffoon for moving all of this in since it was clear Julie would never get the house. But whoever will be investigating my death will be led right here. No brainer.

With a smile he placed the rope on a hook that was very easy to find. Ther was even a hook for the drill bit to be hung, with a perfect piece of shaved wood still interwoven in it. Fresh from the beam in the basement of the lake house.

Nostalgia overwhelmed him as he took a moment to walk around the ranch. So many memories had been made, and so much heartbreak also. First steps by Jared walking, and all through the years up until he stepped into the living room and in on his mother and Clayton in the midst of depraved acts.

On the far end table, the ugly glass style that she picked out was her laptop. Fiddling with the wireless mouse next to it, the screen came alive. Pressing the enter key the icons appeared, and he used the cursor to choose the internet explorer.

Per Julie, no password. Stupid Cow.

Knowing that the cheating couple would be tied up at the cheese plant for a while, Allen spent his time searching for very deep, dark, and incriminating topics. Ones that he had previously surfed on his laptop, and with an intuition that this bad boy would be part of the evidence in their upcoming trial for his death, he made sure that they were even more sinister and depraved. A seasoned investigator knows best what will bring down a suspect.

After one more stroll through the home he loved for almost twenty years, he then went out and fired up his truck. Soaring away from the property and grinning. This was a clean break for both Marshall men in Allen's eyes.

*

Very few people wake up knowing that today is the day that they will die. Instead, the ending date of one's story is hidden until a majority of the final chapter has already been printed. Yet some set their own demise. Their own finale.

Men on death row, or ones who take their lives, but few wake up knowing that they would not be returning to bed due to spite, and due to resentment. But Allen Marshall was one of them.

The curious aspect of said resentment is also a peculiar one. One that many would say was a waste of time. Resentments are like drinking poison and wanting the other person to die from it. Although this will be the same analogy, hopefully with an execution poison cocktail served straight up and into an artery.

The key to a perfect vengeful masterpiece happening was also to ensure that nothing was out of place that day. Therefore, his plans would not be foiled. In the morning, he made Jared the perfect breakfast, and luckily the boy had time to eat it. Savoring the moment, Allen watched his offspring take every bite. A usual hug and kiss followed. Then his son, his pride and joy, ventured off to school, very excited for the his that night.

There was a sadness that he had to pick this day, of all dates on the calendar, for his mission. Being an active father he loved watching his son perform and thrive. But to really make hurt he had chosen Julie's birthday on purpose, so she really would feel the impact.

Running into work Allen made sure nothing was suspicious. Reviewing cases and discussing future actions on potential suspects.

Of course he received more emails from that crazy Swartson guy.

Delete. Delete. Delete. Can't have any other suspects other than Julie and Clayton floating around.

Cutting out midafternoon for the day he gave Frank a hearty handshake and smile. The guy really wasn't that bad. Hopefully he will mentor Jared a bit during everything that was about to come. It will be a tough trial. Allen knew that being a federal policer that his "murder" would be prosecuted to the fullest extent.

AKA a final requested meal and a little shot in the arm for both. Hopefully their food is served cold, just like how he was serving ultimate revenge on them.

Next was the toughest trip. But as he crested over the small knob off of Wolf Creek Road his tires roughed through the snow, and the damn dogs surrounded his truck. Great protection for his mother, horrible companions for anyone who was neither her nor Jared. But at least they will keep her safe when he is done with the day's mission.

Opening the door, he saw his mother at her favorite recliner, her soap operas were blaring and she was nodding along with the storyline.

"Mother!"

Jolted, she turned. "What on Earth are you doing, Allen?"

"Oh, got out early. Thought I would swing through."

"That's good. It is supposed to storm something wicked tonight, will you record Jared's concert for me?" This request was made as she was steadfast with her drama watching. "Oh, I made your favorite linguine in red sauce. There's a container of it on the countertop for you." The upcoming absence disappointed Allen, but he had to keep the day normal, so no waterworks or emotions to be dispensed from him in front of anyone. But now he knew what his final meal would be. One of his treasured favorites.

"Of course, Ma. I will head out then."

"Okay. Talk to you later."

"Love you."

Outside he realized she had not expressed her love for him, yet he knew that it was there. And strong. And he knew that she knew his adoration for her.

Once he was home came the tough work. Squeezing into those size nine boots was tough for Allen. But walking around in them was fine for a small time to make a dual set. Then taking that broom to make the second set of tracks in the snow confusing to identify clearly was a total brainstorm that he had used from watching a forensics show on television in preparation.

Allen was a total mastermind in respect to this morbid occurrence.

This was when he took a break and savored every morsel of his mother's cooking. Times of the past shuffled through his mind. A stern realization smoldered in his mind about how his life was superior to most. And he ached that this was how it had to be.

Slowly he crept onto the frozen waterscape that he had adored since he was a child. Using some adrenaline he had pulled the tools to cut a small opening into the ice in order to get the key ingredient to his clandestine recipe.

The technical pieces needed to extract it were on the hand cart, and he was careful not to slip and fall. That would be ironic, but there was too much resentment to let his former spouse off without some retribution. And firing up the rusted chainsaw made him feel like a man again. A true country fellow and close to his roots. There was guilt that he had brushed Jared off for ice fishing this year, but he did not want to add suspicion to the lake itself being intertwined in this event. In the back of his mind, he hoped that no one would connect the dots of the procedure with his demise. But there had to be some risk in the battle for the reward to be worth it.

Sizing up the right chunk he allowed the remaining pieces to fall into the frigid water. Then he hauled everything back and placed the evidence in the far back room of the cellar. Nothing could be amiss.

Upstairs in his bathroom while staring at the mirror he was thinking of ways to make it more like an attack. A shiner would do, he thought.

Using all of the rage, and drawing power from his hatred for Julie and Cayton, he pulled the heavy, century old wood door of the powder room backwards, then swung it forward, making damn sure that it struck his upper cheekbone. Using the rage he had felt for almost a year that his life was being shortened he would extend his arm with the door nestled in his palm then slam it against his face with every bit of his being. The disgust that he would never see his boy have his own boy. Fury that he was dealt half a hand instead of the full deck he was promised when he took his first breath.

A swing and hit. A swing and hit.

Fuck you, cruel world.

With a final crack of the wood on bone he felt his face pulsate with pain. Success. Much satisfaction came from this self-bullying. There was already proof of the broken blood vessels. Quickly he glanced in the mirror and saw his skin start to darken, and the sign of an attack to appear.

A black eye is very incriminating.

Carefully he was going through his mental checklist over and over again. The boots were dried and then thrown in the fireplace. Minimal evidence was key. With parts of the remaining rope from what he had planted he made loops around his wrists, as if he had cuff restraints. Rubbing furiously, he made sure he had reddened the areas and left plenty of DNA. That was when he dropped them by the back door.

Murderers always make mistakes, right?

Using a larger piece, he rubbed it again and again roughly around his neck, leaving marks as if he had been in that struggle. From there he went downstairs and tied a perfect noose. For this he did use a step ladder that he brought back upstairs and into the attic, making sure it was far from any discovery when investigated upon.

Any remnants of that rope he threw into the fireplace also. Along with that he tossed every single document in relation to his medical issues. Along with that he tossed the hard drive from his laptop. There was no way he wanted any of his internet searches to be found. The week before he bought a new mainframe and inserted it into the skeleton of the old.

This plan was to be flawless.

Once the items that he needed destroyed were lining the bottom of the fireplace, he placed two dozen or so logs on top of them. More than he normally would ration for a typical winter's night. Intertwining papers and kindling wood he ensured that the fire would be massive and consuming.

A bit of lighter fluid had been added in the various layers for the utmost success. And with a toss of a simple wooden match the pile was consumed with a fiery rage.

While waiting to ensure its ability to become simply ashes at the end, Allen sent a simple work-related text to Frank. This was to set the timeline for his death.

This overall malicious act was one in which Allen revealed the pleasure of it being airtight. Maybe his "slaughter" will be on a forensics television show?

Sadly, in the kitchen he smashed the beloved candy dish from wonderful Aunt Charlotte. Allen knew they would not be ending up in the same afterlife due to his sins, yet he was sorry for this act. Ironically, he was feeling more guilt for the destroyed heirloom than what he was doing to two truly innocent people.

This was not an eye for an eye, it was an eye for a life.

Unclipping his hip holster, he slid his handgun under the china cabinet, then disheveled the chairs and table for the dinette. Resting at the top of the staircase was another block of ice, the same size as the test sample he used to gauge the time for it to melt.

Picking it up it felt heavier than its eight pounds. There was a permanent weight to it. A finality by using it. A permanence that he knew he could not undo once the act was over. But mustering up his strength, he walked down those wooden steps one final time.

Placing the block so that the long end, which measured nine inches, was upright, he stepped on it and used his arms to secure the noose around his head. Wanting the disappearing step to be far away in case he was found earlier than it could dissolve, Allen put his tip toes on the edge and curled them over the edge. Squinting, his eyes he said a prayer for his family. And remembered why he was doing this.

Feeling the frozen texture through his socks he then pushed the ice block backwards with all of his might. This propelled it as if it was a football beingpunted, soaring about four inches off of the ground until it hit the wall behind them, a few chunks did break off even, and the parts sliding to rest against the foundation. Melting away and perfectly hidden from the pending investigation.

When his weight fell, and gravity did its job, he felt the snap of his neck, and an unreal sensation of floating, yet falling at the same time.

As his breaths were starting to wheeze, he could no longer feel his appendages. And slowly his mind was simply replaying a scrapbook of memories, ones long forgotten. Yet intertwined with his life, and those that were now going to be without him. For he had performed a deception with precision.

III

A dated buzzer rang, shocking the one who pressed the initial bell asking for entry, announcing that the cold, sterile door was temporarily unlocked, and the visiting trio could enter the first access point of the massive institute. Two of these souls had been through this process before, while the other was quite used to such endeavors, yet never had explored this option. Once inside the establishment they proceeded to the greeter. This was a middle-aged man who allowed their admittance who had a tightly shaved head with a bulky build and dressed in a basic light gray uniform. A badge adorned the left side portion of his chest directly over his heart. Due to desk duty, he was not in the best form, which was fine for him. Enjoying the government pension in ten years after dedicating the previous twenty was his motivation for said line of work.

"We are here to see Superintendent Hacket."

The jailer before them assigned to the task looked up and nodded. "Name."

"Joseph Stevvins, and company would work." Looking back at the others he grinned at his name for the gang. "He knows that we are coming."

"Of course, and I need identification from all three, plus a quick trip through security and the metal detectors."

"Michael and I have been here, so we know the process." Glancing at the newest addition, the lawyer smiled. "Have you been to this facility?"

"Nah, but others like it I have. Part of my niche field."

Since the trial lives had been altered in many ways for the various participants. Joseph Stevvins became a higher end defense attorney that worked throughout the state and on many other murder cases. Even though he had not won this exact ordeal, there was a decent amount of respect for him in the legal community due to the work he had done and aspects he had explored. Any current work for Julie and Clayton was pro-bono since he had made money hand over fist since then, and it was the least he could do to thank the couple that launched his career into overdrive.

As the lower ranking officer called for the highest ranking one at the Terre Haute Federal Detainment Center, the three visitors from New York started their processing to ensure that they would not be breaching the Indiana prison with any contraband. Nerves were not in the atmosphere that day since it was not a stressful meeting. Yet much had to be discussed pertaining to potential freedom.

After the mandatory inspection was finished, and as the gentlemen were re-buckling belts and putting their shoes back on, they were instructed to go down the hallway to their left and knock on door 107. The head guard was waiting for them.

Once they had followed the orders, and entered the office as instructed, they all took random seats in random cushioned chairs, but just for a moment. This was not their final destination for the appointment there. Just a minor pit stop for a stern warning.

"Gentleman," initiated Nathan Hacket, Superintendent of

said facility. "I want to emphasize that this larger size of a meeting is rare. And this will be a one time, and done, occasion." While seated his hands and forearms danced along with the stoic and strict words he was speaking. "I believe that every inmate has a right to due process, and for fairness to be abundant. Especially being a death penalty case. And this one being so far down the process that the Judicial Department will be calling to set their dates to meet the Lord anytime soon. There is no denying that fact."

Being the orchestrator of the conference Joseph Stevvins replied. "I appreciate the flexibility, along with everyone here, and my clients. We have a Hail Mary here, and we have to try for it."

"There will be correction officers stationed outside of the door. I expect no suspicious behavior. No touching, hugging," for this he looked at Michael specifically, "and so on. You will be on closed circuit cameras. They are not sound enabled, and only used for an emergency, as if the inmates start an issue. I do respect that both inmates have only a few blemishes on their records, however, we give very little wiggle on such visits."

The solicitor nodded, "I respect that."

Standing up and adjusting his suit, the host initiated their movement down the hallway. As described, there were two guards outside. Entering the room, they saw one final cop watching Clayton and Julie, who were both handcuffed and tethered to the table, which was affixed to the cold, barren cement floor.

As the three walked in, Joseph inquired, "Anyway that they can be uncuffed."

"No," stated Hacket, "but thanks for asking." With that blunt response he closed the door.

The free persons sat and smiled. The convicts had been slightly chatting amongst themselves. It was rare that they had seen each other during their time in the federal penitentiary. Being opposite sexes, and co-defendants, they were not permitted much time together. There was also a loss in their vigor and love for each other. What started as a fun love affair was now a life or death fight, so simple flirting, or affection, was long buried and forgotten.

Each of the detained had aged tremendously during their seven years since the trial. Crows' feet etched and bore themselves around Julie's eyes. There was a sadness and despair that sunk into her irises, and an extra forty pounds that encased her thighs and love handles. This was from a carb high and sugar-intense diet, with very little nutritional value. Plus, the additional commissary junk food that Michael had been funding added to the poor diet. Feeling desperate to find any way possible in order to uplift their spirits, the kind surrogate son always made sure both had plenty of money on their canteen accounts for such treats.

The same for Clayton had occurred. The once skinny factory worker had a defined pouch for a stomach. Gray had invaded his hair, just as it had done to Julie. Their salt and pepper combos were now just aged and frizzled messes. There was no sense to take care of it anymore for either one of the incarcerated attendees.

Sleep was also negatively affected during their stay. Being a killer of a federal agent, a true low man in the judicial totem pole, the guards in general were not fans of theirs. During midnight rounds it was nothing for a patroller to bang their industrial style flashlight on the bars of their cell. Wakening them and adding more agony to their sentences.

Overall, there was a strong sentiment of exhaustion, in physical and emotional facets for both. They knew of their innocence, and the profound truth of it. While this was a bad dream that kept repeating itself over and over. Their screams were muffled by a tale of murder, that they were not parties to. Yet their lives, and their will, became suffocated. Even they were unsure of what caused the demise of Allen Marshall, yet they were the true victims of the calamity and its impaling aftermath.

Clearing his throat, Joseph started the session. "Clayton,

Julie. I know it has been a while since we met."

Nodding, Clayton confirmed this in his country style voice. "Yeah, about a year."

"That is correct," started the lawyer, "the last time that we all sat down was when The Supreme Court finished reviewing our case thoroughly," his eyes dropped in shame, "and had decided to pass on changing the ruling."

Sighing, Julie shed a tear of defeat. "Is this the investigator that you hired, Michael?"

The implicated guest smiled. "Yes, I am Patrick Foreman."

Slightly rising, the tall gentleman, with deep toned skin, the shade of hot asphalt, then bent to shake the shackled hands of Julie and Clayton, and lastly he politely resumed his seat. Wearing an impressive suit, fitted and tailored perfectly, he had a sense of professionalism, yet a bit of charm to him. Around thirty-eight years old he exuded experience in this section of law yet was at the right age to dive deep into a case. "I am an investigator for various attorneys, and also some prosecutors."

Clayton stared directly at Michael for a moment who shrugged in response. The ever-devoted son had taken another mortgage on his Olean home in order to pay for such services. To him, this was nothing if it meant saving his father from the grisly sentence handed down previously.

"Now, Julie, Clayton, I am going to be honest. And I need you to be also. So that I am not wasting my time and resources. There are two ways to go down this path, and I will give my extreme vigor in both."

A perfect pause allowed this statement to sink into all those around.

"And what your answer is will not change that I will dig into this, but it will determine which path." While discussing options his hands were unclenched, yet his fingers stiff like a karate chop. They accented his words and enhanced his opening spiel to his new clients. "If you are truly innocent, then I will deconstruct the prosecution's case. And if you are guilty, I will find any single strand of a technicality to get the initial verdict overturned. Either way, you get one hundred and fifty percent of my attention and devotion." After a strategic inhale he concluded his spiel. "Am I clear?"

"Yes," rang in unison from both of the involved. Then Clayton took over. "We are innocent. I do not know how this all happened, but evidence was planted. Someone put the blame on us."

"One hundred percent?" The interrogator stared deep at both.

"Absolutely." Clayton pounded his tethered wrist on the tabletop. "We are innocent. Get us the hell out of here."

*

Shaggy patches of grass with a lush feel were deflecting the rays of sunshine and giving contrasting shade to their counterparts. The blades were allowing the reflection of illumination to change their hues and added a wonderful aspect to such a simple expanse. There was a maturity to the terrain in respect to the foliage that it entailed. The smell of midsummer flora rang through the Enchanted Mountains and enriched everyone's senses.

Sitting in her yard was Virginia Marshall with a small toddler on her knee, bouncing him up and down in varied tempos and heights. There was joy in the heat, and pleasure with how nice the day was going.

Feeling a bit of energy, she sat the youngster on the turf and let him crawl a bit, yet was carefully overseeing every movement, like any loving great-grandmother, or caretaker, would. Rotating from on his stomach to sitting up, he was in a playful mood. Coos were plentiful along with smiles. A floppy fabric hat in faint blue with some yellow flecks shaped like little duckies kept him cool, and free from a sunburn.

The sound of tires grinding on the gravel and ascending from Wolf Creek Road caused them both to look, and to simultaneously grin.

"Look at that little man. Your father is home from work."

Once parked by his indigo colored cedar shingled bungalow home Jared hopped out of his bright fire engine red SUV and walked over to the duo. Wind was blowing his paisley tie in a few directions with an agreeing breeze that added more rich aromas coming from the forest on that August day.

"Hi ya, Gram, was Allen good for you?"

"Of course."

"Is Austin awake yet?"

"I doubt it. Those damn overnights at the hospital."

With a smooth maneuver Jared snagged his son then adjusted his pose. From there he stood at an angle, his hip as an impromptu seat for his offspring. "It is better this way. I am guessing you didn't walk down to get the paper from the box?"

"Not yet." There was a startled essence to her voice, and she looked perplexed. With this she sat back into one of the two rustic Adirondack chairs painted in a peach color that were situated nicely for relaxing and enjoying their communal side yard. With the child in tow, Jared did the same.

"The front page of the paper is about how Julie and Clayton somehow have a new investigator working for them to try and get them out." Sighing, he shook his head. "Probably that damn Michael spending every penny he can trying to push a round peg in a square hole and living in a constant state of insanity, and delusion."

Holding back tears Virginia shook her head. "I am shocked that they didn't call one of us for a statement or something. Pretty one sided if you ask me."

"I imagine that the wanna-be detective will swing through at some point. But even with the appeals and the case being looked at a few times, and no one changing their mind, I doubt that this guy will do anything."

"I know it. I just can't wait until they finally do them in for all of this."

"Seems like in the past seven years everyone else involved ended up better off than us."

Huffing loudly his grandmother was quick to correct her heir. "Jared, you need to be grateful for what you have done since then. Your father is looking down from above and is so, so proud of you." With her wrinkled and pale fingers, she squeezed the chubby cheek of the youngest of the trio. "You finished college way ahead of schedule, then got your Master's degree."

"I know."

"Starting with the county agriculture department, and someday you will be right there where he was with the USDA."

Nodding, he agreed.

"Plus starting your family. Happily married."

"Yeah, and sadly that only happened because of all the money that I received between the life insurance and selling the Beebe Hill house."

"We both would become poor people for one more day with him, but sadly my boy, that is how the cookie has crumbled for us. But you have so much to be grateful for. Your father did provide for you in many ways without him knowing his fate."

The side door to the newer of the two homes opened and Jared smiled in that direction. "Did you get enough sleep, Babe?"

Walking up to the three who were relaxing, Jared's lover spoke. "Plenty, and Gramma Virginia, thanks for watching him so that I could do so."

The new addition with loosely curled medium brown colored hair, a stunning jawline, and radiant green eyes kissed Jared's cheek, then tousled the little bit of hair that their kid had.

*

A neurotic Michael sat in a random booth halfway through the dining expanse, its padding covered in a forest green shade vinyl. The structure of the seating arrangement was a highly glossed maple and hand crafted. There was a semi-formal ambiance at this popular restaurant, yet the booth made it feel cozy.

With so much going on his mind was racing, and

there was a decent bit of fidgeting and restlessness happening. Overall, Michael's nerves were a complete mess, even though it was unnecessary. Especially when there should not have been any such emotions at this specific occasion. Since he was the one who hired the private investigator and was cutting the checks meant that he was somewhat in control. But rather than being distraught over this preliminary encounter, he was more petrified as to if the work he was paying for would truly be a waste of many resources.

Finally, a hostess led the stranger to town and used her open hand to direct Patrick Foreman to where Michael McBride was anxiously waiting.

Nodding, the sleuth sat down and smiled. "This is quite the joint."

"The Weck and Keg is an Olean staple. Best Beef on Wecks in the world."

"I had to google them, and I happen to be a fan of beef. So, I am game. Just get me what you plan on ordering." A wise grain appeared, his bright white teeth showing. "Especially since you are paying, Boss."

Both laughed as the waitress approached. "Are you boys ready?"

Michael jolted his head a few times. "Two Olean Tier IPAs, and two Beef on Weck Platters."

"For both?"

"Yes."

"And sides?"

"Fries with gravy and some potato salad."

"German or American?"

"American."

"Coming right up."

Trying to ease into everything the newbie began with small talk. "I see that they have guys slicing the beef?" Another smile. "In bow ties?"

"That's the thing here. Good prices, amazing food. And an unbeatable atmosphere."

"True."

With ease the server dropped off the beers, and Michael took a hefty draw of his. "I read the article in the paper today."

"Good, good." Rubbing his hands together he was confident that his impromptu boss would like that move. "I always want to get the area involved and have the portrait painted that they are innocent."

"Which they are."

"I believe it, but does the area? Are they all split?"

I will be honest; it is not even close to being fifty-fifty. Most of the people in the area think that they did it. And because of that my life has been hell. I am lucky to have kept my job at the cheese plant even. Everyone sees them as monsters."

Patrick took a swig of his ale. "I got that from the reporter."

"Now I am not complaining, but you didn't interview the Marshalls. You got information to pass along from Julie and my dad. And me of course. But left out the detectives, prosecutor, and some others."

"See," leaning in, he explained, "there will be a second part in a few weeks once I speak with them. Because they will want their version of events to be covered since they are feeling it is one sided." Tapping the tip of his index finger to his temple he pressed on. "This is a mind game. And when they feel pressure, they will give up information that will help us. It worked with a case in Philadelphia a few years back for me. That did end up with a new trial. They lost it, but I did my part."

Various chortles erupted between them and helped to calm Michael down quite a bit.

"However, after this much time, and how severe the punishment is, a lot of new witnesses will come out of the woodwork."

"I saw that you included an email address."

"Exactly. Never a phone number." With confidence he performed a small chopping motion with his hand to emphasize the fact that he cuts out the needless battering while working a case. "Because then I would be bombarded with hate calls, instead of just hate emails that I can simply delete."

More subtle laughter ensued, helping the mood.

"For right now Patrick I have you booked and paid for two weeks."

"That should be fine. If I need more time, I will let you know. But I won't drag my feet and eat up your money. You are a working man, trying to save your father and Julie. Not a millionaire."

"I appreciate that."

Noticing their deep conversation the waitress dropped the platters of beef on wicks, and while she was there the head of the table ordered another round of local brewskis. Which the guest approved, since he enjoyed the first one.

Between bites Michael asked, "What can you tell me how you go about with this process?"

"I am going to track down as much information about Allen Marshall as possible. After reading through the casefile I received quite thoroughly, I have plenty of questions."

"Oh?"

"This guy seemed legit. And was handling the divorce well. No known enemies. Nothing stolen, and not even staged as a robbery."

Pointing a gravy covered fry at his counterpart Michael made his comment. "Even my dad never really said nasty things about him. All that he and Julie just wanted was to start their lives together."

"So, what is your theory then?"

Quickly eating the saucy tater treat he shrugged.

"Honestly, I don't know. It could've been suicide. But no note. No way to stand and get into the noose. Nothing around to help him." Shaking his head, he looked down at his sandwich. "What is your theory?"

"I think Allen staged it. But I don't know how, or why. But if he did, I will get to the bottom of it."

*

Six brown official manilla envelopes entered the postal service's logistics system and found their way to six different recipients. Each contained a duplicate of an official document of utmost importance. They were overwhelming and nerve racking, to say the very least.

"Mail call," yelled the corrections officer. Completely bald, and with much extra weight, he resembled a bowling pin. His pale skin was a shade or two off of one. Walking along the cellblock he fed the first of said thin parcels into Julie Marshall's cell, bending it to make its entrance through the steel beams.

Same guard went to the male's side and did the same action with Clayton McBride.

A small mail truck roared up the driveway of the Marshalls' small compound and another copy was signed off by Virgnia, since Jared wasn't around. There was unease from her since anything could be sealed inside.

One of Joseph Stevvins' paralegals let the mailman have her John Hancock and she quickly opened it, even if he was the addressee, since she oversaw all of his legal matters for all of his cases.

Michael McBride was trying to unwind with his own toddler and Piper in their living room when that postman gave a hard knock on their door, and also needed his name in ink to verify a successful delivery.

Senator Jackson Steele had one of his aides handy to sign for his version at his office in Washington D.C.

Now Jackson occasionally received mail from the President. So, this was no big deal. However, for everyone else copied in on this mailing it was a once in a lifetime opportunity. Especially when the leader of the free world signed off on a Death Warrant.

*

R   ubbing the upper portion of his partner's back, Austin Sunn-Marshall was not sure of what to say to Jared. They had met during college and just knew instantly that they were a match. Eventually Jared enlightened his new love of the family drama that was broadcast throughout the country as a televised event. Austin remembered the coverage but was not an expert on it. And being such a deep wound, it was a subject that they never really discussed. Therefore, consoling his husband was not easy for him, but he was trying his very best.

Virginia remained stoic while sitting with them in their dining room, her pride and joy vivaciously smiling while bouncing on her knee. Being in the autumn of her life, she was unsure if she would ever see the execution of her utmost hated enemies. There was a fear that she would never see justice served. That life would cease for her before it would for those heathens. Now that it would happen in Terre Haute, Indiana for both of them, she was a bit torn, yet steadfast on seeing them both inhale one final time.

The government was having a double header and taking care of business one hour apart from each other. Clayton first, and then Julie afterwards.

Ironically, ladies last.

As for Jared, there was an angst in him. There was no doubt that he and Virginia were making the trip. In those years since Julie had written to Jared on a regular basis, yet the words only maintained her innocence. Not to say she was sorry. And that irked him. After a few letters he knew the rest would tell the same lies so he would clump them together and send them back to her in that prison hell.

This was compounded on the failed attempt that she did rearing him. The hurt she kept placing on his chest like cement blocks, one at a time until the anxiety and pressure made him feel stifled and breathless.

With overwhelming impulsivity, he jumped up and went

into his office of their home where he began ruffling through the drawers of his desk. Pushing documents and junk aside, looking for the one business card he had held in storage with him since the trial.

Dialing quickly, he heard what he wanted to hear oh so badly. "Captain Wingard speaking."

"Hey, it's Jared Marshall."

"Jared Marshall! Are you calling to get out of another ticket."

"No, no," the joke went over his head due to the circumstances. "Did you see the article about some private investigator trying to help Julie and Clayton."

"I have read it. Gotta love how they never called any of us for the facts."

"Well, they will now. I just got a copy of the Death Warrant for both of them. Thirty days from yesterday."

A deep exhale from the trooper was his reaction. Due to his stellar work on that case he was promoted twice since the trial. Being the head copper in the region for the state troopers meant a lot more stress, yet more satisfaction in his work.

"I bet that will speed up this Foreman guy. Let me know if he calls you, and I will do the same, okay?"

"Okay."

A nanosecond before Jared was about to hit the red button to end the call, Cecil's voice made him pause. "And call me more often when you don't need a favor, okay Kid?"

"You got it."

*

His elbow, encased in a stelar jet black suit, pushed the door to the suites of offices in the Capitol building that was his political expanse. The small crew of aides and secretaries that helped Senator Jackson Steele were working in their own worlds while passing one another. Disconnecting the call from a fellow public servant, Jackson smiled at his head aide.

"Tabatha, good afternoon."

"Afternoon Senator. I just read this over, and it might be out of place, but there is a Death Warrant from Indiana that was sent certified mail. The president signed it and everything."

Freezing his mind raced to the possibilities. Then it hit him. With grace he received it from said helper and smiled. "The case that got me national attention back in Buffalo. I guess that they are serving paperwork for everyone involved."

Nodding, he then went into his private space and closed the door, signaling that he did not want to be disrupted. There he read it over and decided to conduct an internet search to see what was new in the case. With this query he found the news story from the small city about Patrick Foreman and his fight to get justice for the doomed couple.

Reading it over he rolled his eyes and laughed a bit. There was some mention of his prosecution of the case, and it was respectful and stated that no technicalities from either side could be brought forward and create an appeal. The former lawyer and now politician was impressed that the PI had such dignity and did not push others under the murky water just to make him look good.

Shrugging, he looked at his day planner on his smartphone and was deciding if it was worth it to take the trip out west to complete what he had started just over half a decade before. There were a few meetings that could be adjusted for other times. And he did owe the Marshalls quite a bit since they were steadfast in campaigning for him. They were proud to participate in all of the stereotypical marketing platforms for him. Handing out buttons and being an advocate. Jared even spoke at local colleges and helped enlist new voters to cast their ballot for Jackson.

And this was his landmark case after all. Law school pupils were studying it even and writing papers on its validity and stamina. Solid, well prosecuted, and fairly earned as a win for the people, in his semi-biased opinion.

*

A soft knock was followed by a timid voice. "Mister Stevvins."

With a slight irritation the solicitor looked up. "Yes, Catrina."

"Are you in a good mood?"

Annoyed, he took off his glasses and let them drop on the table, then squeezed the bridge of his nose. "What is it? Do you need to take the day off or something?"

"No, Sir." The secretary in a short black pencil skirt, an ivory hued sports jacket with large shoulder pads and in glossy ebony high heels walked to his desk. "The Death Warrants for McBride and Marshall were just sent, certified mail even." Her voice was soft, high pitched, and had a minor squeak to it. "I've never seen the president's signature before."

Showing irritation and defeat, the lawyer slapped his desk blotter. "Shit. I don't have to be in court today, correct."

"No, Sir."

"Then move whatever I do have on the schedule off for a few days. Michael McBride will be coming in any minute now since he probably received his copy. Lord knows he won't take no for an answer. And he will have Foreman by the ear dragging him in too."

"Okay, Sir." As she was about to leave the boss also informed her. "Only forward his calls, if he indeed takes the time to do that. If not, and he suddenly appears, just send him directly back."

When she closed the door, he sighed.

There was a sense of gratitude that the attorney had for this couple and that exact case. Having national coverage his career soared from being an ambulance chaser in a tiny town, to becoming a respected criminal defense member of the bar. However, with this new line of defendants, one thing about this trial stood out. And this was that he truly believed that they were innocent.

Sure, he had wins where there was a technicality that dropped the state to their knees, or simply not enough evidence for the jury to find whatever suspect guilty. And they would walk free. While Joseph knew that they had indeed done it. Sometimes even having the whole crime laid out for him in order to have the best strategy.

There were days when he did feel guilty for those wins.

When it came to this case, the one with the most national coverage and so much exposure that he still has to turn down clients, there still was a pit in his stomach that something did not align right. That maybe they did not do it after all.

*

A s the first standing domino had fallen, others began to do so in the wave of motion with the announcement of the pending executions.

After a few moments of contemplation Cecil Wingard reached out to the Buffalo branch of the FBI. The number luckily saved in his phone.

"Special Agent in Charge Morris, please."

"Please hold, Sir."

"SAC Morris speaking."

"You have to be all formal to me, Jake?"

"Well, if it isn't my favorite Trooper. Are you calling about the Marshall case, and that PI who wants to reopen it all."

"Yes and no." There was a muffled laugh. "Get this. Everyone involved got a certified copy of the Death Warrant this morning. Signed off in the Oval Office yesterday."

"Well, I will be. I heard that Stevvins doesn't charge them anymore since after their convictions somehow he became an overnight success."

Laughing, the Southern Tier local spilled some tea before getting back to business. "Stevvins bought himself a nice house with an inground pool over on Circle Oak Drive in Allegany."

"You are speaking a bit of Greek to me, Amigo."

"Imagine Amherst, but down here." With feeling the small talk had died Cecil pressed on. "Well, I wanted to give you guys the heads up. I am sure that you still have all of the evidence."

"We keep it until the suspects are cold and deep in the ground."

"If this Foreman guy wants to interrogate us, or peek at the evidence, I am fine with it as long as he is supervised by us. That way he can see how cut and dry it all was."

"Sounds good. How did you find out?"

"Jared gave me a call. Kid touches base whenever he gets a ticket."

Both laughed.

"Well Captain Wingard, let's see what this city slicker is trying to do to our case."

*

Patrick Foreman has a certain process that he traverses in any case that he picks up. There is a thorough process of researching paperwork and records, along with police reports and other documented details. While the internet contains much of this, however, he has spent nights in the library basement on various endeavors while he worked on cracking cold cases.

With a solid decade in the field, give or take a season, there is a precision that he has finessed and developed, along with a steadfast work ethic that he has incorporated, no matter the severity of the file at hand. There is a slight discrimination that he will engage when selecting his next investigation. They do vary from finding a loved one, following a philandering spouse, or even tracking down stolen items. The variety keeps him invigorated. And this is not his only query into a situation where the death penalty was in the equation. Three other such opportunities presented themselves where he was able to take on the role of the sleuth, and did get a stay of execution for one person. The others, well, it was a losing battle when they were guilty as hell, and Patrick was the Hail Mary with a deflated pigskin.

Although this case was vastly different in his eyes. Even meeting the accused he could tell that they felt the world had turned on them. Plus, speaking with Michael really ensured that it was a wrong place in their lives at the wrong time to him. So at least there was some hope and expectation to uncover some truths that were deep in hiding.

In his hotel room the truth seeker had one bed for his own use, and another covered in paperwork, along with the built-in desk and along the top of his dresser. These had police reports, warrants, background information on everyone involved, along with the death certificate and other needed relevant documentation. Uncensored and raw pictures of the scene were also placed about from the scene and the medical examiner's autopsy. Multi-colored sticky notes were attached on various sheets of paper with notes jotted down. With a jet-black marker and vibrant yellow highlighter in his right hand he was steadily working when a pounding startled him and brought him back into the world.

"No service today," he replied to the raps on the door. There was an assumption on his behalf that this was a chambermaid.

"It's Michael. Open up."

Sighing, the host of the room did so, but was blunt with his answering, and set a boundary with his temporary boss. "I need you to contact me first before just appearing. I am working on a lot right now."

Unphased, the surprise guest pushed through, the brown official envelope in his hands against his stomach. "I sent you a text message."

"Which I have not checked because I was focusing on the case. You get my undivided attention for the next two weeks."

"We have a problem."

"Your check already cleared, so I do not see one."

His face becoming mangled due to tears wanting to explode from his eyes, the guest handed over the file, recently signed by the head of the free world.

Puzzled, the contracted detective opened it.

Then a steady pause ensued allowing the depth of the situation to sink in, and to allow Michael to regain his composure.

"I can see the reasoning behind your mania," announced Patrick.

"We should go see Stevvins. Maybe he can conjuncture something."

"The word is injunction, but I doubt that they will at this point without any new information to present."

"Let's go anyway."

Handing back the paper the informal detective cut to the point. "The best work that I can do is not get tied up in something that I cannot control."

"Well, well..."

"Well, well, and run to him if you want. But I am trying to save your father, and the woman he loves, from a federally mandated deep sleep."

"I guess that I will just go and see him by myself."

"That works for us all then. And when I am ready to, I will properly update you."

At the door Michael turned back, "So later today."

As he closed the door Patrick announced, "I never said today."

Alone again he went back to his painstaking task of evaluating all of the raw data before him. There was a legal pad with a light-yellow hue to its paper that was being utilized to help organize and keep memos about parts that he wanted to explore deeper.

An hour of pure, sweet silence had passed with a concentrated examination on the gumshoe's mind while meandering through various points of evidence when he finally muttered, "There is no way in hell that those two did this."

*

Even though they were far apart in the penitentiary they were moving as if they were one soul deep in agony. Pacing back and forth in their single person cells, their hands mangling and grabbing their palms, fretting over the fact that their lives were now like milk. Stamped with an expiration date.

This was not how it was supposed to be. Not at all for the two lovers who just needed some change in their lives. Clayton had been long widowed from his wife, so he was prime for starting anew. And at first, he did respect the Marshalls' sacred vows. However, there was an undeniable spark between them and their passion grew as they were working together. Chemistry, one that she never had with Allen, started to stew and grow.

Excitement was at the commencement of their taboo tango. Keeping it on the downlow from their job and also Jared and Allen had an element of spunk and espionage. As if they were two teenagers kindling love and afraid of their parents finding out.

There was a slight amount of guilt on Julie's behalf, yet not enough to cause this to cease. Her marriage had died the day that Jared was born since Allen became a helicopter parent and forgot about his wife.

Long before this decimation of their nuptials due to her risqué passion had Julie thrown in the towel. Realizing that she played second fiddle to both of them was enough for her after a few years. Many instances she had tried and tried to maneuver balance and a healthy core to their home, yet time after time the two males of the household kept circling back and leaving Julie out of the mix.

Enough was enough when finally she was moved to the front seat and out of the trunk. A man who wanted her to feel loved and special had appeared. A man who could say no to a child, and still have a relationship with his son. Who respected her more than her own child and supposed life partner.

And somehow that all was pulled away, on her birthday of all days, and thrown into a hell, where she was not the sinner. Yet she was cursed to burn.

*

A hoagie from a little deli Joseph loved was strewn on the left portion of his expansive desk. Creme soda in a brown plastic bottle and some chips were dispersed with napkins under. A large one was tucked into his collar and over his dress shirt to keep it somewhat pristine. If he had known that the afternoon would take such a turn, he would have dressed more casual. But such is life.

A few days prior he had given a carbon copy of his file for the McBride/Marshall trial to Patrick Foreman, and due to the turn of events he had pulled the hardcopy and was reviewing it just in case he needed to recall anything pertinent.

As a few crumbs dropped off of his chin from said thinly sliced fried taters a very distraught Michael McBride stormed through and into his office. Everyone was betting on when he would come, and they just let him barge through since taming him was not a possible option.

But if your father was going to be executed for a crime he did not commit, wouldn't you also be a bit motivated.

"Hi, Michael."

"I guess that you received the Death Warrants."

"I did. I was expecting you."

"Can we call in a juxtaposition?"

"I am assuming you mean an injunction. And not right now, unless we have new evidence proving their innocence."

"I only have Patrick Foreman for just under two weeks to do that. And then I don't know." Anxiety riddled his voice and shook his body.

"Listen Michael." the host sighed and smiled, "I have decided to foot the bill for him for two more weeks if we feel that there is some new evidence that could sway the judges."

Realizing that he had been standing and straining himself in a subconscious attempt to over exaggerate the circumstances, the guest sat and sighed. "So, we just have to pray that he will find something."

Shrugging, the attorney agreed. "We can just hope there is something from a fresh set of eyes that can start the process."

*

A quarter filled pint glass which still had a decent amount of lukewarm ale in it sat on the end table next to his recliner, which was fully engaged for optimal comfort. Chances were it would not be finished, and instead dumped down the drain later that evening. Jared had two before it, but this was pushing his limit, especially for four o'clock in the afternoon. When Virginia had called earlier with the news of the morbid delivery, he had rushed home and taken the rest of the day off. There were plenty of vacation days that he had accumulated and before him was a smorgasbord of emotions that had to be processed.

Austin had taken the wee Sunn-Marshall out to play for a bit in the yard so that his beau could have some time reflecting on all that had occurred. There was also a subtle agenda to allow the matriarch of the land to have her own period of the day alone. Her hurt was radiating in the air also. And again, the newbie to this unique nuclear family was unsure of what he could do to soothe any of their emotional ailments.

Appreciating this time Jared was relaxing with a slight buzz and allowing the television to be background noise when his phone buzzed in his pocket. Usually this would be a time to ignore such a distraction, but Jared perked up when he saw the caller and answered, trying to sound semi-sober.

"Senator Steele."

"Jared, just call me Jackson. How are you doing?"

"I'm okay."

"Understandable with a date finally being set."

"Yeah, and Clayton's idiot of a son is paying some private eye to re-investigate."

"I saw the article, and how they never reached out to you, or anyone else, for a statement. But then again, he did emphasize that there would be at least one more article published."

"And with them scheduling the execution we will have some national media annoying us again."

"Yes. Now with this Foreman guy, just answer honestly, don't act like you want to hide anything because he wants to win with the court of public opinion, not on any facts."

"You think so?"

"Absolutely. I had a few of my fact checkers do some research this afternoon. There is an incline to his career right now, and he is quite good at what he does. And what he is intensely looking for is a massive turnover like this to launch him."

"Gotcha."

"Morris and Wingard will be questioned also, he probably got all of the case file from Stevvins. I would bet my life that he is already doing his homework and trying to find strings to pull apart the conviction."

"Gotcha."

"And make sure that you take care of yourself emotionally. This is tough, it's closure, and also losing another parent."

The beer this time decided to respond to that comment using unfiltered feelings. "That bitch has been dead to me since the moment I found my father hanging."

*

There was strong reasoning for Patrick Foreman to not set up appointments with those he intended on interviewing yet have it obvious that he would speak to them during the investigation. This was the whole point of having the article in the local paper as a blindside to those close to Allen Marshall. With the revelation of the date for the convicts' termination, another article was published the day after the warrants were issued. This was to add some fuel to the fire, and also to have anyone in the area who held back some tidbit of information on the case to come forward since it was now the eleventh hour in the proceedings.

It had been two days since the death notices had been serviced, and one day after the press release dictating the enigmatic progress. In turn, this was the day that the sleuth lived for. When everyone was talking about it. Where he could dive in and get some work done, and stumble on some weaknesses of those involved, and verify his new gut feeling that the duo is in fact innocent.

Leaving his hotel before dawn Patrick wanted to ensure he would meet his first intended target on his list. Pulling into the local federal building at moments before seven am he was glad to see the USDA trucks parked. Easing through security he went to the correct suite. Using more leeway than he should have he did enter since the door was unlocked, sans any knocking.

"Is that you Lisa? In kinda early today?" This was a bellowing question coming from Frank Lyons.

"Not quite."

Confused at the rich, deep voice answering, Frank stuck his head out of his office then cocked it to the side. "We have another hour until we open."

"I was hoping to catch you beforehand." With a smooth action Patrick flashed his private investigator's badge and smiled. "Patrick Foreman here. I just wanted to ask you a few questions."

Frank went from being perplexed to being annoyed in an instant. Sighing, he went on. "I really do not want to talk to anyone who is trying to get my late partner's killers out of prison. Especially when they are exploring federal buildings improperly."

With his open palms and hands up showing a non-threatening stance the unwanted guest pleaded his case. "I am undecided at this point on their guilt, and I get both sides before picking one." This was a small fib since he had made his initial stance but needed some credibility on his neutrality. "I throw a fresh set of eyes on everything and go back with what I find."

Rolling his eyes Frank realized it was best to answer this man rather than to fight the process, whether or not he was ecstatic to do so. "Come on, sit down. You get ten minutes of my time."

Without an argument Patrick followed suit. Once settled he initiated the interview. "The weeks before the incident, did you feel as if anything was off with Allen. His actions, personality, or mood?"

"Not really. He was dealing with the divorce and was just busy. He would've been fifty in January."

"That is a milestone."

"Yeah, he had to get a physical for the life insurance since it's a term policy. Well, it worked out fine that he never went."

"Yeah, Jared got it all."

"He'd rather have a living father."

"What doctor did he use for the exam?"

"Same one I do. Lyman. Over by Boardmanville at the medical center."

This was the same physician that had signed off on the death certificate, so Patrick had more reasoning to visit him.

"Did he seem sick at all?"

"Not in the least bit."

"Do you think it could've been staged by Allen?"

"And this is when we finish this. Allen was a damn good man. With ethics and morals. And I will be damned if some outsider comes in and spits on his name." Showing dominance Frank stood and put his hand on his badge, which was mounted on his belt. "Find your way out, or I can get security to do so."

Satisfied, the overstayer ventured back out and really was bent now on seeing said doctor. So quickly he punched in the required information and found a route to Dr. Lyman's office. Since it is such a small town, maybe eight thousand inhabitants in Olean proper, he was able to get to the office building without much haste.

Now that it was barely eight in the morning, he knew that the medical provider would be able to see him before any patients. Again, he was able to mosey into the facilities and rang the bell on the receptionist's desk.

A balding gentleman, pushing sixty in age, came to the front. "Our first appointment is at nine, and we do not take walk-ins."

"Doctor Lyman."

"That's me." There was surprise and angst at such an early caller asking for him. "What is this in regard to?"

Again, with the badge flash.

"I am Patrick Foreman. I am investigating."

Another sigh. "I know. I know. Come back."

This seemed promising so he followed and was settled in the host's private office. The host sat at his desk, the visitor at a simple office chair facing each other.

"I knew that this may come right to me. And I promised myself that if I ever was confronted, then I would let everyone know the truth."

Excited, but yielding any physical signs of it, Patrick leaned in. "What do you mean?"

"Well, Allen Marshall had stage four prostate cancer."

"That was not in the autopsy report."

"It would not be. It does not show up in bloodwork, and he did not receive treatment or surgery for it. And being that the cause of death was obviously a hanging, you won't check a dead man's prostate for the fun of it."

"Why wasn't he getting chemo?"

"His pride."

"Did he plan on it?"

"No. He wanted to die with dignity, he said."

"Were there any symptoms?"

While reminiscing the doc seemed to grow a few tears in his eyes over said patient. "Allen was in a lot of pain. I gave him some light opioids. It appears he took them early enough in the day that they never showed up in the toxicology report at the autopsy in toxic levels. And he was having a lot of trouble with urinating. But he fought like hell."

"Well, he had an exam for his insurance coming up."

"Oh, I know. He tried everything to get around it being found. Even sent me an email to destroy any records I had of him a few weeks before he was killed."

"Do you think this had anything to do with his sudden death? Isn't that throwing a few red flags up?"

"Your guess is as good as mine." A melancholic emotion swept his face. "But it's your time to go. I've lifted that burden off of my chest now, and anything further would be disrupting the sanctity of his privacy."

*

I n order to be a stellar investigator, especially in such an arrangement, discretion is something that you cannot always use. There could be some exclusion of who told you a vital block of information, such as was just revealed, but the cold stone truth must be used as a pick to break the ice. Precisely as the road before Patrick Foreman was showing.

With this nugget he decided to swing into Joseph Stevvin's counterpart in town, JT Dove. Attorneys can go either way, depending on their ethics and beliefs. This one would have to be a "play it by ear" encounter.

Just after nine am he made his brash entrance into the solicitor's office. Being a lowkey and low budget operation JT was alone.

Looking up, the proprietor grinned. "Patrick Foreman."

"Ah, how'd you know."

"Internet searches and intuition. You get ten minutes. Since he is gone, I will use my discretion in whether or not information is pertinent to your investigation." With some arrogance he was playing with an expensive ink pen and swaying side to side in his luxurious office chair which had deep hunter green leather and plenty of tufting with buttons.

"Well let me show you my cards then." Showing more gusto, the visitor sat down across from his latest inquiry. "Allen Marshall was dying of stage four cancer."

The hands of the pompous one stopped fidgeting, and his playful manner dropped immediately. "Nothing was on the..."

"Wouldn't show up unless they probed him during the autopsy since he never tried to get any remedies for it."

"Did Jared..."

"Sounds like he told no one. Only Curtis Lyman knew."

Frozen for a moment, the lawyer was thrown off kilter. "That would explain why he put all of his paperwork in order before he was killed."

"Makes sense... And also makes you question how legitimate it was to be a homicide and not a suicide."

A violent look of disgust overtook the attorney's face. "I barely passed biology and physics, and even I understood that there was no way for the man to levitate a foot off of the ground and hang himself. With rope found at his ex-wife's house."

Using common sense, the interrogator dropped back with his offensive moves and wanted to let Dove feel that he was contributing. "With knowing this, was there anything else that pops into your head now."

"Not really." A long exhale followed. "He was a good man. And Joseph Stevvins did his best with the case handed to him. Defending guilty murderers is not something that I could, or would, do."

*

Most men in Patrick Foreman's comfortable leather loafers would carry onto the next person on the list and keep moving forward. But that wasn't how this truth seeker rolled. Instead he worked the case as if it was a cold one, which in theory it was.

The evidence was still laid out, yet most minds were made up one way, and his was the opposite.

Wanting to decompress from an intense morning and keep his thoughts clear, he ventured back to his hotel room and ordered some lunch to arrive. With coming into these situations blind there is no perfect way to route a map. And so far, the cancer detail really was a spin that was gearing in a good direction.

While enjoying a burger and fries from a small diner over on Wayne Street he focused on crime scene pictures. There was little he knew about the house itself besides that it was usually seasonal on a lake, and that it had been passed along in the family. Where the incident took place seemed like a barren basement with a dirt floor and a bit of moisture on one wall. The beams were high, and it was clear that Allen had nothing around when discovered to stand on. While reading the transcripts from the trial he saw that Jared was firm on not changing the scene, so implying that did occur would not be beneficial to having the son open up willfully and share anything pertinent to the case.

There was no denying that there was a struggle in the kitchen, and a sneak attack seemed like a very believable story. Yet he was starting to disbelieve how perfectly wrapped all of this was. Then he did go back to the thoughts of how Allen was a federal agent. USDA or not. There was training and knowledge of scenes such as this. Building a facade for the world to hide his own weaknesses was completely plausible.

And the ponderer was also lost as to if such a kaleidoscope

of clues could be trained and groomed into a perfect parade that could stage two people to fry for his death.

Dropping his food onto the wrapper with his focus renewed, he became more frantic looking at the exterior photos and reading the notes about the boot tracks, the rope, no fingerprints on the scene. Along with the drill bit and wood shavings. Had this "good man" orchestrated the perfect cover up and really offered his estranged wife and her lover as cruel martyrs just so that his manhood and good name could stay solid. That he could seek revenge on her sins, while committing ones of a greater magnitude and a finality that was now being scheduled in a matter of days.

Standing up and pounding his fist on the desk strewn with so many clues and tidbits Patrick Foreman became enraged when he figured out what Allen Marshall did. And how he did it well. Now he had to discover tangible clues to bring before a jurist in order to save two lives that he was convinced were framed.

*

"I s Joseph in his office." This was a statement, not a question. Patrick was copying Michael McBride by asking and not waiting for an answer. Instead, he kept his stride and opened the unlocked door.

With his feet up on his desk reviewing a file the lawyer looked up. "I am keeping a light schedule the next two weeks since I know that these somewhat comical situations will keep coming where it's pointless to lock my door."

Swinging his body the new guest closed the door. "No one can know this yet. Not even Michael."

With a lofty shrug Joseph replied. "Sure."

Jabbing his finger violently on the desk blotter Patrick was blunt. "Allen Marshall was dying."

Putting his feet on the ground and moving his body forward, Stevvins entertained the introduction. "We all die."

"No." Another jab then he sat down. "Allen Marshall was

secretly dying from stage four prostate cancer."

"Wouldn't they find it…"

"No." Squinting his eyes and shaking his head the hired gumshoe moved on. "I'll cut to the chase. Only his doctor knew. He refused treatment. And only if they had probed him at the autopsy would they have found it. And they don't focus there when it looks like he was beaten and hung."

"That's nice and dandy, but what can we do with that?"

"We are going to sit on it for a few days. I don't want the Marshalls to get any idea of this little secret. We butter them up. Get what we can. Then we throw an injunction in and ask for an exhumation."

With a glare the attorney answered. "So, a small trip to D.C. since this is federal. And piss off half the area. Great."

"You gotta kick up some mud to get it done sometimes."

"I am assuming I am picking that tab up since Michael McBride is up to his eyeballs in debt already due to this."

"I am totally fine flying coach."

"You better be." Both grinned to relieve the negative energy for a moment. "What else do you have up your sleeve?"

"Well, I want to see inside of that cabin."

"Good luck with that."

"Something about it."

"I toured it during pretrial and discovery. It's kinda creepy."

"But there is no way that he could hold himself up and pull his head through the noose."

"Welcome to my biggest obstacle."

"There had to be something."

"Nothing in the entire basement."

"I won't bring up Jared changing the scene."

"God no. One newspaper accused me of trying to hang the son on the stand."

"I read that in the transcripts."

Jumping up, the investigator decided he was done. "I am going to ruffle some more feathers. I'll keep you updated."

"I'll keep the door unlocked."

*

Zig zagging along East State Street while driving his vehicle Foreman decided to not return to the hotel right then, and instead take a little break at a park that he had researched by a quiet walking trail. Pulling away from the industrial and retail area he cruised to a spot in the nearly empty stone lot and parked his rental sedan. From there he exited and found a plethora of picnic tables in a decent sized pavilion right by the hidden forest pathway. Tranquility at its finest. The sounds of the Allegheny River behind it were soft and calming. Exactly what he needed to help bring in his attention and to pivot around all of these new facts.

Setting out just a few documents on a rough lumber table top he nestled onto the matching bench and was reviewing information about both the autopsy. Over and over he was impressed that there were two medical examiners present at said morbid inquisitive event. In his mind he knew that this would make his job more difficult than a blatant check and balance medical review was conducted. Deep in thought he was suddenly disrupted when his phone buzzed for an email alert.

Allowing his eyes to pander over to the mobile device he noticed that it was indeed related to the case before him, and in fact it was not a negative based message, as many tend to be in this field. Curiosity won him over and he pressed the required buttons to unlock the correspondence.

With electricity his eyes blared open and he was diving deep into the email itself. This was from a person who owned a small hardware store in the region who had sold various items to Allen Marshall in the weeks leading up. With some hesitation in the tone of the note they did state that a meeting of anytime could happen at the shop.

Inevitably one was scheduled as soon as Patrick could get there.

With excitement and a core emphasis on the fact that

time is of the utmost importance Patrick corralled his work material and headed back to the car. This lead would be in some small town named Friendship, which was on the other side of Cuba heading east. Luckily there were others in that area of Allegany County that he could swing by and pester in a friendly, professional way for more information on the case.

Gaining speed on the expressway Patrick's head was swarming with details about this witness. There was some mention of a gut feeling and weird purchases. Also that he felt like no one would listen to his side when the investigation and trial were going on. Very common for those who are trapped with knowledge of innocence when guilt is already seated in stone with such controversies.

After a solid half an hour on his trip he pulled up to the Friendship Hardware Shoppe and parked at the most convenient spot, which was on the street by the front door. There was an elegant and aged aura of the building with large display windows and a sturdy and well used front door which was mostly built with toned lead glass and rich hardwoods harvested almost two centuries before.

A soft mechanical ding announced his entry, and a gentleman of about sixty was at the cash register. A few other customers were mingling about as the obvious caretaker was eating his lunch, ready to ring up their purchases.

"Are you Daniel?"

"I could be, or my son could."

"Did you email me about the article in the paper?"

Sighing, the proprietor answered. "You want Skip." Contorting his body on the oak barstool he was on he bellowed out at a higher volume. "Skip. That investigator is here already about that murder." Swinging back to his correct position he rolled his eyes. "I told him to not play with fire. For some reason he thinks that this is some smoking gun. When he just needs to stay out of this whole ordeal."

A man in his mid-twenties who was a dead ringer for a younger version of the greeter came from the back and smiled.

"I am guessing that Pops told you that I should stay out of this."

"We were just making small talk."

"Well, come back here to the office."

Passing the elder Patrick smiled and nodded his head. Another loud exhale was the response.

Once closed in the small ten by ten basic office, a typical one with an aged desk exploding with useless junk mail that should be thrown away and a basic standard computer in the midst of it. Being polite Skip pulled over a folding chair for the investigator to sit while they talked.

"I was a senior in school when this all happened."

"Okay."

"Allen Marshall came into the shop and bought rope, a drill, and a bit for that in his first trip."

"Are you sure that it was him?"

"Yes, because a few days later he came in and bought a size nine boot."

Patrick's ears perked and excitement roared in his chest. But he was one to not let emotions escape and let his practical mind proceed. "That is great, but it's been seven years. Anyone can say that."

With a mischievous smirk the informant moved the mouse to the desktop and the screen quivered, then illuminated. On the main program open was a still image of Allen Marshall opening his wallet with said items from his initial trip there on the counter."

"Well, I be damned."

Then the tech wizard opened a second screen with Allen holding the boots.

"This is great. Circumstantial, but great."

"I'll email some shortened clips of them to you."

A complete rush of confusion ravaged Patrick next. "I am quite perplexed as to why you still have these now."

"Well, the first time he came in he seemed a bit off, but that was okay. Then when he came back, I saw his badge flash in his wallet and I asked him about what field he was in, and he got very defensive. Wouldn't even answer me, and forget about him being polite. Luckily, I saw the USDA on it and moved it to the back of my head."

"That is quite the memory. And what about keeping this surveillance feed for so long."

"When I heard a USDA agent was killed, I remembered this. And reading more I knew something was up. I moved those dates to a separate file so they would not be auto-deleted by our system."

"Why didn't you go to the police then?"

"Pops was dead set against it. That trial really rocked the area. And being a business, he didn't want us to get any bad press."

"Gotcha."

"I did call at the beginning of the investigation but got cold feet. Hung up on the cop even."

"That happens. Is there anything else?"

"No."

"You do realize that this could be a game changer though. You could be saving two innocent lives."

*

Once he was settled back into his rental Patrick checked his email again and was relieved to find that the clips were received and working fine. This would not totally shift everything, but these small details were more pieces of evidence that could be used for an injunction.

Smiling for the first time that day, Patrick pulled up the address for Winters' Funeral Home and was relieved to see that it was a fairly close trip from Friendship. With the added momentum and feeling of accomplishment Patrick made his way over.

As it had been presented seven years before, the home/business was kept up nicely. Patrick enjoyed the simplicity of the drive through the county, and of its structure all together.

More of the small town aura was invading his mind and body.

Doing his own due diligence he had ensured that there were no services being held that day. After parking he then made a few steps up to the main entrance where he rang the bell. Promptly the mortician opened the door and cocked his head. Swiftly Patrick pulled his wallet out of his back pocket and showed his badge.

"Come on in. I have been expecting you." There was a coldness to his tone, and overall essence the moment that everything connected on who his impromptu guest was. Without a guided tour he moved their progression to his office. Being alone in the structure there was no need to close the door, so both sat. "Ask away. I just want this put away and those two put six feet under."

"I appreciate the forward attitude. I read over the autopsy. Everything seems cut and dry."

"Because it was." This answer was curt, and the responder now had his arms aggressively crossed over his chest while seated.

"But you did miss one thing."

Snorting he rolled his eyes. "I know for a fact that he was never exhumed, so therefore that's malarkey."

"Allen Marshall had stage four cancer. He was going to die."

"No drugs came up on his tox screen."

"He wasn't receiving treatment."

"And no examiner would subject a subject in an autopsy to that type of exam unless there was a blatant reason why."

"But isn't it bizarre that a dying man then gets killed, and it looked like a suicide, but ruled a homicide?"

"Stranger things have happened, as you may know."

"I really believe that he hung himself."

"Listen," Roger Winters stood with his own face starting to blush. "Two of us came in with open minds, as we have to in this profession. There was no way he could have hung himself unless he had a jetpack on. Cancer or not." Memories of the week in question and all of the chaos involved came rushing back, raging a fire in his being. Slamming his fist on the desk blotter he abruptly stood and began to walk out of his office. Sternly he looked at Patrick. "I have other duties to tend to other than getting two killers off the hook."

Midway through their descent from the meeting space Roger turned around again to face his counterpart, "And how about the bruising, the black eye. There was too much work for no reason to stage this. And even then, it is not practical."

At the door Patrick turned and was tempted to let the tidbit about the incriminating purchases on his previous visit slip out, but Roger slammed the door and engaged the lock. Truly shutting the sleuth out of any rebuttal.

*

With only a semi-worn white wife beater and some navy blue running shorts on, Patrick was in the gym of the hotel after his arrival back. Trying to look less suspicious he had changed from his semi-formal attire and into work out material. But in the gym he was focused on a pull up bar. With him he had a tape measure, and some painters tape he always brought along on investigations. With physical evidence he was very hands-on. Time after time he was measuring and using ratios to compare how far off the ground the supposed noose would be for Allen versus himself.

Each attempt was futile, and even with him being in wonderful shape he could not maneuver himself up and then back down with his head cocked forward to catch the imaginary loop. Having a rope tied true to the experiment in said setting would push into being quite bizarre, and instigate possible inquiries on his own mental health from any accidental onlookers. Being sent to a psych ward was not on his agenda that week.

Plus, in the back of his mind he had to take into consideration how sick Allen Marshall was during that time. Doing some research on stage four cancer of the prostate he had come to see how Allen probably was numb due to the prescribed pain medication while fighting truly a losing battle.

Soreness did cause him to end the workout/experiment so he retreated back to his room at the dated inn and proceeded to take a shower. Even in there his mind was spinning as to what could have been used to propel the subject high enough. It was as if his mind was now being rewired to only think of this essential missing piece of the story.

Toweling off he headed back and sat on the bed, tossing the towel to the side. After tossing on a fresh pair of gray sweatpants he got back to business and checked his laptop for any messages, and then got started on outlining his next steps in the conundrum.

Scrolling along his electronic messages he deleted a few that were spam, plus the ones that blatantly called his clients cold-blooded killers. These were daily memos sent to him that never penetrated his tough skin. But then there was a lengthy one from the reporter he had coordinated with previously for the article. They had discussed a sequel, but now she was elated in informing Patrick that a national daily periodical wanted to pick up her piece for a total of three. Her premiere installment would be updated and re-published coast to coast, and possibly around the globe. Afterwards two more installments would be in the works. The second shows progress, and the finale the day of the planned executions, whether or not they actually would occur. Gotta keep up the suspense.

This was just the right amount of vigor and spice that the private investigator needed to help the momentum of this case move forward. Without haste he responded with his enthusiasm and gusto about more coverage, and on the national level too.

Rotating his thoughts he decided to focus primarily on the pictures from the autopsy. Oftentimes most truth seekers will just scan them, but there was a desire to become engrossed with them. Not letting any notes or reports soil his impressions of the details of the images. Rather let his impression of what the photos speak to his virgin mind about the story they were ready to tell.

With the dozen or so taken of Allen's face there was indeed bruising which was showing that some type of hit was taken near his right eye. Yet something was not quite precise with the shiner. It appeared as if there was only three quarters of the half-moon impression that should be discolored. And in a strange way it stopped at precisely a defined ending. Like a line had drawn a dead end just below his socket.

For the best analysis the three or four snapshots of just his face were laid on the foot of the spare bed. All of the lights were on in the room, and he was using a small flashlight to add illumination to the evidence. And with this attention to detail, he kept walking and shining, lowering himself and rising.

That horizontal line where the damage stopped was driving him mad. To the point that he went to the bathroom door and extended his forearm. There he slowly pressed the edge of the door against the flesh of his inner arm for a moment and then released it. To show a perfect line on himself, that explained why the injury on Allen was not quite the same as if he truly was socked in the eye.

*

"Captain Wingard," paged the intercom in his office from a soft, feminine voice. The high-ranking officer was sitting at his desk and computer when the communal secretary of the barracks engaged the option on his phone.

"Yes, Delores."

"You have a visitor."

Burrowing his brows he could not think of any appointments at that time period he was due for. "Who is it?"

"A Patrick Foreman."

"Motherfucker."

"Excuse me?" The elderly receptionist asked, either due to the brash language, or her hearing slowly deteriorating.

"Nothing. Send him in."

A smiling guest appeared around the corner, a manilla envelope in hand, and ascended towards Cecil's desk with his hand out proudly. The host nodded as a proactive way to smother the optimism and set dominance with someone who was set on breaking down the case of his career.

"Thank you for seeing me on such short notice, Captain."

"Zero notice is more like it."

"You know how it is. Snag them when you can."

"Us who took an oath sometimes will use that play. But carry on. You get ten questions or five minutes. Whatever is more convenient for me."

Laughing, and quite used to the rough greetings, Patrick pressed on. "I guess let's cut to the chase before I show you all of my cards."

"Shoot, Cowboy."

"Did you ever have any doubt that this was a homicide?"

"I was first on scene. Unless Allen Marshall was a Houdini reincarnate, there is no way at all he could have hung himself."

"I agree that nothing points to that."

"Pretty cut and dry that the killers fumbled there and forgot to find a stool, and did not stage it properly."

"Okay, but here are a few things that I uncovered."

"Amuse me, but don't expect me to waver in my vote for slaughtering of a law enforcement officer."

"Allen Marshall had stage four prostate cancer. He was in pain."

"Why didn't the..."

"He was not receiving treatment and had no surgeries. And only if they had done a physical exploration, would they have known that he was so sick with a tumor so big. I had a chat with Doctor Lyman"

"People with cancer can be murdered before they succumb to it." Sarcasm dripped from Cecil's mouth during this perfect response.

Ready at this objection the lead debater of the subject pulled out the first sheet in his evidence folder. "Here is a picture of the black eye that Allen had."

Wingard shrugged at such a basic photo.

"Notice how that bruising stops at an abrupt spot, rather than making a half-moon around his eye."

"Now that you point it out."

"Well, I believe it was self-inflicted from slamming the door into his face in order to cause some type of injury."

"Your imagination is quite active. Maybe becoming a novelist in the field would be better for you."

"Nah, it would never be profitable," with excitement he pulled out the last two slips of clues. "How about going to the Friendship Hardware Shoppe and buying, all in cash mind you, a drill, bit, rope, and size nine boots." Slapping down printed proof of the bits of his findings Patrick grinned.

"A man buys tools. Stop the press and call off the executions. A newbie to the case, and area, has found that us in the country like to go shopping."

"But don't you think that..."

"I think you are getting paid to twist facts around. Now I am calling it quits here. Flatlining in my corner of the ring. And asking you politely to leave here. Thank you for your time. I hope you enjoy the area. Be sure to visit the Zippo Museum over in Bradford."

"You don't think that...:"

"I think you really don't want to get a disorderly conduct charge for not leaving when asked politely."

Grasping the files he exited the office and headed out. Once Cecil was sure that he had left the station he got up and closed the door. Returning to his desk he flipped through an old rolodex until he found the right number.

Trilling thrice the person on the other end answered. "Special Agent in Charge Morris."

"Hey, it's Cecil."

"Hey my man, what's up?"

"That rent-a-mistrial scapegoat chaser for Stevvins' clients just left."

"Oh jeez, be sure to sanitize the place. That sleaze can be contagious."

"Well, the fucker found out a few things we didn't catch."

"Happens. People think of something they imagined or made up."

"Well, his doctor held back that he had stage four prostate cancer."

"Why didn't..."

"Imma stop you there. Doesn't show up unless they physically investigate that region of him at the autopsy. They had no need to. He refused treatment and told no one."

"Okay."

"Second piece that doesn't line up is that the bruise looks like he slammed a door into his face to get the bruise. There's a weird line."

"That's a new one."

"Last though. Well, he bought rope, a drill, boots, and drill bit all at the Friendship Hardware Shoppe."

"Why does that ring a bell?"

With a sigh that could move mountains Cecil pulled out a bit of memory. "Remember sometime in the first few days we had that weird hang up call."

"Yeah. Shocked that you remember it."

"They were calling from the Friendship Hardware Shoppe."

"That's bizarre. And people shop for stuff. Not enough to get anything turned over. Superman didn't hang himself.":

"Well before he makes his trip up that way, I just wanted you to have a heads up."

"I appreciate it."

"But seriously, between us. Did we get it wrong? Did Allen stage this?"

"Come on. The man had more honor than to do that."

*

The combination of rumble strips on the shoulder of Route 219 southbound and the same horrid dream sequence that reappeared after every time that Patrick Foreman nodded off was the reason why he woke up before nailing the guard rail. With an attempt to keep his composure he redirected the sedan into a proper straight line driving down the winding country highway. After checking every mirror and every direction he could in order to verify that his minor infraction was not noticed by any cruising police officers, he then used his large ebony hand to slap himself across the face and wake up. This was an aggressive way to redirect his attention for getting back to Olean safely.

In order to keep conscious, the private eye kept repeating the sequence of events from his surprise visit to Jacob Morris. Or rather the lack thereof.

There was the awkward initial introduction followed by the lead agent keeping a firm stance on how everything was legit, by the book, and a solid conviction. There was some hope that he could talk to Agent Morray and check out some of the evidence that they kept locked away, but this was a strong no.

After Patrick chatted with Cecil, then Wingard speaking to Morris and explaining the small leaks that were forming in their case, the bureau guys decided to block any peeking of the artifacts of the case. By doing so any inspiration to show off their box of clues was not going to happen since they did not need any other facts to become debatable, and any more room for an injunction. So, Jake spoke with Isaac, and this was a giant lock down. There was no way unless PI Foreman showed up with a court order, or if there was a reversal in the case resulting in a mistrial, that they would play ball. Both scenarios were unlikely based on the few tidbits revealed so far.

So there the informal detective was. Driving back feeling somewhat depleted, and definitely fatigued.

This returning nightmare had shattered any attempt of rest the past few nights since the pieces of the puzzle were now working in his favor. Instead of it being a celebratory dream, it was actually a revolving terror.

It starts with him running up the granite steps of a giant courthouse with a massive file under his arm. It's a cold wintery day, similar to the one on which Allen Marshall died. The wind is blowing, and he slips on a thick sheet of ice and tumbles the fifty or so steps and rolls to the bottom. In the midst of this ordeal all of his paperwork flies into the air, and a picture of Allen Marshall standing in the basement with the tied rope above him lands next to him and gets his attention. From there Allen rises and enters the noose as it closes and he laughs at Patrick. His mouth opens wide. So much that it takes over the entire dream and leads to a shot of Julie Marshall in the execution chair with terror in her eyes. Just as the needle slips into her arms Patrick wakes up again.

Gripping at the wheel hard he keeps his focus on the lines before him. It was just after one in the afternoon with little less than half an hour before he would be back at the hotel room. Due to his self-discipline, he would ensure that he was ringing out at least four more hours of some type of work on the file. Then try to rest early and pray that the reel in his head ceases to replay over and over with no end in sight.

Shaking his head while driving on a straight away without any other cars close by, he threw his arm backwards with moment and slammed his palm across his cheeks and mouth again. This held a duo purpose. One to keep his awareness going, and the second to get this night terror out of his head. Never before had he let an investigation eat at him like this. But then again, he wasn't fighting for truly innocent clients in any such predicament before this one either.

*

"Holy shit, Patrick," the fresh morning newspaper dropped from Joseph Stevvins' hands and landed on his desk blotter. Adjusting from a relaxed position to a proper sitting form his head lifted higher and his eyes widened. "I just met you, but I could tell that this past week must have taken its toll on you."

With poor posture the exhausted one took a seat across from the solicitor. "I even managed some sleep last night when I got back from the FBI office in Buffalo."

"Really... Well, at least I know I am getting my money's worth." A sly grin, one true to his occupation, crossed his mouth. Then it abruptly adjusted back when Patrick failed to find any amusement in this. Trying to save face, the lawyer adjusted the tone. "Should we get Michael McBride over here for a quick update."

"Absolutely not. I have news, but he will take it and probably show up at the Marshalls' homestead waving it in their face. I want to get an injunction and an exhumation. I am going to call him for an abbreviated and censored update. Especially since it is Friday."

"That it is. So, we are going to D.C. so I can file all of these motions and try to see if we have any footing."

"Yea." Quickly he looked down at his phone and then back up again. "I just emailed you flights for Sunday."

A dinging notification rang from Stevvins' desktop computer, and he wiggled his mouse to waken the monitor and start exploring the travel accommodations. "And you probably want to talk to Senator Steele while we are at it."

"Two birds, one very large stone."

"He won't be so easy to drop in on."

"It is what it is."

"What about the Marshalls? Are you going to bombard them with all of this when we get back?"

"Not at all." With confidence he leaned back. "I always like to scope out the locales of those I need to talk to. And thanks to a Benny Franklin being passed along, his neighbor at the lake house let me know that on Fridays in the summer at four in the afternoon Jared opens up the house, relaxes on the deck, and eventually his husband and grandmother join with their baby. Maybe a friend or relative may swing through."

"Well, it's Friday at one right now."

"Exactly, a little trip over to the lake is in store so that I can see the cabin and try to work on unveiling some more evidence. Drop a few bombs on the kid, and give them warning about our Capitol trip that you are taking us on."

*

With a rush of adrenaline his eyes roared open, and he bolted up in the armchair that he had dozed off in. The alarm that he had set for three-thirty had properly executed its purpose, and somehow Patrick had managed an hour or so of solid sleep. The nightmare had gone through a rotation or two, but he forced himself to sleep through it so that it could have an ending.

That ending was the tombstones of Julie and Clayton in an eerie cemetery appearing. A thunderstorm was blaring in the distance, and when the lightning cracked it exploded on the grave, and then the blood of the two he could not save rushed over his hands, while a cackling Allen Marshall was heard, arrogant that his plan had been pulled off.

Splashing moderately warmed water on his face, Patrick was starting to feel remotely refreshed at that point. It was time to face Allen's number one fan, the one who was fooled the most, and was made the fool of the most, in the investigator's eyes.

With caution he prepared his tanned leather briefcase. Its edges colored in a darker cinnamon hue while the main cowhide in a lighter shade. There was some trembling in his slender fingers and generous palms. This was due to the lack of sleep and some slight nerves for the pending encounter. But he checked his documents and pictures, assuring that they all were ready to be in tow with him. And with some confidence gained he proceeded out to the rental car and hopped in, ready to go and tackle this massive beast hanging over his head.

Sailing across The Expressway, eastward bound, he opened his driver's side window, an attempt to keep both his mind and body alert. Also to get a feel for the land. A small sliver of an opportunity to breathe the same air that everyone in this quandary had inhaled before that fateful night nearly eight years before. Plus, it helped with his rehearsal for when he spoke to Jared upon his surprise attack.

With the breeze whisking by, yet still maintaining his pledge to safely drive, he practiced a few lines, specifically the hard ones.

"Jared, I appreciate the tour." Mentally places himself sitting down in a chair, therefore encouraging/forcing the orphan to do so also. "Were you aware of some facts pertaining to the case." Keep it cold, ice cold. Remove the bond and any emotional connection when it comes to how your father fucked over your mother and the love of her life. Especially when it came to the talk about the cancer. The lying. And the framing.

For ten of the fifteen minus enroute he kept badgering an imaginary Jared. Until he exited the local highway and took the left onto Route 305. There in the prime of the land he enjoyed the scenery and allowed his blood pressure to lower and enjoy a more normal rate. That way he did not seem so wired and fired up about the pending interrogation.

Finally, he pulled up to the quaint abode, and noticed that the driveway only held Jared's vehicle, which his target was offloading a few picnic style items. The rocky driveway had barely enough space for his car to be housed also, and the aged gravel moaned and creaked against his tires.

*

F ocus enveloped Jared on getting the house ready for their weekly bar-be-que that he did not notice the intrusive sedan pull up and turn off. There was a dedication to getting the necessities out of the truck and into the kitchen. The first few years after his father's death he had come to check on the house, although the nosy neighbors kept him up to date with any issues. Mostly his trips over were in the winter to make sure that the pipes did not freeze. And back then in the summer for a quick swim, or to perform the tedious ten-minute mowing job that was associated with the lot.

It was not until he and Austin married that he felt a need to enjoy the heirloom more, especially after baby Allen's adoption was finished. Also, it was a way for his grandmother to appreciate everything associated with it. A fun summer weekly tradition. Jared always took care of the necessities, and that was okay by him. The running rendezvous implied that he could be in the spot where his father's heart took its final beat.

"Mister Marshall?"

This inquiry into his identification started him so much that Jared almost hit his head on the door jamb of his pick-up. Turning around his mouth stayed frozen until the pieces of the puzzle clicked into place. "I am assuming you are Michael's private investigator."

Reaching out his open palm, the guest smiled, expecting a handshake.

Instead, there was a void of greeting from Jared.

"Do you have a minute?"

"Very few for the man who is trying to get my father's killers off the hook. But I spoke with my attorney, and some others. Come on." Closing the door he began to walk to the back door. "Let's get this over with."

The intense beauty from the lake caused Patrick to be in a trance for a moment, and Jared did break this by huffing as the door was kept ajar for him. Inside there were very few changes made. This was purely used to do minor cooking, and then some went into the second-floor bathroom for any such needs.

Due to the hours and hours that he had already spent on this case, the sleuth was quite familiar with this room. Squatting down he touched the mid-century linoleum flooring. "You never cleaned up the circles that they marked where the pieces of the glass fell."

"Nope. They used a black permanent marker, and I minimize how much time I spend inside."

Standing up, the justice seeker faced the orphan. "Nice home like this, don't you spend the night now and then, especially in the summer?"

A sharp cackle erupted. "Tried that a few times. Can never fall asleep, and I even hear the basement stairs creaking. My Dad's ghost is here. And is still pissed, so he can't finally rest in peace."

There was a tension that arose from the chatter between them. One that scared Patrick, so he stared at the basement door.

"The worst is when I smell his cologne right here in the kitchen. It reminds me that he still looks over me. But it also takes me back to the day he was killed. Bittersweet visits from a ghost."

There was an awkward silence, then the temporary sleuth looked at the basement door again.

"Go ahead. I've only been down there twice since that horrendous night. Enjoy where my father was massacred by your clients"

Doing so immediately kept Patrick from being harsh, or dropping any hints of what was to come too soon. So, with the hushed light in the cellar, he moved around. There was the spot where a saw was used to cut a chunk out of the beam. And nothing else in the room just like that day. Moving to the rear room he saw the tools and ice fishing material. Shrugging he ascended back up to the ground level.

"How's the ice fishing?"

"I haven't been since I was a kid. Way before Dad was

slaughtered."

Without permission Patrick moved to the living room. "Looks like you use the fireplace now and then at least. "

"Wrong again, Sherlock. Same ashes as the night my father was hanged by my mother and her lover."

Edging closer Patrick looked down in the soot and ruins of said fire. Lowering his body, he picked around and then lifted up a small metal rectangular box. "What is this?"

"Like if I know." Walking over, with some annoyance in his aura, Jared knocked it out of his hands. "Really shouldn't be digging around in places that were peaceful for so long."

"I am sorry." Which was a blank statement. Nonchalantly Patrick laid his briefcase on the floor and took the armchair next to the sofa as a seat. "I did find out some things."

Without realizing it, Jared fell for the subtle trap and found a seat for himself. "Doubt that there is anything new."

"This is tough, but your father was dying of stage four prostate cancer."

"But in the autopsy..." In response to Jared's partial statement Patrick politely raised his open hand and palm. "He never went for treatment. This type doesn't show in blood work. And they never examined that part of him, so it was never found out."

"But how reliable is the source?" spatted Jared.

"Doctor Lyman and I chatted recently. Feeling guilty he let that detail come to surface. And before you say it, yes people dying of cancer can be murdered."

With a stoic fashion Jared allowed this tidbit to float away for the moment and would be sure to deal with it if/when it orbited back.

"We also have evidence that your father bought some of the materials used in the supposed attack."

"People buy things in life."

"I have proof from the Friendship Hardware Shoppe." With confidence he placed numerous still shots from the videos from the days that Allen had bought the items in question.

There was no denying that it was Allen.

"I won't be shopping there again if they are spreading false propaganda against my dead father. And if there is nothing else, my family is coming very soon. And I want whatever this whole witch hunt is after a dead federal agent to be long gone."

"Sure, but can I use the restroom?"

Glaring like Patrick had run over his puppy, Jared turned red and pointed upstairs. Relieved Patrick did go to the restroom area, yet focused on the doors and their edges. In a clandestine fashion he used his phone's camera to take various pictures of the doors, especially the one for the washroom.

Once back on the main level he was excited to see that Jared was on the deck, so acting in a sly fashion he grabbed the steel box from the fireplace and placed it between his body and his briefcase, totally hidden from anyone else.

Outside Jared was playing with the grill on the rear deck. Hearing the guest exit he addressed him, yet faced towards the gorgeous water landscape before him. "This murder ruined many things. And I know for sure that my mother and Clayton did it."

"I am confident of their innocence."

"It's so easy for a wanna be national investigator to come in, get paid someone's life savings, and try to make guilty people innocent."

"Jared, some of the marks your father did himself. His life insurance was about to expire, and he needed a physical. One he couldn't pass due to him dying."

Spinning around, electricity fired in Jared's eyes. "That's a nice fairy tale. But no judge will buy a few things rammed together when they have less than two weeks left until Uncle Sam does them in."

"That's fine. Joseph Stevvins and I are going to Washington D.C. to file an injunction Monday morning. Especially to exhume your father. The cancer detail is make or break." This was a bluff since it was a needle in a haystack chance that a judge would unearth Allen Marshall just to confirm this one detail about his life leading up to his death.

"With a giant metal spatula Jared was striking the air between them, each in a different corner of the porch. With a voice like fire and thunder Jared unleashed on the unwanted bystander. "Then I will go down there for any, and every, hearing. You are not digging up my father. If you think that he did this to himself." With a fiery tone in his voice, he then twirled the cooking utensil and shoved it in the middle of his chest for emphasis. "And left me without a parent for the rest of my life, then you should be committed to a mental institute." Lowering and rotating the cookware so that now it was pointed in his enemy's direction his voice also became cold, almost eerie with a malice undertone. "Now get off of my property, before there will be a heinous murder here that I will need to cover up."

*

The venomous words that Jared spewed did not affect Patrick. He knew that there was a host of emotions flowing through his mind at this time. This also showed true with his loyalty to his father. But evidence was piling up on the other side which all together could be undeniable in a court of law. And plenty of pull for a reversal on the deadly upcoming deed. Or at least a stay in order to dive deeper.

Heading westward on The Expressway, Patrick called Joseph on his mobile.

"Stevvins here."

"It's Foreman."

"How'd it go?"

"About as hostile as expected. But only one death threat."

"I get one a week myself from an array of people."

"So, I may have acquired the hardware for a laptop."

"Oh really. I have a few cords, maybe we could wire it into my desktop."

"I am going to say that's a no go. Do you have a computer guy"

"I do…"

"On payroll?"

"One that will bill me. And I will take care of the tab."

"Perfect."

"A guy over on Seneca Avenue."

"Text me the address."

"Sure… But what condition is the hard drive in?"

"Burned."

"Burned?"

"Yup. But I have seen worse be salvageable and seen."

"And Jared gave you this?"

A quick rustling and a few curse words came from Patrick. "Sorry, a deer just jumped out in front of me."

"Welcome to the Southern Tier at dusk."

"I didn't know Bambi was suicidal."

"Anyway, off of the record, how did you get Allen Marshall's roasted hard drive?"

"I guess I should clarify, it is a hard drive that has been in the ashes of the fireplace where Allen died since that night."

"So it could be anyone's."

As he was exiting I-86 Patrick saw a cop in a black and white patrol car sitting on the edge of the road, so he dropped his phone to his lap. Once safely around the corner and a mile from his hotel he picked it back up. "Sorry, fuzz was close by. Didn't want a ticket."

"You would've just billed it to me, don't lie."

There was a good chuckle or two at that jab.

"So, Jared gave you the burned part directly to you?"

"Let's just say he left the room, and I was able to acquire it."

"Great."

"So just text me your tech guy's number."

"Doing so now." Joseph cleared his throat. "So why do you think this was from Allen?"

"In the report it stated there was a raging fire in the living room. Jared told me he hasn't used it since that night because he doesn't come in the winter. And never stays overnight."

"He does live across town."

"And he believes his old man haunts the joint. Hears noises. Smells aftershave when he's alone."

"Maybe Allen is tormented in the afterlife. If he indeed pulled this off as we now both believe, then he deceived us all. And perhaps reflecting on it all now, his soul might have a conscience that his body did not."

*

"Jared, Honey," Virginia spoke as she sat next to him. They were on a weathered built in bench on the rear deck. "You barely ate."

"I did eat."

"Darling," her withered hand tapped his kneecap, "I have been watching you eat since you were a day old. I know how you are." Motioning her head towards the lake she continued, "Austin is taking the baby to the water to splash a bit. You can talk to me, Sweetheart."

After another slug of ale from the bottle he kept next to him he went on to explain the visit that occurred prior to her arrival. "That damn investigator that Michael McBride hired for Mom and Clayton showed up here. Just before you and the boys came."

"Well, that's not good." With true annoyance her face scrunched. "What did he have to say?"

"Well for starters that Dad had stage four cancer and never told any of us."

"That is the biggest load of bullshit I have ever heard."

"Language, Gramma."

This caused her to give a loving scowl, then press on. "We would have known. One way or another. Probably just some Olean gossip."

"Doctor Lyman told him."

"Doesn't that breach some kind of privacy agreement?"

271

"Not if Dad's been dead seven years."

"Well, maybe he did. But people who are dying from disease can always be murdered."

"Yeah. But also, he showed me some pictures from surveillance footage. Dad went and bought some of the materials needed to hang himself. The rope and drill. And then boots that were too small for him to wear."

"Were those in the gifts for you we found upstairs?"

"No. And I wore the same size as Dad."

With the absorption of all of this information they needed a moment to just be still and reflect. A solid two and a half minutes went by, and a laughing running toddler broke the quietness with laughter. Being that his grandmother was now brewing with mixed emotions, as he was, Jared just let the detail about a self-inflicted black eye be lost to the conversation. Instead, he picked up his pride and joy and reassured himself that his loving father, the one his son is a namesake to, would never leave a mess like this for him to clean up.

*

"So, what do you have for me?" This came as Patrick flew into the small shop's doors, ecstatic to find out what was the outcome of leaving the crispy hard drive with the shop owner the day before.

"First off, a nice bill."

"Send it to Stevvins."

"I had to deal with some heat damage and melting. But luckily not beyond being able to access some programs."

"Go on."

"Come over."

The two gentlemen proceeded to a standalone monitor which had cords connecting the charred metal box. There was a faint aroma of soot and smoke still radiating from the lucky find.

"So, this was a government issued laptop to an Agent Allen Marshall."

Fireworks and popping bottles of champagne rang in Patrick's ears from his overzealous mind at the fact that they could, for certain, state that this was the deceased.

"I was able to access the internet browser he used." Using a mouse the computer guru selected the icon on the screen and clicked on it. When it filled the screen Patrick took over the controls and went straight to the history tab. From there a lengthy list of each website that was visited and the date it was done so showed itself. All of them from the summer before the mystery began.

The amateur detective was so excited that he let out a small squawking noise.

"Are we all set? And can we put on whatever parts we need to show this as a presentation."

"I have a shell of a laptop that will work with the burnout you have."

"Sold. Put it on Joey's tab, because this is our ticket to an appeal."

*

"Are both you and Virginia coming out for the visit?"

In a meek fashion, Jared closed his bedroom door. His grandmother was not in the house, but he still strived for privacy when it came to her. "No. She's still active, but not enough for this. Although she is driven to get to the executions no matter what."

"She still has that spark for justice," laughed Jackson. "I can put you up in my townhouse. It has a spare room."

"I appreciate it."

"I will be notified about the appeal; I made some calls and will stand in on the hearings since it truly is still my case. They are trying to file at a higher-ranking court since there are barely two weeks left until the execution. And of course I have been reviewing my case files. I kept them just in case they tried to throw a roadblock. I am clearing my calendar so that I am flexible with any hearings."

"You are saying that they are flying in tomorrow, filing on Monday."

"Yeah."

"So, I will drive out early Monday and we can go from there."

"Now Jared, remember that they have been digging up the past. And sometimes the past includes some not so pleasant things that maybe your father hid. Not on purpose. I am confident that your mother and Clayton killed your dad. But they are going to get dirtier than they did in the trial."

"It is what it is."

"Just so that you are prepared."

"But what if they win the appeal."

"You are strides ahead of us, and from what you have told me they have nothing substantial to break the reasonable doubt that we established back then."

*

"I cannot believe that we made it through security with that burned out, smoke smelling, hard drive in your carry-on without a single issue."

"Hey, I am not trusting any airline to get my checked bag safely anywhere when this is a huge part of our case." To emphasize this point the gumshoe slapped a large synthetic fabric laptop bag in a rich black hue that he was using for all the necessary equipment for when they have an appeals hearing. "Plus, I have an attorney with me who would have explained my rights and that it was not a bomb."

"You have more faith in me than I do."

Both laughed at this scenario as they walked down the main corridor of the Buffalo-Niagara International Airport. They still had an hour and change until their midafternoon flight that Sunday so there was a casual feel to this important business trip. All of the information that Patrick had revealed in the prior two weeks they had discussed in great detail together.

As for Michael, they let him know about the trip and a possible appeals process. Of course, he became overzealous at the opportunity of saving his father from this given plight. But they kept the details sparse since they knew how fanatical the client was. His emotions were a rollercoaster at max speed, and there was a battle with holding him back from joining the journey to DC. Yet with short notice, family duties, and the extra cost, he was cemented back in the 14706 before he had a chance to even try and join the big guns.

Which less is more was perfect in said matter.

Seated in simple chairs attached to the lower wall, the upper being windows looking over the runway, they kept bouncing the facts off of one another so that they would stay fresh in their minds. Almost as if they were two teens practicing for a giant debate coming up soon.

"I can't believe you got that Doctor Lyman to sign an affidavit for us confirming Allen's cancer." Joseph had stepped up his game and did some legwork for the investigation, including said document. And this was expressed in Patrick's voice.

"Small town and lots of rumors to help him sway to help us. Plus, I am pushing for details of the appeal to stay sealed afterwards. He doesn't want his patients to feel like they cannot trust him. And I did the same for the Friendship Hardware Shoppe. Skip isn't so much afraid of repercussions as his father is." With this Stevvins shrugged.

"I get it. Small town area and they all have it out for Julie and Clayton."

"Exactly. Now the biggest pain will be getting the hard drive allowed into evidence. This is very, very rocky waters. You did not receive it in a clean manner. But technically it is discarded in the ashes. That is what I am pushing for. If it is rubbish that is intended to be abandoned versus still in the home."

"Sheesh. Tell me you found some case studies to use

before the judge."

"Nope. If allowed, this could set a standard."

"Never thought I would be helping build new laws."

"I never thought as a defense attorney I would be defending innocent people for almost a decade. But here I am."

*

"Drive safe."

"Never."

"Let me rephrase that Jared, drive like you always do with the baby on board."

Both laughed at this truth, and Austin embraced Jared as he was wishing him a bon voyage. "Call me when you are at Jackson's fancy townhouse."

"I will." And with that the traveler jumped into his truck and was rolling down the knoll and onto Wolf Creek, ready to spend most of the day driving. Already he had given his farewells to his grandmother. It was an unspoken ordinance that she would not attend due to the stress of the commute, and of course of the rocky proceedings that the passage would entail. Obviously she was anxious of him traveling, and of this whole final appeal that was happening. Their lives had been treacherous for the past seven years, even after the trial. They were always afraid of some technicality happening and the trial process restarting, and the pain and grief to cycle again.

Yet here they were at the dusk of the ordeal, with a meager ten days left until the execution. One event she was hell bent on going to.

Gaining speed on the country routes while heading south, Jared's mind decided to take an adventure in very peculiar waters. There were the racing thoughts that maybe his father did end his own life. Maybe there was a reason why this all happened like it did. Some explanation as to why his world had to be turned upside down. Plus, a panic that maybe his mother and Clayton would be granted an appeal. Or worse a pardon.

While traversing the long ride he thought of every moment leading up to the demise of his patriarch. Could he really be sick from cancer? Did he have it in him to rip his existence away from those who loved him. To abandon him and Virginia when they needed him the most. To lay this burden of starting his life and helping his grandmother through the final chapters of her own cycle. To be so ruthless as to totally expunge his mother from his life.

But then the thoughts of how his father was a hero and would never commit such a sin against the world as to deceive them all.

Ending the nearly six-hour trip and over three hundred miles accumulated Jared pulled up to Jackson's townhouse. The senator was taking half a day off in preparation for unearthing this whole debacle, and in order to be a generous host to Jared. Offloading his medium-sized mocha hued hardshell suitcase Jared ascended the stairs leading from the sidewalk to the stoop of the brick home. Anticipating this exciting event Jackson opened the door with much vigor and emotion. Embracing in a hug for a solid half minute, they then entered the prestigious, historic home and enjoyed some reminiscing and catching up. Which would be preferred self-care in preparation for the legal drama that would consume the next few days of their lives.

As soon as he crossed the welcome mat, and greetings were complete, Jared looked at his friend and mentor. "So did they file their appeal today?"

"Change into something a bit business casual and let's discuss it over dinner. My treat."

"It better be your treat, Mister Politician."

Mutual chuckling erupted and the guest headed to the spare room to change as requested. Emerging he was wearing a navy-blue polo shirt and a handsome pair of khakis. Jackson was in a maroon button-down shirt along with gray dress pants. Nodding to one another they headed out the front door, the resident leading the way. An aura of a dapper appearance was in the air.

As they casually ventured down a few side streets and one major Jackson was pointing to neighborhood historical spots. Naming off some famous politicians and celebrities who had called the chosen property home, along with some spots where history was made.

Beaming in a beautiful standalone building was a pillared two-story white structure which housed the restaurant that Jackson had chosen. Entering into the foyer there was a grand circular staircase with rich mahogany wood and vibrant navy trim. The host was a female in her college era with a crisp snow colored buttoned dress shirt and ebony hued dress pants.

"Senator Steele, I see you have reservations for two this evening.":

"Correct, Samantha."

"This way, Senator."

With elegance and ease they maneuvered towards the rear of the substantial establishment. A prominent bar, with the same rich tones as the entry, sprawled along the east wall and had seating for two dozen souls, give or take a lobbyist. Everyone was dressed as semi-casual, or in deep, appointed professional attire, depending on the importance of their summit at said stately eatery.

As the hostess directed them to a two-seat option, she smiled again. "Wine list this evening?"

"I don't think my guest is much of a wine enthusiast."

"My palette is not craving vino tonight," laughed Jared.

Nodding the maître d' presented the menus and made her own exit, which were opened immediately. Jared was curious as to the cuisine choice at such a landmark.

"Get a steak, Jared. The State of New York insists."

"Any suggestions?"

"Would you like to hear the specials?"

The diners turned to see their weather, who was a handsome lad around the same age as Samantha.

"Not tonight, Derek. How about two bone-in ribeyes, rare. Sides as Chef Jerome prefers. And two bourbons, as I prefer."

"Yes, Senator." The server left to take care of his duties as Jared smiled at the host. "You must be a VIP here."

"I come with guests. If I ate here every night, I would need new suits every six months since my waist would be ever expanding."

With a subtle and brief appearance Derek placed the libations in front of the men and went back to his station. And after a healthy pull from his Jackson led the conversation. "We have discussed the cancer, purchases, and possible self-inflicted injuries about your father's case."

"Yes." Jared performed a longer gulp from his. This chat warranted it.

"They included those in the appeal."

"The wannabe cop also mentioned digging up my dad."

"A request for exhumation is also included."

"Okay."

"I know the judge from various events, and unfortunately, he is more liberal. There is nothing in the research that my staffers performed to show he is anti-death penalty.":

"That's good. I hope."

Each man finished their drinks and Jackson motioned for Derek to refresh them since it was much needed.

"However, he may be more cautious and may sway things a bit to ensure that they are truly guilty."

"Which they are."

"We know that, but fresh eyes, especially those who are appointed, will want to make sure they aren't allowing innocent people to get the needle."

The drinks were dropped, and more sips were enjoyed.

"There is some motion to include a laptop hard drive."

Jared nearly spit his drink out. "A what."

"Patrick Foreman said that he discovered a discarded hard drive to a laptop and was able to have it restored." With cocked eyes Jackson looked at Jared. "Did you give him your dad's old laptop?"

"No..."

With awkward timing the meals were introduced. Their steaks were confirmed to be cooked perfectly, and they hustled Derek to return to his station since much more needed to be discussed.

"Then we need to figure this out." Confusion and a stern tone were interlaced in Jackson's statement.

Upon this they both agreed to get some of the prime beef into their stomachs, and Jackson was allowing some time to meditate on the quandary pertaining to the computer acquisition by the defense. There were some attempts at off-topic chatter, but Jared was racking his head about how this had fallen into the enemy's hands.

Finally, as there was a third of their cuisine left, Jared shook his head. "In the ashes. At the camp. I never gave it to him." Fire burst into his eyes and he pulled out his phone and dialed. The trilling could be heard by Jackson and then a "Hello?"

"Austin. What are you doing."

"I put the baby down and I am just watching television. How was your trip?"

"I need you to have Gramma watch Allen, and I need you to go to the camp."

"Can it wait until tomorrow?"

"No, Austin. Go there and dig in the ashes of the fireplace and try and see if there is a metal box. It's the hard drive to a computer."

"Are you drinking?":

"Yes, but this is important. I think that investigator stole it from the fireplace"

"Fine, fine. I am walking to your grandmother's right now."

"Call me when you are at the camp."

The line went dead, and Jackson's eyes grew in size and in bewilderment. "Did he go inside when you were there?"

"With me. And he poked around the fireplace and found

some charred metal box. I told him to put it back."

"What a weird thing to do."

"I haven't cleaned that out since Dad died."

"Okay. But you never told him to take it?"

"I told him to put it back. Then he asked to use the bathroom. And like a dummy I went outside."

"If you did not discard it, then he can't use anything on it. And he is saying your father did a lot of research on a variety of incriminating topics. Hanging deaths and a whole bunch about insurance and estates."

A dreary disposition overwhelmed Jared's face. Sensing it, Jackson shrugged. "Let's finish our food and drinks. And see if your husband finds it. If not, then we will fight like hell at the hearing Wednesday."

"No matter what, we are going to fight like hell. Dad deserves it."

*

A small clustering of media outlets had progressed to the hallway before the chambers of the Honorable Judge Lello. Rumors of a last-ditch effort in the federal death penalty case coming to an end was circulating the press. There were hopes of an open hearing happening, but the presiding magistrate squashed those hopes due to the high sensitivity of the material before them.

Jackson and Jared were at one side of the doorway on a dignified maple toned wooden bench. One that had recently been lacquered. They had been waiting for the past hour or so. The previous day the public servant had worked a bit from home while Jared was maintaining a state of fluster over the stolen evidence and the other facts about his father's last months that were compounding bit by bit. After a hearty and filthy search Austin was unable to find the metal box, so it was now a fact among their side that it had been snatched without permission.

This was a bonus for them since, hopefully, the judicial mediator would not allow anything found on said device to be admissible towards an appeal. Or at worst an exhumation of the deceased.

While rummaging the beau did find a piece of a rubber sole to a size nine boot amongst the soot and ashes with the chunks of burned firewood. Using stellar judgment he ended up tossing it in a dumpster behind a dollar store in town. Never will this be mentioned, and never will it be known to anyone else.

Situated on the opposite side of the entrance was Patrick Foreman, and of course Joseph Stevvins. They had extended semi-warm greetings to their opposing side, but the stakes were too high and emotions too raw for anything more than simple lukewarm exchanges. With such a nuclear style weapon that they had in the revived hard drive, they were unsure whether to be deathly afraid, or ready to write a law case study on said revelations.

A mousey court recorder stuck her head out of the door and looked in both directions. "Parties for appeal in the McBride/Marshall case, please enter." A few reporters stood and smiled, hoping for an okay to enter the small gathering, but she gave them a slight shake of her head in a firm, yet apologetic manner, refusing their entry.

The host was a former lawyer, long ago promoted, with age and respect ingrained in his wrinkles and graying hair. A substantial body build ensured his black formal gown was with curves and respect. Situated at his sturdy and respectable desk, his horn-rimmed glasses perched on the curve of his short nose. A small scowl was always on his face, a true poker essence to his emotions.

Four leather guest chairs with high backs and arms, in a lively green forest leather, were positioned for the congregation. All of the men did not waste time in taking an appropriate cushion. The ruling was one that could not come fast enough for their roaring minds.

The professional note taker sat at her small desk that held a petit stenotype machine that she had used for several years in said career.

Once all were as comfortable as a setting could be, the leader nodded, and the stenographer sat poised, ready to engrave each word and reaction to such a somber meeting into permanent records.

"I do not like to take on such cases, yet time for the defense is dwindling. I believe an exact week is our timetable, correct Mister Stevvins?"

"Yes, Sir."

"I have spent the past two days reviewing the entire transcript of the trial. Which was done without any wavering from fair, or any flaws. And I also had an in-depth conversation with Judge Forrester. Everything was on point, so no appeals were possible."

With a deep inhale he pressed on.

"The sworn statement by Doctor Lyman does add some questions to the mindset of the deceased. Along with insurance information and the pending divorce. Not to mention the not so flattering video that was finally released with the late Mister Marshall shopping for items that may have been used in a potential cover up. In the eyes of the law, this is not enough to overturn anything. However, Solicitor, you stated that a computer was discovered which was federal property and contained incriminating evidence that Agent Marshall did investigate ways to take his own life, and potentially devastating topics."

"That we do." Stevvins nodded to Foreman, who pulled out the laptop they had assembled. "We have several websites visited and searches performed."

"Objection, Your Honor," erupted Steele, steadfast on the information staying dead in the drive, and off of any official notes, his hand vibrating in the air, and he stood up. "This was stolen from my client's camp."

"This was not turned over by the USDA, Mister Stevvins."

"No..." The anxious attorney started to stutter and sputter with his words. "But if you let us introduce it you will see that the damning information discovered will outweigh the means of how it was acquired, and in the end, sanctify how it was obtained. This would make a great example of upcoming cases where such evidence is essential in..."

A lateral chopping motion by Judge Lello's hand in the air cut the rest of Joseph's sentence. "Where has this supposed groundbreaking evidence been hiding for the past seven years?"

"In the fireplace at my camp. I haven't cleaned the ashes since my father was murdered." Jared was glaring at Patrick. A chill shot through the room.

"And how did the defense acquire it then? I am assuming you are Mister Marshall, the son of the victim."

"I am. I allowed Patrick Foreman to view the cabin. He picked up a burned-out box from the soot. I told him to put it back. He did so. Then he asked to use the restroom. As I walked outside, he may or may not have used the facilities, but he must have stolen the hard drive when he was alone inside. And without any of my permission. Rather I was forward with him leaving it as it was."

Joseph stood up. "It was clearly disposable and would have been thrown out at some time." This was a true attempt at grasping at straws. "If Mister Marshall had disposed of it that night in the garbage outside of the cabin and Mister Foreman had retrieved it."

"Maybe in New York they play story time, but in my federal courtroom Mister Stevvins, we do not ponder what ifs. It was not discarded. It was blatantly stolen, and you were hoping for a judge who would want to play hero and save two people dying next week. Too bad. Hand the drive back over to the rightful owner, and I will not push for larceny charges." Looking up he glared at the despicable duo. "Is that agreeable?"

Deflated, and obviously upset, Patrick ripped the drive from the laptop shell and aggressively handed it back over to Jared. "Doesn't change the fact that your pops framed two innocent people, Kiddo."

"More like wishing on a Hail Mary, when you just

fumbled, Big Guy." This retort by Jared caused some muffled laughing from Jackson.

Realizing the magnitude and amount of tension flooding into the legal space, the judge wrapped up the hearing. "Appeal denied."

*

The repercussions from the finality of that hearing surged into the minds of many who were aware of the case over the years. The final article was completed by the local journalist and was run in a national periodical. Plus, a network reporter picked up the piece and explored all of the options again. To spoil matters, and increase the drama, Joseph Stevvins had leaked information that the judge had refused to see. It was reported upon in all realms of the case about the magnitude of the new information, and the reluctance to include it in the final outcome of the appeal.

Nationwide there was yet again a split on those who believed that the two scorned lovers were guilty or not. Jared and Virginia did speak to various journalists and continued with their steadfast belief that Allen was slaughtered. More and more fuel was given to the fire and debates were heated and fiery when it came to this quandary. But it was a quick flash in the pan since the execution was not given the option for a delay, or a pardon.

What was done had no way to be unraveled.

Dew was on the grass early in the morning as Jared loaded their luggage, and his grandmother, into his loyal truck. The baby was asleep, and Austin was in just sweatpants and a tee shirt bidding them a farewell. It was the day before the execution, which landed on a Tuesday, and they were making the trip to Terre Haute. Hugs were exchanged, and Austin was hoping that life could get back on track once those nails were driven hard into those coffins.

Jackson would meet them there. Due to his schedule, he was flying.

Michael McBride and Joseph Stevvins were attending, and obviously carpooling on their own. Much sadness was riding in that car. A sense of the underdogs truly losing in this matter, and watching innocent people be thrown to the gallows, when it was just a ploy of zealous revenge that Allen Marshall had successfully induced.

Patrick Foreman felt depleted, and knew it was best for him not to attend. The nightmares were still coming a few times a week and seeing them actually executed would put his mental state into a not so stable frame.

Their trips were poignant. Watching the mile markers come and go while pointing out oddities on their travels. A few unique sites and maybe some memories long forgotten. Bittersweetness enriching their voyage one passing exit at a time. All of their lives had changed in so many ways. Some for the wretched worse, some for the oddly better.

There were very few lodging accommodations in the Indiana town. Michael and Joseph had chosen a modest one. Stevvins had picked up the tab for both of their rooms. And chose against something luxurious since this was such a macabre and non-celebratory stay. A simple motel with a numbered name featuring basic amenities and bland decor.

Jackson had grabbed the bill for Jared and Virginia. A medium-tiered hotel that had some comfort for them in their compelling time. Nothing showy or glamorous. Something also appropriate for the journey.

This was a long ten-hour trip, including any restroom breaks that pinged along various Ohio cities during their venture. But they ended up at their lodging right at check-in.

The first execution of Clayton was set for two in the morning. Then Julie's would be immediately after. Once settled properly into their rooms and suites the visitors had light fares at chain restaurants near the penitentiary. Not at the same establishment since that would have just added fuel to the emotional blows.

Julie Marshall had chosen her final meal of meatloaf and

mashed potatoes. A dessert of spice cake was its conclusion. Cuisine her mother, now two years passed, made on her birthdays from the first, until incarceration.

Clayton McBride had chosen fried chicken with steak fries. A dessert of strawberry shortcake and whipped topping. A simple comfort dish he had craved since the cuffs were slapped on him.

In an unprecedented move, the warden had allowed the two to dine together in the mess hall. Without steel tethers even. Guards were close by, but they could hold hands as they had their last supper together. One where neither had forsaken the other. Rather both had been victims of deceit.

It had been more than seven years since they had dined together. The last being the night before it all fell around them. Talks of making an offer on a new home had been the most memorable part of the meal. Although it had been some delectable lasagna that Julie had baked, which Clayton adored. She had always been a willing cook, but Allen had always pushed her aside and took the role in the kitchen.

There had been some wine that night so long before. And love making after. The last time that intimacy and red zin was on the menu for them also.

And now here they both were, preparing for the finale of their existence. Michael had found plots back in Olean and had somehow raised enough money to fund such a morbid venture. Headstones will come in time. After flares of emotions had subsided and there would be no risk of vandalism to the tombs.

All had been planned out by their most loyal supporter.

After their dinner date, and an extended amount of time to digest it all afterwards together, they were allowed a final kiss. One that was allowed to linger for a moment since it was the conclusion of their love. Then they were brought back to their cells. This was not how they wanted to live out the conclusion of their lives.

*

Such a small, impromptu auditorium that they were being filed into as a group was quaint, although they were firmly divided by the rift among them. Barely twenty square feet in space holding simple metal folding chairs as a barbaric seating arrangement, and two armed guards situated in the rear, ready to break up any non-inmate squabbles that tend to occur during these termination gatherings. A large plate glass picture window assumed the majority percentage of the wall to the left. Each side held large drapes which were to be opened and closed at appropriate times during the enigmatic occasion. Almost acting as a melancholic main attraction to a macabre assembly.

Michael McBride pushed through and sat firmly in the farthest seat to the far wall. Joseph Stevvins followed but was acting in a more professional manner. Not quite overly courteous, rather adding a semi-polite nod as he took a seat next to the already grieving son. Directly facing through the window was the death taking apparatus which was permanently affixed to the neighboring room was where they chose their seating. Illumination was low at that point, yet the major aspects of the un-aliving zone were clearly visible. It appeared as a demonic dentist's chair with straps and cranks for adjustments. Not for the comfort of the seated, but rather to propel the doomed occupant's arm in the correct position to get a sturdy vein.

Jackson led their fleet. With Jared and Virginia hand in hand. Heart in heart. A few cocktails over dinner helped their nerves, and there was an unspoken desire that this would liberate them from seven years of such a horrible streak in their lives.

Who broke a mirror?

Their path was one to the farthest back seats. A desire to be a subtle presence was their reasoning behind such a distant position. Others associated in the case with proper clearance filed in ahead of them. A few were known to the Marshalls, most were not. It was as if the end of their angst was a sideshow among the mighty. Superintendent Hacket was one of those there for the amusement.

Outside of the detention center there was a plethora of protestors, their impact null on the final outcome, brandishing signs from drug store markers and stock white cardboard materials. Messages painted on them, yet useless at this point. Begging for a pardon, when no pardon would be due.

Chanting had forged through the car as all parties were driving in and did not affect their opinions of what would be the final product. Sympathy was divided amongst those in attendance, and no persuasion would void the drugs that were about to be administered to the couple doomed.

Just after two in the morning the warden entered the viewing space and nodded at all. Words were not needed to express that the process was moving, and about to become theirs to view. In the administration room the lights were given more strength. A guard and a pastor peacefully escorted Clayton into the staged area. Another public servant entered and together they tenderly strapped his wrists and ankles to the appropriate spots. On his left arm they fastened the nook of his elbow to the arm of the chair also. Adding some act of humanity they did not tie his neck onto the headrest. There was a silent expectation that he would not act up in his final moments in existence.

Pulling a medical tray with a sterile sheet of hospital style paper laying on it, a member of the infirmary unit entered, with three of their subordinates behind them. On display was the needle for an IV, an alcohol swab, and three filled syringes. They wore professional surgical masks, not for any bacterial or virus preventative reasons, but rather to hide their identities while doing work that can be viewed as disdainful. This was not the first, nor last time for their quad to follow this procedure. Each time rotating their order amongst them. Yet each time they questioned many of their priorities, and beliefs, during the act.

After the religious leader finished a muted prayer, and clasped Clayton's hand once, he exited the mortuary venue. Preparing himself for a repeat of the process in less than an hour kept his mood paralyzed. Propositioning himself during their period about why he volunteered for these endeavors, and if maybe it was time to refrain from them.

Yet he always returned, because he felt every person deserves love at the end of their destiny.

The first of the injection squad used a tourniquet in order to prepare a vein for the matter. Secondly, they discovered it and cued their successor that it was their turn. They swabbed the area with the sanitizing alcohol swab, then inserted the needed. Finding a red flash, they knew they hit liquid gold.

The followers each took turns inserting the syringes and allowing the devil's brew to pulsate into the arteries of the father. The person. The innocent.

As they all stepped back, they left and monitored their patient's breathing from an adjacent room, which was slowing.

The entire time this parade of actions was being performed Michael's eyes never left the sad stare of his father's. Their breathing aligned, and tears formed in their eyes. Tears streaming down their cheeks in manic rivulets, sadness radiating between them and raging for so many memories stolen and ripped from them. Names tarnished and lives tormented in a ravishing, unjust fashion.

Until the air ceased, and his eyes turned to peace. Michael seized onto the floor in anguish, yet relief, that he had lost his father, but now his father was gone from all of the torture that he had been enduring since the moment Allen Marshall had died.

*

L osing the love of your life rips and tears at anyone's soul. But for it to only have an hour of mourning before you make your maker, it has a ripe irony that stuns and annoys at the same time. Especially when you were somewhat responsible, or rather your deranged and revengeful ex, for said soul mate's demise.

And this whole tyrannical avalanche that she was victim to only led a more divided stance for Julie McBride on that fateful day on whether it was time to keep fighting, or just give in to the inevitable that life would be better on the other side than this hell inflicted by the narcissist she was too far in love with so long before.

Both she and Clayton had made sure that Michael, her dream stepson, would make arrangements for them. Collect their belongings. Put flowers on their graves and be the sole speaker of good about them in a world that turned so hard.

They had a slew of supporters, but ones that would let memories fade after the toxins were jabbed into the innocent duo.

Earlier she had thrown away all of the letters that Jared had sent back to her unread. He made it a point to bundle them and send them in a large manilla envelope as a way to keep tormenting her over and over again.

Sitting on the edge of her bed, she knew that Clayton's time was happening, and that she would be called also. Acceptance had helped her to this point, especially after all of the evidence was discovered that should have exonerated them by exhuming Allen was thrown to the curb.

The hard drive she heard had been catapulted into the lake by Jared as a way to wash himself from any truths.

Clinking and clanking from handcuffs rustling while the appointed guard neared her cell was vibrant and everlasting. A reminder that she would never die free, in any aspect.

A whispered apology from the corrections officer was subtle, yet heard. Many staff and prisoners were torn on the validity of her verdict once more news was released on many points that could free the innocent Bonnie and Clyde. This one was a supporter and hated the constitution at times when it barred truths from evading the wrongs.

"I won't put them on too tight, okay Julie."

"I appreciate you, Paul."

Together they walked to the forsaken room, and he even

grasped her wrist a few times in a humane fashion, trying to give her some peace at the battle coming. This did ease her a bit, and once at a side room the same man of God met with her and gave her other words to help soothe her aching soul.

Another torn adversary on the issue.

The same lights rose, and professionals entered. Julie was restrained, and prayers given. Nods were had, and veins prepped and sanitized. Ironically unnecessary since this was her final shot.

With a face the same hues of red and orange of the rising sun on a tortuous day on his face and cheeks, Michael sat in agony. Instead of blaming Julie, he embraced her through the raging waters that were a failed struggle they were obnoxiously handed. After losing his mother a decade plus before, he had wanted a blended family and was taking the stance as another victim of this crime they were persecuted for unjustly. So, through the procedure he kept his eyes on hers, smiling to relieve some of the torment and agony she was privy to. The same that he was.

Shakes of their heads and sobs ensued as each syringe was emptied, and again her fate was measured and timed.

At intervals Julie would glance over at Jared and Virgina. Praying for sadness from them of her fate. Yet they glared and showed boiling expressions of disgust and hate towards her. Not wanting that to be her last view she glanced back at Michael, as they paced their breaths together, until hers was exhausted permanently.

While Jared and Virginia each squeezed the other's hand in a muted celebration, yet they were among many of the perfect victims of a precise deception.

AFTERWORD

The grim issue of harming oneself was a major part of the plot to this story. This was to dramatize the book and add to the twists and turns. Sadly, a few of those close to me who this book is dedicated to passed in such a fashion. And the pain will always be there.

So please, if you are feeling depressed, please reach out to a loved one, or to the SAMHSA hotline at 1-800-662-HELP (4357).

Suicide is a permanent solution to a temporary problem. Please use any tool possible, you are loved.

ABOUT THE AUTHOR

Brandon D. Conner

Author Brandon D. Conner spent a decade of his childhood in wonderful Cuba, NY. After moving to Fort Lauderdale, Florida he started his adventure in crime fiction writing. Realizing the true beauty of his former home town, he knew it was a perfect location for a thrilling tale.

BOOKS BY THIS AUTHOR

Iron City Justice: The Butterfly Effect

Could one wager between two athletes lead to pain, destruction, murder, and kidnapping? Detective Adam Carpenter not only has his own obstacles in his personal life but is also chasing a maniac with twisted revenge on his mind, while adjusting to a new partner. This murder suspense is a page-turner as the detectives pursue a cold-blooded zealot through Pittsburgh.

Made in the USA
Columbia, SC
10 June 2025

f3c4f134-fe73-4d7d-93a7-0ea03acd0885R01